D1274169

THE WORLD IS LIKE THAT

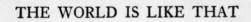

THE WORLD IS LIKE THAT

BY
KATHLEEN NORRIS

PALO ALTO EDITION

New York
P. F. COLLIER & SON CORPORATION
BY SPECIAL ARRANGEMENT WITH
DOUBLEDAY, DORAN & COMPANY, INC.
NEW YORK

MANUFACTURED IN U. S. A.

TO A LITTLE BOY

What though the sky be thick with diamond stars,
   All dull, all pale, all fade to shadows when
Bold among Venus, Jupiter and Mars
   A small new planet swims into our ken.

THE WORLD IS LIKE THAT

CHAPTER I

JOCELYN BRITTON WAS ALWAYS the last to leave the office. She explained now and then to the other stenographers of Fordyce, Sawyer & Fordyce, a law firm in San Francisco, that she did a little work on the side for a social bureau in New York, kept them in touch with the new names in society, watched the obituary columns to inform them when names dropped out.

"It takes real secretarial work, and it only pays me a hundred a year!" Jocelyn might complain philosophically to anyone who was interested or seemed interested. But everyone knew that the real reason she remained late was the hope that Kent Dunham would come down from his studio on the top floor and have a few minutes with her. They would leave the office together and cross to the parking station half a block up Sutter Street to the garage where Kent kept his motorcar. Sometimes he took Jocelyn home, but more often she walked. She boarded in a place called the "Crescenta Loma," in Bush Street, not far away. She did not often ride home with Kent.

All the girls knew this. They knew of the existence of Kent Dunham's wife—a pretty, plump, well-curled little woman who thought a great deal about clothes and furniture. Sometimes Lilian Dunham came to the garage after an afternoon in the shops or beauty parlor and waited for him in the car. She knew Jocelyn, of course, and they acted toward each other like friends. And yet Jocelyn never ran the risk of meeting Lilian if she could help it.

She and Kent usually parted at the corner; two years ago they had often lingered at this corner, and then Kent had walked up Bush Street with her to the "Crescenta Loma," and she had walked back with him. But for the last few months they had been parting, the office girls had noted, at the corner. Perhaps Mrs Dunham was getting tired of tolerating this affair between her husband and the stenographer downstairs. Or perhaps Kent Dunham was getting tired. Certainly it was not Miss Britton who was tired, and her moods fluctuated between happiness and depression exactly as Kent Dunham was being attentive or being neglectful. Any child could see that!

Just how far this affair had been carried by the principals, no girl in the office quite dared say. Some thought one thing, some another. The defenders of Jocelyn Britton's integrity were apt to weaken a little when some voice said impatiently, "Oh, stop talking nonsense! Of course they're lovers!" And on the other hand there was always someone to protect Jocelyn's name if the consensus of opinion went against her, and to say with equal asperity, "Now, listen. I've known her for five years, right here in this office. Her aunt is Mrs Bartley Partridge of Sausalito; they're perfectly lovely people; she's way above most of us in the way she was educated and the way she thinks, and it's nonsense to say that she and Kent Dunham . . . it's just nonsense! They like each other a lot, and that's as far as it goes!"

However far it had gone, it had gone too far for Jocelyn's happiness and peace of mind as she sat waiting for Kent on a certain dark grimy November afternoon some two weeks before Thanksgiving. Office work had been dull today; hours had dragged themselves out endlessly; now it was five o'clock, and everyone else had gone home. Old Mr Fordyce had not come into town at all; Mr Phil had merely walked into his office, with his cap under his arm and his big loose brown coat hanging open, and had glanced at his mail and gone away again. Mr Sawyer had been more disagreeable than ever, and had seized the opportunity to send several of the young clerks to Jocelyn with their senseless immature letters. The firm was constantly taking into its offices young aspirants to legal honors, fresh out of law school, who were to get their training with Fordyce, Sawyer & Fordyce, and they felt their oats. They loved useless research and the throaty young dictation of superfluous letters.

They were gone now; everyone was gone. Most of the offices were closed; the library was locked; two old women with buckets were crawling about the great tiled foyer where the whizzing elevators stopped. Jocelyn worked on, and she said in her heart that he was not coming.

Her heart knew exactly how often he had come in during the last twenty-four nights. Eight times. He had had to go to Portland, of course; that accounted for four nights—accounted for five really, for Lilian would have met him at the flying field to drive him home upon his return; he couldn't have left her that night. That left eleven nights' absence unexplained; not that any explanation would mean anything. He simply—hadn't come. She had sat here in this office, whose every desk and chair, contour of wall and fold of rich long curtain she so hated, so despised, and she had waited for him, as he had known she would, and he hadn't come.

He had known that she would watch the little detestable clock that ticked away so smugly on her desk; he had known that she would seize the telephone with a wild rising beat of her heart, only to lay it down again in cold sickness of spirit; he had known that at quarter to six—at ten minutes of six, she would give him up, start for home, walk the darkening blocks of Bush Street slowly, let herself in with a latchkey to the smells and loneliness of an evening at the "Crescenta Loma."

Why? Why? Why should he deliberately hurt her so much, when he had so many times said he loved her more than anything in the world, more than his job, his position, his wife, his honor? But of course he wasn't deliberately hurting her.

Not Kent, who had scribbled her those notes two years ago,
had treasured every moment he could have with her, had all
but fainted with sheer emotion one day when unexpectedly
she had telephoned him!

Things had changed. An affair, even of so unsatisfying,
so ephemeral a nature, naturally knew its ups and downs. It
could not stay at the trembling peaks it had reached when
first they had known that they loved each other. Jocelyn had
admitted that to her unwilling heart many weeks ago. But for
Kent to avoid her, not to see her sometimes for days together
—when she was so accessible, when seeing her was so easy!
—no, she could not understand that. She could not fit that
into her philosophy at all.

But this afternoon, suddenly, like water breaking through
into the parched cup of a sun-baked spring, the sound of his
foot came along the hallway from the elevator, and his hand
touched the doorknob, and everything was right again. A
wintry afternoon, in the president's luxurious office, became
the time and place for all the beauty and joy of the world to
meet. Jocelyn pushed a last paper into a drawer; the smooth
top of her desk was broken only by the telephone and the
handsome heavy crystal inkwell now; she looked up, the only
lighted thing in the dark place herself; her lambent eyes, her
squared fine shoulders, the glory of her hair.

The man who came in had seen all this too often to see it
now at all. But no man ever saw Jocelyn's face for the first
time without a responsive thrill. It was still a girl's face,
despite her more than twenty-seven years; there was in it, and
in her whole person, something lean, eager, questing, young.

Her eyes were of so dark a blue, so widely spaced and
deep-set that they seemed to shadow the delicate flesh of her
temples and her high cheekbones. Her mouth was wide and
fine; her brows like soft dark brushes; her skin had a fine
clear pallor that was rarely warmed by a flush. But the amaz-
ing thing was her hair; hair of pure baby gold, flyaway as

thistledown, shining in striking contrast to the soft paleness of her face and the shadowed eyes. In any group, in any office, anywhere, everywhere, men looked first at Jocelyn Britton and then at any other girl who happened to be around. She looked mysterious, aloof, foreign, although she was none of these things. She looked as if she might be occupied principally with her own strange beauty; as a matter of fact it gave her little pleasure.

Beauty was made for dancing, for popularity and excitement, for the lure of wonderful new hats and frocks, for moonlight nights on tropical beaches and noonday lunches in great hotel dining rooms. Jocelyn had never known any of these things. If beauty bought them for other women, it had never seemed to bring her any nearer them. She lived in a boardinghouse, where elderly folk were kind to her, and where she had a nice room with a row of good books to keep her company in it. Men had admired her often, and had sometimes asked her to go to movies, or off for Sunday trips, but she had not been free until two years ago to leave an invalided and adoring mother, and for more than the past two years Kent had been all her world.

He came into the office smiling, and sat down opposite her just as he always did, and their four hands met across the flat top of the desk. So far everything was as usual, and yet nothing was. Jocelyn, when she spoke, tried to make her voice sound cheerful and loving and confident, and knew that she failed.

"Well, I was afraid I was never going to see you again! What have you been doing and where have you been?" she began.

"I was in Portland, you know. Had to go up."

"I've seen you twice since you got back, Kent." It was a gentle reminder, delivered with a smile that was understanding. But she hated herself for it. It sounded patient, long-suffering, wifely. Everything that would help a man remember that the speaker had feelings, rights, sensitivities. Just the attitude she didn't want to take, ever, with Kent! Lilian's hurt, virtuous, kind tone.

"Of course you have. But I get mixed up, living in such a whirl. Sure, I was in here last week."

"Thursday. And this is more than a week later," her thoughts said. Aloud she added: "It's all right, as long as things are going well with you."

"They're going a little too well," he confessed ruefully, rushing into the opening. "They're sending me to Portland— Judson talked to me about it yesterday. Well, he really talked to me about it on Saturday night. He and Ruth—that's the wife, and a sweet girl, too—twenty-three, and first baby, all that! They came up and had dinner with us on Saturday, and afterward we talked it over. They want me to go to the Portland office at seventy a week. Substantial raise right there."

This was a blow straight at Jocelyn's heart; she could not rally from it immediately. No muscle of her face changed, but the light that had flooded it faded with the effect of a candle being removed from behind the translucence of a shell. She sat immovable, staring at him, her breath coming from slightly parted lips.

"What—what does Lilian think?" she presently said, vaguely aware that he had been talking on, irrelevantly and uneasily; he had said things about rents in Portland and Lilian's dislike for the fogs of San Francisco.

"Oh, she's delighted to move! Her brother lives there." Lilian had a dull, prosperous brother, Jocelyn reflected; he and his wife and their children would all help in the good work of bringing Lilian's artistic and temperamental husband back into the fold. "But there's more to it than that, Joy," Kent said, suddenly courageous and honest. "Even if we weren't going—even if things were going along here as they always have, I'd made up my mind to—to stop it. That it had to end."

Jocelyn looked steadily at him; she did not speak.

"For your sake, and my sake, and hers," Kent said.

"Hers?"

"Lilian's. She's always been square with me, and I have to be square with her."

"I wonder why, so suddenly, after eleven completely eventless years of marriage?" some remote part of Jocelyn's brain questioned dispassionately. "Lilian has been square." Another detached bit of thinking formulated coldly: "Because no human being has ever tempted her to be anything else." She said nothing aloud.

"I happen to be a horribly honest person," Kent was saying. "I've not been happy about all this. Not a bit! But our friendship was so sacred to me, Joy, I was so proud of it, that I think I lost my bearings for a little while. And now—that's that!" Kent went on, in a lighter tone, "and—you're walking home? Here's your coat; I'm walking, too. I'll go as far as Powell anyway with you. And I was going to say," he resumed—and Jocelyn could tell from his tone that he had thought out all these phrases in advance—"we're always to be the best of friends. Here's the elevator. Good evening, Lenny. My dear," Kent said, steering her along the dusky street past the lighted restaurants and corner cigar stands, "I'll never have another friend like you—I know that. Nothing can take away from us the beauty of this friendship of ours. You're always going to have a place of your own in my heart . . ."

Emptiness; ashes; shadows. Whips falling on her bare flesh, and all the time the dear big hand firm under her elbow in the remembered way, and the marvelous voice close at her ear. The voice that always had a little laughter in it, and a little hoarseness, and an undertone of eagerness and decision.

"Joy," he said, "there've been times when I resented your straightness—your strength, darling. You know that! You know I've been terribly rebellious sometimes—terribly angry at you and your eternal 'We've got to be fair to Lilian!' When I kissed you, when I held you in my arms, and when I knew that I never could take ultimate possession, that the Puritan in you would always win, it used to almost kill me, dear! I've walked up and down opposite the 'Crescenta Loma' a hundred nights, watching for the light to go out in your window, knowing that you were lying there, like a clean sweet fragrant lily, in the dark . . .''

He had always had phrases. It was a part of his charm that he knew poets and loved beautiful words. He was full of charm. For Jocelyn there was nothing about him that did not charm, did not turn her heart to water. If it had been only the physical thing, the hunger of youth for youth, it could not have lasted, in her case at least, for these two years. She did love him that way, too; she would have been the proudest woman in the world to give him all that she had of pride and sweetness and youth, to feel that in that way as well as every other they were indeed one.

But it was companionship that was so wonderful in her lonely life; companionship, and the good talk of books, and the laughter over little things, and the sense that he liked as well as loved her; all this had irradiated the world for her for breathless months. And now it was over. Now in utter chill and sickness of spirit she had to tell herself that it was over.

The drab streets slipped by them; the city was ugly and dull and cold tonight. Jocelyn's chief consciousness was of a hatred of herself so violent that it eclipsed all feeling for him. Fool to play along with a man whose wife could whistle him back so easily, who could take this position of understanding and pity and kindness, and go free, as she could never go free, she told herself bitterly, of his words and kisses again! Oh, if she could have been talking this way to him, rather than he to her!

"Lilian's packing now; we'll be out by the twenty-first. That's a Monday. But she wants to get out the Saturday before and have a day or two with her mother. I'm going up to Keble's place that night. He's away, but there's a lot of my stuff there, and he left the key with me. So it's boots and saddles for the Dunhams! Luckily we have only a cat to worry about . . ."

Afterwards, when she was alone, phrases came back to her. "Luckily we have only a cat to worry about!" For some reason these particular words came back to her, and hurt her more, stirred her more deeply to anger and shame than some of the more significant ones. "Luckily we have only a cat to worry about!"

This from Kent, who in the early stages of their friendship had said to her briefly, unemotionally, more than once: "If we'd had kids, my wife and I! I wanted them, terribly. I wanted a little girl named Sheila, with a mop of hair and a blue smock. But Lilian's always been babied by her mother into thinking she wouldn't get through it. Well, I'm glad now," he had once added, "I'm glad now that there aren't children. Because if ever I have children I want them to be yours."

The quietly expressed feeling had sent a quiver through her, although he hadn't said it dramatically; he had been painting, in his old spattered smock, and she had gone into his studio quite casually, between the setting of the table for their supper and the moment when Lilian would call them for it. He and Lilian lived, had lived ever since she had known them, in an entirely commonplace flat. It had hurt her every time she went there to see how pathetically he tried to make the drawing room seem a studio; he would have liked a big barny loft somewhere, with a curtain across the bedroom corner and a skylight instead of the four small square rooms. In the room he called his studio, a window overlooked a good-sized airwell; Kent said that it had a north light. He had littered the room with sketches and canvases; they were absurd enough, incongruous enough in that small space; he kept a smock or two hanging there, and palettes, and big black tin boxes full of twisted paint tubes.

It had been on Jocelyn's first visit to his home, when she and his wife had been complete strangers, and had handled each other with great circumspection, that pity had begun in her heart for Kent. Before that her feeling had been all admiration for the man who was a real—if only a commercial—artist; a growing affection for him as the friend who stopped in to visit her now and then in the office, and so obviously found her company stimulating.

Lilian had impressed her as uninteresting. A plump, pretty little woman whose conversation was all platitudes about lamps, chairs, beauty parlors and icebox cake. From the very beginning Jocelyn had felt a certain vague resentment of Lilian's complacency. "He's mine," Lilian had seemed to say with every dull little phrase and possessive little gesture. "Admire him as much as you like; enjoy his friendship to the limit; suffer any inconvenience your own feelings may cause you. But he's mine. Mine to pet and feed and scold and know all about: how many shirts he has and how he likes his eggs fried and what he says when he loses his temper and what he says afterward when he's sorry."

Later that attitude was to cause Jocelyn acute suffering. Almost at once she and Kent had begun to fall in love with each other. At first it had seemed to her a frightening thing and a regrettable thing, but she had found the fright intoxicating and the regret in itself something enormously to enjoy. These new thrilling feelings had absorbed her; a married man had completely lost his head about her, and she loved him, too. They had met for countless tea hours and lunches and long walks to discuss how best they could be true to each other and to Lilian.

Sometimes she had gone home with him to have supper with Lilian, and he and she had sat in that enchanted globe of self-absorption that is new love; both being wonderful to Lilian, both more determined than ever not to fail her, but each feeling the dramatic glitter of the situation like something lighted by a glory not of this world. To answer Lilian politely, to turn her starry eyes from Kent's face to Lilian's, to say little, or nothing, while cosmic thunders were ringing in the room—this had given Jocelyn the most acute and trembling joy she ever had known. Lilian had suspected nothing for a long time.

But presently both Kent and Jocelyn had known that she did suspect, and it was then that somehow the bloom and glory of the whole thing had begun to fade. They talked divorce, but there was no more reason for Kent to divorce Lilian than there had been for him to marry her in the first place. If she had been a big, self-reliant woman, or an indifferent housekeeper, or extravagant, or unfaithful, or even discontented, it might have been managed. But Lilian was as complacently satisfied as a good mother; her boy's chair and his hot supper and his newspaper, their little jokes, their pleasures over a well-handled budget and a growing bank account were all so many good stout props under Lilian. Any other woman get her Kent? Why, before he'd been gone two days he'd come running back to her for his clean socks and his mail and his headache tablets and his milk-toast dinner after a party! He depended on her for everything; he was the biggest *baby* . . . !

Jocelyn knew exactly what Lilian was thinking about the whole thing; what she would say when women friends asked her about it. And she writhed with shame and hatred.

CHAPTER II

FOR THE FIRST FEW HOURS after his call in the office it all seemed too bad to be true, and she felt merely dazed and dull. She went through the usual evening routine automatically; conscious that agony was ahead, but neither feeling it nor fearing it yet. She sat through dinner; went upstairs afterward; moved about her room quietly and steadily, making everything right for the night.

It was a pleasant square room on a little hallway of three rooms; the other two were also occupied by single women, and the three had a bath to themselves, which was very pleasant, and also an extra large closet in the hallway. There was also a big closet in Jocelyn's room, and she had a small balcony outside her window; not practicable, but somehow a nice thing to have, and she had a slice of view. The bay, Alcatraz, the Berkeley hills, the bridge were all contained in the narrow strip, and she never tired of watching the changes that came with the changing hours upon them: light and darkness, day and night, fog and sunshine.

The bed wore a tufted cotton cover of red and white by day; Jocelyn folded it carefully and put it on a closet shelf. There was an extra pillow on the closet shelf; she brought it out. She changed her clothes; put on walking shoes; took up a book. She would walk to the big library on Larkin Street. It was just eight o'clock.

Just eight o'clock. The evening was young. She must not think. She looked in drugstore windows as she walked along, saw women making late purchases at the fruit stalls, saw children, bright-eyed and talkative, up much too late. She thought she would ask the librarian for another detective story; she and the librarian had laughed more than once as they had agreed that this book or that was pretty trashy, but had confessed that in certain moods nothing was so soothing and distracting as a good murder mystery.

"That one about the bells—the chimes and the bell ringers —that was lovely!" Jocelyn had argued.

"Ah, well, Dorothy Sayers!" Miss Pruett had agreed, with a nod of her grizzled head.

Jocelyn hoped she would get a good story tonight—a meaty one, long and complicated. She hoped it would be English; there was something sedative about the English scene; even when stories had quite serious settings, like *Of Human Bondage* and Sheila Kaye-Smith's books, they seemed soothing somehow.

The smothered flame began to creep through the smoke; sharp little breath-stabbing points of it. Kent had come into the office—Kent had come into the office—and had said— but she wouldn't think of it . . .

A candy-store window was full of little metal turkeys strutting about. Blue-black turkeys, with tiny red beaks and white wattles. "Turkeys," Jocelyn said aloud, stopping at the window, "I wonder how long it is since I've seen a live turkey.

"Now let me see," she said, walking along. "I've never lived in the country, so I've not seen them there. Mother and I always were in city boardinghouses—except that divine time when we had the apartment just before she got arthritis . . .

"He came into the office—the moment I saw him I knew, of course—I knew—the look on his face . . .

"Oh, how can I go on now?"

She was in the library; she had changed her book, talked to Miss Pruett; she was on her way home again. There was nothing about which she could think; nothing for which to live; everywhere her mind and spirit turned, they met despair.

Back in her room, and undressed, in her heart she was now writing him passionate letters. One after another; one after another. "My dear Kent—Kent, my dear—Kent, it can't end this way—there's friendship, and that's all I ask. Friendship can't hurt anyone. We said we would keep it friendship because then it could always go on, and I need it. My pride's crushed, dear. I can't pretend. I need you in my life."

She brooded, mentally tossing aside these images as she had mentally evoked them.

It must be shorter. "By the way, Kent, I want to see you before you go." Or, "Save me a lunch date next week, Kent." Businesslike. She wouldn't cry or reproach or be feminine and annoying. There were eleven days before Kent would leave for Portland; if he managed a luncheon or tea date at once she would have time to make another engagement with him. If that luncheon or tea went well, it would be simple to say, "If you're free tonight, come round my way about eight and we'll walk."

There had been a time when he had been tireless, ingenious, in arranging for these meetings; there had been a time when they had tucked them in everywhere. Once she had begged off; she had said that she was facing a hard session with a dentist. And he had met her outside Dr Thorne's office with a little ice pack ready, and had taken her to a waiting taxi, tenderly reassuring as to the effect on the swollen face and cut mouth; and when she had reached her room there had been roses there, and a new book, and new puzzles, and someone had been given instructions that Miss Britton would have only hot tea and ice cream for supper, and was to stay in bed.

Oh, memories of exquisite protectiveness and concern! How they burned and tortured now! But she must not think of them now. She must think straight ahead; she must hold firm to what was left. A luncheon with Kent, and afterward perhaps a long walk and tea somewhere. They had once walked through the park from the cliff, past the big Dutch windmill and to the Japanese garden, and they had talked and talked there among the little arched bridges and canals full of lotos flowers and water lilies and fringed goldfish. They could not do that now, in forbidding winter weather. But if Lilian chanced to have a lunch engagement for Saturday—she would not, though! Leave it to Lilian to want Kent that day! But if by some miracle she did have an engagement, then Kent and Jocelyn might walk across the bridge to Sausalito, scramble up hills and gasp with joy at wide bay views, come back by bus to lunch on fried oysters and hot French bread.

Or better, they could go to Keble's place in Piedmont, go through it picking up Kent's possessions; he had said he wanted them when he went away. They would build a big fire to warm the little-used place; they might take chops and buns and a can of tomato soup for sauce. Jocelyn's hands would get grimy from handling books and dusty boxes; there would be hot water in the stark little bathroom with its out-of-door shower and "board-and-bat" walls, and she would wash herself there, tossing her hair back from a soapy fresh face, calling out to Kent, invisible and hammering somewhere, that she was just about done. Then they would have a late lunch, and fall into long talk by the fire. And there would be afternoon shadows on the winter hills and a murmuring fire and perhaps pine branches occasionally sweeping the low shingles of the roof.

Covington Keble was a painter who lived for three or four years at a time in his tiny isolated cabin up in the hills, and then, having sold a picture, or having saved enough money from his small income, left for an indefinite visit to the lessknown towns and roadways of the Old World. He took his bicycle and his dog along, and such luggage as would fit in the bicycle basket; he had various belongings in storage in Paris, and from that base he shifted about, now copying a Tiepolo in Venice, now carrying a sausage sandwich in his pocket so that he might sit uninterrupted for an entire day before a Vermeer in an Amsterdam gallery.

When he was away his friends might use his studio as their own; there was no time when they were not welcome there. Kent was numbered in this select little company— Jocelyn had met him through Kent—and old Keble had capitulated at once to Jocelyn's rare beauty and quiet appreciation. She loved him, and she knew that he loved her. Lilian he tolerated only when there was no escape; Kent was to him an especially beloved son, and he would not hurt Kent's wife or Kent through his wife.

Jocelyn connected some of her happiest memories with the cabin; now Kent had said that he must go over there before he went away. Who would go with him? Not Lilian. She was going to visit her mother for a few days in Portland before Kent followed her to the new home up there. If Covington were here, how heavenly for Jocelyn to join them at the cabin, to steal just that one delicious evening from the bleak empty months to come! It would tie her loss and Covington's together; it would mean she had company in misery. But Covington was in Switzerland, painting blue snow, "which really has a great deal of pink and green in it, too, he had written Kent.

Kent might go over alone, of course. Or he might ask the Booths. If he asked the Booths, it would be perfect, for Una was a darling and Red loved to cook. Jocelyn determined that when she and Kent had lunch together she would find out exactly what was his plan. If he had no definite plan, then why not say lightly: "By the way, if you're going over to Covey's, want Una and Red and me along? Let's have a final jamboree."

No harm in that. If he said: "A few fellows are going with me," that would end it. Her heart sank at the thought of the finality of that ending, for after that he was going away. But between now and the utter inevitable blankness of the future there must be one more meeting.

The days went by, and he did not telephone or send her any word. Early in the week came a summons from her aunt in Sausalito; Jocelyn was wanted for Saturday night and Sunday lunch; if she couldn't make both, Sunday lunch was the important time. Probably, Jocelyn thought, studying the telephone message apathetically, another of the girls was going to announce her engagement. Aunt Nell had six daughters whose ages ranged between twenty-four and fifteen, and one son, Richie, who was eleven. Two of the girls had already married; Jane was Charles Rossiter's wife; Jossy was Mrs Peter Leicester Smith. Madeleine, called Tots in the family circle, had been going with Rusty Livermore for some years, and little Sissy, who was only eighteen, had a beau, too—one Ned Whitehouse. Bam and Peaches, christened Sarah Alice and Adelaide respectively, were supposedly too young for love affairs, but one never could tell with the Partridges.

Jocelyn loved them all; her aunt was the nearest thing to a mother that she had now, and Mrs Partridge's own enormous family did not prevent her feeling a keen affectionate interest in her brother's lonely daughter. She loved to have Jocelyn with her, and Jocelyn usually loved to go to "Maple Den," as the girls had named their home in a mood of high hilarious irony years earlier. There were no maples on the place, and the rambling homely house was like nothing so little as a den, but the name clung, and Peaches and Bam had added a last touch of Victorian reality to it by planting the words in sturdy marigolds and the brushier border flowers across the front lawn. They loved to think of the casual opinion of passers-by as their eyes fell upon this elegant decoration. Jocelyn felt that the Partridges carried their sense of humor too far in this as in other instances, but the family, once having accepted a joke, never grew tired of it.

This week end she dared not leave town, even at the risk

of offending her aunt. Kent might telephone; indeed Kent unquestionably would telephone. If he did not, of course she could telephone him. Why not? Friends telephoned each other. Even if Lilian came to the telephone; what of it? One could say "Lilian, I hear you're going away? Too bad! What's the plot today?"

Lilian would say: "Nothing; why don't you come over for supper and we'll do something!" Or would she? Jocelyn had been aware that Lilian had not been very spontaneous in her messages of late months. Oh well, suppose she was not! That did not matter as long as Jocelyn had a chance to pull her most becoming hat down on her gold hair, button her winter coat effectively up to her ears, plunge her shabby gloves out of sight in her pockets, and walk in on the Dunhams gaily and confidently.

"Hello, people! I'm so glad to find you at home! I was afraid you'd go away without saying good-by!"

Friday came with no message. The hours went by; it was afternoon; it was night. No word. The telephone rang at Mrs Buck's; not for Miss Britton. "I'm expecting a message," she said, loitering in the clean, pleasant, dull hallways.

Friday night. Saturday morning. Sissy Partridge telephoned—"for Mother"—to remind Jocelyn that they wanted her. Jocelyn, in her first keen disappointment, felt that she could have slapped her innocent cousin. Kent, she thought frantically, might be trying to get her on the telephone this minute.

"Tots specially wants you to come, Jocelyn," Sissy said. "I'm not supposed to say why." Sissy's tone was bubbling with excitement and happiness, and Jocelyn could hear Bam and Peaches giggling in the background somewhere.

"Oh, darling, I'm so sorry! But I have an engagement I can't get out of."

Yelling at the other end of the line, of course. They were always yelling in the Partridge house.

"Mother says then come for sup-p-per!" finally screamed Sissy.

"I surely will, if I can." Jocelyn hung up the receiver.

Now she had to do something about it. Now she must definitely find out what Kent's plans were. This was Saturday, at ten minutes to ten. By Monday he would be gone.

Fever burned in her veins. She sat quietly at her desk in the office and tried to concentrate, to think quietly. Was Kent upstairs, in his studio? The advertising agency for which he worked was on the top floor. She could telephone. Better, she thought, with her pulses suddenly hammering, better to go up. There was nothing to stop her. Her absence from the office for a few minutes would not be noticed.

Trembling in a sudden ecstasy of hope, she went to the elevator, pressed the "Up" button; smiled at Tony and said "Tenth, Tony." Here were the doors marked "Wilson & Williams, Commercial Advertising." And here was the one that said "Enter." And here was little Miss Pettigrew at the desk. Was Mr Dunham in?

No, he wasn't. He might be in later, to get his things, but he hadn't come down yet.

"We're losing our darling," said Jean Pettigrew, who was common.

"So he told me, or his wife did," Jocelyn said carelessly, with a nod. "Too bad. We'll miss him!"

"Sad but true," Jean agreed flippantly. Jocelyn said she would leave a message, said she would not; asked that Mr Dunham telephone her when he came in.

"I'll tell little Kentsy-wentsy!" promised Jean. Jocelyn knew she was laughing, deep down inside, at the stenographer who had such a crush on handsome Mr Dunham. Well, it didn't matter what girls like Jean Pettigrew thought!

Then to wait. And how she detested waiting! There was salvation in action, in having anything to do. This was a quiet, empty Saturday morning; the office staff was almost idle. Jocelyn's only moment of real occupation was when

Philip Fordyce came in, to dictate a letter to his wife, who was in New York. They had been divorced for many years, and Janet Fordyce had been married twice since her divorce, but there was a child, Norma, their only interest in common now. Norma must be sixteen or seventeen, Jocelyn calculated, as she dutifully took down the dictation; the letter was about the child.

All the world knew about young Norma Fordyce, for her grandfather had been the great Lockey, inventor of the Lockey car, and had left the bulk of his enormous fortune to his only grandchild. His daughter had been richly benefited, too, in his will, but Janet's extravagances and her matrimonial ups and downs had considerably impoverished her interests. Norma's wealth, on the other hand, left in the original investment in the great motor company and handled by her father, had increased by leaps and bounds, so that to-day she was one of the conspicuous heiresses of the world, followed by newspaper and social sleuths wherever she went, proclaimed as the potential glamour girl of all glamour girls, and already bidding fair to satisfy a sensation-craving public with a diet of steady eccentricities.

She was a beautiful, wild little creature, who had been consigned at the time of her parents' divorce to her father's care, but with a proviso that under proper circumstances she might spend three months each year with her mother. Circumstances had not, unfortunately, always been favorable to either course, and much of Norma's time, since her small-girl days, had been spent in boarding schools and camps and in trips with tutors, nurses, governesses, maids.

Usually letters concerning Norma went through the office of the Lockey family lawyers, Jocelyn supposed; today's note was the first with whose contents she had ever been made acquainted. It was brief.

"Just say 'Dear Janet, I'm delighted of course that the child's coming to me,'" dictated Philip. "'I've gotten hold of Mother, and we're opening the Burlingame place. There are lots of nice kids here and she ought to have a fairly decent time,'" the letter concluded. "And sign it 'Phil,'" said Philip. "I haven't time to wait for it."

Jocelyn smiled at this, involuntarily, and looking up expectantly for further directions, saw that he was smiling back.

"She's on the loose again," Philip explained. "Something's gone haywire with her schooling, I don't know quite what it's all about. Her mother took her to some place in Florence last September, and she's run away—she's in New York now. Janet cabled some Frenchwoman she knew to get hold of her and bring her over, but of course she doesn't want the responsibility of her."

"The Frenchwoman doesn't?"

"No, no, Janet doesn't. She's probably going to be married again."

"Norma!" Jocelyn ejaculated.

"Janet. It's an Italian count this time, I believe. He has estates that need about a million dollars' worth of painting and papering, that's all. She wrote us about it last week. She wants money."

To this, marveling, Jocelyn could find nothing to say. After a smiling moment and a little shake of her head, she went back to the letter.

"You're opening the Burlingame place?"

"Yes, my mother'll be here. She's in Florida now, but she'll come. And we're trying to get an old governess for Norma; she was Janet's governess, as a matter of fact. Miss Sanderson. She'll keep the kid in line."

"The Florence school wasn't so good?"

"She hated it. Climbed over a wall and cut her arms on broken bottles so that we had to get her into a hospital. She's a sweet handful, that kid. I hope she marries young. She'll have a month with her mother, and Janet 'll see that she gets some clothes and see all the good shows, and then she'll be shipped out here. After that Janet will go to Palm Beach, I suppose. She wants to be married at Netty Roger's place."

"What——" Jocelyn's shadowed purple eyes danced, and a deep dimple appeared in one cheek. "What, if I may ask, was the matter with this last marriage?" she asked delicately.

"Well, Count von Sturnberg kept threatening to kill people," Philip answered with a laugh. "It made her nervous. Every time she stayed away all night, he suspected the worst, which generally was the case. She makes no bones about it. When she likes a man she goes off with him for as long as she likes him."

"Oh, she doesn't!" Jocelyn murmured, almost involuntarily.

"She keeps hoping to find happiness," the man began seriously, and stopped. "Well, perhaps all of us do!" he added with a sigh. And in another moment he was gone. Jocelyn looked after his departing form sympathetically. Everyone liked Phil Fordyce. He was a gentleman and a sportsman, polite and rich and appreciative and handsome and clever. He played magnificent golf and bridge and polo and belonged to clubs. He had caught marlin in Catalina waters and tarpon off the Florida coast: he had been everywhere and had talked familiarly with governors and even with a president or two. He rarely became mad about anything, and when he did, it was impressive. He dressed almost too well. All the appointments of his office were magnificent—silver, crystal, ivory, polished steel hammered into polished bronze.

It was now twenty minutes past twelve. No word, no sign from Kent. Jocelyn telephoned his office; he had not come in. She began to tremble with anxiety and nervousness, and presently, with a sudden reach for the telephone, a sudden agitated jerking over the dial numbers, she called Una Booth. When Una answered the telephone unsuspectingly, cheerfully, naturally, Jocelyn felt something like a shock of reaction.

"Una, this is Jocelyn. How is everything?"

"My dear, this great furry cat is pressing himself right against my mouth! Tipsy, get down!"

Jocelyn felt an instant chill. Something was wrong. Una was sparring for time.

"Una, what are you doing today?"

"Well——" Was she really disengaging the cat, or was she looking at Red for advice? "We have no plans, we've been talking of everything," said Una laughingly, after an almost imperceptible pause. "Red's out at this minute, but when he comes back I suppose we'll make up our minds!"

"Horrible about Kent's going, isn't it?"

"Kent and Lilian. It's awful."

Another hint of hesitation. Jocelyn felt a rueful, scornful twist come into her own expression. Una never bothered much about Lilian. This was a new attitude.

"They go Monday," Jocelyn said. The statement fell flatly into silence.

"I know; it's rotten!" Una said. And then briskly, as if she had found at last the swift way out of the conversation, "We ought to do something quite drastic about it, oughtn't we? Lilian's gone, you know; I said good-by to her yesterday. I'll tell you, Jocelyn, I'm just awake and everything's fuzzy. We were out at a Press Club party last night and got home at six. But I'll tell you, let's—— Where'll you be this afternoon? If I can stir up anything——"

"Kent said something about going over to Covey's," Jocelyn put in eagerly, as the other woman's voice again hesitated for a second.

"Oh, did he? Was that yesterday?" Una wasn't giving her any lead.

"No. I've forgotten just when he said it." That sounded as if she had seen him casually, frequently, in the last few days.

"Well——" Another little flag in the conversation. "Well, suppose I telephone you?" Una asked.

"They're going over there without me," Jocelyn thought.

Aloud she said: "I was going to go to Sausalito. But if there was any plan for today, of course I'd put it off. So do telephone me, Una."

"I'll do that very thing!" It was too spontaneous; too carefully sincere; too obviously relieved.

Jocelyn hung up her telephone and sat quite still, feeling a little sick. Something had been wrong with the talk; it left her with a snubbed and chilled sensation. She had done all she could do, and it was no use. Now there were blank hours ahead. The Booths were notoriously dilatory; they idled about in their studio for half the day; they might get around to telephoning Kent at about three; they might put it off until later.

They lived in an untidy apartment back of some old buildings on Post Street; the studio jutted into a garage and had two rooms that impinged upon a flat occupied by the French laundry people who worked downstairs. It was a sunless, gloomy place in the daytime, but Jocelyn had had some wonderful happy evenings there, when she and Una had cooked the dinner, the men had poured red wine, played on the old piano, and done quick sketches of the girls' heads. Lilian hated the place and in a quiet way disliked the Booths and their "influence" on Kent. But that made Jocelyn love it all the more, and there had been happy times when she had known that Kent had liked it the better for his wife's avoidance of it.

Well, those times were over. But something—surely *something* was left?

Why hadn't Una said: "Come right up here, Jocelyn; we'll get hold of Kent and make him do something"? Why hadn't she said that? It would have been so simple, then. Jocelyn, who knew the state of the Booths' finances, could have stopped for a few pounds of sausages, for a couple of pink, cold boiled crabs, for Red's favorite white-iced devil's-food cake. She could have joined them and conspired with them, and it would all have been safe and companionable and happy.

If Kent evaded them all three, then they would have company in misery at least; then they would have been able to criticize him, to wonder what was the matter with him, to say how changed he was.

As it was, she walked home from the office nervously, restlessly, feeling that unless something happened to bring him into the scene during the next two days she would go out of her senses. She stayed in her room, lying on her bed and reading, waiting for a telephone call. It did not come, and at four o'clock, feeling faint and weary and desolate, and having had no lunch, she followed a sudden impulse, dressed herself and started to walk to the Booths' studio. She would go in on them carelessly, explain that she had an errand in their neighborhood to do, for—well, for Mr Phil Fordyce. His daughter wanted—wanted her to find her a wig at the costumer's on Market Street—and so she thought she'd drop in. Kent might be there.

The sudden thought that Kent might be there made her heart jump with fear and joy and brought color to her cheeks. She felt a little dizzy now, and the streets reeled by her unseen. Kent might be stretched in his favorite chair, the old armchair that dribbled stuffing over everything and bagged with unseemly brown straps below its sunken cushions. He would be smoking his pipe; blue haze would circle the cold, shadowed studio in wheeling disks of smoke. Una would say: "It's freezing here!" and Red, fat and bald and good-natured in his spattered smock, would clank open the air-tight stove to throw in a few short chunky logs.

Then everything would be heaven; everything would be utterly blissful and right. Whatever they did would be, of all things in the world, just what she wanted to do. Kent might look up with his lazy smile and say: "We needed you, Joy. We're all going over to Covey's to cook supper."

Or he might say that they would have to dine in town; he could not get away in time to go to Piedmont. Suppose they dined at some Italian place on Columbus Avenue, and afterward wandered through Chinatown and bought each other good-by presents. Then tomorrow they could get an early start for Covey's, and have lunch there on the porch in the winter sunshine, looking down at the great panorama of the cities and the bay and the far blue mountains of Marin, pale under a pale sky toward the north.

It would be the last of Kent for a long time. The last of him for all time, in one way. When he had lived in Portland for a while with Lilian's people, Lilian's old friends, Lilian's influences continually about him, he would not be the same person any more. Kent was impressionable, emotional, changeable. No, she'd never have Kent back. But this good-by time with him she must have, and then she could be good, then she could go on.

"We've never done anything wrong. God, let it go right just this one time!" she prayed, as she walked along.

CHAPTER III

THERE WAS NOBODY AT THE STUDIO. The shock of it stunned Jocelyn, and for a few minutes she could not believe the evidence of the deserted great chill room. For, after her unanswered knock, she went familiarly around through the French laundry passage and up the outside stairs and so unchallenged into the place. They never locked the passage door. Everything was quiet, empty, dreary. Una never dusted or put things in place; socks and combs, plates and ends of loaves were left to lie where they naturally fell, and picked up again when next needed.

Jocelyn stood in the midst of the disorder and coldness, thinking for a long minute. Then she quietly went away again by the way she had come.

But which way now, and why? It was twenty minutes before five o'clock. The day, which had been sticky and heavily overcast, was at its least cheerful moment; it was ebbing fast into dark; street lights were breaking out everywhere. Jocelyn, unconscious of where she walked or what she passed, went home again. When she got to Mrs Buck's it was quite dark. The house smelled, as it always did, of boiling sprouts and furniture oil and furnace warmth.

"Jocelyn," said Phyllis Buck, in the hall. "There was a telephone message for you."

Jocelyn stood quite still. Everything inside her—heart, mind and soul stood still.

"It was from Mrs Johnson," said Phyllis. "They're away this week end and if you're going to Sausalito you can have their car. It's in the garage."

"Oh. Thanks."

"Are you going to Sausalito, Jocelyn?"

"Not tonight, I think; it's too late. I'll probably go over for lunch tomorrow."

"Phyllis!" called her mother. "Did you give Jocelyn her message?"

"I just did, Mom."

"I mean the one that came just after she went out. From that Mrs Booth."

Jocelyn, halfway up the stairs, stood stricken to stone again. There had been a message from Una, then? What? What?

"Your friend Mrs Booth telephoned," Mrs Buck said heavily, appearing stout and wrappered in her bedroom door, "and said—I've written it here. They were going out of town and she would telephone you tomorrow afternoon or Monday."

"Thanks," Jocelyn said, proceeding upward to her room. She could not analyze the meaning of it; she was too confused. She went in and shut her door and sat on her bed. They had gone to Piedmont, then, to Covey's? Hadn't they tried for her? Hadn't they wanted her? The message did not say. If she had been here, Una hardly could have telephoned her without including her in the plan. Why telephone at all if not to do that?

They'd gone over to Piedmont, and she'd missed them. The bitterness of it swept over her like a vertigo, and for a few minutes she could not seem to collect her thoughts at all, or move hand or foot. When she did heavily begin to prepare for dinner, it was apathetically. She wished it were not too late to go across the bay to her aunt; the distraction of the big family, however unsympathetic to her mood, would still have been a tonic.

Quite suddenly she began to pack an overnight bag; there was a twenty-minute ferry service to Piedmont, and she could get a taxi to take her up to Covey's. She would find them all there, with a big fire of logs blazing in the low cabin room, and dinner not half ready. Una was always dilatory, and in the end the men would have to finish up preparations for the meal themselves. She could go in laughing triumphantly: "I had your message, Una, and decided that since this devil is really leaving us Monday . . ."

The joy of getting there, of really seeing him and hearing his voice and answering his nonsense! She had been following him, hungering for him for so long!

Quickly, calmly, she packed. It was good to be determined, to know exactly what she was going to do. Phyllis, seventeen, and a great admirer of the beautiful older girl, came into the room.

"Oh, you are going across the bay?"

"I thought I would."

"Is your cousin engaged?"

"I think so."

"And is he nice? Mr Livermore?"

"He's a darling. He and Tots have been friends since she was a baby. They know him, at least."

"What kind of a car is it?" asked Phyllis.

Jocelyn looked at her, not comprehending.

"I mean the Johnsons' car, that they said you could have."

"Oh?" Jocelyn had forgotten that detail. Of course, she had a car. She could drive straight from Bush Street over the bridge to the cabin in Piedmont; that made it all the more explainable, all the simpler. "I had Ann Johnson's car, and I thought I'd come over and see what you all were up to."

It was all plain sailing now. Fifteen minutes later she was on her way. She stopped at a big market, bought a dozen doughnuts—dark rich doughnuts, chocolate bars, a dozen enormous golden oranges. She bought an evening paper, and hummed with delight and triumph as the little car crossed the gigantic bridge across the dark waters of the bay.

Once on the other side she had merely to drive steadily along the brightly lighted magnificent roads to Oakland, through Oakland's blazing theater and restaurant district, on toward the Piedmont hills. Undulating Oakland Avenue, straight ahead, and then Coolidge until you came to the school, and then past the Tunnel Road and up a slanting cut.

She leaned from the car under the bright lights of an oil station.

"I think I'm off my road. Which way is Wickson Street?"

The white-clad nice young man got out a map, after observing: "You have me there." They looked at it together.

"You'll get wet!" Jocelyn said, for it had begun softly, warmly to rain. He smiled, spattered and cheerful.

"Here you are. You've got to go back to—well, almost to the Tunnel Road, see? They changed it in there, that's what threw you off. Slant through Hodgson Place, see? You cut into Wickson there. What's your number?"

"No number. It's up at the end of Wickson, and over a little crest; there's no real road up there. It's an artist's studio; he's been there since long before the road was put through."

"May find those roads pretty muddy. We had a regular cloudburst here today."

"We didn't have any rain in the city at all. But it felt heavy and muggy. Like rain."

The car clock said five minutes of seven. It would take her only twenty minutes to get up the grade; she would arrive at exactly the right minute. Jocelyn set her windshield wipers to working and drove on into the dark to the tune of their brisk creaking. Rain was falling steadily; her lights bored into a crisscross pattern of silver and black.

She knew this road. It was fun to follow it up and up, finding fewer and fewer houses as the hill rose, finally coming out

on the ridge and seeing the warm squares of light that were
Covey's windows. The lane that led from the broader road into his place was indeed soft and muddy; the car lurched and
bumped on holes; Jocelyn turned it about in workmanlike
fashion and backed it into the empty shed that served as a
garage. Her heart rose on a wave of deep thankfulness and
joy; Kent's blue car was already there. They were here, no
question of that now!

She picked her way in almost pitch blackness to the front
door, carrying her bag and her packages. Rain fell thickly;
the windows gave her the only light she had now; it was not
bright enough to save her stepping into a pool of ice-cold
water here, or into the soft sinking earth of a flower bed
there. Covey had done little in the matter of cultivation, but
there was a path, and there were finally firm wooden steps
under her wet feet, the doorknob in her wet glove.

She dropped her bundles in the dark hallway; shed her hat
and gloves. Pushing her bright hair into a damp cap as she
opened the door of the cabin's one big room, she called chal-
lengingly: "Hello, everyone!"

There was a good fire roaring on the open hearth, and an
oil lamp was lighted. The dear shabby chairs, the long table,
the curtained bunks, the lines of books were all half revealed;
she loved every inch of the place. The warmth of it was
delicious after the bleakness and darkness and wetness outside.

No one was in sight. The rest of the house consisted merely
of a small piny kitchen, walled, as this room was walled, in
raw pine, and a bathroom. In summer weather a canvased
back porch could be used as an additional bedroom; in winter
Covey merely drew an old corduroy curtain across the center
of this room. Women took the berths on one side; men those
on the other, and if a good deal of hilarious conversation
went on across the curtain, it did not tend to make visits to
the place less enjoyable to the artist's lighthearted friends.

Tonight, Jocelyn reflected, she and Una would take their turn at the bathroom, washing shudderingly in its icy chill, but with hot water and fragrant soap and Covey's mismated towels to aid them, and then snuggle under their warm blankets and watch lamplight and firelight shine on walls and faded rugs and the backs of books, and listen to the rain on the low roof.

When the men returned from their ablutions there would be the usual nonsense. "Girls, don't hesitate to call us at the least alarm in the night." "Don't worry, we won't." "Anything alarming you, Jocelyn?" "Only you, Kent." "This is very distressing to me, Jocelyn, you know what a stickler I am for the conventions." "I know, Red. We both feel for you deeply, don't we, Una?"

Then laughter, and their light out, and the men's light out, and finally "Oh, hush up, both of you! We're sleepy!" and then the silence and the dying glow of the burning logs, and once again the delicious soft rustle and patter of the rain overhead.

Jocelyn had stayed here several times under those conditions. They were perhaps the happiest times that she and Kent ever had had together. They had expressed wonder sometimes, that those who loved each other did not find some such place as this in which to be happy. So little money was needed, and so many persons had that much money! A garden, trees, a wide glorious view, wild poppies spangling the hills in May, Michaelmas daisies thick beside the lanes in autumn. And French bread and cheese and good hot coffee, and the utter peace of dreamless sleep and quiet days . . .

And love, they had always said. A man and a woman loving each other desperately, completely, gloriously. She in faded Chinese coolie smocks; he in a daubed shabby jacket and worn cords, and sunrises and sunsets and the whitewash of summer moons and the delicate frosts of winter mornings theirs forever and forever!

Just to be back in the beloved room brought back the old

dream, and it was as if he loved her as much as ever he had, as if she were happy again. She turned from where she was standing, rain-spattered, and with her hands stretched to the fire, when he came in from the kitchen, and the light made an aureole of her gold hair and shadowed her eyes as she laughed at him.

"I had to come! I had Una's message, and I knew it was my last chance. But what a night! I went up to Red's and no one was there, and I'd telephoned and everything was all mixed up. But when I got back to the house Una's message was there, and a message that I could have the Johnsons' car. It all seemed to fit too nicely. Instead of going to Aunt Nell's, I came over here."

He came over to her, and the look she loved was in his eyes. Rain pattered overhead, the fire crackled, Kent smiled, and for a moment his arms were about her, and heaven was in her heart. He did not have to speak, and there was a moment of silence.

When he did speak it was amusedly, tenderly, as she had feared never to hear him speak to her again.

"What are you apologizing for?" he demanded. The tone rather than the words caressed her; seemed to enclose her in sweetness and warmth and safety again. She drew back from him laughing, bewildered, her soft gold hair still disordered and damp, her cheek still fresh and chilly from the cold and storm. "When have you had to apologize for coming where I am?" he asked.

All so much better than her most radiant dream! Jocelyn's face bloomed into sudden radiance.

"But I couldn't get hold of Una, I wasn't sure they were here!" she explained. And as his expression, still amused and tender, took on a new note of mischief and triumph she added, in dawning surprise, "Why, *aren't* they here?" And then with a shocked and half-delighted laugh, "They *aren't?* Oh, Kent!"

"Oh, Jocelyn!" he returned, in the same tone. And again

she was jumbled against his heart, and she felt his kisses on her hair and her temples. Outside, high above the low roof, in the dark, the wind roared, and branches creaked and swished, and on the shingles and dripping from the eaves they could hear the steady pattering and splashing of the rain.

CHAPTER IV

"This is a nice little hour stolen from under the gods' very noses," Jocelyn said contentedly. She stretched her feet toward the fire, and turned the aureole of her bright hair against the cushions of the old chair.

Kent, stretched equally at ease in a companion chair of shabby leather, opposite her, smiled, took his pipe from his mouth and smiled again.

It was half past nine o'clock. The rain had stopped, and when Jocelyn, finishing supper dishes in good housewifely fashion, had stepped out to the back porch to invert the dishpan and hang the towels on the rail, she had seen stars overhead, and had called Kent to watch the white moon struggling in a tangle of heavy rolling cloud. Kent had braced her with his arm, and they had stood for a long while without speaking, staring up at the wild beauty of the night.

Then it had been good to come in, chilled and breathing deep, to replenish the fire and settle themselves there to rest and get warm after the strenuous work of getting a meal in a place as primitive as Covey's.

Never in all the months of their friendship had they two seemed as closely united in mood and spirit as they were tonight. It was as if they had weathered a great storm, been washed apart, and now found themselves flung safely upon a high sun-warmed beach, rediscovering each other with all the freshness of beginnings and all the seasoned joy of known delight.

35

"Kent, I have to go home. It'll take me an hour to drive back."

"When you go I'll go with you," he said, not stirring, except to settle back in his chair again without removing his thoughtful eyes from the fire.

"That wouldn't do any good, darling. We'd be in two cars."

"It 'd be an escort, anyway. But I'll drive your car and leave mine here. I'd have to come back tomorrow anyway, I can take the train. I've not done any packing, really."

"You mustn't do that. No, I'll toast for another half-hour and then be on my way. But Kent," Jocelyn said, her beautiful eyes on his, "this has been so perfect! This has been just what I needed. I've wanted so terribly just another hour with you; and to have it here, just our two selves, and the rain shutting us in, has been—well, I'm grateful. And I do see," she went on a little thickly, but steadily, and with a smile in the eyes that were suddenly misted, "I do see that we have to end it, Kent, and I'm going over to Aunt Nell's tomorrow to begin quite a different way of feeling. Really I am! I've no business to dream dreams and build plans about another woman's husband, not any more than about another woman's baby. We've kept it all at a certain decent level, but I'm not so sure that even that is quite as—as noble as we've always considered it," Jocelyn went on, sometimes glancing at the fire, sometimes bringing her eyes to his again. "We've not given Lilian the satisfaction even of despising us!" she said, on a rueful laugh.

Kent was listening, his head dropped, his fine sensitive mouth biting now and then on his pipestem, his eyes moving moodily to her face, moodily narrowing as he looked into far space again. He did not speak.

"Wasn't it always a sort of lie, Kent, that we were just good friends, that we wouldn't hurt Lilian, that we didn't take from her anything that belonged to her? If we'd been free to marry and had married, I wouldn't want to give any

other woman that much of you," Jocelyn said honestly.
"You've kissed me, you've made me presents, we've met
each other secretly a hundred times, and we've said all along
that it didn't rob Lilian. But I'm not so sure!"

Still he did not speak. He had raised his eyes now and was
regarding her steadily.

"So you see I've come to see it your way," she finished,
gaining certainty with every word.

"I wonder if we've been a pair of fools!" Kent said suddenly in a hoarse voice.

"Fools?" Jocelyn faltered, her eyes widening.

The man spoke in a quiet, thoughtful tone, his body bent
forward in his low chair, his locked fingers dropped between
his knees. He looked at the fire.

"I wonder, my dear," he said, "if we haven't been fools.
You're quite right. What we did take was really much more
than what we prided ourselves upon *not* taking! Companionship, love, longing, we struggled to adjust them for months
and months. You wouldn't give in, and I didn't want you to
give in. I wanted to keep you higher than myself, higher than
any woman who loves and gives and is a man's. Well, we
achieved it. We kept to the letter of the law. I'm going away
on Monday; we'll not see each other again for a long time.
We've killed the beautiful thing, it's dying by inches. You're
mine by every law of our hearts and minds and bodies. But
that isn't the world's law. And we give in to the world's law,
of course."

His voice had sunk so low that she could hardly hear him.
There was no bitterness in it; no violence. It was as if he
were merely thinking aloud.

"But I wonder," he said musingly again, "if we haven't
been fools!"

It was her turn to be silent now. She could not speak.

"I thought I could say good-by to you rationally and
easily," Kent was presently saying. "I'd thought it all out.
My promotion, going back to live in the old town, playing

fair with Lilian. I don't know why that should suddenly have seemed to me important, for she's not especially happy with me. I think that after any break or change she'd very quickly readjust herself, settle down again. But anyway, I felt that she and I were very definitely in the picture, and you necessarily out of it, and that we could work it out that way. Now——"

He stopped on the word and was silent. She took it up.

"Now? Nothing is changed now. Except that we have had this wonderful stolen hour and this talk."

"Everything's changed now," he stated firmly. "I know now that it's only you. You forever and forever, nobody else. That's what I've just been finding out. You're the one wonderful, perfect thing that's ever come into my life, and all that matters is that I don't lose you. I've been an awful fool, Jocelyn; I've been sitting here thinking, just these last few minutes, what a consummate fool I've been!"

He stood up and put his pipe on the low mantel, and came over to kneel beside her and take both her hands in his.

"Darling," he said, "will you forgive me? You have forgiven me, haven't you, or you'd never have come over tonight. Will you trust me that I'll not fail you again? We'll go through with it now. We'll go through with it now!" Kent repeated with a long indrawn breath. "We'll begin tonight a new life that belongs just to you and me, and that the world won't either see or care about! I'll not go to Portland Monday, Jocelyn," he said, "I'll go to Reno. It's best that way, dear, and afterward we'll take whatever chances come along. I'll always be able to take care of you, even if it's only in a place like this. I'll see Lilian tomorrow, in Richmond here——"

"In Richmond?" Her sharp whisper filled the pause as he hesitated. Richmond was but a few miles away.

"Yes; she didn't go to Oregon. Her sister, who lives here in Richmond, telephoned her Wednesday that their mother is down here visiting. So Lilian went over there yesterday and will drive up with them later in the week. Jocelyn, I know she'll be reasonable," Kent said, "and if she isn't, there are ways to get around her. It may take a little time, but it can be managed. I think I knew all along that this was the way it must be, and I've been fighting it off—I've been trying to keep what I had and have you, too. That's over now. I know now I have nothing without you! We'll begin again. We'll have again what we had in those first days, Jocelyn——"

"The blue morocco handbag," she interrupted, smiling with brimming eyes.

"The blue handbag. And the primroses in a green pot. And lunch at 'Julius's Castle.' "

" 'Julius's Castle!' " she echoed.

"We belong together, dear. It's had me all upset and undecided, this miserable business of feeling we ought to say good-by, trying to say good-by. We'll never part again, sweetheart. And when we can—the first moment that we can, we'll be married." He leaned back, still holding her lightly by the shoulders, to smile at her. "You know that, don't you?" he said.

She looked deep into his eyes. Her own eyes were very serious.

"I do know that, Kent."

"Then that's that. And you are mine now, Jocelyn, mine by every vow, every promise I can make to you. I'll leave you here tomorrow and motor over and see Lilian. It's only twenty minutes from here. And after that I'll resign from the Portland thing and get my old job back, and we'll start from there. For love's the only thing that's true," Kent said, "love's the only thing too precious to throw away. It sounds so flat, but it means everything! One glorious week of our life together will make up for all this coldness, this calculation and hesitation and nonsense! You'll not be afraid?" he broke off to ask suddenly. "You trust me?"

"I seem to have been waiting so long to hear you say this, Kent." She leaned forward and rested her forehead against his with a long sigh, and felt his arm tighten about her, and his cheek against her hair.

"Jocelyn, I'm so happy!" he said.

"I'm happy, too."

"It's called burning your bridges behind you, you know, and I've always thought it sounded rather formidable. But what a relief!"

"Kent, we'll never be sorry. For we don't want anyone in our life except sometimes Una and Red, and darling old Covey. And they'd forgive us whatever we did!"

He was looking at her with eyes bewildered with love and felicity, and he answered only in a murmur:

"And it wouldn't matter if they didn't!"

There was a silence. And then quite without warning Jocelyn felt a great boredom possess her, and what they were saying lost all its meaning and was flat and strange. She still felt Kent's arm about her; she was conscious of the nearness and the power of him, but he was no longer he, nor she herself. They were two complete strangers; she was looking into eyes she had never seen before, hearing an unknown voice say incomprehensible things.

Inwardly she shook herself, trying to get her bearings again. This was Kent; she was Jocelyn; they were up in the hills alone at night in Covey's cabin; they were free to live their own lives at last. Everything but their love was to be abandoned.

"Say you're happy that we are going to give up everything else and live just for each other!" he was whispering.

"Happy!" she said with a smile, swallowing with a dry throat.

What on earth was the matter? All the color, all the thrill had drained out of life. She felt stupid and unresponsive; if she answered him what he expected her to answer, it was mere play-acting; if she said what she wanted to say, the words might begin with a burst of disillusioned laughter.

Kent Dunham. Lilian Dunham's husband. A perfectly delightful person and someday to be a successful artist, too.

The sudden revulsion of feeling, or rather death of feeling, frightened her. She found herself speaking gently to him, affectionately, almost soothingly. He must not know how suddenly their whole castle of dreams had come fluttering down; that her spirit was crying out with little Alice: "You're nothing but a pack of cards!"

Absurd to be twenty-seven and a reasoning human being of reputedly more than average intelligence and beauty, and to be up here in the high lonely hills beyond Piedmont with Lilian Dunham's husband, "putting on an act!" Jocelyn phrased it scornfully in her mind.

"I'll go now and write him tomorrow," she thought, even while her fine fingers rested against his cheek, and his words of adoration and eagerness poured on past her unhearing ears.

But that plan he would not tolerate. They had been parted, they had been undecided, long enough! Now they must give to each other every possible pledge of trust and devotion. They would not part again. Their united life would begin here and now, tonight; morning would find them glorified by the peace that her surrender and his triumphant and proud possession of her alone could give them. That had been their mistake from the first, he said. They had not had the courage of their convictions; the courage to love first, and let life adjust itself to love's demands afterward.

He was presently crouched on a hassock at her knee, his arms laid across her lap and his fingers locking her fingers. Both their faces were toward the fire, but now and then he turned his head to look up at her, and she smiled down at him and bent her head so that their cheeks touched, even while she was wondering, wondering how easiest she could escape.

"Jocelyn, I can't plan—I can't begin anything—until we belong to each other! Fate brought us both up here tonight, my darling, and Fate will guide us the rest of the way. It's destiny."

She remembered her wild prayer of a few hours ago; it seemed the cry of a woman who days—weeks—earlier had ceased to be.

"We've never done anything wrong. God, let it go right just this one time!" she had prayed. Even while she listened to him, something deep within her was smiling with irony and pity at that prayer. Only this afternoon; could it have been only this afternoon! Now she was phrasing another prayer, in a new spirit of strange humility and self-contempt:

"I don't belong here. This is all nonsense. Help me—help me to get away!"

"Kent, I have to go home, dear. But come take me to dinner tomorrow and we'll conspire."

"Tomorrow, idiot! By tomorrow we'll have had the most wonderful hours of our lives!" He was talking with all the enthusiasm of a boy; she had never known him so young, so fired, so confident. It was a new Kent, with all the charm of the old Kent and the glory and excitement of hope and joy added. "This is our hour, my darling," he said. "The moment that never will come again. Nothing can take this away from us now!"

Why didn't it reach her? Why didn't it stir her? She looked at him with a slow smile in her eyes, with infinite pity in her heart, with her thoughts far away from him. Already he was out of her life; already the part he had played was far behind her; already she had gone on in her mind to the trip back to the city, the car flying through the dark, the heavenly safety of her room again. Books and silence and the quiet circle of light dropped by her reading lamp in all the shadows. And tomorrow, instead of sharing a love adventure with Kent, up here on the mountainside, she would go decorously to Sausalito and rejoice with Tots and all the cousins over the latest engagement, and feel herself free of the shadow that had darkened her life for more than a year.

"What are you thinking of?" he said, suddenly aware of her inattention, suddenly jealous.

"That I must go home," she answered mildly.

"What for? We belong to each other now. Let the whole world know it!"

"Suppose you lost both jobs and couldn't get another?"

"Then we'd come over here for a while and I'd free-lance. You're not afraid?" he said reproachfully.

"No, I'm not afraid. But I've got to go home just the same. We can make all our plans tomorrow, but I don't belong here tonight."

"You don't trust me," he cried. And then pleadingly, "Ah, Jocelyn, let's have this glorious thing, anyway. Let's steal this much, and then we can be patient, waiting for the rest!"

"After all our months of being good?" she asked whimsically. She could play with words and situations if she liked, now; there was no strain, there was no temptation left. All the misery that she had experienced only a few hours ago had been transferred to him, to Kent, who had been so cool and philosophical and self-possessed ten days ago, when in the office they had had that memorable meeting. Jocelyn felt as if she had been released from long fever and delirium. Peace flooded her spirit like a river.

"After all our months of being good, the time has come when we needn't be good any longer," he reminded her. "Our path is quite clear before us now, and, darling, how good it feels to know which way we're going! I don't think I could really have gone away from you for long, but in any case this saves time. I'll have my talk with Lilian tomorrow; her people will talk and gasp for a few days, and then there'll be a six-weeks' wait, and then—then heaven for us both! Where'll we go, what will we do, what will we live on? Who cares? We'll get along, and in a few years forget that it was ever any other way except you and me, and our garden and our fire, and my paints——"

There was a telephone in the cabin, which was used as a

fire station in dry weather. The forest rangers had placed it there; it was rarely used by Covey or any of his guests. Now it rang sharply in the lonely dark mountain night, above the swishing of leaves and creaking of boughs and the sound of the wind at the mouth of the wide chimney.

Jocelyn and Kent looked at it and at each other and at the clock. Ten minutes to ten. With a shrug the man went and picked up the instrument. It was Lilian, telephoning from Richmond, only a dozen miles away. Jocelyn heard him answering patiently; the married man again.

"I can come back here Monday, Lil, and pick up my stuff and then drive the car to Bertha's and leave it there for you. You wouldn't want it before Monday? . . . All right. If there's nobody there I'll put the key on the top of the screen door. . . . Yep. Tell her I'm sorry not to see her. . . . No, no, don't you girls change your plans; you go do your shopping; that 'll be all right. Bertha'll be coming up for Christmas, won't she? . . . Yep. Need money? How's the tooth?"

Jocelyn went without hurry toward the kitchen, picking up her bag as she went. Kent's back was toward the room; he might be aware that she was leaving the room, but he would not see that she had taken her bag. Her hat and coat were spread in the kitchen, drying; she put them on quickly, and went quietly out the kitchen door and around the house. She did not light the lights of her car when she had gotten into it; it started up almost noiselessly; there was enough disturbance in the air and among the trees and shrubs to cover whatever sound the engine made. As the machine wheeled to leave the garden and turn into the lane, Jocelyn turned up her lights, swept away down into the darkness, heard the mud squelching beneath her wheels.

She drew a long breath; spoke aloud.

"Well, I'm out of that!" she said exultantly. "I'm out of that. Time was when I couldn't have left you, Kent, when just being near you and having you want me would have broken down all my defenses! But not now. Not now! I wonder what's happened to me, I wonder what waked me up all of a sudden?" she went on conversationally. "It was all one way one minute, and just calm—just being bored the next. A man whose wife was telephoning him about car keys and hand baggage and toothache! And I sitting there feeling like the fool I am.

"He'll never forgive me, of course. His pride will be mortally wounded. Well, better his than mine! I would have been ready to kill myself this time tomorrow if I'd gone through with this. Escape. You're lucky, Jocelyn Britton. If you'd been staying up here two or three days with Kent Dunham, and had heard that nice wife-and-husband conversation, what a nice opinion of yourself you'd have had! There wouldn't have been any way out for you then. He'd have had any number of ways out. All a man in those circumstances has to do is say that his wife is simply adamant. He's horribly sorry, and he honors you just as much as before, but—there you are!"

The road wound downhill in pitchy darkness. Rain was again falling, and the little wipers of the car were busily at work. Jocelyn began to speak to herself aloud again, in a different strain:

"Where on earth am I? That glare 'way over there must be Oakland, but how do I get to it? What a road, mudholes and ruts and pools! This isn't the regular road; I got turned off somewhere. Well, by just keeping downward I'll end up somewhere, Berkeley or Alameda or Fruitvale or somewhere. Maybe that time I went up I was going over the ridge, maybe I'm turned around and facing south."

Plenty of gas; plenty of oil; she drove on as briskly as mud and rain permitted. The rain was very trying. It obscured signs; it dazzled and glittered and made driving difficult. Her keyboard clock said eleven.

"I'm taking the nasty new look off the Johnsons' car, fool that I am!" she reflected. "Why didn't I go over to Aunt

Nell's and have an evening playing writing games or dancing
with Rusty and Ned and Pete Smith? Good heavens!"

The last ejaculation was wrung loudly from her as the car
skidded, slipped, and turned abruptly over a low bank to
wedge itself against a tree trunk that was lighted brilliantly
by the lamps. Jocelyn sat still for a moment, weakened by the
shock. Then she realized that nothing more of a dangerous
nature could happen, and peered out to see what she could of
the situation.

All around was the blackness of the rainy night. Her head-
lights showed a dirt road pitted with pools of mud and lumps
of old concrete; this was certainly no part of the highway she
had expected to follow: she had missed a turn somewhere,
and floundered off into one of the hill roads so baffling to the
traveler in these sprawled and scattered hill settlements.
Down below her, where there had once been a chain of lights,
most of the heartening speckles that meant homes and lamps
had disappeared; far away there was a long clean line of
them; the highway between Oakland and Richmond perhaps,
but there was nothing near. No gates, no houses, just empty
road and rain.

She tried to back her car out of the soft mud into which
it had slipped. It bucked; the wheels revolved, but there was
nothing solid upon which they could grip.

"Look here, you've got to move, you know!" said Jocelyn.

After a while she realized that the spinning wheels were
going no further that night, and wondered if she would inevitably get pneumonia, curled chilly and wretched on the
front seat. She got down in the rain and groped for a rug in
the baggage box and found two old blankets. "Life savers!"
she said, rolling herself into them, curling herself up on the
back seat to weather the dark hours until dawn.

After a while the rain stopped, but no car passed her; no
light came along her road. She slept fitfully; saw the first uncertain streaks of day in the eastern sky and realized that she
was on the wrong side of the hill. By the time there was

enough light to see the road, she was a mile away from the car and on the north slope of the hill again, descending through the mud and chill of early morning toward the safety of the towns below.

The first house, the first gas station she reached would mean deliverance, she reassured herself steadily. She could telephone then, get a train and a boat, get home to warmth and a bath and breakfast. These things seemed far away; unattainable. But they were there, waiting, and long before the rest of the world was awake she would gain them.

A muddy car rattled behind her; a muddy little man with a good-natured weak face offered her a lift. Jocelyn climbed in thankfully beside him, and within half a moment everything was normal again. Everything was within reach. Her good Samaritan, his breath reminiscent of alcohol, told her where to telephone for the right assistance in the matter of the car and her bag; told her something of himself as they went along. He had a little boy named Brucie, and had had a girl named Florence, who had died. Oh, too bad! What had been the trouble? Meningitis? Oh, too bad. How old had she been? Just three—that very day.

Jim Scudder had come over to see a feller named Boston— sure, that was a funny name, all right. Bridgie Boston they called him. Jim had won a turkey in a raffle and had left it with Bridgie, who had a back yard. But he couldn't find the street; he always got lost over here in the Oakland streets; it was a heck of a thing, but he couldn't ever seem to find that feller's place. But he knew a feller in town who knew Bridgie, and he could phone him. Jim's wife was off him all right, oh, for boozing and running around, and he hoped to have a turkey sometime today with which to get her over her mad. And here was the railroad station and the lady was welcome. The glorious sun was rising on a clear cold wintry day.

"I wish you'd——" She hesitated, battered and rain-damp and disheveled, but pretty sure he wouldn't take her money.

"No, *ma'am!*" he said.

"Well, thank you a thousand times!"

"I was glad to do it. I hope you have a happy Thanksgiving."

"I hope *you* do!" Her heart was singing. She had gotten out of a wretched predicament pretty well. She felt stiff and achy, but in a few minutes she could straighten up her clothes and comb back her hair in the dressing room on the boat, and afterward have a delicious breakfast: coffee, poached eggs, lots of buttered toast.

"Miss Britton?" said a voice behind her. She wheeled on the station platform, terror seizing her for a second, she knew not why. But it was only Philip Fordyce, in his low-hung dark blue car. He was leaning out, laughing at her. "I thought I knew that hair!" he said. And then, in amazement: "For the Lord's sake, what have you gotten yourself into!"

"Everything!" she answered, desperately laughing in return. He leaned over to open a door.

"Get in," he said. "I'll run you home."

"I'd be ashamed. I'm such a mess!"

His answer was an unsmiling glance and a brief, "Get in!" and Jocelyn got in. Immediately the wide clean roads, packed and trim after the rain, were flying by them. Had she had breakfast? Neither had he.

"We'll go to the 'Palace,'" he said casually. "Good coffee there!"

"Oo-oo!" burst from her gratefully. The "Palace," and coffee!

They parked in the empty orderly stillness of Market Street early on a Sunday morning, and were the first in the dining room when it opened at six o'clock.

"I was over at Claremont last night at a party," the man explained. "Well, I'd promised to play golf this morning, down in Burlingame, and I wasn't sleeping awfully well, and so I got an early start. But what in the name of Sam Hill were you up to? I thought you were one of these real good girls."

Jocelyn, her usual appearance somewhat restored by a session in the dressing room with her own pocket comb and powder compact, laughed unashamedly.

"I did something very silly," she confessed, as the blessed warmth of coffee began to penetrate the chilly fibers of her being. "And then I did something smart to get out of it, and got into worse trouble, in one way anyway, and got out of that, and here I am not quite knowing whether the whole thing was a dream. I have a friend who has a little studio up in the hills," she began her confession, "and some of us love to go there for week ends. Well, yesterday the artist and his wife who usually go sent me a message that I thought meant they would be there, and I drove myself up, in the rain, and found instead that a man I especially like—used to like, was there alone——"

"That's as good a story as any other," Philip said cheerfully, as she paused. Jocelyn laughed again, but her face was red. "You left your car where?" he presently asked.

She told him specifically. She had noted corner posts, street names, as she had come down the hill in the dawn. Philip took out a well-filled notebook and carefully wrote down what she said.

"Give me your key," he said then briefly. "I've a man who looks after my cars; he'll see to it. And it's to go to the Portola Garage? That's—yes, I know where that is. He'll have it cleaned and returned there today."

"I can't have you——" Jocelyn was far away from her usual moorings; she had never talked to Philip Fordyce except in the office, before; she was dazed after emotional excitement and an almost sleepless night, and she could feel in her bones that a heavy cold was threatening her. But still she couldn't let a strange man assume the responsibility for her foolishness. "You mustn't do that," she said.

He paid no attention to this. He pocketed her key, and when the delicious breakfast was over, stopped the car only once before he deposited her at the Bush Street boardinghouse. The stop was at a drugstore; emerging, he placed a large weighty pink-wrapped package in Jocelyn's hands.

"Dissolve two of those pills in hot water and gargle, and take the others about—oh, one every three hours," he said. "I put a hot-water bag in there; I didn't know if you had one. And I put the violet soap in to make it look more like a present."

She would not let him joke it off. Her voice was husky with gratitude:

"You're awfully kind. I'm terribly grateful to you."

"I'm only too glad I happened along. I saw the hair, and thought that you were the only woman I knew with your sort of hair. This is your place? Good-by and good luck. I'll—I took your telephone number, didn't I? I'll let you know about the car. And if you have any fever, don't show up Monday."

He drove away down the dingy quiet Sunday-morning street, and she let herself quietly into the stale cool air of the hallway and went upstairs. She was in her room again, and everything was just as she had left it after her hurried, feverish departure yesterday. It seemed as if she had been away for weeks rather than hours.

Twenty minutes before eight. There was not a sound in the house. Mrs Buck's boarders were for the most part hard workers; they enjoyed their holiday leisure.

Jocelyn had a hot bath, filled her rubber bag with boiling water in the kitchen, returned to her room to snuggle down gratefully under her blankets and fall instantly asleep. But she did not sleep long. She awakened restlessly at ten o'clock, and unable to stand her own thoughts, dressed again, and went across the bay again, this time in the other direction, to join the family party at Aunt Nell's as calmly as if that had always been her intention.

CHAPTER V

IT WAS A DREAMY, unreal day for her. Fortunately the big household at "Maple Den" was far too deeply and happily absorbed in its own affairs to notice anything strange or absent in her manner or to question her as to the abstracted moments into which she constantly lapsed. Tots's engagement was indeed announced, with much kissing and laughing and rushing all over the shabby, spacious, imperfectly warmed house, and at two o'clock a Gargantuan meal was finally on the table and everyone's attention was concentrated upon the hot, delicious, plentiful and badly served food.

The six Partridge sisters, married and unmarried, were all pretty and giddy and witty and bursting with health and spirits; their one brother was a silent little fellow in junior high school, who sat next to his mother at the table and watched with admiring smiles the uproar that held the dining room. The father of the big family was also quiet, also admiring. Dr Partridge was continually being kissed; appeals were continually being flung in his direction; frequently a blonde girl was in his lap, winding up his mustache or using his ears as handles to gently bump his face against her own. But he rarely spoke.

Jocelyn's Aunt Ellen was the ruler and the moving spirit of this pandemonium. She was an enormous woman, weighing over two hundred and twenty pounds and towering half a head over her husband. In manner she was gentle, deprecatory, hesitant. But her family and everyone else who knew her at all knew the iron will and the mulish stubbornness that underlay this mild exterior.

She rarely left her own disorderly house and overgrown garden. She lived for husband, home, son, daughters, grandchildren. Nothing was too good for them, or too much effort to secure for them, and they adored her. Her two sons-in-law were firmly of the opinion that in any crisis she would support them even against her own girls, and the girls considered it one of their richest secret jokes—and they had many—that Mama always talked as if she sided with the boys and then worked things round to exactly what the girls wanted. There had never been much money for luxuries, but they all swam and played tennis and were experts in the arts of picnicking, cooking, game playing. Their home had been a clearing house for the youth of the neighborhood for a dozen years, and such friends as had once pitied poor Nell Partridge, who had those six girls to marry off, now began to realize that her one feeling about their wedding was reluctance to let them go away from home, and that she would have handled half a dozen more without an instant's misgiving.

It was this big comfortable aunt who came panting up to Bam's room late in the gloomy Sunday afternoon to find Bam and Peaches, the youngest girls, in enthralled conversation with Jocelyn, who was lying flat on a bed, with a warm blanket over her.

"Girls, this room is cold! Why don't you make a fire?" said Aunt Nell, sinking into a chair. "Jocelyn, you're getting a touch of flu, if you ask me." She stretched out a hand like a warm pincushion, touched Jocelyn's cheek. "Yes, you've got about a degree," she said firmly. "Bam, you go right down and tell one of the boys to bring up some wood, and get that stove going. Get Jocelyn a nightgown—get her one of Sissy's, Peaches, and Jocelyn, you turn right in, and make up your mind to it. You're going to stay right there over Thanksgiving, or as long as it takes to knock out that bug. Peaches, you get Jossy's hot-water bag, and tell the girls not to let the babies come in here. Now move, all of you!"

It was only when these comfortable preparations were well under way that the older woman delivered the message that had originally brought her upstairs. Mr Fordyce had telephoned to Mrs Buck to say that Miss Britton's car was back in the garage, and that Miss Britton was to take it easy and stave off that cold.

"Isn't that kind of him!" Jocelyn said dreamily. Physical misery had taken possession of her now; she didn't care much, or realize clearly what was going on. Her uncle came up and said that she was doing just what she ought to do; the only cure was rest and plenty of water, and after that she dozed, and wakened to see Peaches and Bam stealthily removing the mattress and covers from the adjoining bed, and closed her eyes for fear that they would speak to her and expect her to speak in return.

After that a lost day or two slipped by, and then they were all spoiling her; it hadn't been flu, just a heavy cold, and it had been nipped in the bud, and it was fun to have Jocelyn here for the Thanksgiving dinner and the games. And somebody had notified the office that she wouldn't be back until Friday.

On Wednesday afternoon, when her aunt was asleep upstairs and she was watching Jane's baby boy, Tim, and Jossy's baby girl, Rosemary, tumbling about in their pen, and when all the cousins were scattered to various office jobs or domestic duties, Philip Fordyce walked in unannounced, and they sat talking together.

He looked handsome and rosy and kind, coming in out of the cold, and he showed an expert friendliness with the two babies, who sat staring at him, slowly and methodically smearing their small faces with some soluble type of round brown biscuit.

"You seem quite all right again," Philip said, when she had answered some questions about her little illness.

"I am. I feel—oh, wonderful!" Jocelyn said.

He looked at her keenly, and she liked the look, even though it gave her a queer little sensation of fright.

"It was an emotional breakdown, as well as the cold, wasn't it?" the man said. Instantly the conversation plunged down from its surface position to something far deeper, and Jocelyn's quick change of expression showed that she recognized it as she responded slowly, with a touch of heightened color:

"That was it."

"You spent the night in the car, on a rainy mountain."

"But that wasn't the worst. It was the shock," Jocelyn said. "The shock of finding that what—what I'd thought I wanted to do wasn't what I wanted at all. Finding that what I thought I'd felt for him simply wasn't there. He—he had been the cool one, before that. I'd been the one that was going slowly mad. And then suddenly it was the other way."

"You'd never cared, really," the man said, watching her.

"Oh, but I had! To think of stopping it all was like having my thoughts—my emotions amputated," Jocelyn explained, with a rueful little laugh. "I've been—sort of—sort of dazed, since. I've lain in bed, all Sunday and Monday and yesterday, just thinking it over—thinking what a shabby affair it's been all along. How cheap it is to say one takes nothing from the wife, one has a right to friendship, knowing all along that one hasn't!"

"Oh, there was a wife?" the man asked, smiling.

"There *is* a wife!"

"You're an honest person," Philip commented.

"I'm not. That's just what I was saying. I'm not! Physically," Jocelyn said, her eyes far away and her voice musing, "we were honest enough! But—I'm beginning to think the mental and spiritual side of infidelity is just as important."

"It's not, though, is it?" he asked, smiling.

"It ought to be."

"It never has been. A man may torture his wife into a madhouse," Philip observed, "but just as long as he stops short of the actual thing there's nothing she can do."

"And whether stopping short makes one feel cheaper, when the affair is over——" Jocelyn began, speaking half to herself. She paused. "I don't know," she said.

"My daughter says it doesn't make the slightest difference whether a girl is straight or not," the man observed dryly. Jocelyn looked at him in sudden interest.

"Norma does? But Norma's only sixteen!"

"She was about fourteen when she told me that."

"She didn't!" Jocelyn's eyes brightened in spite of herself. "What things they *say*," she murmured, shaking her head.

"I think it's a lot of talk, myself."

"But of course it is! They don't mean it."

"You think," he asked curiously, "that the rising generation is really as straight as the present one? I mean—I'm forty-two, of course, and I'm a long way ahead of you. But when I was a kid there *was* a dividing line. Girls whispered a lot and surmised a lot, but they didn't come right out and say that when they liked a man they thought they had a right to live with him, and that when presently they wanted to marry another man he had no right to object. Men did object, then. They liked their wives—what shall I say—exclusively?"

He was half laughing, but Jocelyn's face was serious. They were alone now, for one of the Partridges had swept in to carry the babies off for sun-porch airings. The day had suddenly cleared, and on Thanksgiving Eve the sun was shining warmly and brightly.

"They do still," Jocelyn said confidently.

"My daughter says not."

"Norma is only a little girl, Mr Fordyce."

"I know. But Spotty's a rather sophisticated little girl."

"You don't really think that things have changed, that girls can have these experiences and then go on into safe and honorable marriage?"

"No, I don't!" he disclaimed it hastily, with a little accent on the pronoun. "But *they* do, or they say they do. They say that in colleges—even in high schools they all say it; you see it constantly stated: that the straight girl is the exception nowadays."

The oddity of it struck her, and she laughed, and he asked her, interrupted in his earnest speech and perhaps a little affronted, what she thought funny.

"Not funny. But strange that what agonizes some of their elders, what seems the actual dividing line between wrong and right, should be taken in their stride, as it were, just one more experience among the things youth goes through! But that's not so," Jocelyn said, interrupting herself. "Decent girls grow to be decent women today, as they always have, and girls who take chances pay sooner or later in one way or another! But you stopped in casually to ask how I was, and here we are deep in morals," she added, with an apologetic smile.

"I didn't stop in casually. I came on purpose," he corrected her.

"Oh?" Her color rushed up. "Something at the office?" she asked.

"No. Look here, if you had a sixteen-year-old to raise, a pretty kid who'll someday have a lot of money, what would you do? Lock her up, cut off her allowance, or give her her head and trust that it would come out all right?"

"Give her her head, I think. Or, no," Jocelyn began hesitatingly, "try to win her, to influence her, perhaps. It's a problem, isn't it?" she finished sympathetically, smiling into his troubled eyes.

"It's a terrible problem. Is it one—do you have any ideas, do you think you could solve it?"

"I?" she asked, surprised. "But I don't know very much about girls today. Girls of Norma's age. It's more than ten years since I was Norma's age. And even then——" She hesitated. "I was an only daughter," she said. "We hadn't very much, my father had died, and we lived in boardinghouses. I hadn't much chance to see what a rich girl, one of the Burlin-

game crowd, thinks or doesn't think. I do know this," Jocelyn
went on, "that the girls—the women in the office are a pretty
free-and-easy lot. Quite a few of them are divorced, with
perhaps a child to raise, and they have their affairs—or at
least they say they do, and accept help from men. *That's*
changed, I suppose! But it seems to me that a girl who will
be as rich as Norma, and with your mother to keep an eye
on her——"

"My mother can't do much, except worry and scold and be
horrified. Mother's sixty-six; she says she won't play nursemaid to anyone's child. She adored Spotty, when Spotty was
last with us, but that was two years ago. She spoiled her and
then she bullied her, and Norma had a damnable Fräulein that
her mother had sent out with her, who broke up the whole
house. Altogether, it was a cat-and-parrot time!" the man
said.

"My plan now," he went on, as Jocelyn, realizing that there
was more to this casual call than she had suspected, remained
silent, looking steadily at him, "is to open the Burlingame
house, move Mother there, settle everything before Norma
gets here. Then I'll make arrangements at the Palo Alto
school for French or Italian lessons—I've got a letter from
her mother somewhere saying what she has to study, and her
afternoons will be free. She'll meet her old gang; there'll be
plenty of excitement for her. Sub-deb things, house parties at
Pebble Beach, all that.

Janet, her mother, has picked out a Frenchwoman to come
and be a companion for her, but it seems the child despises
her. Norma wrote me in a fury, saying that if I didn't get rid
of Mademoiselle the minute she arrived she'd run away. She
asked me to get someone young and pretty and sensible, that
she could like, who'd go around with her and understand
what it was all about. I've been trying for her old governess,
Miss Sanderson. Can't get in touch with her.

"And that's where you come in," he finished simply.

"That's where I come in?"

"If you will."

"You mean you'd like me to try it?"

"I want to keep her safe," he said. "I'd like to make her so happy here that I could keep her for a year or two, get her safely married to some decent fellow that I know something about. This Mam'selle, according to Spotty, has got a cousin who's a count, and I presume he has an eye on the family fortunes; I don't know. Spotty met him on the ship, and she says she can't stand him, and that he'd always be hanging around. Well, there's the set-up. D'you think you could do anything with it?"

Instead of answering him she fixed him with a penetrating look, and asked in her turn, with a little difficulty and a heightened color:

"What makes you think I'd be a good person to manage her, instil a little sense into her? You know all about me, what a fool I'm capable of making of myself."

"Yep, I know all about that," he answered, after a second, and without a smile.

"You think I could do it?"

"I don't know quite what there's going to be to do for you or anyone else," Philip said, with a shrug that indicated his entire helplessness. "I don't know that it can be done. Here's a girl with looks and money and position who shows every sign of wanting to get herself onto the rocks at the first opportunity. She doesn't believe in anything or anybody, as far as I can find out. She wants a good time. Well, can she have it safely? That's what I want to find out. It occurred to me on Sunday that you might be the person to keep an eye on her. You can go anywhere she wants to go, understand how she feels. You're young enough to sympathize with her, and yet old enough to run her. If once you got her to like you, that—that might be the answer."

Jocelyn looked at him thoughtfully for a long minute of silence.

"I can't tell you, at least, what it means to me to have you feel I could try," she finally said, humbly. "I've been telling myself all week that you were the vice-president of the company and I just one of the office girls, and that it didn't matter what you thought of me. But it *does* matter. The only thing is," she went on somewhat hesitantly, "that I don't know very much about girls today. And if I tried this—this that you suggest, and failed, I'd feel so terrible about it. I mean if she was unhappy, or if she did something that jeopardized her own happiness for life—eloped, or wanted to go back to her mother, then—then that's the sort of thing one doesn't have a second chance at——"

"You couldn't fail any more than I feel her mother and I have failed," the man said decidedly in the silence. "I've got to get someone. Her mother's suggestion is a Frenchwoman she despises. My mother has in mind this Miss Sanderson from whom Norma ran away a few years ago. You seem to me eminently fitted. You're human, and that's what I'm after. And if it fails, why, we'll always be glad to have you back with us in the office. Will you think it over, talk it over with your aunt?"

For some reason she could not at the moment define, tears were suddenly in Jocelyn's eyes, tears thickened her voice when she spoke.

"I'll be glad to try," she said simply. And then in apology: "I think I'm still weak, perhaps."

"Well, no hurry!" he said cheerfully. "Norma'll not be here for four or five weeks. I'll keep in touch with you. You'll be back in the office on Monday?"

"On Friday."

"Better make it Monday. By the way," Philip said carelessly, "I talked to your pal Dunham yesterday."

"To Kent!" Her cheeks were white.

"A question of a folder for the club came up; I'm on the committee. I thought he might have some idea. He did, as a matter of fact. A very attractive fellow," Philip added, with a smile.

"But I thought that he was going to Portland on Monday," Jocelyn said, quickly and uncomfortably.

"He was in his office yesterday. Maybe he's changed his plans. He was very much upset when I said that you were away from the office with a bad cold."

"I'll telephone him, write him," she said. "I feel very much ashamed of the whole thing. It was all very foolish. Since you—since you were so wonderfully kind to me on Sunday I'd like to say just that much. Sometimes in offices——"

"Sometimes in offices is right," Philip agreed briskly. He got to his feet. "Well!" he said. "I'm very much pleased that you'll make a stab at this anyway. It's a relief to my mind. I'll write Norma's mother that the granddaughter of General Britton has consented to keep Norma out of night clubs and gentlemen's apartments as far as she can."

"You knew about my grandfather?"

"My mother added that bit of information. She knew him in the days when he was at the Presidio. It may smooth your path with her. She's quite a—quite a party," Philip said.

Jocelyn walked with him to the door, gave him her hand.

"You're very kind," she said. "I hope I'll be some help with Norma."

She watched him walk to the gate and get into his car. It went twinkling away into the gathering winter dusk and was gone. Jocelyn stood looking down at the steely surface of the bay and the ruffle of whitecaps, at the descending slopes of roads and oaks and hillside gardens, all looking their plainest and barest on Thanksgiving Eve.

She had not defined it yet, but there was a great peace in her heart. She said bewilderedly that she felt within herself the spirit of Thanksgiving; consciously or unconsciously that the man who had just left her had given her back her self-respect, and the feeling was good.

"Mr Philip Fordyce," she said half aloud, "I think you are the kindest man and the most fascinating gentleman and the most wonderful *person* I ever have known!"

CHAPTER VI

ON FRIDAY SHE WENT BACK to the office, feeling changed and strange, and restfully indifferent to what went on there, for it had been arranged that she should leave just as soon as some new clerk could be trained to take her place. The new clerk, bright and toothy Mattie Stebbins, who had worked for the firm in emergencies before, was there, and the day's work proceeded placidly until the noon whistles were blowing, and Mattie had gone off for lunch, and Kent Dunham came suddenly in.

Jocelyn looked up startled, tried to smile. But the expression on his face did not encourage the smile, and she merely stared at him, trying to find something light and simple to say.

"Jocelyn," he said without preamble or greeting, "will you lunch with me today?"

"Ah, I can't. You see, my cousin Tots Partridge—she's Madeleine, you know—is going to marry Rusty Livermore in March, and we're going to Shreve's today to look at silver patterns."

"I don't care what she's doing," Kent muttered, his hard eyes not leaving Jocelyn's innocent face, "can't you lunch with me?"

"They'd wait for me, Kent. I couldn't."

"You could leave a message here."

"We're not meeting here. We're meeting at Shreve's and then going somewhere to eat."

"And that matters, does it?" he said bitterly. "You didn't write me. I've been in hell all week! What's the matter?"

"Kent, not here," Jocelyn murmured, looking about.

"It's empty!" he said in high scorn. "Nobody'll hear! Jocelyn, ah, sweetheart," he pleaded, suddenly changing his tone, sitting down opposite her, and stretching his hands across the desk, "what's the matter? Where've you been? You don't know what I've been through! I've talked to Lilian; I've seen a lawyer——"

"Oh, you haven't!" she protested, in so distressed a tone that his own tone changed, and he looked at her in suspicion and surprise.

"Why not?" he asked sharply. "Wasn't that the arrangement? What else could I do?"

"Ah, you shouldn't have done that!"

"Jocelyn, I don't understand this. What has happened?"

"Nothing has *happened*. It's just—you shouldn't have. What did Lilian say?"

"She felt very bad. She said she had had no idea of it. But she agreed to the divorce."

Jocelyn frowned. It all seemed far away and unimportant and embarrassing.

"I got a bad cold Saturday night," she offered.

"I know. I was worried to death about you. I followed you by the new cut, and got to the bridge before eleven, and watched all the cars go by until one. But you must have passed me."

"No; I missed my way. I was in the car all night, rolled in an old blanket that the Johnsons had in the back with a grill and coffee pot and a lot of picnic stuff."

"You stayed in the car all night!" He put his head despairingly into his hands, and again with an uneasy glance about she reminded him that they might be noticed or overheard.

"It was all a mistake, Kent—my going over there—the whole thing. I had to get out because I felt it such a false position—so different from anything I wanted it to be. Quite suddenly it all seemed to go—well, flat and wrong, and I wanted to get home. It was a silly thing to do. It was an awful risk, rushing off into that rain. But I didn't think it out."

"You didn't think out what I went through."

She looked at him, knowing what he wanted her to feel, knowing it to be entirely out of her power to respond to him.

"I'm horribly sorry for the whole thing," she said definitely, getting to her feet with an air of ending the conversation. "I'm sorry for your telling Lilian, but I suppose when you tell her it's over she'll forgive you. You said something like this to me two weeks ago, Kent. Now I say it to you. I'm sorry, and—and it's over."

"You can't just—break it off like that," he said quickly, hoarsely. Jocelyn did not reply. She went to get her hat and coat, remembering as she did so the last time they two had been in the office together, and her going out with him into the dreary winter streets, and his walking home with her, telling her over and over again that he was going away, that he must build his life around his new work and his wife now. She felt horribly sorry for him; she wondered if he had felt sorry for her on that former afternoon.

When she came out with her outdoor things on, he was standing at the office window looking down into the street. He did not turn as she crossed to the door, and she went out into the hall and downstairs without a word or a sign from him.

It made her feel sorry and ashamed. But there was no worse hurt. Jocelyn could end her office days with Fordyce, Sawyer & Fordyce with the feeling that she left that whole episode, and all its attendant emotions, behind her. She went on into the new work like a new woman; a stronger, quieter, happier woman, and long before the New Year was well begun she had begun to forget as well as to forgive whatever that two years' friendship had cost her.

Packing her things to leave Mrs Buck's, going over to Sausalito to spend a few days' holiday at Christmastime with her aunt and the big family at "Maple Den," and presently being picked up by the big Fordyce car and whirled down to chilly, wintry Burlingame, these were experiences novel enough to wipe the past out of her mind; never in her life had she felt so free, so ready for new experiments and experiences. Jocelyn had some new clothes; her young cousins had assured her with passionate earnestness that she needed them, and she had felt an odd pleasure in being persuaded into the purchase of a stiff taffeta gown that somehow enhanced her natural air of dignity, a plain long velvet for evening wear, a smart sturdy suit with pockets and a white frill for street wear. Everything else that she owned was cleaned and relined and mended and made as presentable as possible, and even Tots, ecstatic over her trousseau, was not much more pleased than Jocelyn.

She reached the Fordyce mansion a few days after Christmas; Philip had told her that she would be the first member of the newly assembled family to get there, for his mother would not arrive for several days; he himself would be in New York, and Norma would probably not return until he did. Jocelyn was well pleased with the arrangement; she would have a chance to get settled, to get just a little used to her surroundings before the exciting business of handling young Miss Fordyce set in.

The house was enormous, old fashioned, delightfully warm, comfortable. Jocelyn, upon her arrival, could only guess at the uses of the big rooms behind closed doors on the first floor. The place was ramified into a dozen annexes and bays. Every few years in the past seventy someone had seen fit to add a billiard room or music room or cut through walls to enlarge and supplement parlors and dens and libraries.

She was escorted by a silent, courteous butler upstairs, across a wide, large upper hall faced with many dark, handsome doors, through a passage, and into a suite of two rooms—both hers, and supplemented by a bath, a dressing room and a porch with fluted railings.

It was all handsomely furnished, curtained, carpeted, with a fat satin cover folded over a lace cover that in its turn showed the pink color of a satin counterpane on the bed. There were perfumed soap and bath salts and cold-cream tissues and writing paper, stamps and pen and magazines. In the grate a cheerful coal fire was burning.

Jocelyn's trunk was nowhere in sight; a nice little maid came in to explain that she had unpacked it, and hoped everything would be all right. Reassured, she departed, to appear in a few minutes with a perfectly appointed tea tray. Jocelyn took off her hat and coat and put them away, sat down to her tea, and laughed aloud in sheer excitement. This couldn't last; it was much too much fun to last. But while it did, it was going to be interesting.

She went downstairs at seven to dinner, when Lena appeared to announce it, and enjoyed an evening paper with her solitary meal. It was served in the smallest of several dining rooms, but even this room was darkly furnished with heavy shining pieces of mahogany; masses of silver glittered behind glass doors and on the sideboard; at the two high windows heavy thick curtains had been drawn together. Soup, a squab, a lettuce salad with various mysterious little embellishments making it delicious, a chocolate éclair with pink and green tiny candies strewn on it; she found it an epicurean meal. It was different from meals at Mrs Buck's, and different from meals at Aunt Nell's. Jocelyn, all alone in the elegant space and dignity of the old Fordyce house, smiled inwardly as she contrasted the three. She loved it already; loved the mansion itself, the stately gardens she had only glimpsed on her arrival, the quiet service in the quiet rooms, the atmosphere of stability and security. There had not been too much of either in her life.

In her father's day there had been a good deal of moving about. The time of the great war had seen him shifted and promoted constantly; there had been a hotel in Augusta; another hotel in Washington; there had been quarters in Watervliet. Four postwar years in Watervliet had provided about the longest peaceful domestic interval she and her mother ever had known; then there had come widowhood for Catherine Britton, and after that continual changing and a continual descent of the financial scale. Mrs Britton had been a delicate, irresolute, apprehensive woman; to be left with a spirited twelve-year-old daughter to raise had appalled her. For a while she had visited cousins and aunts, but one by one these places of refuge had altered or disappeared. Finally she and Jocelyn had come back to San Francisco, drawn by the older woman's memory of happy younger days at the Presidio, and there Jocelyn had finished high school and gotten her first office work. By this time Catherine Britton had been crippled with arthritis. Jocelyn's holidays had been spent in only brief overnight visits to her aunt's family in Sausalito. Between her father's sister and her mother there had never been sympathy, and the two older women were merely friendly. No intimacy was encouraged on either side.

So Jocelyn came back from the office to read to her mother, to adjust hot-water bags, to discuss the trivial episodes of an invalid's day, and when she did escape for a night to "Maple Den," it was always with the promise to return at a certain hour, by a certain boat, and not to keep darling Mama waiting. When her mother died Jocelyn had grieved deeply and truly, but at that exact time she had been launched upon the perilous and thrilling friendship with the tall, handsome, clever commercial artist whose studio was a floor or two above the offices of Fordyce, Sawyer & Fordyce. Saddened by the ending of the old life, and tortured by the half-promises and half-hopes of the new, she had felt all her actual moorings gone, and now, as she soberly considered the immediate past, she realized that something of her moral moorings had been swept away with them.

She was already conscious of a wish that Kent Dunham

were out of the picture, safely up in Portland with Lilian, explaining to her that he must have been mad to talk as he had of change and divorce. Knowing Lilian, Jocelyn knew that she would accept these representations on their face value, neither knowing nor caring how deep his repentance went. What Lilian wanted was Kent and security and everyday comfort. She could easily persuade herself that none of it had happened; it had all been Jocelyn Britton's imagination, communicated to poor Kent.

The whole thing had been soiling, somehow; Jocelyn wanted to wash it away as she might an earth stain from her fingers. In this fine old-fashioned house, playing duenna to a girl of sixteen, she knew that she might do so. And if she really won Norma's affection, really steered her safely through some of the rapids of modern social living, then it would seem to be a sort of expiation—a saving for herself as well as Norma.

Alone in the great place, except for the servants, all during the day following, she busied herself happily in getting her effects settled, in writing a long letter to her aunt and a brief one to Kent, and in much wandering over and investigating of "Hill Acres." Acres they were indeed, she discovered. The bay-windowed, turreted, balconied mansion was so placed that from its lower porches no other habitation was in view; only the sloping gardens, the beautiful winding drives with their borders of waiting winter shrubs, the plumy tops of oaks and maples and silver birches could be seen.

From the upper windows neighboring estates almost as imposing as this one could be glimpsed. High windows, red roofs, white gateways peered through the massed trees. But the gates at "Hill Acres" were a quarter of a mile from the house, and toward the west, behind the buildings of house and garages, barns and sheds and fences, the orchards stretched up almost to the Skyline ridge.

There were two tennis courts, being treated now by mysterious laborers with wheelbarrows and scrapers. There was an oval swimming pool, with more men working away at its cement lining, and still others struggling with potted plants and small trees in the freshly turned earth about it. There were many terraces; wherever Jocelyn wandered she found some new group of shallow steps and overarching trees and tiled levels where summer-afternoon groups might form themselves under big umbrellas for bridge games or idle gossip.

Inside the house there was the same evidence of the family's love of luxury and power to secure it. If Jocelyn stretched up an arm to take some book from a high library shelf, Lorenz, the butler, was instantly beside her with a library ladder. If she seated herself in a comfortable chair during the hour when daylight was fading, unperceived some noiseless servitor stepped near enough to light a lamp that illumined her book. Lena brought her her tea wherever she happened to be, on the instant of half past four, whether she herself had completely forgotten it or not. Her room was always in perfect order—bath towels replaced, violets and winter roses in the vases, magazines at hand.

Jocelyn had never enjoyed luxury before. Her grandfather had been a distinguished general, but his day had ended long before hers had begun. Her father had been a fretful and fretted person, humiliated in the exciting war years— the first years she remembered—by having the very men he had trained promoted over him, by having to consider his one-time lieutenants his superior officers. Sometimes there had been a cook in the kitchen of Captain Britton's home; oftener only a striker, or an occasional helper to wash the dishes and sweep the porches.

And after her father's death she and her mother had shared the sort of poverty that helpless little widows on small pensions experience all over the world. Boardinghouses, and the timid exchange of financial confidences with other crimped little faded ladies of the same type. Jocelyn had known in her grammar-school years just what it cost to have

a white coat cleaned, just how much more the Martins paid
for their downstairs front bedroom than she and Mama paid
for their third-floor apartment.

"No matter what these people expect of me, or what I have
to do," she said to herself before she had been twenty-four
hours at "Hill Acres," "I'll remain here. That's *definite*. I
can get a thousand things I want here, things I'd never get
in an office the longest day in the world! If Norma studies
French, I'll study French. If she rides, I'll ride. Thank
Heaven I did do some riding when we were at Watervliet,
and I can drive a car. The old lady may be feeble and troublesome, and Norma may be spoiled, but I'll manage them! I'm
going to stay here from now on."

CHAPTER VII

SHE WAS SITTING AT DINNER on the third evening, beginning to get a little tired of solitude, when suddenly there was a certain confusion in the faraway arcades that concealed the front hallway, and immediately afterward, as she still faced expectantly in that direction, a handsome woman who looked about forty came in, flung aside a smothering confusion of silver and black fox furs, sank into a seat that was opposite Jocelyn and said impatiently to the butler: " 'Do, Lorenz! Get me two old-fashioneds, right away. Where's somebody? That stuff in the hall is to go up to my room! You're—— Phil said he couldn't get poor Miss Sanderson and I suppose you're the pinch hitter? Put the portable radio on the table, somebody."

The last phrases were addressed to Jocelyn, who merely smiled feebly in reply. She had not the faintest idea who this could be, and found it hard to answer a person whose identity was so completely unknown. Lorenz placed a radio on the table, and the newcomer instantly shifted the dials to some desired point. The roar and shouting of Madison Square Garden on a packed night filled the room.

"And plants a light left on the head of—Teddy Parsons," Jocelyn heard. The statement was followed by the somewhat remarkable phrase: "Boy, is stamina and endurance to do their work tonight! This is a—— It's a left, and another, and Joe Rupetti," the voice raced on breathlessly, "—wait a minute, he is counting—three—four—and he's up again, like he was last time—he's up, and he's going—he has landed a light jab, and another on Teddy Parsons' chin . . ."

"I'll bet there was a count while I was getting out of the cab, damn it, I could have held the taxi," Jocelyn's companion said in an irritated undertone. "You," she said to a trim little maid who had suddenly appeared in support of the butler, "go out and see what happened about five minutes ago in the Rupetti-Parsons fight. There must be someone out in the kitchen who's interested. I'm going out to dinner, Lorenz," added the crisp voice, "but I'll have a cup of soup if he's got any—ah, here we are with round seven!"

The fight continued for possibly six more minutes, when there was a knockout, and the lady relinquished the radio and had it carried away.

"I'm filthy," she said then. "I flew from Florida. I should have been here hours ago, but when we came down in Reno I missed my plane. A friend came down to see me at the airport and raced me off to look at some Seel'yum puppies. Adorable, but we were minutes late. *Minutes.* You can't do it, you know; they won't wait. Lovely woman, Cecily Baker—the candy Bakers. Millions. You're—— Phil wired me he couldn't get hold of Miss Sanderson. You're Miss——"

"Britton. You're——" Jocelyn was confused enough to add "Norma's mother?"

"Norma's mother! Darling, how sweet of you," said the lady. "I'm Phil's mother. I'm her grandmother. He told you to say that, I suppose? No; I saw her mother in New York, but Janet never will come out here. Hates it. So you're Miss Britton? I can see how Phil——" She paused. Her voice died away into a speculative murmur. "Dear boy!" she said fondly. "And that reminds me that I must call up Sally McIntosh. And I have to go to a dinner, isn't that repulsive? I need rest. I've not been in bed before three o'clock for two weeks; you know what Palm Beach is. Could you come upstairs with me now and I'll dictate a few telegrams to you. You'd be a duck if you would. You can telephone them in, and it means I can sleep late in the morning no matter what happens. There's only one thing—if a Colonel Dinsmore should call from Boston, I'd like to take that call. Nothing else."

Jocelyn accompanied the mistress of the house upstairs, and inspected and was inspected in turn by the room maid and the personal maid. Mrs Fordyce cast all her clothing about carelessly as she prepared for her bath, stepped into it unembarrassedly, and proceeded to dictate telegrams as she soaked and soaped luxuriously in the hot perfumed water. Immediately afterward she was rapidly assisted into an incredibly small amount of spangles and chiffon velvet, and seated herself with her rather small amount of reddish-grayish hair in sticky clipped confusion around her head.

"Stay and talk to me," she said, as curlers and creams began their work under the hands of Annette Burgier. Silken curls of gray and red were taken from a box; pins and bands were skillfully placed; presently a sort of mask of cotton and wire was removed from her face, and delicate pastes and powders were applied. Her brows were touched; her cheeks brushed lightly with peach color; her lips were carefully dyed, and a dog collar of blazing diamonds was taken from a traveling case and clasped about her soft, almost unwrinkled throat. "Not bad for an old stager who had supper last night in Palm Beach and played three rubbers afterward," she said with an oblique glance at Jocelyn that was almost a leer.

Jocelyn said what she honestly thought, not without a consciousness that the other would like to hear it:

"You must be more than forty. But you don't look a day more than forty."

"When I was forty," said Mrs Fordyce, "I thought I was too old to live any longer. I dreaded forty. I cried on my fortieth birthday. But what wouldn't I give to be forty again! Sit up for me, Annette," she added, "I'll not be late. You'll be unpacking anyway. Is Johnson there? Please telephone—

perhaps you'd do that, Miss Britton? Please telephone to Mrs Addington and tell her that I'm on my way."

A small fleet of cars had arrived at the garages that same afternoon; two drivers in neat chauffeurs' liveries of black-and-gray whipcord had appeared. Jocelyn gathered that one of them was waiting, as the older woman swept downstairs and vanished into the night.

She went to her own room, just a little breathless, with her preconceived ideas somewhat shattered. She had visualized Philip Fordyce's mother as a gentle, beribboned and silk-skirted old lady, fine as porcelain and almost as breakable. To discover in her place this pretty, groomed, vivacious woman, with her beauty treatments and her interest in prize fights, was something of a shock.

She was quietly reading at nine o'clock when there was a knock at her door. Jocelyn jumped with a moment's fright, for everything had been very still until that moment, but immediately she said, "Come in," and got up to meet her visitor whoever that visitor might be.

A rather stern-looking woman of perhaps sixty faced her, a plainly dressed person unmistakably rigid as to ideas, morals, and the corsets that supported her lean, erect form. Jocelyn half suspected who she was before she briefly announced herself.

"I am Miss Sanderson."

"Oh? Oh, how do you do? I'm Jocelyn Britton."

"You've unquestionably a great many qualifications for handling a girl as difficult as Norma, Miss Britton, or you would not have been so suddenly put into this position here."

It was delivered sternly and evenly, as if she had rehearsed the unfriendly little speech on her way to the house, as Jocelyn believed she had.

"I came straight to you," said Miss Sanderson. "Lorenz asked if he should announce me; I said I thought not. Announce me! I know my way around this house. I know this family, through and through. I taught Norma's mother."

"I know Mr Fordyce was trying to get in touch with you," Jocelyn said mildly. The opening guns had been fired with such force that she knew an engagement was imminent.

"I was in Honolulu, and then with my niece in Glendale," said the visitor. "Yesterday I came up to the city and reported at once to Mr Fordyce's office. He is in New York, and his stenographer believed that he had filled the position."

"He didn't hear from you," offered Jocelyn.

"I don't know how you're in a position to know that," said Miss Sanderson sharply.

"I was his secretary," Jocelyn countered neatly. Well, she had sometimes taken his letters, she thought. It was almost true.

"They tell me he is in New York. When does he get back? When does his mother get here?"

"His mother is here. She got back tonight. She's gone out to a dinner, and won't return, she said, until about eleven."

"I'll have Lena make up a room and stay here tonight," announced the other woman, after a second's thought in which she seemed to forget Jocelyn's presence entirely. "I'll see Mrs Fordyce in the morning."

"Would you like me to ring for Lena?"

"I'll ring for Lena!" Miss Sanderson suited the action to the word. "It has always been understood that when Norma finished school I should be her companion," she said. And then, with the first sign of human weakness that Jocelyn had perceived in her, she added, "What happened at the school in Florence?"

"She ran away. She climbed over a wall that had broken bottles on top of it, and cut herself quite badly. Now she's with her mother in New York, and the grandmother has just come back from Palm Beach."

"I know all that," Miss Sanderson said scornfully. "I'm sorry the misunderstanding has arisen. I'll see you tomorrow,

Miss Britton, and we can clear the matter up then with Mrs Fordyce."

She went away in the wake of a somewhat terrified-looking Lena, and Jocelyn tried to settle down again to her book. But it was not possible; the disturbing thought that this formidable old woman and that other preposterously frivolous and youthful one might conspire to put her out of this position, which she was so much enjoying, came between her and the words she tried to read, and she finally gave up the effort and went to bed because there was nothing else to do. She dared not take a walk through the unknown paths and gardens so late at night, and she had written what letters were necessary.

But she slept lightly and restlessly, more upset by Miss Sanderson's intrusion than she would have admitted to herself, and she roused into wide-awakeness when she heard the return of Mrs Fordyce. It was a cheerful, audible return. Good nights were called loudly to the friends who had brought her home; car doors were slammed; house doors, far off and softened in sound, closed with bangs.

Jocelyn turned up her bedside light and looked at her watch. It was ten minutes past three.

CHAPTER VIII

THE NEXT DAY WAS MARKED by a deathlike silence until eleven o'clock, when Mrs Fordyce awakened and everything stirred into sudden life. Maids ran up and down; trunks were bumped upstairs; telephones rang; flowers arrived. By noon friends were coming in, women as beautifully groomed as their hostess sat in the dressing room and gossiped and laughed and drank cocktails. Bert, as they all called Mrs Fordyce, was evidently in her glory; she loved company and excitement, and expressed herself as not having enjoyed a single instant since she had left home.

Miss Sanderson went back to the city at about two o'clock, and afterward Jocelyn was sent for.

"My son has gotten us into a horrible mess, and I'm afraid you'll have to be generous about it," said Mrs Fordyce, who was again alone except for Annette, and again being put through a pretty thorough course of beautifying. "We both tried to get hold of darling Sandy—she was my daughter-in-law's governess, you know, twenty years ago. She's marvelous, inasmuch as she simply doesn't permit anything—goes right along like a Gorgon and doesn't stand for any nonsense. We thought we couldn't get her—the poor thing supposed it was all taken for granted, and didn't take the trouble to cable. She hasn't any money anyway, that may have been the reason; she had a brother who drank it all up. She tells me he's dead, but that doesn't bring it back, does it? Well, she's much older; I confess I had rather a shock when I saw her, but after all, we did send for her, and she was Janet's governess. It makes it so awkward! I wired Philip on the train explaining that she was here and what should I do about you, and caught him at Omaha or Ogden or somewhere, and here's his answer. He says, 'Get rid of Sanderson or Spotty won't come home.' He's evidently told Norma, which is so ridiculous, because a girl of that age ought to have no say at all.—You're sticking that right into my head, Annette!—They'll both be here tomorrow morning, and so will poor Sandy; she's determined to hold her ground, and of course she feels that the way you look has influenced Phil, and no wonder. I love pretty people myself; I always have!"

At this point she paused for a few seconds to rub some injury to her scalp and whimper, and Jocelyn, who was sitting near her, and who had watched her quietly through this long speech, said amiably:

"There won't be any awkwardness as far as I'm concerned. But Mr Fordyce said that his daughter disliked Miss Sanderson. And it does seem to me that even if she was the right person for Norma's mother, twenty years ago, she really isn't—— It would be very trying for Norma—— I can't see that she'd feel enough sympathy there to like it at all."

"Well, of course there's that to consider," the grandmother said on a long sigh. "But then what to say to poor Sandy?" she continued pensively. "She did pack up and get on a steamer, and it was quite pathetic to hear her saying that she'd get Norma out of smoking and all that. She evidently hasn't the slightest idea——! But then I was telling Mrs Verrinder and Mrs Kenworthy about it today," she went on, returning to her anxious tone, "and they said that she'd had the Foster girls and the Griscom girls and the little Yolander girl and been perfectly *marvelous;* she simply kept them in strait jackets! She's just been passed around from family to family—languages, you know, and all that. She speaks wonderful French. You speak French, I suppose?"

"Well, no, I don't," Jocelyn admitted.

"You see, there we are," Mrs Fordyce said plaintively and helplessly, "we have to think of that. Sandy's wonderful at French and at German, too. She lived in Paris for eight years, and then afterward she had Janet there. Well! I wish Phil would get home, because I do feel that with all I have to do, and not having seen Norma for almost two years——"

"When they get here," Jocelyn said soothingly in the pause, "we can settle everything."

"Well, they're due tomorrow, sometime after breakfast. I used to meet them," the older woman said, picking up a mirror and studying her face attentively, "but I've stopped that. The train or the boat or the plane is always late, and someone comes out and chalks it up on a blackboard, or else bawls it through a loud-speaker, and it's so dull! Then you decide to go uptown and have a cocktail, and while you're there the wretched thing comes in. I've never known Janet—when she was my daughter-in-law, that is—to do anything but come in in the middle of a bridge hand. You pick up a good hand, and there's a racket, and of course the opponents throw down their cards gladly, and there has to be a re-deal."

"You had only the son, Mrs Fordyce?"

"I had only Phil. I never wanted him to marry all that money, although I knew Janet's family, knew her from the hour she was born, and I was terribly fond of the little wretch. I am still. She treated him abominably; she used to hurt his feelings and then laugh at him, but I don't think anyone's ever meant to her what Phil does. I believe she'd come back to him like a shot, but he'd never hear of it. She's been married twice anyway, and now there's some count—French or Italian—haven't you noticed that all the newspapers are hinting about it? I hope she doesn't. It doesn't sound any too good. I married again myself, but afterward I took my old name back; I never loved anyone but Philip's father. Married when I was seventeen, and of course a perfect little fool, and when he died I thought all men were like him—— My heavens, here she is!"

The last ejaculation was in reference to a rush of feet suddenly audible in the hall, a voice calling "Granny!" in swiftly increasing volume and nearness, and the violent entry of a running girl, who stopped herself just short of collapse against Mrs Fordyce, protected the beautifully arranged hair with a sudden respectful cupping of hands, planted a kiss with gingerly care upon the very top of the curls and, wedging herself closely against the older woman on the bench of the dressing table, burst into speech. Or rather, she continued more coherently the flow of words that had been pouring from her since her first footfall had been heard.

"Granny, you darling, you're too divoon—the hair-do— it's perfect—I met a beau of yours on the 'Forty-niner,' I'll tell you all about him later! Are you glad to see me? Do you realize how much trouble I'm going to make for you?"

She had been eyeing herself in the mirror as she spoke, and hurriedly applying lip rouge and powder, and catching up a loose strand of her rich black hair; now she reached for a cigarette, lighted it expertly, and observing that it was "divoon" to be home, subsided into a near-by chair.

"No; but I mean it really is divoon," she said. "Phil asked if I remembered Miss Britton in the office, and I said of course I did; I remembered the hair. You'll soon find out I'm a perfect angel, Miss Britton, if I'm not shut up in some Italian or German place where every meal starts with macaroni or potato soup. I grew gross, positively gross. I really did, Gran. Where's the Sanderson? Have we killed her and stuck her body down a drain somewhere, or what?"

She was laughing; she was a little out of breath. But not perhaps as breathless as Jocelyn, who remembered this girl as a clumsy, big, already beautiful young thing of perhaps fourteen, on her last visit to San Francisco more than two years ago. She had been spoiled then, but in a simpler fashion. Jocelyn remembered office rumors that she had to have ice cream every day, and movies almost as often, and that she had been too fat, and inclined to laugh and cry too easily.

This girl was like that earlier girl only in her beauty; she had the same thick, ivory-smooth skin, the same black eyes, with black silky lashes shadowing them, the same rich, smoky black hair and stain of pure apricot on the cheeks. But she was slender now, her hands looked actually delicate and thin, her movements had lost all their old heaviness and had the swift grace of a bird's flight.

There was too much artifice in evidence for her sixteen years, or for any years; her hair hung in soft heraldic locks on either side of her face; it was curled slightly at the tips, and formed into tiny waves and feathers about her forehead. There was rouge on the cheeks whose natural color made it look thick and superfluous; her eyebrows were picked to a thread; her soft baby mouth was stiff with shining vermilion paste. Even her hands, that were still so childishly young, had been scraped and chalked and painted until they had an appearance of ivory claws tipped with wet blood.

And her clothes! Jocelyn had never seen, even in the smartest window of San Francisco's smartest shop, such exquisiteness of dress. It lay in no special thing; not in the tip of the furred little hat, nor the silky lightness and flexibility of the long fur coat she threw aside, not in the severe smartness of the brief silk sheath of her dress nor the foam of frail batiste and exquisite embroidery that could be glimpsed as she crossed her silk-clad legs. It was the sum total of all these and of a hundred other details that brought Jocelyn suddenly to the realization that here was actually one of the little princesses of the world, born to the purple, and wearing it with careless royal ease.

That painted little talon of a hand could write a check today that would mean comfort for some workingman and his family for all time; write another tomorrow; write a third, a fourth, a fifth, and go on writing them for a month, and her great fortune would not be touched or her bank balance seriously disturbed.

Unexpectedly, Jocelyn found herself desirous of being a part of Norma Fordyce's scheme. There was a fearful fascination in the mere contemplation of a life so unlike her own, so unlike that of most girls. There was an intoxication in the mere taste of it. She knew, even now, that it was neither an entirely safe nor entirely pleasant feeling, this reverence for money and for what money could buy, but all the world had succumbed to it from the very beginning of time, and one could not quite ignore it; one could not feel that it simply did not exist, that Norma Fordyce was no more important than some humble little Mary Brown or Betty Baker who might come into the office to register shyly for a possible position.

Instinctively she smiled at Norma, the tolerant amused smile of an older woman who finds a mischievous child engaging, and Norma was quick to respond to it.

"Miss Britton thinks I'm terrible, don't you, Miss Britton?"

"I think you're all completely crazy," Jocelyn said simply. The girl laughed delightedly, and her grandmother said drily:

"Crazy is quite right. Any girl who climbs over a glass-topped wall and gets herself into an Italian hospital——"

"Darling, the hospital was perfectly beautiful," Norma interrupted negligently, "and the nuns were so sweet I almost became a Catholic. And long before I was on my feet Mademoiselle showed up—she'd come from Paris—and then Count Coudeau showed up, and then the Drapers decided that they had to return unexpectedly to America, and Mrs Draper was sure Marie Louise would be a wonderful companion for me, and so we came home in a brigade. And once again, Miss Britton, I was saved from a fate worse than death!"

"Your mother met you?"

"Mother met me, and took me to Mattie Marchand's that very hour to get clothes, and her new beau—did you meet him, Granny? Count Spazzolari, nine years older than I am.

He bought me a puppy. It's being sent. I don't think she'll marry him, I really don't, although it's practically announced and all that. He's revolting."

"Well, I'm glad you're safely here," Mrs Fordyce said, now fully clad and ready to depart, "and I hope we'll be able to keep you happy and give you a good time. I've got to go to May von Bahren's luncheon; I want to sell her all that boiserie I brought home. It doesn't fit this house at all, and it would be divine in hers. Now do you think you'll be safe in Miss Britton's charge, and will you let her know what you want to do, and if Miss Sanderson telephones tell her to get in touch with your father at the office? D'you happen to know if he's coming home to dinner?"

"I believe he is." Norma had gotten no further in her answer when a handsome woman walked into the room and said laughingly:

"I know he is. And so am I. I telephoned the office to see if he was back, and had a chat with him, and Ned Randall and I are coming over to dinner, and to take you on at bridge afterward, Bert."

"Nita, you nice child," Mrs Fordyce said cordially. "It's so good to see you! I hoped you were going to be at May's today."

"I can't be. I've people staying with me—I've sent them on ahead. I've got to give them a dinner, Monday or Tuesday, so hold them both until you hear from me. This is Norma, of course, but so grown up I'd never know her, and quite beautiful, too. Like Phil. Don't you think like Phil?"

"And Miss Britton, who's going to help us keep an eye on Norma," Mrs Fordyce said, with a jerk of her beautiful hat toward Jocelyn.

"Yes; Phil told me that, too. We'd all have taken on Norma and run her without any trouble at all, but perhaps it's better this way. You remember me, Norma?"

"Mrs Royce," Norma said, very much pleased, as Jocelyn could see, with the newcomer.

"Or you can call me Anita, or Aunt Anita or anything you like. I'd like to carry you right off now, but we're playing bridge after lunch and you'd be bored to death."

"She's just in," the grandmother said. "She ought to have a bath and rest."

"She'll have a perfectly lovely season," said Nita Royce. "The younger crowd is having all the fun this winter."

She fell into a gossipy review of a great many personalities almost entirely unknown to Jocelyn. Jocelyn sat peacefully in her deep chair waiting for Norma to give some sign of wanting to go to her own apartments; she knew the talking women supposed her to be entirely uninterested in what they had to say. But even though she did not know the subjects of their chat personally, she knew something of most of them, and she liked piecing the pattern of the group together with this scrap and that.

Divorces, love affairs, scandals, deaths, the qualifications of this girl and the unattractiveness of that other, stories of bridge games and polo games and dinner and opera nights were all jumbled together in Mrs Royce's fascinating talk, and Norma listened to it too, and occasionally asked a question about one of the friends she had left behind her two years ago.

"Meggy Brice is giving a big dance, and there's the Parkers' baby party," Nita said. "You should have had cards to about ten things."

"I imagine they're all upstairs," Norma said indifferently.

"Remember, you're not out, Norma, and don't accept things that will put you into the debutante class," said her grandmother. "Just the school-vacation things. There's nothing so bad for a girl as to force parties too early."

"I'll remember." Norma shot a long-suffering glance at Jocelyn, and Jocelyn perceived, with rising pleasure in her heart, that they were conspirators already.

"It's impossible to think the child is only sixteen," Nita murmured. "She has all the manner of a grown woman!"

"Perhaps I've had a good many of the experiences of a grown woman," Norma said proudly. Jocelyn thought for the first time that she was very young, after all. If Mrs Royce was amused, she gave no sign of it.

"There's no reason why you shouldn't go on with your studies, settle down here, and have your coming-out party winter after next," said Mrs Fordyce definitely. "It's a lovely group here, and you'll get nowhere running around the world meeting new people."

"Nowhere at all," Norma agreed blandly. "But you know it wasn't my plan to stay in Florence," she reminded her grandmother delicately. "Nor to go to that school near Baltimore where we practically lived on horses. I hate horses!"

"What *do* you like, Norma?" Mrs Royce asked.

"Talk, good talk," Norma said in her best grown-up manner. "People with some intelligence. On the boat a little crowd of us used to sit talking sometimes, after the orchestra went to bed, until two or three o'clock."

"Where was Mademoiselle?" Mrs Fordyce asked quickly.

"She was there, darling, cracking her finger joints and yawning her head off. Any attack on me, by René Coudeau or anyone else," Norma concluded, yawning herself, and getting to her feet, "was definitely out. I'm going up for a bath; will you come with me, Miss Britton?"

"Leave Miss Britton here for a minute; I want to ask her to be kind enough to send a few telegrams," Mrs Fordyce said. But when Norma had trailed away, leaving her furs and other impedimenta just where they had fallen, she turned to Jocelyn with a hurried air of warning. "Will you keep a very sharp eye on the telegrams she sends?" she said. "I don't want her to feel that she's being watched. But at the same time we can't have her inviting strange French counts to the place. Do the best you can with her. I don't know exactly how much we can do, but it's possible Phil may have some ideas."

"She's destined to make a *complete* little ass of herself

just as soon as she possibly can!" said Mrs Royce with a rueful laugh.

"Well, she can't marry until she's eighteen, and that's a long time off," her grandmother said in nervousness and annoyance. "They know it, too, these riding masters and princes and counts she's always picking up. Even then, if she marries without her mother's permission and Phil's permission—the bulk of it all goes to a college library. Her grandfather was devoted to Phil, and I don't suppose he ever suspected that Janet would act the way she has—divorcing Phil and marrying people and running all over the country! She was his only child, and probably he hoped she'd settle down after she married. He died, anyway, before the second divorce. Nice old fellow. He could hardly write his name, but he was goodhearted. However, Norma isn't quite as free as she thinks she is, and for a year or two anyway we can keep a pretty firm hand over her. Phil's never hesitated to let anyone who was interested know that he had the right to say what he thought of her husband, and it makes a considerable difference with these counts and earls. I hope she'll marry a good American, but she won't. Not with the example Janet sets her. That was all, Miss Britton, except that I'd like to have you keep pretty close to her. If she wants to go into the city to see a movie, or look up some old friend, you arrange it with one of the chauffeurs. There are two, and there are plenty of cars, and she'll probably send for another car tomorrow! Of course, she loves the Lockey car!"

"You'll be back for dinner, Mrs Fordyce?"

"Mrs Royce here tells me I will, and Phil too, and that we're playing bridge. If you can get hold of anyone to amuse Norma, that's all right. I'll be back about five, and if there's anything, come in and see me then."

CHAPTER IX

JOCELYN WENT UPSTAIRS across the hall to Norma's suite.
She had seen the beautiful old-fashioned rooms before;
weeks earlier an army of decorators had come down from
the city to make everything ready for the daughter of the
house, and Jocelyn had thought that even the Victorian state-
liness and the outdated shape of the apartment had made it
all the more attractive.

It consisted of three big rooms with a large dressing room,
a bath, an enormous square bathroom that had evidently once
been a small bedroom, and a bath and bedroom for the maid.
There was a sitting room with tall windows looking down on
the park and the trees, a bedroom primly ruffled in white
dotted swiss over pink, a guest room similarly treated in pale
blue. These rooms were all in a southwest wing, and when
Jocelyn went into them today bright afternoon sunshine
was streaming across them, to lend an actually summerlike
air to the gay colors and the masses of flowers that decorated
them.

The sitting room was the largest; its windows were curtained with dark rich blue lined velvet draperies that came
down to the floor and touched the pure white velvet carpet.
The old mantelpiece had been taken away and a glass mantel
substituted; vases were all of plain crystal; the only break
on the plain white walls was made by an occasional flat, un-
framed circular mirror.

Confusion reigned everywhere as Jocelyn came in, and
Norma reigned over the confusion. Trunks were standing
about, and out of them had come spilling enough glory to
dazzle any woman alive, as it did Jocelyn, who had never seen
or dreamed of such a display before. Frocks of striped linen;
frocks of stiff checked taffeta; transparent batiste frocks finished with cunning scalloping of dark blue; evening frocks
as frail as tissue and colored like rainbows. Hats broad-
brimmed; tiny hats like birds with wings poised for flight;
hats made all of velvety French flowers; hats as demure as
Quaker calashes with veils and ribbon strings. Gauze stockings in all colors; shining little shoes of every shade and
every material from alligator skin to pearls; underwear so
beautiful, so carelessly heaped and piled in frothy, lacy, fragrant, beribboned whiteness and sweetness that Jocelyn could
get no further; she sat down helplessly with one hand on it,
and presently began to assort it and fold it into something like
order. A nightgown dead white, embroidered in tiny dots of
pale blue and pink, a flesh-colored chiffon nightgown with a
frilled lace long coat to match, deep embroidery, Chantilly
and Irish laces, cobwebby black pajamas with encrusted heavy
Turkish borders in gold and blue and silver and cream and
apricot thread.

A slender girl had joined Norma; evidently a neighbor,
for she could not have been summoned more than a few minutes earlier. Norma was trying to find one special garment
in the general tangle; she kept tossing fresh miracles of
beauty out onto the floor, and muttering "Damn it, where is
it?"

Her personal maids and two of the housemaids were hurriedly getting matters into shape; flowers were continually
arriving; telegrams; letters; the telephone tingled constantly,
and Jocelyn saw her charge get into a rising fever of excitement, almost hysteria, as she was swept upward by the sense
of popularity and the rush of welcome.

She presently found what she sought, a bellboy's uniform

from a Paris hotel, and explained eagerly to her guest that she could wear it when she gave a cocktail party. She then introduced to Jocelyn the other girl—Jean Kimberley. She and Jean had been at Miss Abbott's school together two years earlier, and they had much to say to each other and laughed a great deal. Jean was a year older than Norma, and was to have a coming-out party next winter. There were engagements and house parties to discuss, and Jocelyn felt reasonably safe in leaving the two together while she went to telephone several telegrams for Norma. One to her mother; a few to girl friends; one to a dressmaker; and one to Count René Coudeau. This last one Jocelyn took the liberty of suppressing. Her heart beat the faster for it, but she did not hesitate.

Half an hour later she returned to Norma's rooms, which were rapidly being cleared of trunks and boxes, to find that the girls had planned to go to Jean's house for lunch, and afterward to "have fun somewhere."

"Then you'll have to ask me too, Jean," Jocelyn said pleasantly, in a tone that made no betrayal of her inward quaking.

"No, she won't," said Norma. "Because Mama knows Mrs Kimberley very well, and so does Dad."

"If your father's willing, of course," Jocelyn said. And noting that she had plenty of time, as Norma was in her underwear, and that her maid was only now displaying various gowns for her choice, she went to her own room and telephoned Philip Fordyce in his office.

"Hello!" he said. "Nice to hear from you again. Norma home all right? . . . Good. I'm coming down tonight for dinner. Do they expect me?"

"They do. A Mrs Royce was here with your mother, and she's arranged a bridge game."

"Nita Royce," she heard him say, in a changed tone. And then, still subdued and thoughtful, he said, "Damn."

Jocelyn came straight to her point. Was Norma to go where she liked; was trusting her to go that far?

"Not to the Kimberleys'," he said at once. "The girl's all right, but I don't like that outfit at all. Nope. She stays at home."

"Or I go along?" Jocelyn said.

"Yes, of course," he said in a brighter tone, as if he had not thought of that possibility. "If you'll go along it 'll be all right. It won't bother you?"

"Why, that's what I'm supposed to do," she answered, in a wondering tone with laughter in it. "The sooner she gets it into her head the better."

"You go along then," he said. "Tell her I said so."

"I can't very well do that. The daughter's right here."

"Oh, gosh," he muttered, laughing again.

"I might tell her that you're out of your office, if you'll step out for a moment," Jocelyn suggested, inspired. "Then I can say that I must go with her until I hear from you."

"That's the idea!" Relief was in his voice. "What d'you think of her?" he asked, as an afterthought.

"She's fascinating, and she's a beauty, and a few good lickings wouldn't have hurt her." Jocelyn added the last phrase also as an afterthought; she heard him laugh, and was smiling with excitement and pleasure as she went back to the girls.

"Your father isn't in his office," she announced, "so Jean will have to include me. Is that all right, Jean?"

She said it easily, smilingly, but she knew that a great deal of what the future held depended upon what happened right here and now, in these very first hours of her guardianship.

The two girls looked at each other, and Jean said quickly, with a little laugh:

"There's nothing to be afraid of, I assure you! Mother and Countess von Sturnberg were in school together."

"I'm not afraid of anything," Jocelyn said amiably, and left it at that.

"You make me laugh," Norma said. But she was not laughing. "It's just for lunch."

"And afterward maybe we'll go to a movie," Jean added.

"You don't want to go back to boarding school, Norma. I'll not spoil anything," Jocelyn said mildly.

"The only thing is, whether Mother expected even me back again," Jean said, starting on another tack. "There's probably oceans of food, but I know Mother's at the club, and I'm not sure what we'd get!"

"Stay here then," Jocelyn said cordially.

"That's no fun," Norma said sulkily.

Jocelyn's heart failed her for a moment. There were a great many hours of this day ahead, and a great many days ahead of this day, and she wondered how half of them—one tenth of them—would be filled.

"Why don't we go over to the country club?" she suggested suddenly. "You'd probably see a lot of your old friends, Norma, and there might be something going on— tennis or golf—that it would be fun to see."

To her intense relief, for she was beginning to feel that she was entirely inadequate to the situation, this plan pleased Norma. Jocelyn could see that she liked the idea of appearing suddenly at the club, having arrived from New York only that morning, stepping instantly into her place as one of the most interesting figures in the Peninsula group.

It was arranged instantly that Jean should take her car home, and Norma and Jocelyn should pick her up at her own gate in fifteen minutes, and Jocelyn telephoned to the club to reserve a table for Miss Fordyce, and by this time was more gratified than surprised at the obsequious attention that this simple request received.

"D'you know the Kimberleys?" Norma demanded, when they were in the big car, rolling smoothly toward Jean's gate.

"Just the name."

"She's divorced, you know, and she's trying to marry my father. She's been trying for years," Norma said serenely, "and Nita Royce is after him too," she added. Jocelyn laughed out suddenly in desperate amusement.

"What's the matter?" the girl asked.

"Nothing. Just that it's curiouser and curiouser," said Jocelyn.

CHAPTER X

THEY WENT TO THE COUNTRY CLUB for lunch. It was a
spacious building set in sloping lawns, with shining cars
ranked under the trees all about it; gardeners doubled up over
loamy borders; white clouds billowing across a blue sky overhead. Scattered groups of men and women were moving
over the greens; three girls and a man, mounted on shining
bays, galloped measuredly along the bridle path.

Inside was warm scented air, much pink and green chintz
patterned in ropes of flowers, wide doorways and arches
opening in every direction, and chairs set in half-circles near
the roaring open wood fires and the sun-flooded southern
windows. A heartening and delightful atmosphere, Jocelyn
thought, and as the girls were at once enveloped in welcomes,
her responsibility for their enjoyment was for the moment
lessened, and she could relax and enjoy herself, too. Another
girl and a young boy, Johnny Kimberley, joined them for
luncheon. The boy, home from Lawrenceville for Christmas
holidays, seemed a nice quiet little fellow, but between the
three girls, of whom Norma was the youngest, a conversa-
tional rivalry began that bored, surprised and amused Jocelyn
equally.

Norma was the youngest, but Norma held the cards. Whatever they said she could top with something even more
enviable and brilliant; she had not, like Meggy Brice, been
presented at St James's, but Lord Bullhaven had mentioned
it to Gran. She had not, naturally, been to any of the

Embassy balls in Paris; but she had been the guest while there of the Ambassador. Jocelyn realized that the young innocent boasting was going beyond all bounds, but could think of no effective way of stopping it.

"Of course we were on the Matthews' yacht, so we didn't have any trouble." "My uncle's name let us in ahead of everyone." "Walks up to me and presents me with this adorable diamond—imagine!" "Always stay with Lord and Lady Pierce." "Putrescent." "Fabulous." "Putrescent." "Perfectly fabulous."

As foolish, as vapid a conversation in which three pretty girls in their teens ever had indulged themselves, Jocelyn thought. They were not interested in the food they were eating, or each other, or the sparkle and beauty of the scene around them. They were flushed, eager, almost savage in the race for distinction. They had selected their own lunches from a buffet table loaded with platters of food: chicken, ham, turkey, cold beef, corned beef, salads, stuffed eggs, cheeses, sandwiches, but they hardly touched them. They smoked many cigarettes, and indulged in many side conversations with friends who leaned from neighboring tables or sauntered across the room and came up to talk.

The luncheon had begun with a brief passage at arms between Norma and Jocelyn, but Jocelyn had come off victor, and for the moment could feel herself fulfilling her obligations to her charge.

Meggy, who was in the debutante class, and was giving a large party on New Year's Eve, had ordered five cocktails as a beginning of the meal. But when they had arrived, and one had been placed before her, Jocelyn had placed hers and Norma's back on the man's tray and had said firmly, "Take those back, please."

"They were ordered," the waiter had said.

"They will be paid for," Jocelyn had assured him.

"Mother lets me," Norma had muttered. But without conviction. It was one thing to sneak a cocktail into her stateroom while Mademoiselle was asleep, or to quietly appropriate one when a great trayful came up to her mother's suite in the Waldorf; it was another to drink one openly here before her grandmother's—and, what was more serious, her father's—friends. She had hesitated, and in that second been lost, for the man had actually carried away her cocktail, and Jocelyn had assumed a quiet air that seemed to say that everything was going quite as it should.

Jocelyn, to Norma's "Mother lets me" had not returned "But I don't," but she might well have done so. Norma had given a glance full of patient long-suffering to the other girls, and the moment had passed without further event.

A group of older girls and young married women began to play poker immediately after luncheon, each with her cocktail glass and ash tray beside her beautifully manicured hand. The mild boy with whom Norma and the others had lunched observed that there was a fine movie in town, and it was immediately arranged that they should all go see it. His car would carry the three girls, he said, but it wouldn't be very comfortable for Miss—Miss——

"Britton," said Jocelyn. He must have heard the name fifty times at luncheon, but he was not a very bright boy, she reflected. "Then we will all go in our car," she said. Norma might rebel at any minute; make a scene, run away. She had run away from a good many situations. But until she did there must be no compromise. To let her get the whip hand now would be to lose influence over her forever.

Norma's grandmother had also lunched at the club, although they did not discover her until the meal was over. She was then seen to be at a bridge table in a corner room, furiously sweeping open a pack of cards for the cut. She looked approvingly at the little party as they passed by and said absently, "So glad you're having a wonderful time, darling!" and then, in surprise, to one of the women who made up the bridge quartette: "Didn't that child only get here this morning? Good heavens!" After which she observed, "You,

Harriet. Mine was a club. Blue pack. No bid," all with the swiftness and definiteness of a flash of lightning.

Jean Kimberley's mother was also at the club—a handsome woman of thirty-five or -six; she had come up to the girls, turned a dramatic, intense concentration upon Norma, asked her a dozen affectionate questions, and finally come around to the subject of Phil. How was Daddy? He'd been in New York. Tell him Aunt Jane was glad they both were home.

Jocelyn studied her with great interest as she talked, remembering that Norma had said this attractive grass widow was interested in Philip Fordyce, and when Nita Royce came running down the club steps after them she looked at her too with a little stir at her pulses. She was another who wanted to marry Phil, was she? She was hardly distinguishable from Jane Kimberley, equally animated, reckless in speech, sensationally pretty. But indeed, Jocelyn thought, all these women were pretty.

They went into town in the big Fordyce car, and saw a picture of which Jocelyn had but a vague impression. Life itself was too thrilling at the moment to leave any room for the story of a handsome young policeman who was suspected of playing the gangsters' game until the very last moment. He was actually in jail with every prospect of being sent to the chair, and his delightful comic old mother had been in tears for at last half a reel, when it turned out that he was commissioned by the chief of police himself, just recovering from a severe attack of amnesia, to play that very part.

Afterward they went to a hotel to dance; the girls apparently much amused but, Jocelyn suspected, deeply chagrined at having with them only one young man. However, they picked up two other young men who went to the same prep school as Johnny Kimberley, and after that things became hilarious again. The others had cocktails; Norma had tomato juice and looked sternly at Jocelyn; but Jocelyn, who was beginning oddly to enjoy herself, shook her head at the cocktails and only went so far as to promise Norma that if her father permitted them she should have them the next time.

At six they dropped the others and went on alone, and then Jocelyn spoke seriously to Norma:

"Children your age shouldn't order cocktails in public places like that."

"Children! But my dear," Norma said, dragging the last word into two syllables, and taking the tone of a woman of forty, "you're dating yourself! I mean everyone does it, and everyone goes on being quite decent and I mean what's the harm?"

"I don't think you should, and I'll be surprised if your father does," said Jocelyn.

"Oh, Dad!" Norma said with a pitying laugh. "But he's not, after all, any better judge than Mother?" she demanded innocently.

"She knows there's no answer to that," Jocelyn thought. Aloud she said: "But you're with him, now. And I think it's for you to set the example, Norma," she added, after a moment. "You're a natural leader; if you set a fashion, they'll follow it."

She could sense that Norma was pleased; a vaguely gratified look came over her sulky little face; she said in a mollified tone: "I'm not even out yet!"

"*That* wouldn't matter. You're a gentlewoman," Jocelyn said adroitly. "You've been places; you've had advantages that these other girls haven't. And your position will make you important, no matter where you go or whom you marry. Anyway," Jocelyn finished, "while you're with me I don't want you to drink cocktails. And if you're not with me, whom will you be with?" she finished, smiling. "Miss Sanderson is all ready to take up her duties. She feels that I am not qualified to act as chaperon to a girl of your position."

"Who said she did?" Norma demanded, startled into sudden interest in something other than her own affairs.

"She did, herself. She called on me soon after I arrived here. She asked me if I spoke German and French and how much I had lived abroad, and I don't think I made a very good showing." Jocelyn's mouth widened into a smile; her eyes were still serious.

"Well, the old busybody!" ejaculated Norma.

"You see, you are a very precious little package, Norma," the other girl said. "You'll marry in a few years, and then it will be too late for us to do anything about it. But meanwhile, everyone who loves you wants to be sure that you won't make any mistake that you'll regret."

Norma made no comment upon this. She had been looking out of the car window at the landscape moving by, and she continued to do so. But that she liked this new view of herself and her responsibilities, or possibly this old view worded differently and coming from a new source, was evident when she jumped out at her own doorway.

"Do you mind if your precious little package gets out first, Miss Britton? Otherwise you'll have to climb over my legs."

Mrs Fordyce's voice and Philip's voice could be heard coming from one of the big rooms upstairs, and Norma went in to them at once, leaving Jocelyn to proceed to her own room, to take her bath and get into dinner clothes. It was after seven o'clock when she crossed the upper hall to see if Norma was ready.

On the way she heard Mrs Fordyce's voice again, raised high with resentment and impatience.

"If I marry him, Phil, then I'm in for all that trouble I had with poor Ferdy! He would give me a divorce and he wouldn't, and it took weeks of hanging around Reno to get anything straightened out! If I merely go off on this Catalina trip I *do* get a good sunburn out of it, and I'm horribly white . . ."

Jocelyn went hurriedly on, opening Norma's door cautiously, for she had advised a nap before dinner. After all, the child had gotten off an overland train only this morning; she had had a severe hospital siege in Italy, a rough mid-

winter crossing of the Atlantic, and an exciting month with
her mother in the shops, theaters and restaurants of New
York. All day she had been active, dressing, chattering, greeting friends, dashing about in the car. If she were getting a
little rest now, so much the better, for although there was no
plan for the evening, Jocelyn had small faith that Norma
ever would voluntarily go early to bed.

The trunks and bags were gone from Norma's sitting room
now, and the place was in perfect order; the extravagant
gift flowers in vases; the fire burning behind a handsome
wrought-iron screen with blue enameled peacocks on it.

Jocelyn went cautiously on and noiselessly opened the bedroom door; immediately she stepped in, her face flushing.

The room was striped with tiers of drifting cigarette
smoke; Norma was at the dressing table with her gypsy mop
of silky, smoky black hair in a tumble, and her talonlike little
hands rubbing something into it from a bottle.

"Mattress is at dinner," said Norma of her maid. "And
my head was itching. I think I have lice."

The other person in the room laughed huskily at this, without changing his position. He was a youth of perhaps twenty,
generously built, with a mop of red hair. He was dressed in
golfing wear, and had stretched himself comfortably upon the
satin and lacy surface of the bed, cramming half a dozen
small pillows under his head, and so being enabled to smile
amiably at the women over his cigarette.

"Norma," Jocelyn said, in a tone that did not attempt to
disguise her displeasure and shock. Norma laughed, unem-
barrassed, and the young man immediately sat up.

"Yep; I'm getting your pillows and whatnots all mussed,"
he said. He yawned and flung his long athletic arms in the
air. "God, am I sleepy!" he said. "I played thirty-six holes.
I was so tired I was an emergency case, but I just heard
Norma was back and so in I came, and weaving my way
busily upstairs I just dodged what's-her-name—Mattress."

"Norma, your father wouldn't have liked to come in and

find you this way," Jocelyn said, still too much disturbed to know quite what course to take. "Hadn't you better comb your hair back and come into the other room?"

"No; she hadn't," said the young man easily, grinding out his almost-finished cigarette on a tray and rising to his feet with a fresh series of yawns and stretchings. "For I'm on my way. You'll think about joining the Double Beds Club, won't you, Norma? We need you. I've not been introduced—Miss Britton? How d'you do, Miss Britton? I'm Charles van der Lipp, three words. My mother thinks it's a French name, and she often pronounces the Charles the French way. But it's Dutch. I'm a little meinherr, eating klopjes and skating on the Rembrandt van Rijn. Good-by, my darling," he said to Norma, "I love you with your hair that way. I'm so glad to be free of your boudoir! Que Mam'selle est ravissante dans mes bras! I don't speak French, Miss Britton," the caller went on, politely, "so I don't know what that means. I learned it from my uncle. He said it at the telephone once when I was sleeping in his room. Is it bad? Everything French is, isn't it?"

"Miss Britton doesn't speak French either," Norma said, turned about on the dressing-table bench, and facing them in a cloud of dark hair. She was laughing with mischievous satisfaction in Jocelyn's discomfort.

"Oh, doesn't she?" asked Charles. "What a break for us! I'll get a phrase book at the dime on my way home. Now brace up, girls, I'm going. Ah, don't, dear. It's war. I'm off to serve the colors. I think they're red, white and blue; one's never sure."

He was gone, and Jocelyn had destroyed any effect her dignity had hoped to produce by bursting out laughing at him. It was impossible to do anything else. Norma, after an uncertain glance at her, laughed too, following her lead. But Norma was only faintly amused; other elements in the situation seemed to her more important than its humor. She frowned like a frowning baby.

"Did he actually walk in here as he said?" Jocelyn said, as equably as she could, when he was gone. "Do you know him very well? He shouldn't," she went on, shaking pillows and jerking covers straight, "do a stupid thing like that. Mussing things up with his dirty golf shoes!"

She did not look at Norma as she spoke, but she sensed a sulphurous silence over by the dressing table.

"He's my best friend," Norma said presently, in a voice of suppressed fury. "I played with him when I was only six years old!"

"He seems, in spite of his disorderly ways, a nice boy," Jocelyn commented mildly, still busy.

"I happen to like him very much!" Norma said icily.

"You are a silly little fool, and I am another to keep a job like this," Jocelyn thought, "but there is something about this whole madhouse that fascinates me." Aloud she said, glancing at a tray containing two small glasses, "You sent downstairs for cocktails?"

"Certainly!" Norma answered haughtily.

There was a silence. Jocelyn sat down and looked at the other girl.

"Norma, that's not nice," she said. "If you don't know that, he should."

"I suppose *you* know what is nice?" Norma murmured to her own reflection in the mirror.

"I seem to know what isn't," Jocelyn answered, a trifle more sharply than she had intended to speak.

Norma began to speak steadily, in a sort of drone.

"I won't be spied upon, and reported, and talked to," she said. "I don't do anything anyone else doesn't do, and I've not three heads, and there's no use people following me around and making out that everything I do is monstrous! I'm perfectly able to manage my own affairs if I am only sixteen; I'll be seventeen in about another month, and when I'm eighteen I'm of age! If people are nice to *me* I'll be nice to *them,* but if my father thinks for one second of an instant . . ."

"Why, she is a mere infant!" Jocelyn thought, watching her part and fluff her hair, and pout as she surrendered it to the ministrations of Mattress, who at that moment came into the room. And she tried to remember the impression this girl had made upon her only a few hours ago; only this morning, when Norma had first arrived, the very incarnation and picture of sophistication and coolness, and had successfully impersonated, if only for a few moments, a woman of the world in the person of a girl not yet seventeen.

"Norma, if you had a daughter of sixteen——" Jocelyn began patiently.

"Which I haven't!" Norma snapped, seeming to feel this a rather apt reply.

"Which you haven't. But if you had, and she was—well, pretty, and was someday probably to be very rich, would you let her go about alone to parties and restaurants and dances?"

"Certainly, if I trusted her and if she wasn't a fool, and I'm going to tell my father so!" Norma answered warmly.

"You wouldn't feel that she might get herself into difficulties, find herself in awkward situations?"

"I think people like my father and grandmother and, well, like you too," Norma said calmly, "have filthy minds! What do they think we're all doing all the time? I should hope we had sense enough to keep ourselves out of trouble!"

"But Norma, girls *don't.* You were talking today of the little Patterson girl who was driving on the Skyline——"

"But that just meant she didn't know how to drive; it didn't mean she wasn't behaving herself!" Norma said, and as she was a creature of brief and changing moods, and as she had pretty well talked herself out of her ill temper, when Jocelyn laughed, she laughed too, reluctantly, and they went downstairs to dinner with no further words.

The dinner party consisted of the bridge foursome, two college boys who had come over to pay their respects to

Norma, and who were so shy and inarticulate that they needed a great deal of encouragement, and the pretty, talkative girl who had brought them along. Covers had been accordingly laid for nine, and Jocelyn found herself facing her first formal dinner quite composedly, settled as she was among the young people and not obliged to speak during the entire meal if she felt so disposed. But glib as the girls were, and politely responsive as were the boys, they did need some help, and Jocelyn was presently guiding the conversation with all the skill at her command, and was rewarded by more than one flash from the group, and by a sudden description of a submarine's machinery by young Buddy Taylor that amazed them all.

She noted that only one of the boys took a cocktail; the pretty girl, Janey Trent, observing that it gave Mama fits if she did. Philip had been in the group when they came down-stairs, looking handsome, Jocelyn thought, in his dinner jacket; he smiled at her once or twice absently as he talked to the other women during dinner; he did not once address her directly. She was glad to be more or less ignored, because the glitter and elegance of the whole scene was rather breathtaking to her. The handsome, richly furnished old-fashioned rooms looked their best at night, when soft lights illumined only their better points; there were fires everywhere; on the table candles shone in silver candlesticks, and the low-spread flowers and the chocolates and nuts were in silver swans. She had dined on the previous nights in a smaller dining room; if she had seen this room before, it had been so darkened and swathed as to be practically unrecognizable.

In this stately setting the clear bright skins of the girls, their curled shining heads, their fresh gowns, and the handsomer gowns of the women, made what was to her a dazzling picture. Jocelyn wondered what her little group would want to do after dinner, but they left her no doubt. They played a wild game of bridge; they turned on the radio and danced; they finally subsided in a sort of heap upon a particularly

deep and soft davenport, discussing their costumes for the
Brice party and advising Norma as to her own.

It was at this time that Lorenz appeared to say to Jocelyn
that Mr Fordyce would like to speak to her, and she went
into the adjoining room, one of the many drawing rooms,
libraries, game rooms, reception rooms, living rooms of the
main floor. Here again was a fire, were big chairs and soft
lamplight, were flowers and order and silence. Phil was
standing; he said smilingly that he would only detain her for
a moment.

"I happen to be dummy," he said. "I just put my mother
down eight hundred, and of course she's in a frenzy. She all
but accused me of cheating. Tell me, how goes it?"

"It goes well." Jocelyn smiled gallantly, but there was a
certain subtle significance in her smile. "At moments she
likes me, and at moments she's going to tell you all about
me," she said. "But on the whole, as an alternative to Miss
Sanderson or boarding school, I think we'll manage."

"What d'you think of her? Of course she's spoiled."

He wanted her to contradict this. But instead she nodded.

"It couldn't be helped, I suppose. But she's fine, too. I'm—
I'm liking this."

"Not sorry you tried it?"

"No."

"I was afraid—you see, I hardly know her. I've had her
on the train three days, but I'd not really seen her before that
for years. I was a little afraid, from the way she talked, that
she didn't quite know the difference between a—well, a companion and a lady's maid."

"She doesn't," Jocelyn answered seriously. He looked at
her quickly.

"Want me to speak to her?"

"No," she said thoughtfully, unhesitatingly.

For a minute they looked at each other, and then the man
laughed.

"Philip, you crook!" called his mother's voice from some

room undefined. "We're waiting for you, it's your deal!"

"Good luck!" Philip said. There were a dozen questions in Jocelyn's mind: questions about cocktails, about overnight visits to other girls, about hotel dancing, but she perceived even now that she would have to answer them herself. Norma's father knew as little of the situation, was as unprepared to solve her problems as she was herself.

She presently joined the sleepy group before the fire in the dimly lighted room adjoining, which had the effect of breaking it up. The visitors drowsily departed, and she and Norma went upstairs. Mattress and another maid were in Norma's suite; Jocelyn turned her over to them with a deep inward sigh of relief. She felt completely exhausted.

Lying in bed, reviewing the incredible panorama of the day's events, she felt completely unequal to the inevitable demands of the days to come. If this was Norma's first day, the moment of her arrival, what would the next one be, and the next, and the next? Apparently the girl expected to be, and was accustomed to being, amused every minute. She must be putting on new frocks, driving, dancing, eating, drinking, talking for fourteen hours out of the twenty-four, and Jocelyn was the person upon whom would fall the responsibility of seeing that all this went on safely and sanely.

She knew that she would be bored by Norma, ignored, snubbed, shocked; she knew that her hold here was precarious, that it might be loosened any instant. But the scene was so brilliant, so new; the spectacle of a girl in Norma's position so fascinating at close range, that Jocelyn, snuggling deep into fluffy blankets, sinking off at last into wearied sleep, knew that she would keep herself in the picture if she could.

Just as sleep claimed her, she started back into a moment's consciousness. Kent. Kent! She had not thought of him for hours. And in that fact alone lay ample reason for her remaining at "Hill Acres." It was such a relief to forget him, to return to the thought of him rested and fresh! He was out of her life now, and no harm done. No harm done. She had run away from the harm of that night in Piedmont; she had never been so close to capitulation before.

What sudden impulse had saved her? What strain of Puritan coldness and strength had come down to her, to show her that scene in the cabin in all its reality—a young woman with everything to lose, a man indifferent to her for so long and now again impassioned, a wife in the background with her rights also to be considered?

Why had Kent, who had been for so long a figure of glamour and romance, become so simply just an attractive man, torn between wife and sweetheart, undecided which he must follow? And herself, by what lucky chance had she seen herself infatuated, blinded, just one more foolish woman believing that today's wrong might become tomorrow's right, that stupidity might bear the fruit of wisdom?

Alone in the dark she felt her face flushing with shame. There was something very flat in surrender; it was not glorious and triumphant and courageous for either man or woman. A man knew well what he was taking, when he took away a woman's honor, and a woman knew what it meant, too. Her last defenses gone, she might reason and plead and laugh and tease a man into this further concession or that, afterward, but her power over him had now shifted to his power over her. And for what? What did she ever gain by weakness?

"Well, it's over," Jocelyn thought, turning on her pillow, settling down to sleep. "I hope I never see him again. I wish I might never think of him again."

A night wind stirred at her curtains and went through the room like a ghost. But she did not hear it; she was sound asleep.

CHAPTER XI

THE BURNING CONSIDERATION of what she was to wear to the Brice party was absorbing Norma when Jocelyn went into her room at ten o'clock the next morning; they discussed it thoroughly, and took up the discussion afresh when Janey Trent came in. There was the Parkers' baby party on the second, too; Jocelyn, with one eye on the clock, was delighted to see how time slipped by while the young ladies idled over their breakfast, while Mattress set Norma's curls and helped her dress. Every hour that Norma was amused was an hour gained.

Any simple ideas that Jocelyn might have had of Watteau costumes or coroneted Queen Elizabeths were dashed when the girls explained their own views of the subject. Jane was going as a baby smiling in the basket shouldered by a peasant mother. Jane's legs would do the walking; the upper part of a bowed female figure in gay rags would be fastened in front of her, and her own head and arms would protrude from the basket supported on the dummy's shoulders. The man who was taking Jane was going as a notorious criminal whose name had lately appropriated the headlines; he would not only wear prison stripes, but have a shaved head, a face painted yellow, a revolver from which blank shots would occasionally be fired to enliven the proceedings, and a string of filthy cans hanging from his belt, from which he would occasionally offer his dance partners cuts of dry bread, canned beans shoveled forth on a strip of shingle, and cigarette stubs. "We must save all our stubs for him!" the girls said enthusiastically.

These details drove the girls into ecstasies, but still the question of Norma's costume remained unsettled. Charles van der Lipp, it seemed, was escorting Norma. Norma, nearly seventeen, seemed young to Jocelyn to be included in this party at all, but it was becoming increasingly evident to her that the heiress to the great industry of the Lockey motorcars was subject to few of the rules that restrained other girls.

"You wouldn't like Carmen, Norma? It would be lovely with your dark hair."

"Darling," said Norma to her chaperon patiently, "I went to a party as Carmen when I was three. I remember Gran gluing a little cigarette to the corner of my mouth."

"You must have been simply divoon," said Jane.

"I ate the cigarette and threw it up," Norma said, with a certain twist to her mouth that meant that she thought she was being funny. Jane laughed hysterically, and another girl who had come in to join them laughed in an exaggeration of appreciation.

"They all know she's important; they've all been warned to make much of her," Jocelyn thought. "Good heavens, into what a false atmosphere money like that puts a girl! Little Van der Lipp is here to bag her before anyone else gets her for the dance; everyone flattering her, trying to amuse her! Well, she's pretty, she'd probably have a beau if she was clerk in a cafeteria, and lived out on Shotwell Street! But it's funny."

It was by this time almost decided that Norma should go as a fish bowl with real fish swimming in it. Jocelyn would have been incapable of imagining such a thing, much less would she have known where or how to find it. But once again the power of unlimited money was evinced; when she telephoned the San Francisco costumer, there was instant reaction to the name of Fordyce, and it was promised that the very best that Lewis could manage should be sent down for inspection the following morning.

Norma was now in a state Jocelyn particularly disliked—a smug, elated mood that said that Norma Fordyce was smarter and more ingenious than anyone else, and had been more places and seen more of life, and that she could show these backwoodsy Peninsula people a good many things that would surprise them. She was laughing a great deal, often finishing her laugh with tears in her eyes; she was getting noisy, and the addition of two strange boys to the party, when they all went downstairs for a one-o'clock luncheon, did nothing to quiet Jocelyn's uneasiness or improve Norma's manners. Her hilarity rose to shrieks; she grew silly; she extended affectionate overtures to the boys, and accepted their familiarities in return. Ponny, who was an enormous fellow, caught the small girl up by the hands and swung her around in a circle until she and her clothes were a whirling blur, and it was Blick, the rougher and noisier of the two, who finally caught her, held her to steady her on her feet, and smoothed down her disordered clothing with a remark or two that Jocelyn felt in very bad taste, to put it mildly.

"Ponny, stop!" Norma screamed, as his big hands gave her frothy underskirts a straightening jerk; Blick, laughing good-naturedly at his brother's boldness, as Jane was, added a comment that rather sobered both girls with its vulgarity, and the four sat down to their luncheon in suddenly gloomy spirits, Norma sending more than one tentative glance toward Jocelyn as she did so—half defiant, half afraid.

When conversation recommenced, it was at a rather more rational level, but Jocelyn frankly did not like or trust the confident, coarse, big Sears brothers, and when Norma proposed to go and spend the following night with their mother, she seized her first opportunity of slipping off to telephone Philip.

"No; not to that house," he said. "Tell her I said so. That is, unless you go along! Much more of this and I'll have her committed to an asylum. I don't think she ought to go to the Brice show, myself, but my mother says you'll be there, and she'll keep an eye on her. But don't stand any of that Sears nonsense; that woman would be so glad to get Spotty compromised with one of those big bruisers she'd turn handsprings. Patsy Carter telephoned me this morning; they're nice people. They want Spotty for dinner, but I said you'd call for her at half past ten. That's tonight. But go easy on that Brice dance. I understand it isn't going to start until about midnight. Kids that age, and they go to bed after dinner and sleep two hours before the party!"

Jocelyn went back to Norma to remind her amiably that a court tennis match was going on in the city and that her father thought they might all like to see it; he was going to try to be there, and as Norma coldly turned down the Sears brothers' suggestion of a ride, it was finally decided that they should go into town for the tennis.

Philip met them here, and carried the younger crowd, which by this time had swelled to about a dozen, off for dancing and what was called "tea," and Jocelyn had a free time in which to report to affectionate Mrs Buck, to telephone her aunt in Sausalito, and to pick up some small things she had left behind her at the boardinghouse. At six she was herself picked up by the Fordyce car. Philip was staying in town for a club affair tonight, the others had all scattered, and Norma was alone. She said at once, at her weary and sulky worst, that she wished Miss Britton would not tell tales to her father; there was no possible reason why she should not stay at the Searses' house tomorrow night; she liked the Searses very much, and her grandmother liked them, and so did everybody else. And again she repeated that she considered the suspicions of the grown-ups disgusting.

Jocelyn chatted along comfortably, quieting her, and presently interesting her, and they were friends again as Mattress dressed her mistress for the Carter dinner. Jocelyn accompanied her to the actual drawing room, saw a gracious quiet woman and some girls and boys take joyful possession of her, and then went thankfully home for the blissful quiet of a solitary dinner in her own room, and the utter restfulness of a book.

So another day went by without mishap, but on the eve of New Year's Eve she heard by telephone from a woman who haughtily described herself as Mrs Pauncefoote Sears, and who laughed quite shrilly at the idea that Janet von Sturnberg's child could not come to her house without a chaperon. Mrs Sears described this situation as impossible and too delicious, but she was eventually convinced that it was quite within the realm of possibility, and any deliciousness it might have possessed was angrily altered into stupidity.

"Stupid, to disappoint the poor kid!" she ended the conversation pityingly. "I only want to warn you, Miss Britton, that I am her mother's closest friend, and she may not find this so very amusing. I don't mind tonight, of course; it's just a lot of children, but believe me you'll merely drive the child to some silly or desperate step! I know that blood!"

"And I know your type, too," Jocelyn thought, hanging up the receiver. "And if any more women tell me they're the Countess's closest friend I'll believe she was pretty popular! I wonder how far these dear old friends would go if Norma were somebody's penniless niece just on here for a visit!"

The next day was the great day that preceded the Brice fancy-dress dance. It began with hysteria on Norma's part because her costume, when duly filled with fish and water, proved far too heavy for her to support, and frantic costumers were at the house by eleven o'clock to see what could be done. The scaly great fish head was perfect; the mermaid's shining plated tail was perfect, but the glass tank was too heavy. Norma cried bitterly in despair, and was for asking Jane for Jane's costume. "She must have thousands!" she whimpered, when Jocelyn shook her head at this idea. No; she mustn't spoil Jane's fun. There must be some lovely tancy dress in Norma's wardrobe that could be furbished up for this occasion?

Oh yes; Norma had costumes. But she hated them all; she hated this silly dance; she hated everybody! She had a Portuguese costume, complete with embroidered cotton pockets and white blouse, the full striped skirt as gay as Lusitania itself. She had a Dutch costume ornate with round silver buttons, starched crown-shaped cap, gold ear-blobs. She had a Turkish lady's robes, delicate tissues superimposed upon delicate tissues: sari, gondola slippers, diamond for the left-hand side of the nose.

None of these would do. Norma feverishly telephoned in one direction for a friend's snake suit, all diamond stripes and scales; failing that, telephoned to another friend to borrow a "Miss America" outfit consisting only of a span's length of bathing suit and silver brassières. Discouraged in these attempts she flung herself on her bed, refused her luncheon, and sobbed.

At this point the costumer arrived with a new idea: a light harness, a fish tank cunningly made of a transparent bowl within a bowl; no glass at all, only a mica-like material almost as light as paper.

"It may break!" Norma protested, smiling through her tears.

"But how delightful if it does!" exclaimed Charles van der Lipp enthusiastically. Charles and other friends had been coming and going all day; they had sympathized deeply with Norma's trouble, consumed endless trays of sandwiches and cocktails, and were now ready to rejoice with her in a brighter hour. Charles would reveal to no one what he was to wear, but the others enjoyed comparing notes and discussing the ingenuities of their plans.

A car was sent to San Francisco for the special purpose of collecting forty Japanese goldfish with wide feathered tails. The cost of all this appalled Jocelyn; the fish head and tail had come to more than four hundred dollars, and several tanks had been tried and abandoned before the final one was complete. But there was no one she could ask about it; Norma's father was away in Yosemite; her grandmother had been out playing poker until half past three that morning, and as she too intended to go to the fancy-dress ball, she had requested not to be disturbed until six in the afternoon.

CHAPTER XII

TWENTY YOUNGSTERS were to dine at the house in simple evening dress, some afterward going to their own homes to dress, one or two dressing at "Hill Acres." Jocelyn had a firm word with Norma about cocktails before dinner, but most of the others indulged freely, and it was nine o'clock before they sat down at the table.

Even after that they made no hurry. They played bridge; they called the local moving-picture house to ask what was playing. The time between half past ten and half past twelve must somehow be whiled away; no one wanted to be early at the dance. But eventually it was time for Norma to go upstairs to take off her gauzy silver-and-white dinner dress, undergo a careful process of beautifying from Mattress, and get into the fishy disguise. When they started, Riggs, the underbutler, mounted seriously up to the front seat of the car, with the goldfish tank held steadily in his hand; Jocelyn maneuvered Norma, with her scales, tail, empty transparent bowl, into a jump seat and managed to insinuate herself in behind her. Charles had left them half an hour earlier to dress; they were to pick him up.

When he come down to the car at the Van der Lipps' pretentious gate a mile away, he and Norma began to laugh so violently at the impossibility of his getting into the car that for a while there was no prospect of getting started at all. But eventually Charles, who represented an artichoke with Hollandaise sauce, hung on, half in and half out, and driving carefully, not to spill the fish or dislodge Charles, the chauffeur eventually landed them safely at the Brice mansion. It was close upon midnight now, but they were not the last; cars were wheeling about in the black winter night, and the first horns were blasting in the New Year.

There was another delay while they stood in the drive and Charles and Riggs and Jocelyn, from pitchers brought along for the purpose, poured water from a garden faucet into the circular tank that surrounded Norma's slender body. Then everything was ready; they advanced up the steps, and Jocelyn was quite unnoticed in the uproar of enthusiasm that greeted the artichoke and the fish bowl when they went in.

As with every fancy-dress party, this initial outburst of admiration exhausted the interest shown in the fantastic apparel of the latest arrivals. Other extraordinary effects were coming in: a rajah on an elephant with six dancing girls, a Popeye nine feet high, Snow White and all her dwarfs. In no time Norma was merely one of a pushing throng, laughing, good-natured enough, but too much crowded together to notice anything except individual comfort and appearance. The fish bowls were crushed together, and the water in such danger of spilling and ruining a hundred stately gowns and period slippers that Norma was easily persuaded by Jocelyn to slip home with her, hurry into exquisite evening wear fresh from Paris, and return to the dance to enjoy comfort and the consciousness of her own beauty undisguised. The fish the obliging Charles carried out into a strange pantry and confided to a strange caterer's man, and the fun was resumed with as much vigor as if it had not been interrupted.

Norma paid her respects to the hostess and was greeted by some old friends. Then Jocelyn, who was moving inconspicuously about the revels, noticed to her uneasiness that the girl was drinking cocktails with anyone and everyone, and in the special company of Pauncefoote Sears was growing excited and noisy. There was nothing to be done about it; her grandmother was there, clicking chips in the comparative quiet of a card room, snatching cards with agitated hands, groping for the cigarette or the drink that was always at her side. If anyone should check Norma it was Mrs Fordyce; but Mrs Fordyce had lost heavily the night before, and was determined to get her own back tonight, and her granddaughter's activities interested her no whit.

It was about three o'clock when Charles van der Lipp found Jocelyn, who was leaning against a window sill in the dimly lighted conservatory looking out at the bare lawns and the moon, and wishing that there might be an end to this wild scene of noise and drinks and music and decorations and jaded girls and men whose make-up had sweated into their hair and their collars.

The girls and boys who had discussed this dance with Norma had all spoken of its lasting until dawn, and ending with scrambled eggs and coffee served in the disheveled ballroom. No hope there. But the older women, including Norma's grandmother, had said lightly that a girl Norma's age would only "look in" on the fun, only have a "little glimpse" of the brilliant pageant; girls who were not out were not supposed to stay too late; and Jocelyn was wondering if she might not approach the excited, perspiring, smoke-scented, liquor-scented child who was her charge with the suggestion that it would be a good idea to go home. She was wearied beyond bearing with the whole scene; the costumes that had cost so much care and time and money had lost all their appeal; the brimming glasses of champagne seemed to have been circulating through the milling and dancing crowds forever.

"Miss Britton, could I speak to you a minute? Would you step out here?" Charles van der Lipp said. Jocelyn looked at him in surprise; his tone was serious. She had liked this ridiculous boy from the first, even though her first view of him had been the prejudicial one of finding him sprawled in his dirty golfing clothes on Norma's bed; she followed him into a sort of backwater of hallway, and as she saw his expression she laid a hand on his arm.

"Charles, something's wrong? What is it?"

"I'm a skunk for telling on them," he said unhappily, in a furtive, cautious manner. "But it's Norma. She's an awfully decent little kid, and I kind of hate to see her get in wrong."

"Where is she? What's she done?" Jocelyn's thoughts leaped at once to drunkenness; Norma had been fairly on her way to it when last she had seen her. Two thirds of the youngsters in the room were by this time silly with drink, and some of the boys had frankly, as the girls expressed it amusedly, "passed out."

"She and Peggy Wilson and Ponny Sears and Larry Bickford said they wanted to go down to Santa Barbara and swim and have breakfast. They said they all felt too hot."

"Santa Barbara!" Jocelyn said in a sharp whisper. "Why, they couldn't! That's three hundred miles!"

"They went off about ten minutes ago in Larry's car. They were all laughing, and they said they'd get there about eight."

"Charles, you're not serious!"

"Well, that's what they said."

Jocelyn looked distractedly about.

"Where's her grandmother? I must see her grandmother!"

"I went to find her first. But they said she felt kind of sick and they'd been giving her lemon sours, and they thought she'd gone home."

"Charles, don't say anything about this, will you? Peggy— but Peggy couldn't have gone! She's older than Norma. She'd know better."

"I know. I swore I wouldn't tell. But I got so worried."

"Don't tell anyone until we know, Charles. They may be around here somewhere. Let's look for them everywhere. And then I'll go home and see if Norma isn't there. She was terribly tired and—and excited."

"I know," Charles said wretchedly again. "And she's such a nice little kid."

As miserable a half-hour as Jocelyn had ever known ensued. She threaded the thinning crowds, crossed endless hallways and shining floors, peeped into corners from which absorbed couples eyed her resentfully, went into the banquet room, the dressing room, the card rooms. Norma was nowhere to be seen. She could not see either of the Sears boys or the Wilson girl either, and the terrifying conviction that Charles had been right deepened with every minute.

She found her coat and went home, dreading to go up to Norma's room for fear of destroying her last hope, knowing well that she would find there what she did find there: quiet lights, perfect order, Norma's bed turned down to display luxuriously pale pink linen sheets, pale pink fluffy blankets, pale pink satin puff; Norma's pale pink nightgown, heavy with delicate lace, also waiting, and Mattress half asleep before the fire.

Jocelyn went on to Mrs Fordyce's room. But that was empty, too, and Mrs Fordyce's maid, sleepily appearing in her nightgown and wrapper, reported that her mistress had telephoned—or someone had telephoned for her mistress—that she would stay that night with Mrs Royce.

Back in her own room, desperate, Jocelyn stood perfectly still for a long minute, her hand to her cheek, her forehead knitted into a frown, her eyes seeing nothing that was about her.

Presently she said aloud: "I may be a fool!" But with rapidity and decision she went back to Norma's room. It was now four o'clock in the morning; things had an odd stale look, as if night had gone on too long. After a brief talk with Mattress, Jocelyn returned to her room, changed her clothes, put on her heaviest coat. Mattress had a packed suitcase ready; she gave the maid only a final warning about not alarming the house, not saying anything to anyone until she had further directions, and descended to a waiting taxicab.

"Mills Field," she said to the driver.

"What plane are you taking, lady?" the man asked. "I don't think you can get one now until seven."

"There'll be a plane waiting. I ordered one," Jocelyn said briefly. "Don't lose any more time, please. I have to be in Santa Barbara at eight o'clock."

CHAPTER XIII

SHE HAD NEVER BEEN in a plane before. There was one bad moment: the moment in which she climbed in and was advised to buckle her belt about her. Then all other sensation than one of pleasure and excitement and amazement disappeared. To rise on a great easy sweep into the dark; to see the lights wheel and lessen below her and the sleeping world rush backward under the last of the moonlight, was all sheer delight.

There was a soft pillow under her head and a warm rug over her. Jocelyn was tired; she was almost immediately asleep.

When she was roused by the pilot's voice it was to a second of alarm again.

"What is it? We're coming down?"

"We're at Santa Barbara," the man said. Jocelyn started up, staggered out to cold air and the chill winter dawn, stood unsteadily, dazed and thrilled and unutterably triumphant.

"I don't believe it!" she said, still stupid with sleep.

"Here you are!" the pilot said. He carried her bag to the taxi; the sun was rising over the sleeping city; it was twenty minutes past six o'clock.

During their desperate search at the New Year's dance for Norma, Charles had told her that it was the plan of the runaways to go to the big hotel which fronted on the ocean. Jocelyn went there at once.

When she asked at the desk to register the reservation of a suite for Miss Fordyce, it was after a little reflection. The decision to use Norma's name was made because Jocelyn felt instinctively that there must be no attempt at a secrecy that could not possibly be preserved. Burlingame would know of this, and what Burlingame knew the whole world would know, for Norma's name was world news. The fact that Norma's chaperon was there with her, that Norma was expected, that a change of clothing had been provided, were all important.

She was immediately glad that she had taken this course, for as she mentioned Norma's name the clerk remembered that a reservation had already been made for Miss Fordyce; by telephone, about half an hour ago from Santa Maria. The rooms were ready; Jocelyn took possession then and waited, and everything had the unreality of a dream.

At eight o'clock she went downstairs and had coffee at a dining-room window commanding the driveway at the front of the hotel, and a few minutes before nine, when she had taken a chair on the veranda, the party arrived and she went down to meet it.

Ponny Sears was driving; Larry Bickford beside him. The girls were huddled into the back seat. Peggy Wilson, a big, bold, overdeveloped girl, with a very white skin and very black hair, looked frightened as she saw Jocelyn. Larry had jumped out of the car, and he and Peggy helped Norma out. Norma, in her draggled evening attire and big white fur evening wrap, looked white and bewildered. She had evidently been asleep; there was a bright red spot on the cheek that had been resting against Peggy's shoulder. Her eyes fell on Jocelyn, concerned and serious, and she began to cry.

The others, all in their early twenties, were young enough and scared enough to show relief at the appearance of authority, and to begin their apologies at once. Some feeble attempts at laughter died away; they surrounded Jocelyn, in their fantastic attire, with the men's overcoats striking still another incongruous note in an unbelievable scene, huddled after her into the hotel and up to the warm, comfortable, orderly rooms to collapse into chairs and onto beds with all the frankness of exhausted children.

Jocelyn paid small attention to the half-hysterical girl and the jaded-looking men. She concerned herself exclusively with Norma, who was pale and quiet, and who confessed in a whisper that she had been "damn fool enough to be sick in the car. And they *wouldn't* go to the hotel in Santa Maria," sobbed Norma, "because they said the people there didn't know them, and Peggy's uncle knows the man who owns this hotel!"

"It was all a sort of joke," Peggy Wilson began impressively. "We were fools to try it, but it sounded like so much fun to leave a New Year's party and go swimming in Santa Barbara! We were going to telephone for clothes . . ." Her voice died away; no one was listening.

"I think you boys had better go into the next room; there's a bath there, too," Jocelyn said quietly, cutting across this explanation without apology. "I want Norma to get into bed for a while. I brought you a change," she said to Norma, "and I brought something Peggy can wear. Now the first thing is a bath."

Norma, who had had the fearful and humiliating experience of being actively ill in a small car occupied by three other young persons who had also had too much to eat and drink, submitted meekly to Jocelyn's ministrations. To Peggy, Jocelyn did not speak at all, and Peggy was silent, too; she evidently was feeling the same physical sensations that had attacked Norma earlier in the morning. Her color was ghastly, her breath reeked of liquor and tobacco smoke, and when Jocelyn suggested breakfast she merely leaned back with closed eyes and whispered "Oh, God!"

On the other hand Norma made a rapid recovery. A warm bath, a change into fresh suitable morning wear, a cup of hot coffee resuscitated her at once. Her embarrassing illness in the car had at least had the effect of relieving her of the symptoms that were making the others wretched, and after breakfast she lay down, was covered with a light blanket, and slept peacefully during the entire morning of New Year's Day.

It was a queer morning. The spacious hotel rooms were warm and peaceful; from the windows Jocelyn could see the beautiful Pacific and the cheerful holiday movement among the cottages and garden homes. The young men, appearing unshaved and in rumpled fancy-dress clothes at about nine, had mumbled some awkward apologies and departed in the car. They observed that if they needed sleep they'd stop at some auto camp on the way. Peggy had said impulsively, with a challenging glance at Jocelyn, that she would go with them. Jocelyn had made no comment; her bland silence had been sufficient indication to Peggy that she was not in the least concerned with that young woman's plans or conduct.

But Ponny and Larry had objected. Both had splitting headaches and bad color; they did not want a girl along to-day. So Peggy remained to nurse her own headache, yawn over the glossy pages of a hotel magazine filled with photographs of Monterey cypresses and film folks' homes, and mutter at intervals that she felt "like hell."

At three o'clock the Fordyce car with two drivers arrived; the girls and Jocelyn got in, and they started on their long drive home. Norma was subdued, friendly and almost timid in manner; it was Peggy's turn to feel ill, and Jocelyn could see that Norma enjoyed the sight of her friend's discomfort thoroughly, and was ashamed to find a certain reflection of the same feeling in her own heart. Eventually, at about nine o'clock in the evening, still without a word of reproach or cross-examination from Jocelyn, Peggy was deposited at her own door, and the others went on to "Hill Acres."

"I didn't know exactly what I was doing," said Norma then. It was as near to an apology as Jocelyn would ever have from her. "I'm glad you came," she said. "I was sick of them all. I hated them all! I didn't know what to do."

"No more liquor, Norma."

"Oh, it wasn't the booze; it was everything!" said Norma.

Her father and grandmother were in the latter's room. Mrs Fordyce was in bed. She explained that some fish she had eaten the day before had been poisoned. Nita Royce had been scared to death about her.

"Have a lovely time, lovey?" she said to Norma. "Another time let your father know when you're going to Santa Barbara. You might have told them to let us know," she said to Jocelyn.

"What was the idea of driving down there so late, Miss Britton?" Philip asked, quiet and unsmiling.

"Those crazy boys weren't half sober," said the older woman. But indifferently, and snipping at her nails with a microscopic curved scissors as she spoke.

Norma gave Jocelyn a quick glance.

"We were so hot, Dad," she said.

"I think I'd discourage that sort of idea another time, Miss Britton," Philip said coldly. "Well, those pills will be making you sleepy, Mother," he added, kissing his mother's hair when he got up to go. "Get a good rest."

He was going downstairs for a man's poker party a few minutes later when he met Norma and Jocelyn in the hall.

"No more of those night runs, Norma," he said seriously. "I'm surprised that Miss Britton permitted it. And I don't like that Sears boy, or any of that lot! It was all right, I got your telegram when I got home here, before dinner, Miss Britton, and my mother knew only what I told her of it. But I think a party is enough excitement for a sixteen-year-old, and I don't like night driving, especially by drunken boys."

Jocelyn said nothing, not because she intended to keep silent on the subject, but because at the moment she could not decide exactly what the strategic course would be. Just how far to protect Norma, just what to admit and what not to admit puzzled her for a second, and in that second Philip had turned and started to descend the stairs, and Norma had given a triumphant caper and had giggled in delight.

"He thinks you were with me all the time!" the girl had exulted. "Oh, what luck!"

"I don't know what he could do even if he didn't think that!" Jocelyn said, betrayed into ill temper. "It doesn't seem to me that what anyone says has much effect on you! I don't know what Miss Sanderson would have done in my place last night. Had you sit in her lap all the time? Held your hand while you were dancing?"

"Poor Britty!" Norma crooned pityingly, still with her triumphant giggle.

"I think you let me down," Jocelyn told her.

"I never let anyone down!" It was Norma at her worst again, self-confident, arrogant, childish. "I don't see why they all make such a fuss about me," she went on complacently, as they reached her own room. "Loads of girls have money! Anyone can have money! It's only stupid dirty people who haven't got sense enough to work and save that are poor. Miss Wykoff said so, in our political-economy class."

"I don't know or care who Miss Wykoff is," Jocelyn said warmly, "but that's not true. A great many fine and splendid men are poor, and their wives are working all day washing and sweeping and caring for children, and they never earn even enough to be comfortable——"

"Why, look at my grandfather, darling," Norma yawned. "He was the stupidest man that ever lived. I don't think he could do much more than write his name! He had a little bicycle-tire shop fifty years ago, and what did he do? He loaned Jim Fortesque three hundred dollars to start the Lockey car, and now look at them. Miles of factories and sheds and a town called Fortesque and thousands of employees who always give me a darling car when I go to the plant, and Lockey libraries and hospitals and memorial parks and I don't know what all! And a statue of my grandfather in blue jeans with an oil can. If you call *that* hard to do!"

"Ze poor dwess!" said Mattress, displaying a ruin of striped gauze and gold and black ropes.

"Throw it away," said Norma. "I adored it, too," she said ,exedly. "Damn everything!"

She sat down, drawing the telephone toward her.

"If you telephone people," said Jocelyn firmly, "I'd go very light on what you did last night. It's not at all to your credit. It's not funny. Don't say more than that all of you and Miss Britton had breakfast at the hotel, and you and Peggy were so tired you rested all day and came home in your own car."

Norma, telephone in hand, looked a little dashed.

"I hate them all anyway," she said, as if in partial exoneration of herself.

"You'd hate them more if you'd gotten into deeper trouble."

"Ah, but you see I don't get into trouble!" Norma gave a confident laugh. Immediately her face clouded. "Dad 'll know when he gets the bill for the plane," she said anxiously. "Did you tell them to send him the bill?"

"I did."

"Well, I'll telephone tomorrow morning and send someone over with the money. I wonder they'd trust you?" Norma added curiously.

"They didn't. They telephoned here five minutes after I called them to confirm it."

"All in the middle of the night!" Norma giggled. She eyed Jocelyn uneasily, as Jocelyn settled herself in a chair with a magazine. "You don't have to stay," she said sweetly but rudely. "I'm going right to bed."

"I think I'll see you into bed," Jocelyn said grimly. "And if your father really expects me to keep an eye on you," she added in her thoughts, "I think I'll have my bed moved in here."

After a moment of annoyance Norma began her telephoning. But what had evidently been intended for a long period of gossip and giggling about last night's party turned out to be a rather flat failure. It was New Year's night, repentance and fatigue and satiety had set in everywhere; family parties and early good nights were the rule, and after a few attempts Norma gave it up, and somewhat disconsolately asked Jocelyn what game she liked.

From long heated Saturday evenings in the heart of the Partridge family Jocelyn knew a great many games. Backgammon appeared to be the one Norma fancied, and they played three games before Norma collapsed into sleepiness and was put to bed by Mattress and Jocelyn. While they played, Jocelyn found herself describing various phases of life in the big family of girls in Sausalito, and Norma showed a more eager and natural and youthful interest in the story than Jocelyn would have believed possible. She could not hear enough of the older sisters' troubles with the smaller sisters, and the sharing of rooms and frocks, and the cooking of meals.

"I think Mama was a dirty scut to have only me. She could have had three others and she wouldn't," said Norma, moving a white ivory counter.

Jocelyn felt her throat thicken.

"She went to doctors. You can, you know. There are doctors in New York who do nothing else except keep you from having babies," said Norma. "Mama got a chinchilla coat, for having me. Her father told her if she'd have a baby he'd give her anything she wanted. First she wanted an elevator in this house and then she wanted a chinchilla coat. So he offered to give her both and she had me. But then they decided against the elevator because they weren't living here, and they were divorced when I was two. But the next time, when she was married to Uncle Barry—that was Barry Caverley, you know, who was amateur tennis champ for years—she didn't want any more babies."

"Who told you all this, Norma?" Jocelyn took off a black ivory man. Her whole being felt chilled and sick.

"Mama. Damn it, you're ahead!" Norma replied, absorbed in the game.

CHAPTER XIV

AGAIN JOCELYN WENT to her room exhausted. But not to sleep. She was reading in bed, her pulses still throbbing to the excitements of this strange New Year's Day, when Lena came softly tapping at her door.

"It's Miss Norma, Miss Britton. Mr Fordyce asked me to call you."

"Miss Norma! What is it now!"

Jocelyn sprang out of bed, reached for a dressing gown, groped with her feet for her slippers, and was flying after the maid within a minute of the alarm. She had only opened the door from the wing into the upper hall when she heard Norma's voice, screaming, sobbing, hysterical. It ceased for a second, and she could hear Philip's accents, stern and commanding.

"Stop it, Norma! Stop it. Damn such fools as that Wilson girl, anyway!" And then more gently: "Ah, don't, dear. Quiet down, Spotty. Talk to Dad about it."

Jocelyn went in, her face colorless with terror. Norma was sitting up in bed; her father, on the edge of the bed, had his arm about her.

"Come in, Miss Britton," Philip said quickly. "I'm glad you've come! See what you can do for this poor little girl here. That Wilson idiot has just telephoned—at eleven o'clock! It seems—it's too bad—terrible thing, but those boys have had an accident, coming back."

"What boys?" Jocelyn whispered, sitting down weakly.

"Pon and Larry!" Norma whispered back, beginning to heave with wild sobs again, "and Pon was killed! Peggy said so. Larry's been all smashed up and Pon's dead! Oo-oo-oo— he's dead! And we all had breakfast together, and it was my fault——" And Norma began to sob and twist again, writhing against her father's shoulder and trying to free her hands from his grip.

"You never should have gone down to Santa Barbara," said Philip. "It was a mistake. But I can only thank God that you weren't with them. I congratulate you, Miss Britton," he added, with a glance for Jocelyn, "that you telephoned for the car. Otherwise——"

"Dad, will it all get into the papers?" Norma was quieter. Jocelyn's mere presence had had the effect of calming her. But she was still white-cheeked and frightened, and she clung to her father like a storm-blown bird.

"Darling, I'm afraid so. But Miss Britton was with you. That lets you out of any responsibility."

"Pon's dead!" Norma whimpered, beginning to cry again, but with less violence. "Oo-oo-oo——"

"Larry badly hurt?" Jocelyn asked.

"They say so. They're bringing poor Sears home, but they've taken the other boy into a hospital in Watsonville. It's too bad. It's too bad. They slept all day, it seemed, and started back about six."

"Larry told them that I was with them, and Peggy too, and Peggy's mother fainted, and she said that she was going to put Peggy into a convent in Belgium," Norma gibbered. "And Peggy said two reporters telephoned from Watsonville, and they said that Miss Britton flew down and got there before they did——"

"What's that?" Philip said sharply. "What are you talking about?"

"I suppose the papers will have the whole thing tomorrow, if Larry has been talking," Jocelyn said. "You see, the children went down without me," she explained, turning to Philip. "They got away from the dance and went down in Pon Sears's car. I didn't know it until they were gone. I'd seen Norma dancing with Charles van der Lipp——"

"Oh, if I'd only stayed there!" Norma moaned.

"You mean you weren't with them? You mean—— Spotty, you didn't go down there alone with that lot?"

"We were just fooling," Norma murmured, tears beginning to run down her face again. "The boys were kind of edged, and we all felt so hot, it was so hot in there! And so we said what fun it would be to go swimming at Santa Barbara—I'd never been there, Dad," she interrupted herself with trembling lips. "And I wanted to see it. And so we sneaked off in Pon's car—oh, poor Pon! Poor Pon!"

"Go on, Spotty. You went off in his car."

"Yes, and Pon was plastered, so Larry wanted to drive, but he was sort of silly, too. And they went so horribly fast, and I was sick——"

Philip and Jocelyn exchanged glances; Jocelyn faintly shook her head. The thought of the little befuddled heiress being rushed over the dangerous long roads by a pair of irresponsible half-drunken boys had haunted her all day.

"How'd you get there?" Philip demanded, looking at her.

"I flew," Jocelyn answered simply.

"You flew?"

"I telephoned for a special plane."

"At what time was this?"

"About—around half past four."

"And you joined them there?"

"I got there before they did."

"She had rooms and clothes and I had a bath and went to sleep," Norma said. She leaned weakly against her father's shoulder, shut her eyes.

Philip's eyes met Jocelyn's.

"I owe you an apology," he said. Jocelyn flushed brightly.

"That's all right," she said uncomfortably.

"You were there, and you took charge," he said. "And the boys started home ahead of you?"

"They were in their costumes. They were both sleepy and upset."

"My God!" Philip said. "Well, you've had your lesson, Spotty. You might have been in that car; you might be dead tonight. Now try to quiet down and get to sleep. I was up all night myself, and I feel groggy. I'm going to break up that poker party downstairs—none of the fellows will feel much like going on with it. I'll look in on you again in a few minutes."

He went away, and Jocelyn sat for a while with Norma, talking with her. Having recovered her self-control, Norma was in a manageable mood, broken and mild. Jocelyn sat beside her and held her hand and found her for the first time a simple, natural, scared and honest little girl.

"Can't we—isn't there any way we can keep this out of the papers?"

"I'm afraid not, if Larry talked."

"They *can't* print it! Dad can stop them. I mean—everyone can't be talking about me. Not—not with those boys— why, people thought I shouldn't go to that dance at all, that I was too young! And I'm not out yet," Norma said feverishly, her hands tightly holding to Jocelyn's. "And my mother—my mother'll be wild. Mother said that Dad couldn't take care of me, and now she'll think he can't, and I want to stay here, and now they'll all get started arguing—they're always talking about what to do with me——!"

Poor little thing, Jocelyn thought, as Norma gradually relapsed into drowsiness, into sleep. She had had a grilling forty hours since they had discussed costumes in this room only yesterday morning. She was exhausted, and it was not long before Jocelyn could put out the lights and slip away. Norma slept, but Jocelyn lay wakeful and shivering for hours.

She overslept the next morning, and guiltily rang for her breakfast at nine o'clock. Philip had gone; Norma was still asleep, but Mrs Fordyce was walking about her room in great agitation, her lavender draperies floating about her, and her two callers, Nita Royce and a handsome efficient-looking woman of perhaps forty, who was introduced as Mrs Verrinder, stared hard at Jocelyn as she came in.

"You sent for me?" Jocelyn asked.

"I've been lying awake practically all night," Mrs Fordyce said sharply. "I suppose you've heard of the perfectly terrible thing that has happened? Miss Britton, I hold you—and everyone holds you—largely responsible."

"Holds *me* responsible!" Jocelyn echoed, proudly and angrily.

"The idea," said Norma's grandmother, "of permitting that child to start for Santa Barbara at that hour of night! She had been drinking, too, Phil tells me, which never should have been allowed!"

"But you were quite right, Bert," Nita Royce said soothingly, "she was much too young to go to that party. Poor kid! It isn't right that she should be submitted to all this miserable publicity."

"You knew that I didn't know they had any such plan, Mrs Fordyce?"

"My dear Miss Britton, I don't know anything. I ate some poisoned fish at the club, and I was desperately ill at Mrs Royce's house; how could I protect my own grandchild? We'll hear from Janet about this," Mrs Fordyce went on ruefully to the other women, "and of course I'll get the blame. All I can say is that if Miss Sanderson had been on the job it couldn't have happened. Because, I mean, it simply never *did*."

"It was just a wild idea of the poor youngsters," Mrs Royce said. "Larry Bickford was telling Tom last night that he doesn't know why they did it, they just did it on the spur of the moment. 'Oh, come on, let's go swim at Santa

Barbara!' You know how it is. Like that awful party years ago when the men and women all changed clothes——"

For some reason this recollection did not appeal to Norma's grandmother, and she said hastily, "That was all nonsense. But at least we all—they all—were grown up! The thing is that Sandy never would have let Norma get into a condition when she would have considered such a thing. Mrs Foster telephoned this morning—Sandy was with Doris and Yvonne until they got married, and she asked me why I hadn't kept Sandy, and *why* we'd given Janet a chance to criticize our way of handling Norma. It's just about killing me, the whole thing. And the Sears funeral tomorrow—that glorious big strong boy——"

"You don't think," Jocelyn put into the tearful pause, "that Norma was at all to blame? For drinking when she had been forbidden to drink, for letting them talk her into such a thing?"

"No, I don't!" snapped her grandmother, and Mrs Verrinder shook her lovely, smoothly curled head and said in gentle reproof: "I think we can hardly blame a child that age for a piece of folly, Miss Britton."

"No, we can hardly blame Norma; she's full of fun like the rest of the kids," Mrs Royce added. "You've *nothing* to reproach yourself with, Bert," she added, to her hostess.

"I reproach myself for ever letting Sandy go! Poor Sandy, in a hotel on Post Street that advertises that it has baths!" Mrs Fordyce lamented. "Well, Miss Britton, we sent for you to discuss this with you. We don't think it's wise to keep Norma here for several days—possibly a week. She could go down to Hollywood, of course, for her mother's intimate with April Moon, but that doesn't seem just the right thing just now. I mean, it 'd be more parties and all that. So we're thinking of the Yellowstone or the Grand Canyon or some place she's never been, only it's a terrible time of year; she ought to go to New York and have a lot of opera and concerts, but her mother's there, and that would mean trouble for poor Phil. He's simply wild about the whole thing, says he doesn't know what to do—that it was a crime the child ever got into such a mess—and here are the bills for the costumes and everything—he thought they were much too high—I confess I left that to you——"

"Oh, they all spend too much money and go too many places and they haven't the faintest idea of moderation!" Mrs Verrinder said heartily and impatiently. "I confess I don't know what they're coming to! The day my Joan announced her engagement she danced around her grandfather and said, 'Oh, am I glad I'm a virgin, am I glad I'm a virgin!' I thought Daddy would smack her down. He said to me: 'Daze, I didn't even think she knew what the word meant!' He said: 'My mother never used that word in her life!' But they teach these things in schools now. Teach everything. I think it's awful. My father and mother never were alone together five minutes before they were married. He called her 'Miss Maggie' and she called him 'Colonel' until the end of their lives. Southern fashion, you know. Oh, well, the old South! Girls like flowers——"

"A telegram, Mrs Fordyce," said a maid, offering a yellow envelope on a tray.

"Would you please read it, Miss Britton?"

Jocelyn took it, ripped it open.

"It's signed 'Janet,' " she said. " 'Absolutely horrified at this disgusting scandal,' " she read. " 'Must insist that Sandy be given full charge of poor darling Spotty and if necessary both placed in some good school. Dull for Sandy but I will make it up to her. Otherwise I will come at once to California to take charge which will upset my plans here. Am sending Spotty two hats which she can return if she wishes. Please inform me at once of what steps you take and get her out of headlines for God's sake.' "

"You see?" Mrs Fordyce asked, spreading her hands, shrugging her shoulders helplessly. "That gives me absolutely no choice. But it means we have Norma to deal with!"

"I just waked up," said Norma, trailing in in peacock-blue and silvery-gray striped chiffon, looking pale and weary, and seating herself on her grandmother's bed. "I wanted Miss Britton; Mattress said she was in here. When I was asleep," she said, with watering eyes, "I thought it was all an awful dream. But now it seems that—that Pon really is dead, and they'll all look at me, they'll think I'm an awful person—and I'm no worse than anyone else——"

"Read this telegram from your mother," her grandmother said as she paused. "We know you weren't to blame, darling," she added. "We blame ourselves. We never ought to have let our little girl get into such a horrible fix."

Norma took the telegram and read it apathetically; read it a second time. Her pale face flushed. To Jocelyn she looked young and helpless and pitiable—a little girl, disheveled and tired, among all these groomed and definite and flashing women.

"I'll not go anywhere with Sandy. I loathe her!" said Norma.

"But darling, you can't go to Janet," Mrs Verrinder said quickly and lovingly. "Isn't she going to be married to Count Spazzolari?"

"I don't want to *see* Sandy!" persisted Norma. "And I won't live with Mama and Mario, either! He kisses me and I hate him."

"Hello, girls," Philip said in the doorway. "Dressed enough for me to come in, Mother?"

"I'm just over a terrible touch of ptomaine," Mrs Fordyce said pathetically, "and I feel as if I wouldn't care if I never got dressed again! Come in, dear. We're all discussing this thing, and there really doesn't seem to be any way out— there truly doesn't," she went on, with a deprecating smile for Norma, "except to—to make a change, and get our poor dear strict old Sandy back—she's always been so *devoted,* after all, Phil——"

Philip had taken a chair, and Norma had gone over to get

into his lap, and from the stronghold of his arms to look defiance at the court that was sitting in judgment upon her. Jocelyn, who felt as if she were playing a part in a play, looked from face to face, and wondered to think how much money could not buy.

"I'll not go to school with Sandy as if I was a baby!" said Norma, in deadly finality.

"We've had a telegram from Janet, Phil," his mother said disconsolately. "I'm sure I don't know what we're going to do! She says it's Sandy or she'll demand Norma back."

"She can't have Norma back. Norma spends nine months a year with me," Philip said, tightening his arm, as he read the telegram.

"Oh, I love you when you're kind to me, Daddy!" Norma, becoming artificial the moment she was made the center of attention, said effusively. He looked down at her thoughtfully, unsmilingly, but did not speak.

"Phil, isn't this awful?" asked Daisy Verrinder.

"Well, we all love this little girl, and we've let her get herself into an awful mess," he said in his kindest tone. "It does seem to me that with so many of us here to look out for her we might manage better than we have. All I want for you, Spotty," he went on, "is to keep you happy and keep you safe and see that you have a reasonably good time until I hand you over to some better man. Now here's your grandmother, and here's Aunt Daisy and Aunt Nita all ready to lend a hand, and here's Miss Britton to help out, and one of the nicest crowds of boys and girls in the world to play with. What's the matter with us all that that isn't enough?"

"That *is* enough," Mrs Verrinder said, perhaps really touched by this appeal, or perhaps, as Jocelyn uncharitably thought, just one more of the striking grass widows of the group who would have liked to play the role of the second Mrs Philip Fordyce. "And I think the sensible thing is for us to forget this catastrophe, which wasn't Spotty's fault at all, and have lovely, happy simple times with games and little home dances. I know my Billy, big as he is, would like to take care of Norma——"

"But Billy's at Yale," Mrs Royce put in sweetly.

"But he's coming home to Stanford for these two last quarters," Mrs Verrinder countered with equal amiability. "I had a wire from him this morning."

"And he had a wire from you first that Norma Fordyce was at home," Jocelyn thought. She said nothing; she waited expectantly. These extraordinary people never failed one!

"I've been in town all morning," Philip said. "I've fixed everything as far as I can. I went to all the newspaper offices, made a statement that Norma and Miss Wilson and Norma's governess were all down there together; I've quieted it down as much as was possible. Nokes has put five plain-clothes men on the place, watching the gates; we won't have any photographers here. The main thing is to wait until this all quiets down a little, and then start over."

"Yes, but there's Janet and what she says of Sandy! Please stop pulling my hair, Annette. Phil, I will not—I cannot have Janet come on here, especially with one of those foreigners!" his mother said. "You know how she upsets the whole place. Last time we had to have the bathtub torn out, and those men in white clothes were climbing all around the roofs and look-ing in my windows and I know one of them took my bracelet. You remember my emerald bracelet, Daisy? Mr Castro bought it in Paris when we were first married—I hated the name Castro because Castro Street is so dull—dreadful flats! But he was being perfectly darling then. Now, Phil, do think out something! We can't just go on this way, we've got to wire Janet something that will be completely reassuring. What can we say about Sandy? We could tell her she was dead. That would sort of quiet that down."

"She's very probably in touch with Sandy, Mother."

"Oh, perhaps she is. How horrible! Let me see."

"Why not send Norma to me for a few days?" Mrs Ver-rinder suggested smoothly. "Diana'd love it, and as I say,

Bill's coming home. He ought to be here tomorrow or next day. I've always kept my children *children,*" confessed Daisy, with a complacent little laugh. "They may not have had as much fun, I'll grant you *that——*"

Nobody was listening to her. Mrs Fordyce said:

"I'm so sorry about making any change, Miss Britton. But you see Miss Sanderson was my daughter-in-law's governess before she went to the Griscoms and the Fosters. Mrs Foster really bribed her to come to her, and Mrs Griscom didn't forgive her for years, so you can see how valuable she is. And the French and German are important, don't you think so, Phil?"

"I'll act worse than I ever have," Norma promised calmly.

"No, you won't, Spotty," her father said kindly. "You're only a little girl, and you know we're all doing this just to protect you. I have to go on to Washington in a few days; no help for it. It's a Federal case, and Uncle Bill's too old to go, and Mr Sawyer can't. It may keep me there for weeks, and I won't have a happy moment if you aren't being a good girl. Why, Spot, you have everything to make you happy! You're only sixteen—well, nearly seventeen—and that's a beautiful age. You ought to have the happiest years of your life ahead, and marry some nice man, and have some cute little kids, and buy yourself a beautiful place at—say, Tahoe, and another in France, if you liked, or along the Riviera——"

"Pebble Beach," Norma said, smiling sulkily.

"Well, exactly! But we want you to learn a lot more, first, and take things quietly. Leave something for the later years. Your mother's idea was for you to take special courses at Middlefield School, work away there with nice girls, go to simple little parties, as Aunt Daisy suggests, and let Miss Britton get some sleep. How about promising that you'll toe the mark for a few months? Then it'll be summer, and we'll talk about Honolulu——"

"I want a place in Honolulu!" Norma said, petulantly, but mollified.

"Well, why not? You can have any damn thing you want in the world if you'll just steer clear of scrapes."

"But I won't do anything if Sandy's around!" stipulated Norma.

"Well, now let me see how we can work that. Miss Britton, what would you suggest?"

"Suppose we telephoned the Middlefield School," Jocelyn said, feeling like Alice as they all looked at her seriously, and conscious of a deep inner impulse toward angry laughter. "It's vacation, and they'd have plenty of room. And suppose Norma and I went quietly down there and boarded for a few days. We could make arrangements for her studies with all her teachers and get her books and get started. Then you could telegraph her mother that she was at Middlefield, and that nobody could see her or get in touch with her for several days."

"I think that's the answer," Philip said, with a quiet triumphant smile of approval.

"But that doesn't solve Sandy, Phil," Daisy Verrinder said, in her gentle regretful way. "Dear, dear!" she added with a light laugh and a glance at the other women that made the remark the merest nonsense, "if it wasn't for the dreadful eight years between us I'd marry you with or without your consent, Phil, and move right in here with Bill and Di, and then we'd not have any trouble at all!"

"Are you only fifty, Daisy, with that great boy?" asked Mrs Royce innocently.

"Forty-eight, dear," Mrs Verrinder corrected. "Although poisonously close to forty-nine," she added hastily, almost as if in prevention of some correction.

"Phil's still in love with Janet," his mother said.

"Say, listen!" Philip protested. "Cut it out! I'm not asking Sandy to chaperon me, or Miss Britton, either!"

This drew all eyes to Jocelyn, who was infuriated to feel herself flushing.

"What—what do you think of the Middlefield School plan?" she asked, stammering a little.

"I'll tell you what I think," said Mrs Fordyce suddenly. "Send Sandy down there with Norma for three days. Then wire Janet that Sandy and Norma are at Middlefield. She's always thought Norma ought to go to Middlefield."

"If it's a school where every girl has her own horse and takes care of it, and the head mistress wears hunting coats and things, I won't stay," said Norma.

"You'll not have to stay," said her grandmother. "You'll be home in a few days. Meanwhile we'll tell everyone you're in a rest home, your nerves have been all upset by this terrible accident, and in a week they'll be thinking of something else, and you'll be home again."

"But why Sandy?" the girl protested.

"So we can wire your mother you're with Sandy."

"I don't know why everything's so horrible!" Norma muttered. She had left her father's arms to go curl herself uncomfortably on the foot of her grandmother's bed. Now she turned her back on the company, toppled over, pulled a fat satin puff over her, and apparently returned to sleep.

CHAPTER XV

JOCELYN AND PHILIP went into the hall together. The girl, above a sense of hurt, was trying to smile and speak understandingly.

"I'm afraid I've let you down terribly," she said.

"I don't know what gets into them, or how they raise them," Philip said, shaking his head. "A child that age, causing all this fuss and uproar! And the appalling thing is," he added, as he and Jocelyn moved toward the door that opened into the wing where her rooms were, "we're probably going to have six or seven years of this. I don't know how people get them through it. I wish to God the girl was twenty-three!"

"But that seems such a tragedy," said Jocelyn. "A father ought to be getting such joy out of a daughter as pretty and smart as Norma."

"She's pretty enough," he conceded, "but I don't know why you say smart."

"She's smart enough, too, only it's been all twisted sideways, Mr Fordyce," Jocelyn said, suddenly turning to her own problem. "I think your mother would be happier with Miss Sanderson here; to have me gone. And I do think it would be a good thing to send them down to the school tomorrow. Norma's frightened enough to go now; she doesn't want to go back to——" She hesitated, changed somewhat the phrase she had been going to use. "She doesn't like New York, and she doesn't like Count—what is it? Spazzo-something. And of course she doesn't want to go back to a European school."

"So here we have the question of one of the richest little girls in the world," he said, with a troubled smile and a shake of his head, "with a mother and father and grandmother, with five or six homes, and nowhere to go. Well, we'll pop her and Sandy into school for a week and see where that gets us."

"And I'm slipping away," Jocelyn told him. It gave her an odd little twinge to say it. She didn't want to leave this fascinating tangle. "I've not been much of a success, and it's possible that Miss Sanderson's Victorian methods will work better."

"She'll not stand Sandy long. That's really to pacify her mother. I feel very badly about the whole thing," Philip said. "I wish you'd kept a stricter eye on her at the party, but at the same time, if you hadn't gotten down to Santa Barbara when you did, and taken charge of them all, she might be lying in her grave, like poor young Sears, tomorrow night."

"I really want to go. I feel as if the tempo had been a little swift for me," Jocelyn said. "I'm going to my aunt, I think. There's going to be a wedding there, and there are two small babies in the house, and I generally straighten out my uncle's bills for him and collect a lot of money he never would. And I feel as if that sort of thing might be good for me, for a while."

"You haven't had much fun. You've been here—what? Just a week," he said.

"It seems like a year," Jocelyn said fervently, and they both laughed.

"Well, when 'll you be back in the office, Miss Britton? For I'll be going away next week, and I want to report first, of course."

"I was thinking perhaps I wouldn't come back. It's been— pretty strenuous for me," Jocelyn explained. "You remember under what circumstances you gave me a lift home from Berkeley? I suppose that took it out of me a little. And then this, and the feeling that I've let Norma get herself into such trouble—I'd like to get away from it all for a while."

"You mean you're still in love with Dunham?" His voice, with its sudden ring of authority, its quality of having the right to question her, thrilled her oddly, and she felt a little shaken as she answered him.

"No, I only feel ashamed about all that. That's over. It seemed so—so easy a thing to get into. But when one sees it from a little distance——— However," Jocelyn interrupted herself, smiling, "you've had enough of that affair! But I'll always be grateful to you for what you did, and glad I had this experience here. Perhaps Miss Sanderson wouldn't have lost sight of Norma, even for that minute———"

"No," he said, as she hesitated, "I don't think she would."

"Well, maybe not. Maybe she knows girls better than I do. I'm sorry, anyway. And if you'll be here until—say a week from today, I'll come into the office and tell you whether I can come back or not."

"But we can't get along without you!" he said, really troubled.

"Oh yes, you can. Only I am glad you want me. I've been four years with Fordyce and Sawyer, and of course I feel at home there. But I really would like—I'd like awfully to go to my aunt's for a few days."

"I think you should. I think you've a holiday coming to you, putting in a New Year's Day like yesterday. But if you'll be in the office a week from today we can settle everything then."

"You weren't going before that?"

"If I was, I'll wait." He said it with so significant and friendly a smile that Jocelyn felt her pulses respond again to some breath-taking emotion.

"Shall I say good-by to your mother?" she asked. "To Norma?"

"No, because I hope it isn't good-by. I'll explain to them that you are very considerately clearing the tracks for Sandy, and I'll see you, positively, on Wednesday."

"Wednesday, then."

"They are having such a powwow in there," he said, with an annoyed glance in the direction of his mother's bedroom door, "that I suppose the cooler we keep the whole thing— the less complicated, the better for everyone. It's all worked out very differently from what I thought it would. I wish to goodness I could be more with the kid. I liked the way—it sort of broke me up, the way she came over to me this morning! Lord," he said with a weary sigh, "what a mess!"

Silence hung for a moment between them; they looked at each other almost in inquiry. What was not being said? Then they both laughed.

"Incidentally," Philip said, ending the pause, "if it interests you, I thought I would just mention that Mrs Verrinder's kindly plans to move in here with Bill and Diana do not seem to appeal to me."

Jocelyn laughed outright. But afterward, when she was packing her bags, when she was leaving "Hill Acres" and on her way by train and boat and streetcar to Sausalito, she did not smile at the memory of this and of other things he had said.

Instead they gave her a strange feeling of richness, of warmness at her heart. Her last talk with Philip, rather than making her feel cut away from the Fordyce interests, had seemed to draw her nearer to them. He was the most important member of the group, after all. He was Norma's official guardian and had the last word in everything that concerned her, no matter how her mother, grandmother, how she herself, and Sandy, and fondly interested friends might argue and plan. And he had included Jocelyn in his problem. "We'll pop her and Sandy into school for a week," he had said, "and see where that gets us." And the pronouns had meant Jocelyn and himself, his expression had left her in no doubt of that.

He felt now that Jocelyn was his adviser and conspirator where Norma was concerned. "We can't get along without you," he had said. "I hope it isn't good-by. . . . You've a holiday coming to you." And then at the end those few words about Mrs Verrinder, mischievously added, with Philip's own careless air of dominating a conversation or a situation, of not caring very much what anyone thought of him or the varied predicaments in which he found himself. It was a hard manner to define; Jocelyn found it infinitely fascinating. There was something generous, definitely male, pre-eminently sophisticated about it.

She thought about him a great deal, and analyzed and re-analyzed the talk they had had in the hall, wringing every possible iota of meaning and significance out of it. Her aunt, meeting her enthusiastically at the side doorway of "Maple Den," observed that she had never seen Jocelyn looking better.

"The change," said Aunt Nell, "has done you good."

"Something," said Jocelyn joyfully, "has done me good!"

She caught up the nearest baby and kissed him, burying her face in his soft warm little neck. And when her aunt heard her chattering and laughing with the other girls, it seemed to her that sober little Jocelyn, who had always been a rather pathetic and lonely figure among them, was the gayest of them all.

CHAPTER XVI

JOCELYN HAD OFTEN THOUGHT that her aunt's way of calming any particularly confusing domestic situation, or simplifying any too complicated home program, was to propose fresh confusions and complications, and in some mysterious fashion whose secret was known only to herself, to thereby straighten everything out into pleasantness and peace. Therefore it was no particular surprise to her to discover that with a houseful of daughters, babies and sons-in-law, with wet weather making all out-of-doors one great mud problem, and with Tots burdened with the dual responsibilities of a job in the bank and an approaching wedding, they should have decided on a Sunday picnic.

Winter picnics to the Partridges were of quite a different stamp from summer picnics. In summer they toiled up mountains, through all but impenetrable chaparral, with the boiling sun of July or August beating down upon their heads, and the water warming in canteens. In winter they chose bleak hill walks over windy ridges to the barren beach, sought out rocks behind which, and behind which only, it was possible to keep a driftwood fire alight, and devoured their food in a light rainfall if necessary, with sweaters and thick stockings getting wetter every minute.

Still, nobody who could possibly be included in one ever avoided a picnic with the Partridges. Charles Rossiter and Peter Smith, who had married Jane and Jossy respectively some years earlier, were now ringleaders in preparation, and

Jocelyn noted that even quiet Rusty Livermore, who was so soon to assume responsibility for Tots, was showing a dawning enthusiasm for the whole crazy plan.

"It's going to pour," the one son of the house predicted.

"Oh, I hope it does!" Jane, who was oldest, and about Jocelyn's age, said fervently. "Oh, can you ever forget the time it poured so we simply couldn't see anything, and we got off the road, and slumped into absolute morasses!"

"And had to hold arms," contributed Bam.

"Oh, and just before Jossy's baby came," exulted Sissy, who, engaged to Edward Whitehouse, was pretending unconsciousness of his adoring glances. "Remember that one? Remember Dad trying to keep Jossy from slipping, and both of them sliding down a bank, and Dad looking up with his face streaming and saying, 'This is anything but good for your sister'?"

Upon which they all laughed delightedly.

Various disreputable utensils and familiar burdens gradually were assembled in the laundry, a basket whose contents were covered with a piece of dark green oilcloth, a large blackened coffee pot with a swing handle, long forks, tin cups strung on a cord. Dr Partridge appeared in full picnic regalia: a weather-beaten topee on his gray hair, an old leather jacket buttoned snugly about his neck, high boots into which old jeans had been stuffed. On his hands were shabby gauntlets; he buckled a canteen about him, picked up a stout walking stick, and was ready to start.

The girls wore caps, raincoats, old sweaters, old plaid skirts. Each member of the expedition carried something; Jocelyn found herself let off easily with the coffee pot, which, with only the coffee grounds sewed into a cheesecloth bag within it, was manageable and light. Two of the young men took the basket whose handles had been ingeniously altered by the doctor to swing in balance from a pole. Everybody took a few matches, for there had been one picnic upon which they had been forgotten, and Aunt Nell, who was remaining

at home with the babies, asked everyone more than once
about the butter. It was unfortunately customary to leave
the butter in the icebox until the last moment, and thus run
the risk of forgetting it entirely.

Jane had to nurse her baby at eleven, so they had to wait
for that. Half an hour earlier everyone was circling about
restlessly, looking at the cloudy sky and at the deep café-au-
lait puddles in the yard and the road. It was after eleven,
and the baby had almost finished his meal, when Bam came
out to the side yard where the bundled picnickers were passing the time by trying to hit a certain branch of the big syca-
more with rocks, to announce to Jocelyn that Kent Dunham
was there to see her.

Jocelyn's face flushed brightly as she turned to go into the
house, but when she reached the large shabby room that was
the parlor she was pale. She still carried her big black coffee
pot; her hands were still covered with old chamois gloves;
a small felt hat was pulled down over her shining hair.

As they met she did not smile; she looked strained and
anxious. Kent did not smile. He looked nervous and anxious
too, and she thought, looking at him in cool, strange detach-
ment, that the romantic appeal of his beauty was all the more
marked for that. Anyone looking at Kent would know that
he was an artist, keenly intelligent and sensitive. Not because
of any affectation like long hair or flowing tie or exaggerated mannerisms—he would have despised such superficial
absurdities—but because of something keen and eager and
boyish in his manner, something that showed that to him the
world never grew old, and that any moment, any turn of the
road might discover to him a fresh kingdom of love and
laughter.

He was eight years older than Jocelyn, but this morning
she felt herself the older. She put down her coffee pot, and
he gripped both her hands in his and stood half bending
above her, for he was tall, and looking down at her with pain
and pleading in his eyes.

"Jocelyn, it's been two weeks! I've not seen you since before Christmas. I had to come! I've been in Portland, you know. I only got down here yesterday, and telephoned the Fordyce house and they said you were here. You're not going to be there any more?"

But he did not wait for an answer. He rushed on, too full of his own misery to stop once he had begun.

"All these days," he said, "ever since before Christmas —we had Christmas with Lilian's family—I've been counting the minutes until I could come down again and see you. You've got to talk to me, darling; this is my one chance. You're not going out in this rain?"

"It's not raining now." Jocelyn was conscious of feeling sorry for him. He was unhappy; anyone could see that. And he was growing unhappier every minute, for naturally she could not pretend that she was as excited as he. In fact she could not awaken any emotion in her heart. In a detached way she saw herself as well as Kent; saw this man and woman in Aunt Nell's bare, airy, double parlor that smelled this morning of damp and book bindings, and realized that the man was troubled and importunate, and that the woman felt as far away and unconcerned as if years and not days had passed between today and their past emotional interviews.

"But where are you going?"

She indicated the coffee pot.

"Picnic."

"In this weather?"

"Well, rain's the best time. It's not so hot walking. It's fun."

"But we have to talk!"

Jocelyn spoke gently, sympathetically.

"No; we don't have to talk, Kent. We've only to say that we liked each other too much for our own peace of mind for a while, and now it's—it's over."

"Too much for our own peace of mind!" he echoed, angry and aghast.

"It's all like a dream," Jocelyn said, in a tone that was like a dream.

"Like a dream! You can't talk that way! I've broken up my whole life for you. I've told Lilian. Ah, Jocelyn, don't be like this! Don't, dear. You did love me once. You're not the kind that changes. I've said that to myself a thousand times, that you don't change. Won't you give up your picnic and let me take you somewhere to lunch so we can talk?"

"I have to carry the coffee pot; we've all got something," she said, feebly. Even to her it sounded inadequate, and the man brushed it impatiently aside.

"Anyone can carry a coffee pot!"

"I know; but I couldn't let my uncle down," Jocelyn reasoned, dutifully. Making excuses to get away from Kent! It all became more and more unreal. She, who had hungered so to see him, to have him telephone, stop in at the office, send her some word or sign that he thought of her, to be wishing that this interview were over, that he would go!

He looked at her a moment, puzzled. Then he said quite gently:

"What changed you, Jocelyn?"

"Why—why——" she began stammeringly, and stopped. When she spoke it was in a lower tone, and slowly, as if she were formulating her idea for herself as well as for him. "Don't things sometimes change that way?" she asked simply. "That afternoon, before Thanksgiving, you know, when I went over to Covey's house, I was tired—I was *tired* of wanting to see you. My heart was—just *tired*. I'd hoped so long, waiting for telephones or for you to come in; I'd wanted you so horribly. And then suddenly, that night over at the cabin, it just—wasn't there. There was a blank. It had burned itself out, as I suppose it always does if it isn't right.'

"How d'you mean, 'if it isn't right'?"

"Well, that it wasn't. Not with us. If it can be an engagement and kitchen showers and a wedding and all that, it leads —don't you think so?—to a different kind of feeling. But ours wouldn't have."

"Ours can now," he said firmly. "Lilian is considering it. Of course her family doesn't want it. They're the sort who hate that kind of thing. But it's only a few weeks of unpleasantness, and then we are free. And Jocelyn, if that meant for you and me spring over there in Covey's cabin, and afterward work together somewhere in some other place, that would mean happiness to you, wouldn't it, dear?"

She looked at him wonderingly, kindly.

"But don't you see, Kent, it's—just dropped. When you came into the office that day to see me, when you said that you had made up your mind to stop it, that this was the end, how did you feel? Didn't you feel that the glow—the joy had gone out of it? That we were carrying on a dead affair?"

"No, never. Not for a minute!" he protested. She knew that he believed it. "I was thinking only of you," he said, "that I would be in Portland, and that you were too fine to be thinking of me, that some other man had a right to love you since I couldn't."

"And you don't think that now?" she asked simply. She saw that he was for a second caught in his own net, but he came back courageously.

"Now that we're talking of divorce, that changes it."

"But last year we didn't talk of divorce."

"No. No; we didn't think it was possible."

"And what makes it possible now, Kent?"

"Because—don't you see, don't you remember?—suddenly, that night at the cabin, it was all so clear. That we didn't have to—to pacify everyone, to look out for everyone. That *we* were what matters, you and I! That Lilian must find her own way out, and I must find another job, if I had to, if it was impossible to stay where I was then, in San Francisco. Don't you see how it all slipped about and became—became not only possible to do, Joy darling, but the only thing, the inevitable thing! I'd been on the other side of the wall, thinking that I couldn't have you and Lilian, and couldn't let Lilian down. But just in that flash, when you came to me, you darling, when I realized that we had only to take our happiness and stop fussing and worrying about it, it was all changed!"

He was warming to his argument as he went along. Now he had both her hands, and had drawn them up to his chest, and their eyes were close together.

"Joy," he said gravely, almost reproachfully, "if you'd stayed that night, if you'd had the courage to give yourself to me that night, to trust me, it would all be straightened out now, it would all be so simple. Lilian thinks we were lovers; nothing I can say will make her believe anything else. She says that if you will write her, saying that we belong to each other, she'll make no further objections to a divorce."

Jocelyn's head went up proudly; she freed her hands.

"Lilian says that!"

"She said that before I came away."

"Well, I like her nerve!" Jocelyn ejaculated forcefully and inelegantly, too stunned to choose her words.

"But darling, she knows how we care for each other."

"But—but——" She came to a full stop, remembering those days when she and Kent had shared all but the ultimate intimacy, had been lovers in thought and soul, had longed to break down the last barrier and challenge the whole censorious world as to their right to happiness. "One wonders what use Lilian would hope to make of such a letter," she said scornfully.

"No use at all, of course! Except perhaps to convince her family that there was real reason to divorce me. And what do we care about her family! We'll be off somewhere, Brittany maybe, or Italy. I'll be painting; we'll have a couple of sunburned barelegged little boys."

Jocelyn had walked to the window, and was looking out

upon the bare garden and the dripping shrubs, and between the low gnarled limbs of the crouching oaks down the hill the troubled gray waters of the bay.

"You just said, Kent," she began presently, turning her head a little to glance at him as he stood close behind her, "that quite suddenly, that night at Covey's, everything seemed to change and become clear to you. Why can't you believe that everything seemed to change and become clear to me, too? Up to that time you'd been liking me—oh, loving me, I know that! But other things had seemed equally important, other things had had to be balanced against it. I'd been just the other way. I'd loved you so that nothing else seemed to matter.

"Well, that night we changed places. Don't ask me why. I don't know why. I'd been frantic to see you all day, telephoning Una and Red, going up there, not knowing what to do. You were going away on Monday, and I felt as if I had to see you or die.

"But then when I did see you," Jocelyn went on, "everything went flat. I thought, 'How silly I am to want this man, nice as he is, fascinating as he is, when he belongs to another woman, and all sorts of humiliating and—and uncomfortable things stand between us!' If Red and Una had been at the cabin, as I thought they were, we would have had the evening together, and perhaps I might have thought, 'He's being nice to me again!' and perhaps it would all have been different. But being there alone with you, knowing that that evening decided everything, one way or another, had a— well, a funny effect on me. I wanted to decide it one way, and I ran away from it."

There was a long silence. Then Kent asked, clearing his throat:

"Is there anyone else?"

"No," Jocelyn said quickly. But her color rushed up.

"Then I am going to get my divorce," he said firmly, "and follow you wherever you are, and win you back again."

"Kent, I do ask you not to do that! You know how it is when a thing *stops*."

"It will come back. I thought it had stopped, too, when I talked to you that first day before Thanksgiving. It hadn't stopped. It was just that I was confused; I didn't know how to work it out. But when you came to me that night in the dark, Joy——"

"Jocelyn!" shouted a dozen voices somewhere out of sight toward the rear of the house. "Come on! We're starting!"

"I have to go," she said. "You wouldn't want to go along? It may be wettish."

"No; I'll not go along. When can I see you again?" he asked, shortly; deeply hurt.

"Do you go back to Portland?"

"I have to, of course. Tonight."

"How's the work going there?"

"Very well."

"And are you and Lilian——?" She stopped, not knowing how to go on.

"We're not living together, if that's what you mean. I have a brother there, and I'm living with him. He's not married. But we keep the surface smooth for her family's sake. Her father's a bishop, you know. She's staying with her family, and I'm practically living at the office until I get things broken in. I see her. I was there for Christmas dinner."

"She wants you back, Kent?"

"Does that matter?" he asked fiercely.

"Jocelyn!" came an augmented scream from the picnickers.

"I have to go," she said again. There was no other word between them. They exchanged a look that was placating on her part and savage on his. Kent picked up his hat and raincoat and was gone. Jocelyn, after a moment in which she stood perfectly still, with her heart sick and her pulses throbbing nervously, took her coffee pot and went out to join the others.

They were milling about by this time in a state of wild impatience. The moment she appeared, an advance guard was off up through the narrow strip of orchard, across the muddy road, and into the meadow that stretched upward toward the long straggling windbreak of eucalyptus trees that staggered across the hill. The sun had broken uncertainly through the slowly moving battalions of the clouds and shone brilliantly upon wet branches and sodden earth. The air, for the moment, was suffocatingly hot.

Rejoicing in this temporary truce, the party struggled upward, its drabbled appearance enhanced by the various unshapely and cumbersome bundles it bore. The doctor strode well among the foremost walkers, his topee pushed back, his shoulders straightened, his gray hair blown by an occasional puff of warm wind.

When they reached the ridge they stood panting, gasping, looking back in triumph from the heights they had scaled. The hill fell away below them to the roofs and treetops of the town, hanging precariously upon a hundred steeps. Framing all was the bay, flowing about Angel Island and Belvedere, on past Alcatraz to the ports and piers of San Francisco.

Clouds were massing again now; a tremor of wind ran over the world, and as they started the downward slope to the ocean a soft warm rain began to fall freely into their faces. But this only raised the spirits of the party to wilder levels. They leaped and ran and shouted in the pure sweet envelopment of the rain, and took the downhill miles almost at a run.

Then they were at the old Portuguese farmhouse, and under the shelter of a cowshed scented richly with manure and hay and wetness, were entering upon the usual debate. Stay here and build a fire, where there were water and milk and protection, or go on, and take a chance that two miles farther at the beach it wouldn't be raining or the tide would be low enough for them to camp in the cave?

As usual, the latter policy won; they bought milk and filled their water cans, and set off afresh, along the line of eucalyptus that had carpeted the ground with wet leaves and that scented the air with intoxicating balm. And presently they could smell and hear the ocean, breathe the sweet cleanness of salty air, hear the rush and gurgle of waves among rocks.

New madness now seized everyone, and they were off like a pack of hunters, mounting the high barred gate in a flight, taking the last half-mile in a brisk ten minutes, flinging themselves and their bundles on the sands, laughing, screaming, chattering like the gulls that flew in disturbed circles above them.

For a while everyone lay panting, or crawled about contented to mark the wet strand with bits of driftwood, bore tracks for flea races, or spread coral seaweed in fan designs on smooth planes of sand. Then suddenly hunger seized everyone at once, and while the men went in every direction for firewood, the girls expertly built a support for the grill, got their coffee started, opened up boxes containing an incredible number of strings of red sausages and a corresponding number of buns.

The sausages popped and sizzled on a hot grill, the buns were toasted and buttered, mustard was passed to lunchers whose mouths were too full for a "thank you," coffee went in boiling dark gold streams into the tin cups.

"Oh, Lord, this is good!" said the party, in true thanksgiving, as it feasted, and for some time there was no other attempt at conversation.

They were halfway through the meal, and beginning to feel that they might at some remote time be satisfied, when a man's figure emerged from the eucalyptus at the ranch, scaled the gate, and was seen advancing rapidly toward their party. Up to this time they had had the beach all to themselves. They regarded him with suspicion, dislike and surprise, except Jocelyn, who had a horrible fear that it might be Kent, come down to be near her, and sulk and be silent and annoy her uncle, who was rather strict upon the subject of love affairs with married men.

But as he came nearer she saw that it was not Kent. It was Philip Fordyce.

All the blood in her body rushed to Jocelyn's face, or at least that was the sensation she had, and she knew that as the others heard her ejaculate his name they saw her color.

But she had no time to study their reactions. She put down her bun as she recognized the newcomer, wiped her greasy mouth with a paper napkin, and went to meet him.

"What on earth—— You couldn't have just——" she stammered, as they turned to come back to the fire.

"No; I didn't just chance it," he said, laughing, out of breath, quite ready to sit down on a convenient rock, and panting as they all had been panting an hour earlier. "I came over to the Sausalito house, and Mrs Partridge told me how to get here. Up through the orchard, and over the road and to the top of the hill, and then straight down the old wagon road to the ranch. And at the ranch I asked. I needed a walk, I knew I couldn't get in any golf anyway, so I came after you."

"Uncle Bart, do you know Mr Fordyce?" Jocelyn said. She introduced the others, even while Jane was putting a hot bun and a sausage into Philip's hand, and Bam was discovering by nods and shakes and raised eyebrows whether he liked sugar and cream in his coffee. He ate ravenously as the chatter and laughter began again, and presently said fervently that never in his life had he tasted such food.

"We all say that!" said Jossy. When the clearing-up scramble began, Jocelyn was pleased to see that her uncle and Philip had fallen into a serious conversation upon state politics, and pleased again to hear her uncle's earnest: "You are absolutely right, sir. You are absolutely right!"

Later they all went exploring and wading and adventuring along the beach, through the cave, over the rocks and cliffs.

Jocelyn, who had been rather silent, perhaps instinctively trying not to betray the wild confusion that reigned in her heart, found herself with Philip, and asked him if he had ever been on a picnic like this one before.

"But this is the way all picnics ought to be. Just weenies and coffee and molasses taffy."

"The taffy was an afterthought. Uncle Bart used often to bring us chocolate bars when we were little, and we felt that we ought to have something sweet along, even though this was really an impromptu walk. Everyone originally intended to do something else this morning; the girls were going to a lunch at Ross, but something went wrong with the car, and they didn't have it fixed, and Jane and Jossy and the boys were going to town to a concert, only Charlie left the tickets in his office and couldn't get in, and so Aunt Nell said why not picnic? She had the weenies anyway, so we just got buns, and Bam and Peaches made the candy this morning. Nothing else, naturally, with fourteen of us and two babies in the house," Jocelyn finished with fine irony, "was going on at the time in the kitchen."

He laughed joyfully.

"Are you much with these people? I think they're perfectly marvelous."

"More since Mother died than I was before. Aunt Nell is my father's sister, and she said something about Mother years ago that Mother never forgave. Women," Jocelyn explained with an apologetic smile, "used to be like that. I don't know what it was. But I think it was that my mother looked so delicate that if she ever had a baby it would be a paper doll! Isn't it funny to remember a thing like that? Mother was very gentle, too, usually very kind to everyone. But she thought Aunt Nell had too many babies, and lived in too sloppy a manner, and she used to say that Uncle Bart would have been a very successful doctor if he hadn't had so many children to support. Oh, they were civil enough, she and Aunt Nell, but they didn't really like each other."

"And isn't he successful, this fine old doctor?"

"Uncle Bart? Oh yes; he has a fine practice and all that. But six girls and a boy, you know, and all their schooling and shoes and trips and two weddings in the past two years, and one more this year, and maybe Sissy, too. All that has kept things rather scarce."

"It's just the family I would have liked. It's just the way I'd like to live," he said steadily. Jocelyn, pacing beside him on the smooth sand just above the tide line, turned to give him a surprised glance.

"You?" she asked, amazed.

"Yes. And I think every man," Philip answered seriously. "I think men like things much more simple than women suppose they do. They get sick of having rooms decorated and commenting upon new clothes. They like walking over hills with girls who kiss them and tease them. And love them," he added in an undertone. "Well!" he interrupted himself in a different voice, "what I came down here to say to you is that we want you back."

Jocelyn's heart leaped. She looked at him with light welling in her eyes; she was not to be exiled, after all.

"Yep," he said. "You saw the paper this morning?"

"The paper!" she echoed, fearfully.

"Oh yes," Philip said resignedly. "Another story on Norma. Didn't anyone see the paper?"

"They don't come up until late, and we were all buzzing around. No." Jocelyn was actually pale. "I didn't see anything," she said.

"She says herself she needs you; we all seem to need you," Philip went on. "Everyone agrees on it. We've had a bad time with Norma since you went away. The school telephoned the second morning, at about ten, that she was gone. Miss Sanderson, in her thorough, old-fashioned way, had taken away Norma's purse, and Norma had very simply started to walk home."

"Good heavens!" Jocelyn exclaimed. "She oughtn't to do that!"

"We notified the police; we thought it might be a kidnaping. Of course there was no question of keeping it quiet. My mother got quite hysterical, and began telephoning all her friends to ask if the child was there. The police scoured the roads; I came down from the office; we had Pinkerton's on the job, and Norma walked in. She'd had two lifts; anybody could have picked her up. She'd twisted her ankle badly, she's got it in a bandage, so it was no question of her going back. Miss Sanderson came back, furious and crying of course, and my mother didn't do much to quiet things down, and in the middle of it Norma said she'd give me her solemn word to behave and to study if Miss Britton would come back."

Jocelyn laughed.

"Is there the slightest possibility that she means it?"

"Yes; I think there is. I had a talk with her this morning, and she seemed very serious. She seemed tired, as well she might, and sick of the whole thing. She's got to stay in bed for several days and amuse herself, and it 'll be a good thing for her. You'll come back?"

He said the last phrase suddenly, turning toward Jocelyn. The girl answered him doubtfully, after a perceptible hesitation:

"If you think I'm any good. I'm good at some things," Jocelyn admitted, "but I don't feel that I made much of a success of Norma."

"We've none of us made much of a success of Norma," her father said sadly. "And yet there's no reason why she shouldn't be just like other girls."

"Oh, I think there is," Jocelyn said, surprised. "Her not having her mother. Her being passed about from hand to hand. And then, of course, the money. It's very hard not to have that affect people, affect their attitude toward her. It affects me," she added honestly, after a moment's thought and with a little ashamed laugh, "it fascinates me. There's a sort of thrill about it, like royalty, or any high position—the President, or a maharaja or something like that. It's made her different; her whole attitude toward life is different from that of anyone who ever has to think about money."

"It shouldn't be," said her father.

"But it is. She can't think of herself except as she is, with anything and everything she wants in the world hers to buy."

"That shouldn't make her unhappy. We all love her. Her grandfather simply adored her. The night she was born, I think, was the happiest of the old man's life. He would have liked Janet—my wife—to have a houseful of children. He gave Norma a check before she was twenty-four hours old that made me realize that my baby was going to be richer than I ever could be. He kept chuckling and saying that there would be a boy with his name in a year or two and that he meant to take care of them all. But before Norma was two, as it turned out, her mother had asked for her freedom. He tried to make the best of that, poor old Lockey! I think he hoped Janet would go on having children, anyway. But she never had another. So it all came to Norma in the end. And it seems as if there must be some way—there must be some way of making these next five or six years happy ones for her, and starting her off into a sensible marriage with some decent fellow who'll take care of the money and of her."

"I suppose men will be after her in no time at all," Jocelyn said thoughtfully.

"Her mother wrote my mother that they were already. Well, we can only do our best. And you will come back? It won't be so hard from now on. She's had her lesson. She'll go right ahead with her studies—there won't be so many parties, anyway, with most of the boys going off to college. How d'you feel about it?"

"I'd be glad to try again," Jocelyn said simply.

"Is tomorrow too soon?"

"Monday. No; if you like I'll come down Monday."

"I'll send for you. Eleven? He'll be here at eleven, after he takes me into town." It was the touch of luxury again; the easy solution of any problem that money and service and possessions could affect. She could not help liking it. She could not help being glad that her fortunes were again to be linked with those of the Fordyces. Jocelyn thought of Philip's mother, of Miss Sanderson, of Norma, and her spirits rose with fresh courage for the fresh attack. She would be at home again in the big extravagant house; this time she would not fail.

They wandered back to the others, to find that the old doctor had just issued marching orders. There must be no more lingering on the beach. It was presently going to rain again, and they might all catch cold if they walked home in wet clothes in a wind.

The lighter picnic paraphernalia was gathered; the group started up the long slope, more slowly now, for everyone was tired and sleepy and the day was bleakly unfriendly. But eventually they did reach the ridge again, and, as was customary, broke into loud singing as they went down through the meadow and across their own orchard, and so into the laundry.

Here a wild scene took place, as muddy garments were discarded and decisions as to bath turns were made. Aunt Nell reported on the babies; Tim had taken his bottle like a little soldier, and everything was well. A royal Sunday supper was in course of preparation; hot baths were soon running; laughter and voices echoed all over the house.

In the confusion Philip slipped away. He and Jocelyn and the old doctor had been together as they climbed the hill; he had been urged to stay for an unpretentious supper. But he explained that his car was at the door; the man had been waiting a long time, and within twenty minutes he could be at his club, where there was always a change of clothes. He confirmed the arrangement that would take Jocelyn to "Hill Acres" on the following day, and was gone.

But he left something behind him: a glow in Jocelyn's heart, a sense of restored self-respect that warmed her veins like wine. She had been rather discreet in relating to the family the events of her stay at the Fordyces'; she had felt hurt and humiliated over the ending of the adventure and had not been anxious to speak of it.

But now she could allude to it without reluctance, telling them at the same time that she was wanted again. They all protested; they did not want Jocelyn to go. But her heart was already straining toward the scene to which she was going; she did not know exactly what the situation would be, but she knew it would be thrilling and unexpected.

CHAPTER XVII

It was just noon when she went into Norma's room the next day, to find the girl exquisite in a cascade of billowy chiffons and laces, and Charles van der Lipp playing a marble game with her. Norma was banked in pillows on the wide couch; a light taffeta cover was drawn over her knees; Mattress was moving unostentatiously about the big room; there were flowers everywhere, winter sunshine streamed through the windows, and a wood fire blazed in the white grate, reflections in the white tiles showing a hundred other little fires.

Norma had been laughing with the exaggerated loudness that was characteristic of some of her moods; she sobered instantly when she saw Jocelyn, a somewhat doubtful look came into her eyes, and she said lifelessly: "Oh, hello."

"Hello," Jocelyn said amiably. She had thought out in advance that her approach to Norma must be all casual friendliness, completely devoid of anything like reproach or questioning. "Norma," she added immediately, after a nod to Charles, "Lena tells me there's a puppy downstairs. Do you want him to come up now?"

"Oh, has he come?" shrieked Norma. "I thought he wasn't coming until tomorrow! Oh, get him, get him! The darling!"

"Looka what you've done!" Charles protested, aggrieved, as the marbles went all over the floor. "I was winning, too!"

"I know you were!" Norma giggled, at her silliest.

Jocelyn went to get the puppy, wondering if, after all, there was anything in this spoiled child worth developing.

The puppy was engaging as only a tiny Sealyham can be. His little bearded solemn face was watchful and yet innocent, suspicious and yet eager for friendship. Just to watch him walk solemnly sniffing about the rug was enough to enchant them all, and when he decided that Norma was his predestined mistress, snuggled his little muzzle contentedly into the crook of her arm, went peacefully to sleep with his small legs stretched out to their full length behind him, Jocelyn saw a look in the younger girl's face that she had never seen there before, and felt that her question of a few minutes earlier was answered in the affirmative.

"Where's Sandy?" Norma demanded, as soon as she and Jocelyn were alone.

"Is she here?" Jocelyn asked, unpleasantly surprised.

"Is she here! She's wild," Norma said carelessly. "Wadda pooda pooda pooda," she murmured above the dog's unconscious little tangled head. "She thinks I let her down. I'd promised not to pull anything too fancy—you're paralyzing my arm, fella," the girl went on, only half attentive to what she was saying to Jocelyn. "I'd said that I'd stay put. But when she didn't believe me, and sneaked my purse away, that was a little too hot! I started to walk home, but I thought they'd lend me money at any gas station, you know, when they knew who I was. But I didn't have the nerve after the first try—the man just grinned politely and said that he was the Duke of Windsor, but that their instructions were never to cash checks or give credit. So I walked on, and I'd have made it too, seventeen miles or whatever it is, if I hadn't wrenched my damn leg!"

"So now you're going to be a good girl for a wnile?" Jocelyn asked, sitting down on the foot of the bed for a moment's chat.

"Maybe," said Norma, with a wicked smile.

"No; seriously. Seriously, you hurt only yourself with this sort of nonsense, Norma. To have the papers constantly reporting what you do, and all of it so silly, won't help you at all. Your father wants you to grow to be a fine woman, gentle and cultivated and self-controlled, and every time there is one of these breaks it—it sets you back."

"Do you suppose I could grow to be anything *else* than a fine woman?" Norma asked with her childish shallow air of pride.

"Of course you could. Money isn't any protection against your—well, making a fool of yourself," Jocelyn answered, smiling.

Norma scowled, still with her arm bent protectingly about the puppy.

"My mother sets me a swell example," she said bitterly.

"But even your mother," Jocelyn reminded her adroitly, "hasn't the responsibility that you have. You are a much richer woman than your mother, Norma. People know about you, and they want to look up to you, admire you. They want to feel that you are one of the rich women of the world who sets a good example."

This view of her importance pleased Norma, and she brooded upon it with thoughtful eyes fixed on space.

"I'm a natural louse," she confessed at last.

"I don't think you are at all. I've never seen any signs of it. Just—just impulsiveness and recklessness. You do too many things without thinking."

"I suppose if I lighted a cigarette I'd wake him. . . . No, I'm a louse," Norma repeated. "The only reason I asked Dad to see if you wouldn't come back was to make Sandy wild. She hates you."

"I'm sorry that was the only reason," Jocelyn commented mildly.

"Oh well, it wasn't the only reason," the girl said hastily. She laughed loudly, in embarrassment. "I didn't mean that.

But you should have seen Sandy's face when I said—they were all yelling at me, of course, and I was crying and my ankle hurt like hell, and I said that you had had a good influence over me and that I'd do anything they wanted if you'd only come back. Sandy looked ready to burst."

"That wasn't very kind."

"I know. But why should you always be kind? It sounds silly to me."

"Well, here's your lunch," said Jocelyn. "And now you'll have to disturb this little gentleman. Wake up, puppy."

Norma caught at her hand as she lifted the puppy from the bed.

"Look, honestly," the girl said awkwardly, "I wanted you terribly to come back. We'll have a lot of fun. And I'll work with my languages and everything."

"I know you will."

"Mrs Fordyce would like to see you in her room, Miss Britton," the maid said, steadying the tray as she set it before Norma.

"I won't eat this if I can't have a cocktail," said Norma. "The doctor said I could. I told Granny I wanted a cocktail."

"I know what you want," Jocelyn said, in an undertone.

"What did you say? You said you knew what I wanted? How do you mean?" Norma demanded, always interested when she was the topic.

"What you want is a good spanking," Jocelyn said. "A cocktail with luncheon! Go ahead and eat now, and I'll be back in a little while and see if there's anything to do."

Norma looked at her for a moment with a clouded face; then she laughed.

"Nobody ever spanked me in my life," she said.

"It's quite evident!" Jocelyn returned. They were both laughing now, but Jocelyn's face sobered as she crossed the hall and was admitted by Annette to Mrs Fordyce's room.

She found the mistress of the house prone upon a couch, with every evidence of a nervous crisis about her. On a tray were two empty cocktail glasses; on a crystal saucer were the stubs of a dozen cigarettes, heavily marked with lip red; more cigarettes, unsmoked, monogrammed with a neat "Bert," were waiting, and also in view were salts, a glass of water and a headache tablet on a plate, an electric footwarmer, the telephone, and a dark green sleep shield.

"Miss Britton, I'm glad you're here. We're all desperate; I've not slept for two nights. Phil told you, I suppose, what's been going on; I don't know what on earth we're going to do," said Mrs Fordyce, in a monotonous chant, her eyes closing as she spoke, her words flowing forth almost without accent or punctuation. "I wish he'd marry Jane Kimberley; she'd jump over a church to get him. We'd at least have someone here who belonged here, great friend of Janet's too, and the child likes her——"

"It's been pretty strenuous, counting the New Year's party and everything else," Jocelyn conceded, breaking in at the first pause, sitting down by the bed.

"Miss Britton, you don't know! We've had eleven wires from Janet; they're all there—each one wilder than the last. She wants to know why anyone else was ever with Norma except Sandy, and she says that unless Sandy has full charge of her she'll begin court proceedings to overthrow the judge's decision fourteen years ago, and try to obtain guardianship of the child; she says she's coming out here, and I don't know what all. We tried bribing Sandy to go, doubling her pension —nothing would work! Janet trusts Sandy, she knows that Sandy is a perfect jailer and never gives a girl a ghost of a chance—you can depend upon Sandy always to think the worst and get ready for it—I will say that——"

"But she ran away from Miss Sanderson when they were at school, didn't she?"

"Janet doesn't count that. She blames it against the school. You can read her telegram there. The consequence was—my heart is really killing me," said Mrs Fordyce. "Put your hand here, feel that jump? Two doctors have told me that the instant that started again I was a dead woman. The consequence was," she resumed, "that here we all were with Norma on our hands, and she's got to *live,* you know; we can't put her into a box for six or seven years; and poor Phil looking simply *haggard,* and Sandy like a marble image saying that she only wanted to do her duty by Norma and the countess, and Norma in floods of tears saying that if Miss Britton would only come back she'd do anything. It's my conviction that she said that to annoy Sandy, who looked daggers at her——"

"She admitted that much," Jocelyn said, smiling. "But this is a pitiful situation," she added, more gravely. "I want —like all the rest of you—somehow to get *at* Norma, somehow to understand what she is thinking, what her own idea of her future is. If this goes on, at twenty she'll be not only well known, she'll be notorious. And nobody'll ever attempt then to understand her, or put a generous construction on what she does. Being dragged about this way, seeing so much of life that is—is sensational, being able to buy anything she wants; it's all bad for her, it's demoralizing her."

"Exactly!" said her grandmother triumphantly. "And this is where she belongs, in this quiet, simple place, where all her father's old friends are. She certainly shouldn't be turned over to her mother, at her age!"

Jocelyn hardly had time to analyze her own amazement at several phrases of this statement, for the old lady was proceeding calmly:

"Now, we've had to pacify Sandy, or she'll report to Janet, and there'll be trouble. So she's the—well, the formal governess, and she'll go with Norma down to school now and then, and keep a sort of eye on her. And you'll be the companion, someone for Norma to play with. Can you—do you think you can manage that?"

Jocelyn felt a strong sudden resentment. This was the last arrangement in the world to which she would voluntarily have given consent. She was about to say with dignity that she felt it better to withdraw until both Norma's grand-mother and her father felt that another readjustment should be tried, when Mrs Fordyce quite unconsciously produced the argument that decided her definitely and instantly for the experiment.

"Sandy, to tell you the truth," said Norma's grandmother, "has an idea that you're not very deeply interested in Norma. After all, you were in Phil's office, you know, and as Sandy says, these office friendships! Sandy is perfectly confident that you'll not stay under that arrangement, that Norma can't have two governesses, and, as Sandy says, the child will very quickly find herself too busy and too taken up with her friends to worry about it any longer. I'm telling you this quite frankly, because I want you to understand that, what-ever happens, we can't make Sandy angry, because she's in constant touch with Norma's mother."

When Jocelyn spoke it was smoothly and sweetly; she had risen as if understanding that the interview was over.

"Mr Fordyce is going to Washington on Wednesday," she said. "Perhaps since there have been so many changes and so much confusion, it would be better to leave it as it is. I'll see Miss Sanderson now, and I'm sure we can come to an understanding."

Philip Fordyce returned from Washington five weeks later. He came somewhat doubtfully, somewhat curiously, into his mother's room on the afternoon of his arrival, to find her dressing, and his daughter idling in a big chair.

Norma jumped up to greet him, and he held her at arm's length and looked at her with great satisfaction.

"Well, Seventeen-years-old," he said, "I hear good things of you."

"I'm an angel," Norma reported complacently.

"She really has been good?" Philip asked, kissing his mother.

"Very good," said his mother, unenthusiastically.

"I told you so," Norma said. "It's Jocelyn."

"Jocelyn, is it?" The man smiled. "I brought her a little present from New York," he said.

"You shouldn't have," Mrs Fordyce said. "My God, Annette! You're putting eyebrows on me," she added forcefully, "you're not operating on my brain!"

"And what 'd you bring me, Daddy!"

"Everything in sight. I picked out a nice senator for you, but he had a wife."

"I wouldn't marry a senator and live in Washington and have to be tactful," Norma declared. "We're having a party tonight, Dad. Friday night. Jocelyn lets me have a party every Friday night if I'm up in lessons. We have fun! Pencil games. We nearly go crazy."

"All that sounds very normal," Philip said, hardly believing his ears. "How's Sandy?"

"Awful. Jocelyn will tell you. But there hasn't—been— *one* thing she could report to Mother!"

"Look here, are you behaving yourself to spite Sandy or to please Granny and me?"

"To spite Sandy!" Norma answered joyfully. "We don't have dinner with you tonight, Dad; we have it in the old billiard room Friday nights, and we sing. It's fun!"

She presently went off to dress, and Philip followed suit. His mother had informed him that the Randalls and Jane Kimberley were coming to dinner, after which they would play bridge, and it occurred to him that by being ready a little early he might see Jocelyn for a few minutes, and get her report upon the state of affairs.

Descending to the library at seven, he sent Lorenz to summon her. But upon entering the room he discovered that he was not to see Jocelyn alone. Jane Kimberley, graceful, gentle, with touches of pure silver banding her dark hair, rose to meet him as he came across to the hearth, and held out a welcoming hand. She was dressed for dinner; diamond clips sparkled on the emerald-green velvet of her gown; she had fine brown eyes, and tonight as she smiled at him they wore their most affectionate expression.

"Home again, Phil."

"It feels good, too. I'm hoping to stay here for a while now. I hear everything's going well."

"Everything goes well when you're back," Jane said. "My dear, dear old boy!"

She put her hands on his shoulders as she spoke, and Philip quite naturally put his arms about her and kissed the upturned face.

Jocelyn had come flying downstairs at his request. She had known he was expected tonight or tomorrow night; he was never very definite about his comings and goings. But the whole house felt different for his mere presence, and as she and Norma had arranged the last details for the Friday-night party her heart had been singing. He was home again, and she would have a good report to make him of her trust.

She was halfway down the last broad shallow flight of stairs when she saw, as if it were a little scene from a play, the two figures in the library; the tall woman with her dark silver-streaked head close to his shoulder; the tall man with his arms about her.

Jocelyn stood stricken for an endless minute. Then she turned and fled up the stairs as if followed by Furies. She went blindly, dazedly, to her own room, and stood there panting, with one hand to her cheek.

The room went around slowly, more slowly. In the quiet and emptiness of it Jocelyn spoke aloud.

"So that's what keeps you here! So that's what you're thinking about, Jocelyn Britton? You idiot! You *idiot!* Well, now you know! Now at least you know!"

CHAPTER XVIII

EVERY WEEKDAY MORNING at quarter to ten the car came around the drive to the front door, and Jocelyn and Norma descended, with books and school binders, and were driven to Palo Alto, where in the dozen low-roofed, oak-shadowed buildings of the school they spent three hours at various studies: Italian, history, English letters. Jocelyn from the beginning entered into the lessons wholeheartedly; it amused and flattered Norma that, in the matter of languages at least, she was far ahead of her companion. She spoke fluent French and had had some years of Italian study; she had heard both languages spoken more or less correctly, and with Jocelyn's urging she could easily keep up with the class of four special students in which she was placed. The history and English work was easier for Jocelyn, and it was a pleasure to her to make it interesting to Norma. Norma was abysmally ignorant here; she loved to dash off a glib opinion of some historical event, expressing herself as to the basic causes of the Civil War or the injustice of the fate of Marie Antoinette, garbling some account she had heard of the Russian royal tragedy, misquoting an English statesman who was always "right next to the King" in importance, who had "had a crush on Mama," or detailing at great length the story of an Austrian countess who was supposedly "the most beautiful woman they ever had seen in Europe." But she knew absolutely nothing.

Jocelyn put up with these fantasies, patiently, awaiting the occasional yet steadily increasing minutes when Norma was merely an intelligent, nice child, gradually drawing her to quieter manners and a less exaggerated speech. Norma, even at her worst, was always exciting, and the drama that was life at "Hill Acres" increased rather than lessened in fascination as the days went by.

There was something magnificent about the waste, the extravagance, the luxury of the place. And in the ideas and ideals of its inhabitants Jocelyn found the same elements—a constant wasteful abandonment of one pleasure-seeking plan for another. Norma's short life and her grandmother's long one had been broken into the irreconcilable scraps of a jigsaw puzzle: Antibes, London, somebody's yacht, somebody's villa in Hawaii, with the Freddy Wilkinsons in their adorable Palm Beach place, with the Blossoms in the gorgeous Irish castle, with the Mallards at Tahoe.

These had been only a fraction of Mrs Fordyce's activities; to Norma's had been added innumerable schools, countless sessions with governesses and companions, countless educational lectures and musical Saturday mornings, encounters, always unsuccessful, with stepfathers, and a series of escapes and flights.

Both had interspersed these interests with much shopping, much trying of new clothes and new haircuts, whatever movies or plays or circuses were available, baby dances, little-girl parties, older parties, dinners, bridge games, and then the sudden reappearance of all the trunks and a start through the same procedure all over again. At seventeen, Jocelyn calculated, Norma had lived in about forty different places and sets of apartments, and temporarily inhabited about twice that many more in hotels, trains, ships, clubs, schools.

To reconcile this particular girl to a quiet-home-life program that included plenty of study seemed to Jocelyn, at first, an impossible undertaking. But she soon discovered that beneath Norma's sophisticated and bored exterior was the hungry heart of a little girl who had been cheated of real affection and real small-girl pleasures. Norma was starved for love, for companionship and fun; she never had had any real interests in her life, and as Jocelyn somewhat doubtfully offered them she seized upon them like the child she was.

Jocelyn began with a small dinner party and pencil games every Friday night. At first she had to carry these affairs pretty much on her own shoulders, but by the third evening the young persons were enthusiastically managing them themselves, and when she broke up the meeting at midnight it was always under a storm of protest.

The opening event was arranged for fourteen and enjoyed by only eleven, for three of the invited and expected boys did not come, sending no word and making no subsequent apologies. This infuriated Norma, who immediately became noisy in scornful laughter and bravado, and long before the pencils and papers came out Jocelyn was aware, in sickness of spirit, that the girls were angry and humiliated and the boys supremely bored, and that she would lose ground with Norma accordingly.

But once the games were started, competition and excitement began, and flushed and excited youngsters, who had for the moment forgotten the exact balancing of the sexes that is supposed to be the very foundation of all social gatherings, were shouting and arguing and laughing wildly together in honest youthful fashion, and the evening flew.

For the next Friday after the one on which Philip arrived at home she selected her guests with more care, confided the problem of their coming or not coming to Charles van der Lipp, who was her right-hand man, and achieved so hilarious a success that Philip, coming home somewhat early for him, found them still laughing and circling about Norma in the hall at a few minutes before one o'clock.

Then the Parker boys' mother, one of the few women of the group who had won Jocelyn's admiration, asked if she might not have the same sort of party, with no cocktails and no punch, at her house on Sunday nights, and Norma exulted that she, Norma, had started a fashion. "Graveyard brawls,"

Charles called them, in scornful allusion to their liquorless character, but he came regularly, and Jocelyn was pleased to see growing up between him and Norma a real brother-and-sister affection and understanding.

She learned many subtle little ways of influencing her charge without ever expressing her wishes in words. Norma, Jocelyn told her, was "the only girl in Burlingame who would dare entertain without cocktails." Norma was illustrating, for the benefit of this effete little group, the value of dignity and decency.

"With just baby games," Norma said once, doubtfully.

"Not baby games at all. These are exactly the games that the smartest people in the world play. When they get together in the evening to be amused, they don't go to the theater or a movie; they get out pencils and paper. They started crossword puzzles about ten years ago, revived them, and now wherever you go—England, France, China—you find crossword puzzles in the papers. Everyone likes games, Norma, and everyone hates to be bored with the same old business of dancing to the radio."

"Well, at home, perhaps," Norma, who was in one of her contrary moods, conceded, "at home dancing is dull. But when you go to a big hotel and they turn the lights down and somebody croons—it's fun then."

"Not for you! No night clubs for you while Sandy is stalking in the background!"

Any reference like this always made Norma laugh, and restored her good nature. For Miss Sanderson was indeed stalking about in the background of all she and Jocelyn did or planned, and fear of her reporting to Norma's mother, and a malicious youthful pleasure in annoying her with especially cautious conduct, were two of the elements that were keeping Norma in order.

Miss Sanderson's alleged position was now that of companion and adviser to Mrs Fordyce and superintendent of Norma's activities and those of Norma's youthful governess.

"You've got to stay, Sandy dear," Mrs Fordyce, hating and fearing her, had said cordially. "You understand Norma's mother and you understand her, and no matter what temporary arrangement we have to make to keep the child quiet, we'll need you. Go drown yourself, you old ghoul," Mrs Fordyce had added, in her soul.

But Sandy had accepted the meaning of the spoken words. She had settled down in a comfortable room, had begun to drive and irritate the maids to madness and had devoted herself to a discontented and scrupulous watching of Norma and Jocelyn. Everyone in the house knew that the moment either one slipped, Sandy would get in touch with Norma's mother, and machinery would instantly be set in motion to remove the child from Philip's guardianship.

"If your mother is really going to marry Count Spazzolari, Norma, I should think she wouldn't want her pretty daughter around," Jocelyn said once speculatively.

"Whoever has me manages my money!" Norma returned promptly. "Of course Dad and the lawyers here handle the investments," she added. "I had to go to the bank once, and they talked to me and everything, and I was quite thrilled! That was about my grandfather's money. A man there—he was president of the bank, I think—said, 'Is this the little princess?' But my allowance would go to Mama and the count, and of course she'd like that."

The tragedy of it, Jocelyn thought, hearing the gay, unconcerned young voice, watching the young undisciplined mouth that rattled off the story so unconsciously.

"Hasn't the count any money?"

"Oh, not a cent! An old lady brought him to America so she would have someone to dance with, but Mama got him away from her, and he used to take Mama to parties and everything and they said the old lady just about died of rage. She promised to settle a lot of money on him if he would come back to her, but she couldn't marry him because one of her sons said he would take out guardianship papers if she did. So he stayed with Mama at the Villa, but then when they went to Nassau, Mrs Pontifex tried to get him away from Mama, and got him started selling some wine his brother makes on his place in Italy, and Mama says it's lousy wine, so they all buy it and pour it out into the garden nights and put other wine in the bottles to please Mario."

"And where's Count von Sturnberg all this time?"

"Oh, Mama paid him to go back to Austria. But he writes her now and then, if he's lost at the races or something."

"Ugh!" Jocelyn said, half aloud.

"Yep, I think it's awful," Norma agreed serenely. "I don't think I'd like to marry a title. That awful Mam'selle who brought me back to America before Christmas had a cousin who was a count. He smelled."

"Norma!"

"He did. Of perfume. What I'm going to do," said Norma, "is marry an American and buy a place in Italy or in Minorca or somewhere like that, and build a white stone house, all white stone, with loads of trees around it, and a pier for a yacht."

"But the thing about that is, Norma, that any fine man would want to work, want to be in business. He wouldn't want to idle around in the garden all day."

"That's because American men think of nothing but money. Now in England and France they have leisure classes . . ." Norma was off on one of her ill-informed foolish tirades, jumbling together with her own young impressions half-remembered things that she had heard older women say. Presently the diplomats, the titles, the world's most notorious capitalists were all involved in the story, with yachts, diamonds, privileges generously thrown in to embellish it and make her point.

And when she was once started like this there was nothing to do but wait patiently for silence, and by skillful degrees change the subject.

But Jocelyn had this great advantage now, that Norma

loved her. She would do nothing without her "Jotsy." Jocelyn had moved into rooms adjoining Norma's own, and often the younger girl would come in at night when Jocelyn, thoroughly wearied after the strain of the day, would much have preferred to go on with her reading, to sit on Jocelyn's bed and talk on unwearied into the night. She was insatiable in her interest in Jocelyn's life; she wanted to hear all the details of her childhood, what she had worn, what she had wanted for Christmas, what her friends had been. Norma would be quickly jealous of the Sausalito cousins, if Jocelyn quoted Bam or Sissy; she wanted to visit them and know them all and have them like her. Her affection was overpowering at times; her constant desire for Jocelyn's company was anything but restful, but Jocelyn was wrapped in a dream now, and day by day what Norma did seemed less important and less real.

CHAPTER XIX

For the first few weeks after her return to "Hill Acres" she had seen Philip not at all; he had been absent in Washington on a law case. During this time she had concentrated upon what she hoped to do for Norma, or at least begin to do for Norma, and when Philip returned she was secretly elated to realize that he found a real change in his daughter.

After that he was again often absent, but only for a night, or for a few days now and then, and when Easter holidays came he announced that he was going to take Norma and Jocelyn to Honolulu. They would be gone only fifteen days, eight of which would be spent at sea; they would have just a week in the islands.

This prospect seemed to excite Norma more than any other her life had offered her. It touched Jocelyn to realize that to be with "Daddy" and with her adored Jotsy on this trip would give it an element of freedom and pleasure that Norma's outings never had known before. The prospect of no lessons, no Sandy, no Granny, just sheer fun with the two persons she liked best in the world raised Norma's spirits to their wildest pitch. Jocelyn was not far behind her; she was experiencing in these days the deepest joy a woman's heart can know; she loved and she knew now that she never had loved before.

Just how she had come to care for Philip she could not quite have said. There was no necessity to say it, even to herself. She was too sure for that. Sure, without a word from

him, without a kiss, without a touch of his hand. A thousand
insignificant trifles became all-important when her memory
joined them; his expression of amusement and affection when
they talked of Norma; his consideration for her; his concern
that she be made comfortable; the moments he spent occasionally with her and Norma, teasing them, questioning
them, at ease as she never saw him at ease under any other
circumstances, these and many other little circumstances like
them confirmed in her the feeling that burned in her veins
almost like a fever, that possessed her with hope and fear,
self-contempt and a wild pride, day and night.

There had been almost from the moment of his return from
the Washington trip a feeling that she knew at last for love.
Everything he did and said thrilled her to the very depths of
her being; at night when she was lying wakeful and happy
and unhappy in the spring moonlight she remembered the
tones of his voice, the casual glance he had given her from
the bridge table when she and Norma went through the hall,
the meaning that he somehow put into his most careless
morning greetings, his briefest messages to her.

Spring was in full flood over the orchards and gardens, the
blue mountains and the high meadows now; spring glorious
with acacia and blue wild lilac, with apple blossoms and
tasseled eucalyptus, with long fences draped in magnificent
red and pink roses, with the steady humming of bees, the
flash of blue jays; the heartbreaking cry of the upwhirling
larks. To Jocelyn there never had been such a spring, and as
she heard Philip's quick step on the stairs, the gayer notes of
his voice, his readier laughter she told herself that it was
spring for him, too.

If she had needed any confirmation of her dream, she
would have had it in a rude awakening when one Friday evening Mrs Kimberley came out from a bridge game to watch
the games and to ask Miss Britton for a word aside. The
younger crowd was busy over a frenzied struggle with the
Prince of Paris and his lost cap, and Jocelyn could go with

the other woman into the adjoining room and face her with merely curious eyes. But the moment she saw her guest's expression her own changed and her heart sank.

"Miss Britton, I've promised dear Mrs Fordyce to speak to you, and I know you'll understand," Jane Kimberley began in a bright, nervous, yet determined tone.

"What is it?" Jocelyn asked.

"It's—— Miss Britton, you know we are all very fond of you here, and that you and Sandy have done wonders for Norma. But you're not going to Honolulu on the fifteenth with Norma and Phil—Mr Fordyce?"

Blood rushed into Jocelyn's face and she felt her throat thicken.

"Why not?" she asked.

"Because—my de-ar-r-r!" Mrs Kimberley protested, with an eloquent spreading of hands. "A girl like you," she elucidated it, "can't possibly go on a trip with a—a stunning man like Phil, without a great deal of criticism. Without incurring —incurring a great *deal* of criticism! You must see that?"

"I'm Norma's governess," Jocelyn offered, selecting words somehow from a wild confusion of heart and mind. "It seems to me that to go on a two-weeks' vacation with her and her father is a perfectly natural thing to do."

"It's an impossible thing to do," Mrs Kimberley said, chilled by opposition into something like anger. "Miss Sanderson is Norma's governess."

"Only in name. Sandy does nothing for her now, except now and then talk to her teachers about her school work, perhaps."

"Excuse me. Mrs Fordyce speaks of Sandy as Norma's governess," Mrs Kimberley said icily.

"She may speak of her as Norma's governess, but Norma does all her work with me."

"Mrs Fordyce calls you her 'companion.'"

"You're in love with Phil Fordyce, that's what's the trouble," Jocelyn thought. Aloud she said: "Mrs Fordyce knows of this trip. She and Norma and I were buying clothes for it yesterday."

"And if the Countess von Sturnberg hears that Norma has gone to Hawaii with her father and a very pretty girl?" Mrs Kimberley said, almost archly. Jocelyn had a strong impulse of hate; the humiliating thought that the other woman might have some justification for what she said was just beginning to possess her; she felt the hot blood in her face again.

"It would be too bad to disappoint Norma now," she said. "She has set her heart upon going."

"It wouldn't necessarily mean *that,*" Mrs Kimberley said delicately. "I told Philip—Mr Fordyce last night that if I could possibly arrange it, Jean and I would go. That would regularize the whole arrangement. In that case Sandy says she would go, just to sit up and watch the dancing if Mr Fordyce and I were playing bridge, and keep an eye on them in the mornings and all that. Tennis, of course, and swimming and deck sports—it's just as well to have an older person around."

"I can consult Mr Fordyce about it," Jocelyn said, her heart sick with anger and disappointment. Norma had been happier, more like a normal girl, over this prospect than Jocelyn had ever seen her before. They had discussed every detail of the trip with the eagerness of complete novelty and pleasure on Jocelyn's part, and a real girlish unspoiled enthusiasm on Norma's that had delighted Jocelyn. They had selected bathing suits, sport clothes, evening dresses; they had gone down to the docks and inspected the boat, one happy noontime, with Philip as escort. The lounges, the dining rooms, the deck chairs under awnings among palms, the fascination of narrow passages and high white boat decks, and above all, the charm of their own luxurious suite had opened up for Jocelyn a dream of delight she had never before experienced; she had told herself a hundred times that such fun could not be for her; that something would happen.

Now it had happened. Jealous, watchful, suspicious Mrs Kimberley and the dissatisfied Sandy had brewed this nonsense between them, and Norma felt with a dismal prescience that in the end it would wreck the whole plan.

"I don't think consulting Mr Fordyce would quite do," Mrs Kimberley said. "Men don't see these things quite as women do, and he would probably think there was nothing irregular about it."

"There *is* nothing irregular about it!" Jocelyn said proudly, impulsively. To this Mrs Kimberley made no audible answer. She narrowed her eyes and looked into space with a little half-smile on her lips. "Surely," Jocelyn went on, despising herself inwardly for wasting so much time on this woman, "surely a man may travel with his daughter and her governess without starting any scandal?"

"Oh, if it's Norma's *governess,* if it's Sandy, then there is nothing to be said," Mrs Kimberley countered neatly. "If you speak to Mr Fordyce about it," she added, "please don't quote me. I am merely suggesting to you that, as dear Mrs Fordyce doesn't want Janet rushing out here to make trouble, it might be wiser to make some other arrangement. And now I must go back," said the visitor sweetly. "I was dummy, and I thought I'd just slip out here and give you a hint. You see, with a man as attractive as Mr Fordyce, Miss Britton, it's very easy for a girl to put herself into a false position."

Graceful, with her smooth hair beautifully curled and her slender figure lovely in soft brown lace, she flitted away, and Jocelyn, bitterly ruffled in spirit, went back to the younger set. She felt distracted and uncertain; to whom could she speak, who could advise her now?

Philip had seemed to take an interest almost as keen as the girls' own in the prospective trip. He had picked out a trunk and two bags for Jocelyn, who had no luggage of her own except an antique suitcase, and had had them marked with her initials. Their creamy stiff smartness was now displayed in Norma's sitting room, with Norma's own beautiful bags. Scattered about were new stockings, white shoes with their straps and silk laces still immaculate, hatboxes, frocks on hangers. Norma and Jocelyn had been looking at their new purchases before dinner, rejoicing in them, trying on a white taffeta coat or a broad-brimmed flowery hat.

Norma's were of course the more varied and numerous and handsome, but Jocelyn had her own thrills, too. Philip had assured her that she must have at least three dinner dresses and one or two afternoon frocks to add to those she already had, and that this expense must be considered his, not hers. So there were a frail black lace and a striped blue and black-and-silver organza, a full-skirted pale green swiss for afternoons, a white small hat, a hat wreathed with roses; there were three linens and two coats, and finally there was a formal gown that took Jocelyn's breath away every time she saw it or even thought of it: an effect of almost transparent silky organdy over an effect of hoops; clustered tiny gardenias and rose-point; an underpetticoat that was a foam of frills. "I hope I shall have a great many clothes in my life," Jocelyn had said, seriously, when she had tried it on in the shop and had come forth from the fitting room to see what Norma and her father thought, "but I shall never forget this one! I oughtn't to take it!"

"Nonsense," Philip had said. He had been led to a much less expensive department in the big store than the one in which Norma's select models, straight from London, Paris and New York, had been displayed. "All this stuff of yours doesn't cost what that one silvery evening wrap Spotty just bought cost," he had assured her. "Twenty-seven fifty and twenty-two fifty—I didn't know women could get clothes at all for that price!"

"There are women buying dresses for six fifty and four forty-four!" Jocelyn had reminded him joyously. "If the trip had no more fun to it than this," she had exulted, "I'd have had enough!"

But to discover that these preliminaries might really be all that was to be permitted Norma and herself daunted her nonetheless. She knew that she herself was the main attraction of the whole plan for Norma. To travel for the first time in her life with an adored companion, with a friend young enough to enter into her interests, a companion whose honest enthusiasm would inspire her to enjoy things that once would have been boring to her, to feel no longer either shy or foolish; all this made a prospect that was new and intoxicatingly pleasant in Norma's scheme. She wanted always to be with Jocelyn, always to get Jocelyn's reactions before she was sure of her own, she loved her new role of the protected and self-controlled little princess who owed a duty to the world as well as to herself.

All this would be blasted if the Kimberleys took Jocelyn's place; almost as completely blasted as if Sandy did. Norma's grandmother certainly would not offer to go. Mrs Fordyce had said frankly that she hated Hawaii because when there you had to keep admiring things.

"Whether it's poi or tapas or those women sitting in the damp shade making wreaths or breaking your heels going up some volcano, you can't say anything but, 'Oh, delicious!'" she had said, when the Hawaii plan first had been broached. "If there is one thing I feel about poi and volcanoes it is that they ought to be kept in books, where they belong! Sally Ingerfield, who has a divine place down there, still owes me six hundred and twelve dollars from a poker game! I hate the place."

Jocelyn confidently expected an outburst of fury from Norma at the first suspicion of a change of plan, and she dreaded it. She was working hard with her studies, anticipating holidays all the happier for her industry when the big ship sailed just a week from tomorrow. Friends were coming down to see her off; there would be music, and leis of gardenias and confetti, and ropes of colored paper to hold the vessel with a hundred rainbow tentacles to the pier until the whistles boomed forth their hoarse farewells and the littered water began to churn wildly in a widening channel between the moving mighty hull and the fog-wrapped water front.

What a moment that might have been! To know oneself safe on board, with all the charms of decks and lounges, libraries and ship's shops to explore, to watch the hilly city and the great jaws of the Golden Gate slip by, to be out on the fresh open circle of the wide Pacific with the band playing and voices laughing and Norma reminding her, "We don't have to dress, sailing night!"

Oh, she had never had such fun in all her twenty-eight years, and she had had more than her share of loneliness and responsibility and work and dullness! If this could only be———!

CHAPTER XX

ON SATURDAY Norma went to a matinée luncheon with the Parker boys and their mother, and Jocelyn utilized her free hours for a trip to Sausalito. Aunt Nell would decide the point for her! Aunt Nell, who always thought anything the girls wanted to do was right.

She found the mistress of "Maple Den" in a foggy back yard, under the fresh new green of the trees, watching two sleeping grandchildren, and fortunately alone. Two married daughters were on a shopping trip for the midsummer bride; two were at their office desks; two still in school, as was the son of the house. Jocelyn, eager, frowning, scornful, appealing by turns, lost no time in putting her problem.

Her aunt was equally prompt and much more definite in her answer. Of course it was impossible. Some other arrangement would have to be made.

Jocelyn was stricken. She sat facing her aunt with eyes that were tragic in a suddenly paled face.

"But Aunt Nell, surely girls and their fathers and governesses are always traveling together!"

"Not always. It could happen, of course. But not with this girl. She's had considerable newspaper notoriety already. Her father's a rich and important man. And you're a pretty girl, Jocelyn."

"Aunt Nell, that's—that's nonsense! How can people be so—so vulgar and—and censorious and suspicious! It seems to me if they are, it would be just a good idea to show them that one didn't care a rap *what* they thought!"

"You can't do that, dear. Women—and men, too, for the matter of that—are always trying to do it. They go off on islands and try free love, or they are married by some ridiculous service that doesn't hold either for church or state, or they go nude——"

"But Aunt Nell, this is just a man and his daughter going on a trip, and taking a companion for the daughter who isn't out yet!"

"Isn't out yet?" Mrs Partridge said leniently. "Why, that girl is so far out in society that it's a nice question as to whether you can ever get her in far enough to have her come out again! She has been out since she was born. No, Jocelyn, you can't take chances with a girl like Norma Fordyce. You tell me she's happy now, that she's beginning to act like a human being. For God's sake keep her so. Don't get her grandmother and mother and father and this Sanderson woman all worked up again! Keep things quiet."

Jocelyn stared into space, a mutinous expression on her face.

"What do they suppose I am? Mr Fordyce's mistress?" she presently demanded resentfully. "Am I supposed to be in love with him?"

"*Are* you in love with him, Jocelyn?" her aunt asked quietly, when the angry words had had time to die away into the quiet, still foggy air.

"Aunt Nell!" the girl exclaimed, freshly indignant. But if she had more words ready they did not come; she looked at her aunt for a few seconds with her face reddening, and then covered her hot cheeks suddenly with her hands.

"If I see it, probably they see it," Mrs Partridge said dryly, and for a long time nothing more was said.

After a while Jocelyn took down her hands and looked far away into space and laughed.

"How long have you known it, Jocelyn?"

"Oh, not long. I thought—I never dreamed anyone else would know. Everyone loves Philip. There are two or three

women who are just—open, about it. I suppose of course it
makes a difference! About the trip, I mean. Now don't say
anything, Aunt Nell," Jocelyn said quickly, as her aunt made
a movement as if she would speak. "Don't. I know what a
fool I am! I thought it would always be my secret, that no
one but myself ever would know. You see," she went on,
trying to laugh, "he's wonderful. He's quiet, but he's so
definite! He puts things into just a few words. He's—I don't
know, he knows everything about international law and
maritime law, and fishing and golf, and plays and London
clubs and everything. I always used to think, in the office,
that there was no one like him, but now—now—when he's so
good to Norma and me, and so pleased that she's happy——"

"He bought you some lovely dresses for the trip, didn't
he?"

"Well, not expensive dresses! The whole lot didn't come
to what one of Norma's did; he said so. I'd have to have
clothes, Aunt Nell. And I've never been to Honolulu!"
Jocelyn ended, on a wail. "And now I'll never get there!" she
added, despairingly.

"I suppose Miss Sanderson couldn't go?"

"Oh, that would ruin everything!" Jocelyn said, so frantic
in her disappointment that her aunt realized suddenly how
young she was.

"Well, you'll have to get out of it somehow, dear. To go
would be to put yourself and Mr Fordyce and the child, too,
in a false position. Especially with the mother anxious to get
hold of her and her fortune. It seems to me the best thing
would be to go to Mr Fordyce and explain, and ask him what
he would suggest. If there were some friends of his going on
the trip, who would join the party——"

"But that wouldn't be so much fun," Jocelyn interrupted,
still unreasonable. "We had everything p-p-planned and we
were going to do s-s-so many things——" And twisting her
body about and putting her head down on the back of her
chair, she burst out into bitter crying.

Mrs Partridge, who had risen with a grandchild in her arms, with the intention of carrying the baby into the house, looked down at the bowed bright head thoughtfully for a full minute. Then she rapped it gently with her thimble.

"You're behaving very foolishly, Jocelyn; I don't know that I've seen you act quite so silly," she said calmly. "You're a woman, now, and you have to act like a woman. To get yourself mixed up in a scandal wouldn't do you any good, and would undo everything you've done for Norma Fordyce. Now you stop it. Let her go off with her father under the charge of some married woman who is making the trip, and you wait here. You're no worse off than you were before this whole thing was talked of a few weeks ago. Bring Rosemary in, will you, dear? They both are awake, and I think I'll let them play in the kitchen. It's nice and warm in there. There are conventions, Jocelyn; there are things that you just can't do. So you should be glad someone reminded you of them in time!"

When Jocelyn picked up Norma at the theater an hour later the younger girl looked at her sharply.

"You've been crying, Jotsy?"

"Yes. I got upset about something. You've got good eyes!" Jocelyn said smilingly.

"Who was mean to you?"

"Nobody. It's only—now be a sport, Norma, and don't tell anyone I've told you this. But Sandy and your aunt Jane feel . . ."

Jocelyn went into the matter somewhat hesitatingly, wondering just how much to say and how much to conceal. The effect, surprisingly, was to make Norma laugh.

"Old snooty busybodies!" she said. "What business is it of theirs! Never mind, darling, we'll be off a week from to-day no matter what they say! If Dad's satisfied and Granny's satisfied, what does it matter what anyone else thinks?"

"Well, my aunt seemed to feel——"

"Oh, I love it! What do they think you're going to do?"

Norma went on joyfully into speculations, and Jocelyn said: "Norma, dear, it really isn't nice to talk that way."

"Well, *they* do, with their spying and suspicions! Why don't you talk to Dad?"

"I thought I would. And promise me you'll not say anything until we see what he thinks."

"I'll do anything you say, dearest. But if they think for one minute that we aren't going to sail next Saturday, they can go sit on a tack!" Her confidence, baseless as Jocelyn knew it to be, had the effect of cheering them both, and when she had a chance to speak to Philip of the matter that evening, it was with considerably more hope in her manner.

He listened to her opening words thoughtfully, not looking at her. Jocelyn, beginning to be made slightly uneasy by his manner, presently came to a stop.

"My mother's just been saying something of the sort," Philip muttered then, kicking at a log in the fireplace, looking up to smile at her dubiously. He was going out to dinner; he was in formal evening dress, looking his groomed and handsome best.

"Your mother! But she was the one who talked it all over with us. She's known about it from the beginning."

"I know. I suppose this is some of Sandy's work."

"And Mrs Kimberley."

"That so? Did Jane put her hooks in? Well, they evidently worked to some purpose on my mother. She was all agog tonight. I mustn't let Norma in for any more publicity or we'd have Janet all over us. All that!"

Jocelyn was unable to say anything; the bitterness of her disappointment seemed to come up into her throat and choke her.

"I'd been looking forward to it; it seemed as if we might have a few days' fun," Philip presently said. "But we can't take a chance on Norma's mother."

"No, of course not," Jocelyn agreed dully. "Norma'll be disappointed," she added, with a little effort.

"She'll not be any more disappointed than I am!" the man said, half aloud. "But it's had the effect—I mean all this women's nonsense—" he went on, "of making me see something that I mightn't have seen quite so quickly before. Of course you know what I mean?"

Jocelyn looked at him quickly in the soft half-light of the library. A good fire was blazing, but only one lamp had been lighted. Philip took both her hands, and for her the world seemed to turn upside down, revolving about her in slow circles.

"You know that I had to find out sooner or later what had given me back my daughter, and why this trip meant so much to me, don't you?" he questioned her again.

Speechless, swallowing with a dry throat, she looked steadily at him.

"Can't you say 'yes' to that, Jocelyn?" he asked.

"I don't know what you mean," she whispered after a long moment.

"Why, it means that I've found you," he said simply. "Everything's been twisting about and changing, and I've not known what was the matter with me, and now I know. While my mother was talking to me today it came to me like a flash. So there's something for you to think of while I'm at my dinner, my dear!"

It was all an act in a play: the handsome man in evening dress standing beside his own library fire in the incredible old-fashioned luxury of "Hill Acres," his daughter's governess with her hands in his, staring at him as if he had lost his wits, or she hers.

"Don't go!" she managed to say.

"I have to go." His tone was amused, kind, not at all flustered. "But I want you to know how I stand. I've fallen in love with you, as if I were a boy," he said. "I'm forty-two, I've a daughter of seventeen. She'd always be a problem to us both, even after she married. You know exactly what a madhouse this is. But the fact remains that I love you. Just how it will all work out, I haven't any idea; you'll have to be the one to fit the pieces together. But if we aren't to be allowed to go to Honolulu without a chaperon, perhaps if we got married, they'd worry less about us. Now I'm going, but you think it all over, and we'll talk some more tomorrow! If you'd be down about half past eight we might have breakfast together. No, we couldn't talk then. It's Sunday, isn't it? And I'm playing in the tennis semifinals with Carter. Well, I'll be back for a late lunch, and if you can amuse the kid somehow suppose you come in and sit with me at about half past two? Don't look so astonished," Philip finished, laughing. "The most natural thing in the world for anyone who is in your neighborhood at all is to fall in love with you. This may be the solution; anyway, I hope it is. Good night, my dear."

He was gone, and Jocelyn was standing perfectly still in the big shadowy room, breathless, ecstatic, wondering if she had imagined the whole scene. His cigarette was still smoking on the cinnabar tray; the sound of his voice was still in the air; she could hear his brief word of thanks to one of the men, as he took his big coat and silk hat in the hall. No, it hadn't been a dream.

Norma came downstairs, calling for her; they went out to dinner together. The inevitable Charles had appeared; they were three.

"This time next week we'll be having our first dinner on the *Malolo,* Jotsy," Norma said. "Don't you wish you were going, Charles?"

"I am," said Charles calmly. "Handle the black trunk carefully and mark it 'Needed on Voyage.' I'll be in it."

"Did he really say that?" Jocelyn thought. "Oh, my God, help me. What shall I do? It couldn't be that he meant that!"

"I'll go as a stowaway," Charles further pursued it. "They'll drag me out from behind a binnacle, dripping bilge water. I'll tip me cap——"

"Oh, Charles, do, do! It would be such fun! All the papers would have it!" Norma was falling in love with Charles as rapidly as only a girl of seventeen can fall in love with a handsome collegian four years her senior. But Jocelyn could find no objection to this affair. For the first time Norma was companionable, easy, happy with a man friend, and since it must be someone, and soon, why not Charles, whose record and whose background were both beyond criticism?

"It might be just as well to try to keep out of the papers," Jocelyn said mildly. She hardly heard what the others were saying, answering them automatically, wrapped in her own thoughts.

He couldn't have said what she thought he had said! Philip Fordyce, the most important man her fortune had ever brought within her circle of friendships. Wanting to marry her! Her head whirled.

Why, that would mean—that would mean everything she had ever wanted in the world! That would mean security, a place of her own, a home, a chance to establish friendships and build what she wanted into her life. That would mean that these brilliant, enviable, maddeningly arrogant women would have to take her into their calculations, would have to consider her seriously, whether they liked it or not. It would mean that she had magnificent Phil behind her, sustaining her and loving her in everything she did.

Loving her! That was the miracle. She couldn't help loving him. It was inevitable that she should. Nobody could live under his roof and see him daily, nonchalant and handsome and sure of himself, always adequate, whether the problem came from Federal headquarters in Washington, or merely concerned the bidding of a bridge hand, and not love him! Jocelyn had told herself days earlier that it was this man's fascination that kept her here at "Hill Acres." It was impossible for her now to think of living anywhere but near him, if only to hear his voice occasionally, if only to catch a glimpse of him now and then. But for him to love her? Why should he?

Half the glamour of the proposed trip to Hawaii had been

because Philip was to head the little party. She and Norma were to have been his constant companions, lunching with him, dining with him, wearing their new frocks on beaches and ships' decks to please him.

The moments of her bitterest disappointment, as the plan had faded from probability, had been caused by the thought, not quite recognized at the time, but recognizable now, that she would be parted from his company for a long two weeks.

Now that consideration was banished. Those few incredible minutes in the library had killed it; in its place was a confusion of hope and fear that made her feel an actual physical exhaustion. Long after Norma was asleep she lay awake, staring up into the dark, her head resting on her crossed arms, thinking.

In the end she said to herself that Philip had perhaps spoken in an unthinking mood of gaiety and good nature, and that he might never make another allusion to the subject. She would never bring it up again, naturally, and therefore she must begin again to plan for whatever alterations in the plans for the trip were necessary. Someone must go with them, that was obvious. The question was, who could go suitably, adequately, without destroying all the pleasure of Philip, Norma and herself?

The next day Philip was gone off for his tennis game when she and Norma came downstairs at about ten o'clock. Some girls had come over to talk of a charity rummage sale with Norma, and Norma delighted to take them upstairs again to her sitting room and dazzle them with the magnificence and variety of the things she was giving to the sale.

Slippers and belts and clips; Italian vases and bowls; gloves from Paris that had never been worn, but that were no longer the last word of fashion; detective novels, big books of engravings, more than one smart little traveling clock; sweaters, sweaters, sweaters.

Meggy Brice and Peggy Wilson quite shamelessly appraised the sweaters at a dollar apiece, and bought several with no further formality. Meggy bought two French hats, and Jocelyn was stung into sudden realization that she was paying a dollar and a half for a Bond Street top coat, of tweed so soft it was furry, and so flexible that the whole thing might almost have been put through a hoop.

"We never price anything at more than a dollar and a half!" Peggy said, with a meritorious air.

Mattress came in and was asked to ask someone to pack all these things and have then sent to Miss Wilson's house, and the young ladies, after some beautifying processes, decided to go to the club for lunch. This was a gay, neighborly thing to do on Sunday, and Jocelyn always enjoyed it. Norma was greeted affectionately on all sides, and some plan for the afternoon was usually developed.

This afternoon she and Norma had a special reason for wanting to watch the tennis, for at luncheon time the surprising news spread through the big dining room that Phil Fordyce and Joe Carter had qualified for the finals in a 6-4, 7-9 match against Bill Trent and the senior Ned Randall that morning. The finals would begin at two.

It was exciting to find places in the bleachers, and see the umpire climb up to his high perch, and watch the easy pendulum movement of the first rallies. Every boy and girl Norma knew was also watching; the girls' hats moved like flowers about the stands and the green lawns; the little flying balls went *tap, tap, tap,* and Jocelyn watched Phil, and thought that he was the most wonderful man in the world.

The sun shone down on his brown hair and his burned brown skin; his sport shirt was open at the neck, and from the brief sleeves and beneath the flannels he wore, his rounded, firm arms and legs worked with the precision of pistons. Now and then, between games, he brushed back his hair with his forearm, wiped his forehead with the same movement, and looked over to laugh at Norma and Jocelyn. The spring day was still sufficiently uncertain to make the sunshine welcome, and the women huddled their shoulders in it gratefully; all about the sharp angle of the court were lawns and trimmed borders packed with flowers, and the shadows of great trees on fresh grass. In the shade cinerarias displayed their smears of solid bright color: deep blue, pink, scarlet, purple, flawless white; and in the sunlight pansies and stock, wallflowers, Shasta daisies and delphinium were massed together in one riot of bloom.

When the game was over, Philip jumped the net like a boy, shook hands, laughing and gasping, with his triumphant opponents, and came over to the chairs where Norma and Jocelyn were sitting. Friends gathered about him, but Jocelyn was conscious that he was disposing of them with surprising rapidity, and presently he joined his daughter.

"Whew!" he said. "Those boys are too much for your poor old dad, Spotty!"

"He gave them every decision," Norma said accusingly, and everyone within hearing laughed.

"Are we out without Sandy?" Philip said, falling into step beside Jocelyn as they turned toward the clubhouse.

"We haven't seen either her or your mother this morning. As a rule she comes in, if only for a minute. But no sign of her today."

"I'm going to take a shower," said Philip. "You going right home? . . . Good. I'll follow you and come up to Spotty's room and we can talk. Been thinking over what I said to you yesterday?"

"I've been trying to believe that you said it." Jocelyn looked up seriously from under the brim of a new hat; her face was a little pale, but that only made the shadows about her eyes and the contrasting gold of her hair the more startling. For a second he looked down at her with a thoughtful half-smile on his face, then she felt his fingers catch hers in an instant's grip.

"I said it all right," he said, and Jocelyn had those words to ponder as she went home. Just that much certitude she had wanted during the long hours of the night. Now that she had it, her heart was already making fresh demands. She was sure; but she wanted to be more sure, to have everyone know, to have it settled beyond dispute or question. These women would laugh at the mere idea of Phil Fordyce seriously considering marriage with the governess. They must not be allowed to laugh. It must all be settled, and quickly.

"Oh, I couldn't ever do anything else now!" Jocelyn said to herself, trembling, as she and Norma went into the big house and turned toward the great vault of the stairway. As they did so a woman began to descend, stopped, assumed a pose and bent a smile of incredible sweetness upon Norma. A slender, girlish-looking woman with soft lusterless fair hair, dyed to a color that was not quite gold, not quite brown, braided about her head, and a soft, powder-blue gown of filmy silk wrapped tightly about her body and buttoned snugly up her long throat to her chin, and spreading and flowing in waves about her knees and feet.

"Norma, darling!" said this exquisite apparition. The rays of the descending sun poured through the high stained-glass window and speckled her cool beauty with tiny dashes of scarlet and green.

"Mama!" Norma said, stupefied. She ran up the stairs, and the lady put her arms about her and kissed her.

"Precious," said Janet, Countess von Sturnberg, "I got worried about you and your daddy, and I wondered what on earth they were doing to you! I've been thinking about Daddy ever since he and I had a little talk in New York a few weeks ago, and wondering if perhaps 'Hill Acres' wasn't the place I belong, after all! From what darling Granny and our marvelous Sandy have been writing me I haven't felt one bit happy about my big girl, so here I am, and if Daddy'll forgive me I think I'm ready to begin all over again!"

CHAPTER XXI

JOCELYN FELT BITTERLY WOUNDED, felt completely left out of it. From the moment Norma's mother appeared there was nothing for her to do except obliterate herself as much as possible, and wait for such crumbs as might fall from the family table.

Sandy, on the other hand, was warmly included in the Fordyce councils. Sandy, rigid, gray-haired, spectacled, clad in a brown silk dress as unyielding as iron, with iron-stiff ruchings around the high collar and decent plain cuffs, went into Mrs Fordyce's room immediately after the countess and Norma had disappeared therein, and when Philip came home he was immediately summoned to join them. Jocelyn, loitering in Norma's sitting room, through the half-open door saw him come upstairs, his hair still wet from the recent shower at the club, his face sunburned to a brown even deeper than usual, and went impulsively across the hall to meet him.

"What's this Brooks was telling me? Janet here?" he said sharply. "Did you see her?"

"Yes, I was in the hall with Norma when she came downstairs."

"What 'd she say?" He was too deeply disturbed to smile at her, to say anything that would make the troubled situation easier for Jocelyn.

"Just that she had been worried about Norma, and wanted to see—I think she said what we were doing to her."

"Great Scott!" he said in angry desperation, under his breath. "This is a sweet time for her to show up! This is my mother's work."

"And Sandy's," Jocelyn couldn't help saying.

"I suppose she had her finger in it, too. It makes it nice for Norma!"

He said nothing more, immediately crossing to his mother's bedroom door and disappearing as it closed behind him. Jocelyn stood irresolute for a minute; then she went back into the sitting room.

She had always imagined Norma's mother to be a hard, flashy woman; flippant, insensitive, selfish. It was a shock to discover her in this gentle, gracious person with the caressing soft voice, the graceful slender body, the appealing eyes. Jocelyn felt suddenly forlorn and helpless. She had no defense against this sort of thing.

Waiting alone for Norma's return, she tried to recall every detail of the vision that had come slowly downstairs in the last shafts of afternoon light. Braided hair, not quite gold, not quite brown; a blue gown wrapped tightly about a tall thin body and spreading in waves about silver-slippered feet; nervous long hands covered with rings.

"I haven't felt one bit happy about my big girl!" Janet had said. "If Daddy'll forgive me I think I'm ready to begin all over again."

"Hypocrite!" Jocelyn said to herself angrily. "She's been married twice since she left him, and is talking about getting married again! And now she walks back into the house as if nothing but a married quarrel had happened!"

All their plans for the happy holiday in Hawaii were wrecked now. They couldn't go off and leave Norma's mother here with old Mrs Fordyce. The wearing of new clothes, the packing, the excitement of going up to board the big ship and sailing off into the south seas would be canceled because of this new development.

The countess had decided quite suddenly upon the Western

trip, Jocelyn knew. She had heard her say affectionately to Norma, as the two had preceded her up the big stairway: "I'd no more idea of coming than you had at this time yesterday, sweet. But I had a letter from Granny that made me so unhappy . . ."

They had both ignored her. Natural enough, a mother and daughter reunited after months of separation. They would ignore her from now on. Why not? She had no place in the story. Sandy hated her, and unquestionably the countess was all ready to dislike her heartily, to resent her having ever been made a member of the household. Philip, trying to protect his child's interests, would be helpless, and Granny would always be for the line of least resistance, for the easiest course. Norma might say a word in defense of her beloved companion, but nobody would hesitate for a second to drown out her voice; if Norma wanted anything really important, that was in itself almost sufficient reason for her being denied it by grandmother, mother and governess.

So Jocelyn loitered about the room in a miserable state of indecision and apprehension. What were they all saying, in that room across the hall? What attitude could Philip possibly take toward this woman who had deserted him for another man, fifteen years earlier, and who had twice married since? She had felt no maternal yearnings toward Norma when the poor child had been shuttled from school to school, from governess to governess. She had gone her giddy way then, being reported in the hungry newspapers as buying a diamond here, chartering a yacht there, opening a mansion at Palm Beach, giving a party to two hundred friends in a New York penthouse. All this time Norma had been lonely, misunderstood, unhappy, growing more twisted and self-centered every day. Now, just as the child was developing a natural affection for her father, just as she was finding a suitable group of friends, this mother must turn up to wreck the whole scheme once again!

Norma's reaction to it would be all-important. Jocelyn

was not long left in doubt as to what that would be. About an hour after the conference in Mrs Fordyce's room began, she heard voices, opening and closing doors, and Norma's voice in the hall.

When the girl came in she was in the excited, talkative mood that Jocelyn especially disliked. She held out a hand upon which blazed a magnificent ring of two pearls and an oblong diamond.

"Look what Mama's given me, Jotsy! Did you ever see such a rock! My grandfather gave it to her when she graduated, and she had it reset for me. My dear, such goings-on! It looks as if my delightful parents were going to agree about me for once in their lives. A coming-out party in Honolulu this summer, instead of next fall, with people coming from all the corners of the earth, China and London and everywhere! Mama says she's tired of worrying about me, and of course I am a handful, and consequently the entire committee is going to camp on little Norma's trail—imagine the excitement when everyone around here gets news of the great reconciliation!"

Jocelyn could make nothing of this jargon. It was Norma at her worst; Norma slipped back to the spoiled child of a few months ago; chattering glibly of what she knew nothing, tossing off airy references to distinguished persons Jocelyn did not know, elated with her own position and power, wild for freedom.

"Norma." It was Sandy's most triumphant, smoothest voice from the doorway. She came in, elderly and rustling, for the moment ignoring Jocelyn completely, speaking only to the younger girl. "My dear," she said, "I think Mama will want to sleep in here with you tonight. Did you speak to Mattress about the change? We are moving you back to your old quarters, which are quite ready," Sandy continued, turning to Jocelyn without looking at her. "The countess naturally wants to be with Norma. So I think, Mattress, if you'll see one of the girls about getting the room Miss Britton has

been using in order, we'll move the countess in as soon as
you're through. Have them help Miss Britton move her things
back to her old room, will you? My dear child," the old
governess added to Norma affectionately, "this is exciting,
isn't it? To have our Mama suddenly appear with all these
beautiful plans."

"We're probably not sailing Saturday, Jotsy," Norma announced importantly, following Jocelyn to her room, as
Jocelyn went in and began to gather her things together.
"Mama wants to go down to Honolulu for three months, in
a few weeks, and have my coming-out party there, with all
the guests—about two hundred of them—invited to come
down and stay two weeks! Can you imagine it, beach parties
and dances and swimming! Mama says nobody ever did that
before, and it'll make it different from any other party that
ever has been!"

Norma did not accompany her when Jocelyn followed the
maids, laden with her clothes, books, small possessions, to her
old rooms. She found the place in the same exquisite order,
filled with the same comfort and beauty that had impressed
her upon her first arrival at "Hill Acres," four months
earlier. She had been a complete stranger to all the mystery
and unhappiness and folly of this big house then; she had
been amused, curious, anxious to stay and become a part of
the life of one of the richest little girls in the world. She had
been humiliated by her own weakness in the affair with Kent
Dunham, glad to find here in these lovely little rooms, whose
windows commanded one lovely park view after another,
healing and help.

Now everything was changed. Now she had been tested in
the fire of these feverish excitements and superficialities and
found wanting. Now she had learned to love Philip Fordyce,
to ache in every fiber of her being to be near him, to be with
him, to count somehow in his life, and just as in his careless
generosity he had offered her the dazzling position of his
wife, it had all been snatched away. He liked to solve

problems easily, Philip. And unquestionably he liked his
daughter's young governess. But how much? How much
would whatever he felt for Jocelyn count against the power-
ful batteries of his child's mother, his own mother and the
implacable Sandy? Jocelyn felt helpless and confused, uncertain what to do, what action would be wisest now.

She walked restlessly about her rooms, now determined to
pack up all her belongings and leave for her aunt's house in
Sausalito, now fiercely determined not to be worsted at this
first encounter but to wait and see how matters would shape
themselves. No word came to her; no message. She was
afraid to go back to Norma's rooms, to try to get in touch
with Mrs Fordyce. She could only wait.

The Sunday afternoon faded into darkness, and night came
down with chilling fog from the hills. There was a tap at
Jocelyn's door at half past seven o'clock, and Lena came in
with a supper tray, and stopped to light her fire.

"Et get colt," observed Lena.

"It is cold," Jocelyn agreed. She was sitting in a big chair
now, with a book. The sudden warmth of the blazing logs
was grateful indeed. Lena drew the curtains; the room assumed the snug, homelike air that Jocelyn remembered having
loved when first she came to it.

Another tap at the door, while Lena was still busy.
Jocelyn's heart rose. It must be Norma!

But instead it was Miss Sanderson who stepped in; in-
clining her head sideways with a bleak imitation of a frozen
smile that was characteristic of her and that Jocelyn particularly disliked, and not meeting Jocelyn's eyes as she sidled
to the chair opposite her. Often, before Norma had taken her
wholly to her heart, in the days when Jocelyn had still
occupied these rooms, she had seen Norma curled there, chattering, listening, growing fonder of her young governess
every minute. Now the stiff dead-leaf-brown silk of Sandy's
pleated and ruched old-fashioned garment was spread there
instead, and Miss Sanderson, with a little preliminary "hem!"

as sharp as a bullet, and a little dry sound of clearing her throat, was ready for battle.

"Miss Britton," the older woman began, as Lena went noiselessly into the bedroom and closed the door, "just a few suggestions. The countess has moved into Norma's room; you knew that. It seems as if she can't get near enough to the dear child, now that they're together again. I brought up Janet Lockey," Miss Sanderson continued, after another sharp "hem!" as Jocelyn said nothing, but sat watching her steadily. "You knew that? I had her from the time when she was eleven. She had lost her mother, dear child. I was with her everywhere. When they put her into a German school, an Italian school, I boarded there with her. And I think I may say I discharged my trust carefully. Hem! To the best of my ability, at least.

"She was very young, of course, when she married Mr Philip. Too young, perhaps, but her father never refused her anything, and indeed he was very fond of Mr Philip, too. Three years later, unfortunately, they quarreled, as young people will——"

"I thought she left him for a man named Caverley," Jocelyn put in coldly at this point. Miss Sanderson's expression, which in an acidulated and reluctant fashion had approached an indulgent smile, altered instantly. She scowled.

"She was very young," she said frigidly, "and whatever she did was done more in mischief than in—in any spirit of— of recklessness. I was with them at the time," the old governess went on, gathering dignity as she proceeded. "It was after I had been with Mrs Griscom's daughters. I was trying to organize Miss Janet's household; she had had great trouble with the baby's nurses. She had been dancing with Captain Caverley a good deal, and I suppose I may say flirting with him——"

"I suppose you may," Jocelyn said dryly in the pause. The other woman gave her a glance, and her face darkened with a dry flush.

"I heard them laughing one afternoon, down on the lawn. That very lawn out here, under your windows. And quite suddenly Miss Janet—as I called the countess then—came flying into the house and packed an overnight bag, and they were gone. It was an escapade, she herself had no idea how serious, and we know now that she afterward regretted it very deeply. She was only with the captain two years, and after that," said Sandy, with the tone of one giving her great credit, "she did not marry anyone for seven years. Not anyone!"

"That was something," Jocelyn said approvingly. Again Miss Sanderson looked at her sharply, but the girl's round eyes were innocent of significance. "How long before she and Mr Fordyce were divorced?"

"A year. He applied for a divorce immediately, but under the California law it took a year. She wanted him to go to Reno, but he said he could not be spared for six months."

"*She* didn't go to Reno?"

"She couldn't. The captain was stationed in some New York place. She lived near him, and after the year was up they were married. It was very uncomfortable for her, of course, but her father was with her."

"Oh, her father was with her?"

"Certainly. He joined her immediately. Otherwise—hem!" said Sandy elegantly, "it would not have looked very well."

"Under the circumstances how was it she got Norma for a quarter of the year?"

"Under what circumstances? There was nothing extraordinary in the circumstances."

"When I first worked for Fordyce, Sawyer & Fordyce," Jocelyn said, "the girls in the office said it was an elopement with Captain Caverley."

To this Miss Sanderson made no reply.

"It was because of her father that she got the baby some of the time," she said shortly. "But indeed, we mustn't gossip this way," she interrupted herself, drawing her shoulders up primly. "I came to say that Mrs Fordyce and Mr Philip and the countess and Norma have all gone over to the club for dinner. I see Lena's brought you yours."

"All together!"

"Certainly. The countess has a great many friends here, and she said she wanted to give them a surprise."

"But—good heavens! Fourteen years after their divorce!"

"They have seen each other in that time. As a matter of fact Mr Fordyce saw her in New York the last time he was there, in the banker's office," Miss Sanderson said stiffly and uncomfortably.

Jocelyn was silent for a moment, looking into the fire, her head whirling, and the other woman was silent, too. Suddenly Jocelyn asked over a sick sense of defeat:

"And what is the plan now?"

"I dare not hope for a reconciliation now, although I pray for it, as his mother does," Sandy said piously. "But I do dare to hope that there will be a friendly adjustment. It is my confident belief that Mr Philip has never loved any other woman, and I think her coming to him tonight stirred him to the soul. Hem! Stirred him to the soul."

"Norma said something tonight of taking a place in Hawaii and having a coming-out party there."

"Her mother wants to take her there for a few months, her father perhaps joining them later. Just what the arrangement will be, I don't know. But Mrs Fordyce asked me to give you this."

She leaned forward, a pink slip in her hand. Jocelyn looked at it blankly; looked up.

"What's this?" she asked, her cheeks reddening.

"That's the countess's check for three months' services, Miss Britton, and she asked me to express thanks for all of them for the kindness you have shown to Norma."

A dozen phrases came to Jocelyn's mind; she discarded them all and sat silent, staring at the paper. Sandy was not worth her fire.

"Now, when would you want to go?" Miss Sanderson pursued it gently, inflexibly. "Any one of the men can drive you into town whenever you like. Tuesday? Wednesday?"

"I would like to say good-by to Norma and Mrs Fordyce tomorrow," Jocelyn said after a moment. "I could leave in the afternoon."

"I'll arrange that, then." Miss Sanderson's voice sounded as if she strove to conceal her content. "You see none of us will be wanted, since the countess herself is taking Norma in charge," she went on tactfully. "Of course, she's always been devoted to the child, but moving about so much——"

"I may accompany them to the Islands," she recommenced after a moment, as Jocelyn remained silent. "But that would only be as the countess's companion. She may want me to go."

Jocelyn was too crushed to speak. Even if she had been able to express her resentment that this other woman had been sent to dismiss her, her offended pride at the presentation of the check, her desolate sense of being unwanted, of being no use to anyone now, whatever her earnest efforts at usefulness had been, she would not have given Sandy the satisfaction of witnessing her agitation. Before Sandy she would display nothing.

She stood up, folded the check small and put it under the mantel clock. Her look indicated to the other woman that the interview was over. Sandy rose, too, and moved with her usual stiff effect of posture and deportment to the door; her grizzled head was inclined toward Jocelyn, but her eyes as always evaded the other's eyes.

"I'll tell Mrs Fordyce and Norma that you'll see them in the morning?" she said on a rising inflection.

"Please."

That was all. The door closed softly on Sandy. Jocelyn was alone.

For a few minutes she would not let herself think. She stretched her arms on a long "A-h-h-h!" and stood in the

center of the room, deliberately routing her thoughts, deny-
ing the swarming emotions as fast as they arose.

"I'll read," she said aloud. She seated herself, picked up
her book. The fire crackled softly, and the spring night wind
whispered about her windows. Jocelyn turned a page; turned
another page.

It was no use! She flung aside the book and went to the
window and opened it, kneeling down with her elbows on the
sill and her eyes straining out into the dark. There was no
moon, but the stars were all the brighter for that, and by their
light she could see the outlines of the great trees and the
faraway silhouette of the westward hills. "Hill Acres." She
loved it; every inch of it. It had already gripped her with its
extravagances and its beauty, the mad life that went on under
its roof. Jocelyn felt that she could not do with less highly
seasoned fare, now; these crazy people would forever be in
her mind.

The drinking, smoking, gambling, dancing, gossiping
grandmother, her head piled every morning and every evening with a fresh set of gray red curls. The spoiled child,
whose pudgy little hand could write checks for any and every
absurdity she fancied, who had never known home life or
home love, who had been flattered and quarreled over and
shifted about until she was almost incapable of simple youthful emotion of any sort. The three-times-divorced mother, so
gentle and sweet in manner, so sensational in history, always
on the front pages of the newspapers, always involved in
some fresh story of extravagance and folly. And finally the
quiet, decent man who was the one steady reality to which
all these other whirling elements clung; Philip, who had perhaps like other men only wanted a home and children and
reasonable peace and affection, and who had married the
Lockey heiress eighteen years ago.

But even Philip——! When Jocelyn's thought came to
him she winced away from the keenest hurt of all. Even
Philip had been so long used to the strange moral—or im-

moral—code of this particular set that he could placidly accept the monstrous situation of a wife's return after fourteen years, after two unsuccessful marriages, offer her his arm, escort her and his mother and daughter complacently to a country club, a spectacle for all the world to see.

Philip, who had spoken to her only today of so different a plan! Who yesterday had told her that she had given him back his daughter, that the Hawaiian trip meant much to him because he had found Jocelyn.

"I've fallen in love with you," he had said, in his own amused, unemotional way. "The most natural thing in the world for anyone who is in your neighborhood at all is to fall in love with you."

And now—now——! Jocelyn drew in her head, got to her feet, looked across the room to where her new luggage had been piled by the curious maids who had moved her things from Norma's suite an hour or two ago, and suddenly put her head down into her hands and began to cry.

CHAPTER XXII

IN THE MORNING she had her breakfast upstairs and finished her packing, hoping, praying every minute that Philip would send for her. But ten o'clock came, and eleven, and there was no word.

It was almost noon when Lena came in to say that Mrs Fordyce would like to see her, and Jocelyn, with a fast beating heart, went to the big beautiful bedroom to find the mistress of the house at her dressing table, Annette busy with her hair.

"Yes," said Mrs Fordyce, lightly, nervously, as Jocelyn came in. "Good morning. What's it trying to do, rain? Well, I suppose Sandy told you last night that all our plans have changed."

"That's what we must get used to, in this world," Sandy herself said with a resigned smile. She was sitting knitting industriously in a chair close to the dressing table.

"The countess is going to take Norma with her to Honolulu," said Mrs Fordyce. "Whether they'll sail as soon as Saturday or not I don't know. But Norma's clothes are all ready, and I suppose Janet has brought trunks of them from New York. Phil could turn his reservation over to her, I should think."

"Mr Fordyce isn't going?" Jocelyn asked, instantly heartened by the thought.

Mrs Fordyce made no answer to this, apparently absorbed

in the jerk Annette had given her head in placing one of the curls.

"Damn you, Annette," she said quietly.

Miss Sanderson held off her knitting and eyed a row of purling.

"He will follow later," she explained.

"Then there's nothing to do but say good-by," Jocelyn said. She had been standing since entering the room; she extended a hand to Mrs Fordyce, who wiped cream from her own hand on Annette's apron before taking Jocelyn's hand and saying, through the mirror, "Good-by, and thank you so much!"

"Good-by, Miss Sanderson," Jocelyn said, retreating.

"Good-by and good luck I'm sure," said Sandy, sweetly, and without punctuation. She did not look up from her knitting.

Across the hall in Norma's rooms Jocelyn found the girl scribbling away madly at her desk in a new gold-bound diary that, she explained, her mother had brought her.

"No more lessons!" Norma exulted. "Mama says I'm too advanced for them. After all, travel educates, Mama says, and meeting all the strange people I do, and having my own way of judging them. Mama laughs and laughs at me, she says I'm not quite like anyone else, and I guess that's true, because I remember when I was only a tiny baby . . ."

It went on and on. The old mad childish babble of things she didn't understand, didn't remember correctly, was quoting from some boasting tale of her grandmother or mother. Jocelyn listened for a while, a careful half-smile on her face, and then asked Norma if she would say good-by for her to her mother and father.

"It's a shame about Honolulu!" Norma said, by way of reply to this. She looked pale this morning, last night's lip red still smeared on her mouth; her rich dark hair giving off a scent of tobacco smoke, her breath indicating that nobody last night had limited her as to liquor. "But of course

we'd only have had a week there," she went on, "and Mama
and I intend to stay for months, rent a beach place with lots
of garden, or maybe buy one, and have parties! If I have a
coming-out party Dad 'll come down, and loads of yachts—
the fun! Mama says it just suddenly occurred to her, 'Why,
here's my little girl, the most interesting personality I ever
knew, and I'm letting everyone else have the fun of her!' It
seems a letter I wrote her—remember that funny letter I
wrote the day I just felt funny——"

The stream this time was interrupted by the entrance of
the countess, who also looked pasty of face and seemed
weary in manner. A beautiful dressing gown trailed about
her, her hair was in a tumbled disordered mass of curls.

"She really is beautiful," Jocelyn thought. Immediately
she was under the spell of the cultured, lazy voice.

"Miss Britton, I'm so glad you came in. You had my
check? And Sandy tells me you're going today. That's not
hurrying you? I'm afraid I've upset your plans and Norma's
for the Honolulu trip, but my little girl here has forgiven me
and I know you will. I just got what I call 'Norma hungry,'
and out I had to come to see her for myself. What I didn't
realize was that I was going to find a little beauty for my
daughter; I'd have adored her just as much if she hadn't been
a perfect little Countess Powtowka. You know that picture
with the ribbons around her hair? I'm going to try Spotty
here with ribbons someday and have her painted. We used
to have a copy of that picture in my room when I was married to Captain Caverley—old-fashioned, but I think this
child here has something deliciously quaint about her. Anyway, I'm going to give her just the bestest—bestest——"

Norma had gone to take one wing of her mother's chair
as a seat and was cuddling up against her. The countess
punctuated the last words with little bitelike kisses against the
girl's cheek.

"Yes; she's going to have a happy summer," the countess
pursued. "You know it never stops, down there. Dances,

beach parties, fascinating men playing ukuleles. She's only seventeen, but that will make the girls of nineteen and twenty perfectly wild, and I think it might be fun! Darlin'," said the lady, rubbing her temple against Norma's, "you've not had a very good Mommy so far. But she's going to make it up to her Spotty-baby. That's what I used to call her," she finished, smiling at Jocelyn for sympathy. "I wanted a boy, of course; everyone did. And when this measly little bunch of black hair and red skin was put down beside me I asked the doctor—the man nearly died, he adored me, anyway—what I'd ever done to get such a spotty baby. Of course it set the whole hospital in an uproar, because it seems most mothers don't speak at all for hours and hours, and then it's to praise the baby."

"Measly little bunch of black hair and red skin!" Norma echoed in delight.

"That's what you were. But now you're my little princess, who's going to have the happiest time of her life. But we mustn't keep Miss Britton, darling. Say good-by and trot along and have your bath, don't let Marie-Thérèse dress you until we know what we're going to do. Miss Britton," the countess went on, when she and Jocelyn were alone, "I want to explain this situation to you. You, of course, think of me as a frivolous, selfish woman who has neglected her child all these years. I haven't," Janet said, tears of maternal devotion in her eyes. "I've always tried to do what was best for Norma, for I've realized that she was an unusual and excitable child, and ought to have careful handling. Two years after I eloped—which was of course all a girl's silliness and imagination—I divorced Captain Caverley because I knew he was a completely unfit father for Norma. As to Count von Sturnberg, he fell in love with the child long before he did with me. We were on a cruise on my father's old yacht, Norma and her nurse and a dozen friends and I, and we picked the count up at Hamburg. The instant he saw her he was completely bowled over. He paid absolutely no attention to me; he simply followed that seven-year-old baby about like a slave. She adored him, then. She hates him now, of course, but on the old *Janorma* she did really adore him."

Jocelyn wondered contemptuously why they always had to justify themselves, deceive themselves. Janet must know in her heart that she had destroyed Norma's life, and that of Norma's father as well. But she was presently in tears of self-pity as she described effort after effort, sacrifice after sacrifice gladly made for her child, and so often futile.

"Spotty wrote me such a happy, funny letter about her Easter trip to Honolulu," Janet said. "It waked me up, suddenly, I mean it really did. I thought how affectionate and forgiving Mr Fordyce always was, and that perhaps we might have a home together down there someday, in the Islands, with Spotty. That's the way it ought to be, and that's the way I hope it will be. He worships Spotty, and Bert—his mother—tells me that he's never quite forgotten his bad Janet. So," she finished sweetly, "you understand, don't you? That we do appreciate your goodness to Spotty, and that you've perhaps done something to reunite a family that was just a little bit off the track. And now, I'm sorry, but I must run and dress."

That was all. Jocelyn was out in the hall again, with nothing to do but find a butler to carry her bags downstairs, and to follow them to the waiting car. She moved through her good-bys to the staff automatically, with a queer numbed feeling inside her, and as she drove away she seemed to be driving into a great void, in which nothing was of interest, nothing mattered.

With a last gesture of luxury she asked the man to drive her all the way to Sausalito, and descended at the gate of "Maple Den" shortly after one o'clock, weary and dispirited and fighting a maddening impulse to cry. But five minutes in the household of the Partridges were enough to dissipate any self-pity, and to plunge her at once into the roaring life of the household. It appeared that in the middle of Tots's wedding plans for June, Ned Whitehouse, who had for several years been Sissy's beau, had burst in upon the family only an hour earlier with the news that he had been promoted, that he was to be in charge of the Bakersfield office, and that he wanted eighteen-year-old Sissy.

This had thrown all six sisters into a very ecstasy of excitement, a mad readjustment of plans. Immediate efforts must now be transferred from Tots to Sissy, announcements must be sent to the papers; Sissy must notify the manager of the shoe store in which she worked that she was leaving at the end of the week. Sissy could be married in white if she would wear Jossy's wedding dress; everyone thought that would be charming. "And carry field flowers the way Margaret Pierce did!" "Oh, field flowers!" cried everyone at once.

Awakening babies were given their afternoon glasses of milk to an enthusiastic description of their aunt's plans. They were going to have an uncle Ned in three weeks, how did they like that? Sissy dashed back to the store to pay what attention she might to afternoon sales, Ned raced back to his city job, but the others circulated about in a close group all afternoon, everyone afraid to be absent for even a minute for fear something might be said that must not be missed.

It was decided that Sissy herself should tell her father, and as he came in, genial and weary from office hours, half an hour before Sissy did, there was a terrible thirty-minute interval in which all the girls were bursting with the great news, whispering in corners, and exploding into apparently causeless laughter at the slightest word from him.

Eventually Sissy was back, and in his arms, and all the others were gathered about to laugh and cry and exclaim over the youngest bride.

"Sissy, you could *easily* have a baby before you're nineteen!"

"Tots, your kitchen shower at Jane's on Thursday night! We'll have to let Sissy in on that."

"Listen, if Sissy wears my wedding dress, and we're just the same size, why don't I wear her bridesmaid's dress, and why don't we all wear the bridesmaids' dresses from my wedding?"

"Now, darlings, that makes it much too much of an affair. If we are going to do it so soon, let's keep it very simple and just have——"

"Listen, Mama, it's just as easy to have quite a lot of people and not hurt their feelings, really it is!"

"Listen, Mama, sandwiches and coffee and two big cakes and let them wait on themselves."

"Sissy—Mrs Whitehouse!"

"Sis, you'll have to have cards!"

"Ned wants her and Jane or Jossy to drive down to Bakersfield and househunt."

"Househunt! Oh, heavens!"

The old doctor kept his arm tight about his fourth daughter; now and then with his free hand he wiped his eyes. Jocelyn, looking at him, benign and gentle and wise, with blooming girls swarming all about him, kissing him, curled at his knee, hanging over the back of his chair, contrasted the parenthood in this shabby house with the other example she had so recently had a chance to study, and wondered once again if just too little money were not, after all, a better condition than much too much.

Ned, of course, came back to dinner. They sat down fourteen to a wild meal of not enough of any one thing to go around, but of plentiful variety. Aunt Nell had expected only seven of them; there were eleven chops. But two cans of corned-beef hash pieced them out nobly, and the round dish of new potatoes was flanked with the oval dish of noodles. A half-pan of corn bread heated up from lunch was supplemented with a sheet of biscuits; there were three kinds of jam, the heel of Sunday's ham, some stale spongecake made into layers with a cream filling, and whatever other odds and ends the icebox supplied: a small bowl of spinach, some cold asparagus, a slab of chocolate custard.

All these things were set about at random, and the young hands reached for them, and the young voices jabbered in a tireless stream. Aunt Nell had her elephant teapot beside her; the doctor as always dined on hot milk and toast; the big coffee pot circulated among the tall milk glasses and scattered cups. Jocelyn sat next to her aunt, and gathered details of family news under cover of the wedding chatter. Richie, the son of the house, sat on the other side of his mother. He was of a gentler, quieter type than his sisters, not good at school work. Aunt Nell asked Jocelyn anxiously as to whether she thought it would be a good idea to have his tonsils out. It seemed a bad time of the year for it, with the flu scare just over.

She paid but a kindly, indifferent attention to such portions of the news from "Hill Acres" as Jocelyn chose to give her. Norma was going to Honolulu with her mother, was she? Never mind, Jocelyn, you'll get your chance another time, dear. Jocelyn could see that her aunt's mind was already working on the number of presentable napkins that the family could rally for the wedding, the probability that there must be overnight provision for Ned's folks, who lived in Portland.

"Sis," Jocelyn said, "why not have Miss Snyder tighten the upper part of your bridesmaids' skirts and sort of full out the lower part and put rick-rack braid all around? That's what I saw at the Freeman wedding last month, and it was awfully smart."

"Oh, Jocelyn, that sounds like an inspiration!"

"I gave Tots three hundred, and I'll give you three hundred," said the doctor, "but anyone who asks me for more wrings my old carcass dry!"

"Daddy, what an angel you are!"

"Ned wired his mother this afternoon, Mom."

"Sis, don't have it Thursday. Have it Saturday and then all the boys can come."

It was all so good, Jocelyn thought, and so good for her. This joyous, wholesome home talk; these pretty eager sisters outvying each other in suggestions and generosities in some way had the effect of soothing her spirits. These were her own people; this was the world in which to find realities and peace.

After dinner everyone but the brides-elect, Tots and Sissy, who were already planning the newspaper notices that should dignify them into Madeleine and Ellen, flew upstairs to find the bridesmaids' dresses of two years ago, and see what their possibilities were. The others attacked the dishes, put the dining room in order, and were ready with suggestions when the younger girls came downstairs wearing the discussed garments, prepared for criticism.

Jocelyn crouched on the floor at her cousin's knee.

"Look, Aunt Nell. A row of fine tucks, see, to lift it? And then chiffon, fluffing out——"

She had gotten so far when a voice from the open parlor doorway said mildly, "What goes on?"

The world turned upside down in a burst of stars. Her heart stood still, began to race deliriously. She scrambled to her feet, laughing, exquisite, her face April. Philip Fordyce came into the room.

" 'The Dancing Lesson,' by Degas," he said, on a rising inflection. They all laughed, and the girls, more like a high tide of roses than ever, clustered about him and explained that while they had been absorbed in the thrill of Tots's approaching wedding, quite suddenly little Sissy had taken the center of the stage. Eighteen days to her wedding!

Philip entered into the spirit of the occasion wholeheartedly. He took out a notebook and said that if Tots and Sissy had picked their silver patterns yet he would send them each a berry spoon.

"Everyone gets berry spoons," he told them seriously,

"and everyone thinks they are perfectly useless. But believe me you can do wonders with a berry spoon. Mush, you know," elaborated Philip, "and milk toast."

They were all in such spirits anyway that they found this irresistibly amusing, and Jocelyn's sweet liquid laughter had in it a note that, for some reason she could not understand, brought tears to her aunt's eyes. The thought of silver patterns had already held Tots in rapt delight for some weeks, but it was new to Sissy, and fresh uproar arose as her sisters voiced their advice. Have it like Jossy's; have it like Sally Brougham's; have formal modern; have lotos flower!

Just how she knew not—for everything had gone rosy and bewildering and vaporous and she was hardly conscious of what she said or did—Jocelyn found herself and Philip Fordyce wandering down the steep garden paths to the side gate, and standing there, with the dusk not yet so deep about them but that they could see the paths and the dim gleam of flowers, and the moon rising large and pale over the eastern hills beyond the bay. Belvedere and Alcatraz and far Berkeley sparkled with chains of lights; toward the west the home lights of San Francisco rose tier upon tier against the dark blue sky. Across the lane the meadow fell away below them to scattered oaks and the dark waters of the bay; the night was warm and still, and the red lights of little boats at anchor were mirrored in the water.

"I came to say I'm sorry it all broke like this," said Philip. "I telephoned home today to get in touch with you, and found you'd gone. I don't blame you. I know you're angry. But I wanted to say that I'm sorry."

"I'm not angry," said Jocelyn. "I came away because Miss Sanderson didn't leave me in any doubt that that was what I was expected to do. She was kind enough to say she'd say good-by to you for me."

"Sandy," he said thoughtfully, and for a minute he did not speak again. "Jocelyn," he went on then, "what did they tell you?"

"Why, when you all went to the club last night——" she was beginning, when he interrupted her.

"Clubs," he said briefly.

"Didn't you go to the country club?" she stammered.

"With all of them?" he demanded in turn, equally amazed.

"She said you did."

"Sandy did?"

"Well, she may not have said it in so many words. But she said—she certainly implied, that you and the countess were friends again——"

"Friends again!" he interposed on an impatient laugh, as she hesitated. "My dear girl, we've been divorced for fourteen years, and in all that time she hasn't made a friendly gesture toward me, or even indicated that she wanted to see me! There can't be any talk of a reconciliation between Janet and me; it would be absurd! If I was angry when she walked out on me and my mother and a little girl of two, fifteen years ago, I've had cause to be a hundred times angrier since. She kidnaped Norma—oh, we kept it out of the papers, but that was what it amounted to. She left her in Paris with three nurses and five doctors, down with scarlet, and went with friends to Cairo.

"I didn't," he added in a more moderate tone, as Jocelyn merely waited in silence, her eyes starry in strengthening moonlight, "I didn't want even to be in the house with Janet overnight. They were all planning to go to the club, I came into town to my club and stayed there. You knew that?"

"No, I—I didn't know that." Suddenly she felt weak and small and helpless, and putting her elbows on the gate rail and covering her face with her hands she began to cry.

Instantly his arms were about her, and so came her hour of miracle, and Jocelyn entered upon the kingdom that is only for lovers, and took possession of it. His kisses on her mouth, his words close to her ear, her whole crying, laughing self leaning against him, safe in his big hold—never had she known such a heaven of ecstasy, or dreamed that it might ever open its doors to her.

Presently a period of comparative sanity set in, and Jocelyn could dry her eyes, and listen and laugh and cry, although she was still shy of words.

"You just went away."

"Of course I went away!"

"And her coming doesn't make any difference?"

"Why should it? It makes this difference," Philip admitted on second thought, "that we don't go to Honolulu Saturday. She'll probably go and take Norma. And after they're gone we'll be married. You'll come down and visit my mother, and we'll have a little dinner for the few people who matter, and after that we'll be married."

"Oh, but your mother'll hate me!"

"You know my mother. The minute you're established there she'll take you entirely into her confidence, gossip about Janet, go to her card games and dinners, and go off to her place on the Rogue River in July. Nothing matters to my mother except that she's amused."

"I really do think it's—it's awful the way rich people live," Jocelyn said, conceding him this with a startled little laugh.

"You know you've never said you loved me, Jocelyn."

"I've loved you ever since you came over here that Sunday to ask me to come to Norma. Perhaps I loved you before that," her tender, shaken voice said out of the dark. "Only— only I can't believe it," Jocelyn added in a whisper, as if she spoke her thoughts aloud.

"Why not? I'm not offering you much. You've just said yourself that money doesn't buy much happiness. I'm offering you Norma, for she'll cling to you like an abalone once you—you belong to us. She's *always* going to be a problem. She'll marry, but that won't end it. Her mother'll always be a problem. In fact, you'll be a working housekeeper for the whole crowd of us," Philip said, "and you'll not get much out of it!"

"I'll get my wildest dream of all dreams out of it. I'll marry the one man in the world who has made me feel that —that I want to marry!"

"Who are you talking to?"

"You."

"And I've a name, I suppose?"

"Phil."

There was a long silence.

"I'm going to try," he presently said, "to make you the happiest woman in the world. I'll be so happy myself, I'll be so proud of you, that perhaps I'll be selfish. But I'm going to try. Just thinking about you as my wife, Jocelyn, has made all the world different to me in these last few weeks. It was Janet, I suppose," Philip went on, in a surprised ruminative tone, "that first made me realize what I was feeling. I had to see her in New York for a few minutes, in the bank. It was about Norma's affairs, of course, and we were merely civil to each other. But she said that my mother's letters had been full of the new governess, and asked if you were pretty. I said that you were the sort of woman in whom looks didn't matter. That you were handling Norma with so much intelligence and affection and imagination that she was an entirely changed girl. I suppose," the man concluded with a chuckle, "that that was what alarmed Janet. At all events the first thing she said to me last night when we went into my mother's room was that I was in love with you! She'd evidently been thinking it over. Well, I had, too. I thought about it in the train, and I thought about it when I got home. And it seemed suddenly to smooth out everything, to be the perfect, the restful, the wonderful answer. And then I knew!"

"But—but can she get Norma away from you, if you marry again?" Jocelyn asked fearfully.

"Why should she? She's married twice since she left me."

"I know. But Norma wants to go with her now, and that may mean that she never wants to come back. They said you were going to join them."

Philip laughed, throwing back his head, dropped his cheek to rest it against her hair again.

"That was pure fiction," he said. "That was to scare you away."

"But surely they wouldn't think that if you wanted to you couldn't get in touch with me?"

"They might. Especially if my mother could persuade me to go with all of them to Honolulu on Saturday. That would have made a long gap. You see, darling, they didn't know that I'd asked you to marry me. They may have thought it was just a passing feeling."

"And you're sure it's not?"

"To whom are you speaking?"

"Phil." For the first time in this talk he heard the characteristic quiet little chuckle under her voice.

"No, dear. I'll not change. You may."

"I'll not change. But if I am the person who separates you from your daughter?"

"Then you might be the person who gives me my son."

"I didn't think of that. I've not had time to think of anything. And oh, Phil, I won't dare tell my aunt or anyone about this tonight! They're nearly insane over Sissy's plans as it is!" Jocelyn's voice had in it some of the notes of young delight and awe that made it sound like Sissy's own.

"As far as separating me from Norma goes," Philip presently said seriously, "her mother never can do that. Janet will take her to the Islands, give her a royal time for a few days, and then forget her, and abandon her to Sandy. Poor kid! Janet will be dancing, drinking, racing about, gambling, and then there'll be talk of schools for Norma again, what on earth to do with Norma, and back she'll come, only too glad to get to Dad and Jotsy!"

"Oh, I hope so!" the girl ejaculated fervently.

"This is Monday," he said. "They sail on Saturday. I don't want to marry you in any hole-in-the-corner way, Jocelyn. I want them to know it, I want the papers to have it, and I want whatever ceremony you and your people here think best. Of course we'll have this whole crowd here invited, and you'll decide how it's to be. I'll see you tomorrow —will you come over and lunch with me tomorrow? We'll find a ring and you can select your own berry spoon. I always give brides berry spoons."

"Oh, Philip, we aren't really planning our wedding!"

"We really are."

"This morning," she said, "I thought I was the unhappiest woman in the world. Now I'm by miles and miles and miles the happiest!"

They walked to his car and stood talking, and he took one more kiss and went on his way. Jocelyn walked back to the house in a dream of heaven. It could not be true, but it was true!

There was still a good deal of confusion and noise going on in the parlor; lights were lighted up and down stairs. Jane met her in the hall.

"I entirely forgot to pick up Timmy!" said Jane. "Jocelyn, Mr Kent Dunham's here. He got here about fifteen minutes ago, and he's in the library with Dad. He says he's got to see you!"

CHAPTER XXIII

THEY HAD A FAVORITE TABLE hidden away among the arches of the big central dining room at the Palace Hotel, and here they sat talking, talking, talking on in an enchanting new intimacy that made every word thrilling, and every subject, shared by their two minds and hearts, of absorbing interest.

Jocelyn wore today a straw hat covered with poppies and wheat. Her brown linen suit was plain in line, the blouse tailored and severe, but the radiance of her face and the light in her eyes made her beauty so unusual that Philip wondered how she could be so serenely unconscious of watching eyes and admiring glances.

"Everyone knows we're here today, Jocelyn."

"I should think everyone would. We've been right in this spot every day this week."

"Next week will be different."

"They really sail tomorrow, Phil? It 'll be such a relief; I'll breathe so much easier when that's over!"

"They really do. At least I imagine they will. We'll send Norma some books, shall we? I've ordered flowers and candy through the office, but I'd like you to help me with the books."

"She came around to it, did she? She said she wouldn't go if Sandy did."

"She had to, poor kid, for very shame. I felt so sorry for her." Philip frowned, pushed away his plate. "Spazzolari's going to be there next month; did I tell you that? Yes; he goes down on the Pelham yacht, it seems. Poor Norma, that started her off again. I was down at my mother's for an hour last night, and we had it hot and heavy. I took down Norma's letter of credit and some other papers. Janet was there, very gay and confident, and putting on an act of great surprise that Norma didn't want to go. Sandy was sitting right among us, so naturally Norma couldn't say a word, but she'd telephoned me in a perfect fury—I told you that yesterday— that she wouldn't go if Sandy went. Janet's almost beside herself trying to keep the child amused—all the lesson books gone, of course, and they are already getting on each other's nerves."

"It would be funny if it weren't so terribly sad, Phil."

"I suppose so. It's exactly what's gone on all through Norma's life, and we don't seem to find a way out. The understanding is now that if Janet has Norma until August——"

"Until August!"

"Yes, I know, it seems an awful long time. But then she's to be handed over to me, and I've about half a mind," Philip said, "to chuck law for six months and travel—you and I and the kid."

"Philip, what she would really like much better, what she really needs, is just to stay on here quietly, having her little Friday parties, going to subdeb things, making friends," Jocelyn said earnestly. "If you—if we had a place at Monterey, or Menlo, or one of the quieter places, and her friends could come to it, and there were tennis and golf and outdoor meals, that's what would save her. She doesn't care about the leaning tower or the Taj Mahal."

"Well, perhaps you're right. She misses *you*. She asked me, when we were alone last night, if you wouldn't go with them."

"And Sandy and her mother, too?"

"She seemed to think it might be arranged."

"Oh, but Phil, that would be worse and more of it!"

"That's what I told her. She said again then that she

wouldn't go at all. But I believe she will. You see," the man
went on, "Norma'll be eighteen next February. Well, that's
a long way off, but not as long as it used to be. I believe it has
occurred to her mother that Norma comes into her accumulated income then. That would settle Janet's debts, if she
could borrow it——"

"Debts!"

"Oh yes; she's deep in debt. Always."

"She couldn't be!"

"She is."

"But didn't her father leave her—at the office the girls
always said——"

"Yes; he left her an immense fortune. But Caverley
wrecked a good part of it, and 'twenty-nine cut it down
again. However, that wouldn't matter; Janet would be in
debt anyway. She really doesn't know what money is. She'll
promise to economize, give up a second car and a third
driver, and on the way home from her broker's stop and buy
herself a diamond watch for thirty-five hundred dollars. It's
always come from somewhere, and she thinks it always will.
She sends Von Sturnberg lots of money, to keep him quiet,
and they tell me that she's been buying this Spazzolari silk
monogrammed underwear. I don't know."

Jocelyn's face expressed her opinion, and he laughed.

"Norma comes into her fortune next year?"

"No; just the accumulated income. We've never spent
half of it. But that accumulated income will run into hun-
dreds of thousands—possibly a million. Pocket money. And
Janet knows that if Norma's with her when she gets it, the
chances are she'll make over to her mother about two thirds
of it. So yesterday Janet was saying in her most maternal
manner that she especially wanted Norma for February—I
could have her until then, but please to remember that for
her coming-of-age birthday she must be with Mama. And I
presume the idea is to give her such a good time now that
she'll *want* to be with Mama."

"She doesn't seem to be making a very good start."

"Well, that's where she'll fall down. Janet couldn't stick to any course very long. And now, sweetheart," Philip changed the conversation suddenly, "we've talked enough about Norma. She'll go off tomorrow, with Sandy and her mother, and if those two women have a modicum of sense they'll keep her happy for a while at least. So that's that. What about Dunham? Did you see him last night?"

"Oh yes. I met him at half past six, and we had dinner, and we talked."

"And is he just as unreasonable as he was Sunday night?"

"Just as unreasonable. But I don't think, Phil," Jocelyn said with a smile, "that it really matters what he says, now. It makes me feel a terrible fool, but that isn't important, either."

"Well, after all, I gave my little girl one of the richest mothers in America," Phil reminded her consolingly. "I've been a fool, too!"

"I know. It seems so strange that one can feel so decidedly one way for a while, and then suddenly it all goes dead, and there's no making it come alive again. Last summer, last autumn, every thought was Kent. And at the end there, when he told me that he thought we must end it, that it wasn't fair to me or to him or to Lilian—I remember he brought his wife in!—I was like a crazy woman. I felt that I had to see him again, that nothing else mattered. And he reminds me of that now."

"He's not divorced?"

"No; Lilian only wants Kent; she doesn't seem to care on what terms. She feels that she's bound to win in the end, and I suppose she will!" Jocelyn said. "All the time I was interested in Kent she knew it; we saw each other; she used to say complacently that while Kent admired me he couldn't get along without her. I was always the outsider. It was only that last night, at Covey's cabin, that he suddenly threw all

that aside, suddenly said that he and I could face the world
and the critics together, and then I ran away——"

"You ran away to me," said Philip.

"Lucky, lucky woman that I am!"

"But now what does he want, Jocelyn?"

"Now he's in despair. Lilian wants to take him back, on
the ground that it was all a stupid mistake. She's the kind
of woman who could easily persuade herself that that was
true. He wants me to be his friend, to enter into all his plans,
to advise with him what can be done. And how can I? I
simply don't want to. It's all—dead. And it's so embarrassing
to have him pleading with me, arguing. Fortunately," Jocelyn
finished, "Uncle Bart was in town for a consultation last
night, and I joined him at the hospital at nine and got home.
Otherwise Kent might have reasoned all night."

"We both have something—and in my case it's plenty!—
to put behind us," Philip said. "Once you're married we'll
hear no more of that."

"Oh, I hope not, I hope not! He manages to make me feel,"
Jocelyn explained ruefully, "that I'm responsible! Perhaps
I am. And he reproaches me with changing toward him.
Well, of course I have. But surely it would be worse to pre-
tend that I hadn't!"

"You've not told him about me?"

"I didn't dare, Phil, because I'm hardly able to believe it
myself, yet. And when I put it into words it—really, it
scares me."

"Well, it won't be long. When the *Malolo* sails tomorrow
we'll be one good step ahead. And then when will you come
down to us?"

"I'll have a long talk with Aunt Nell before that and see
what she thinks. But it oughtn't be too soon, Phil, because of
Norma. If she needed you—if she was unhappy—it would be
so terrible to have you off on a honeymoon with me. It would
be letting her down again. In one way and another everyone's
more or less let her down, since she was out of grammar

school. Wait until you get her first letters from Hawaii; those will tell a lot. Or wait until her mother returns her in August. Everything concerning Norma has always been managed so rapidly—in such a rush!"

"August!" He smiled at her. "Well," he conceded, "let's wait until they sail tomorrow and then we'll see."

"You can't think what fun it is to be planning with you, Phil."

"It is fun! But it seems as if we had so many more things to think about than most people have. There's my mother and Janet and Norma and all the ramifications—to say nothing of Sandy——!"

Her joyous laugh interrupted him.

"I love the idea of it all," she declared. "I love the idea of making your life simpler and your mother and Norma my friends. And someday, Phil, we'll have a ranch, with redwoods and a creek on it, and brown little boys, and ponies, and fishing, and you'll do nothing all day but roam about with us and eat picnic meals."

"My God, that sounds good!"

"And you don't know," Jocelyn continued, "that Norma won't settle down respectably and conventionally with the right man, and have children who'll come up and stay with us——"

She stopped, for he was looking at her across the table with the expression she loved best to see in his eyes, and when he spoke, what he said had nothing to do with his daughter.

"I love you, Jocelyn. You are the most wonderful woman I ever knew. Now," Philip went on after a moment, when they had smiled at each other for a moment with all the beatitude of happy children, "when will you come down to my mother?"

"Has she any idea of the way we feel for each other?"

"I don't think so. But it won't disturb her. She lives her life completely apart. You don't have to worry about my mother. What does worry me a little is the other women.

They'll all give dinners and dances and things, and you'll hate 'em."

"We won't go to them."

"We'll have to go to some of them. They'll mean it kindly."

"I've an idea that people like the Searses and the Verrinders will be angry. They'll not be at all in a hurry to entertain me."

"All the better if they're not," Philip said. "We don't need them."

But a cloud had come into Jocelyn's eyes.

"They wouldn't snub Norma?" she asked. "They wouldn't refuse to come to her parties?"

"Not while the Lockey company is solvent," Philip reminded her dryly. Jocelyn laughed.

"Well, we'll meet that when we come to it," she said. "This time tomorrow they'll be out at sea, and we can plan from there. You don't go down to see them off?"

"I don't want to see Janet. I'm bringing Norma into town early, and taking her to the boat; if Mother wants to come back with me, I'll bring her, but I imagine she'll stay until the last whistle blows. Might you and I lunch?"

"I'll be here at half past one. But if you're not here I'll understand."

"Jocelyn, does it seem to you miraculous to understand each other the way we do?"

"It's the loveliest part of the whole thing."

"Come on, then; we're getting books."

And they went off together, too completely absorbed in each other to know or care whether the watching world was noticing them or not.

The next day he joined her with so changed a face that she knew before he could speak that everything had gone well.

"They're gone?"

"Gone. There was a great crowd of Janet's friends to see

them off, and that put Norma into good spirits, and she and her Charles were racing all over the boat, and she had a lei of gardenias, and seemed in great form. I didn't get anywhere near to Janet; it was easy to avoid her in the crowd; but I understand from my mother that she felt quite triumphant. They pulled out on time, and ought to be going through the Gate this minute."

"What a relief, Philip! It seems as if we could breathe now, and get to our own plans."

"We'll have to decide when to tell my mother and your aunt. With Norma gone I feel as if my responsibilities were over, for the time being, anyway. If she's happy, well and good. If she's not, she'll come back all the readier to settle down to sensible living. We'll have our three months anyway, go up to Banff maybe, and on for a look at New York. This is April. Why not plan for early June?"

"It sounds heavenly."

"Oh, and by the way, I've a message from my mother. She asked me never to tell Janet, but to ask Miss Britton if she would come back and act as her secretary for a week or two. She's let herself in for the Garden Club excitement. I believe we're to have five or six hundred women trampling over the place, and a lunch, and Mother has a lot of bridge dates and can't be bothered with lists and telephones and committees, and she was casting about for someone to help her and she suddenly thought of you."

"Do you really mean it?" Jocelyn said, immensely pleased. "I thought she couldn't wait to get me out of the house."

"Oh no; she has no feeling in the matter at all. As a matter of fact she likes you; Annette told me so. But with Sandy and Janet riding her, she didn't want to fight. How about it? And by the way, they tell me you left a check behind you the other day."

"The Countess von Sturnberg's check. Yes. I was employed by you, after all. But how funny it sounds now! Employed by you. Yes; you owe me a month's salary. I'll spend it on a trousseau, and save you money in the long run. Perhaps I shouldn't take it. For you bought me all those beautiful clothes for Hawaii. Philip, isn't it all strange? A few days ago planning for Hawaii. Then fired, and back with Aunt Nell. And now going to be your wife."

"Not any stranger to you than to me. For it's years since I thought of being happy again, Jocelyn. It's years since I've dreamed of anything like companionship, love, having a wonderful woman beside me to share everything I do, and care for what pleases me or worries me. You will come down to Mother, then? When?"

"Any time, Phil. Monday?"

"Monday. I'll be going down about four. I'll send over for you at three. Will that be too early? And let's set that other date. This is the ninth. Let's say—I've got a calendar here. How's nine weeks from today, June eleventh?"

"My cousin Madeleine's being married a couple of weeks later. Yes; that would be all right. Nine weeks—oh, Phil! You won't want me to have a lot of clothes?"

"We'll get clothes in New York."

"It 'll take me days and days to get my breath. Married nine weeks from today!"

"I'll see you, you know. The Garden Club thing isn't for a month; you'll be down at our house and we can plan. Just take it easy, darling, and don't get fussed."

"It's nice to be fussed by happiness," she said.

And when he looked in upon her, working away at his mother's desk a few days later, she repeated the statement. "Of course I'm excited. But no woman in the world ever was so happy!"

CHAPTER XXIV

IT WAS TREMENDOUSLY SATISFYING to get back to "Hill Acres." Jocelyn reveled in every detail of her return. To be again an inmate of the big house, to resume again her old quarters and her old position was pleasure enough. But to be conscious of her secret and to see all this as the domain over which she was soon to be mistress was to feel an enchantment in every hour.

She and Philip saw each other daily now, if only for a few minutes. He was taking an unprecedented interest in the affairs of the Garden Club, and to the great delight of the other members of the committee insisted upon assuming much of the responsibility for the forthcoming festivity. At meetings Philip was businesslike and handsome in the chair, and Jocelyn was near him making notes, taking dictation. It was all like a happy dream to her.

New hats shading her corn-silk hair, new linen frocks cool and smart for hot days, luncheons with Mrs Fordyce at other women's beautiful homes—all these were part of it. Jocelyn was having a more and more complete introduction in the world into which she was so soon to enter, without anyone suspecting what was going on. She was a familiar figure now under the striped awnings, under the great oaks at the country club; the servants at "Hill Acres" respected and liked Miss Britton, and had accepted her as virtual housekeeper and manager; she had become Mrs Fordyce's favorite companion. The older woman liked to talk to somebody, and

Jocelyn was a good listener; there was no long-established family in the fashionable hillside suburbs that did not come in for a thorough dissection and betrayal.

"Her grandfather had a saloon and a girl-house down San Bruno way in the old days," Mrs Fordyce would say carelessly of some fragrant bride, who was all but unable to count her glittering array of wedding gifts. "There's colored blood there," she said of a redheaded animated debutante. "The sooner they get that girl married off the better!" And of a third she might comment thoughtfully: "I remember when her mother was nursemaid in the Garborough family, demure little thing that wouldn't say boo to a goose. She worked away and worked away and the first thing we knew the old man was divorcing his wife and marrying her. He had three boys, too. They never spoke to her. But after he died there was a legal fight that Phil said cost them just half the estate."

Jocelyn lunched with a charmingly suave woman who had been to Paris some fifteen years earlier, and who while there had arranged hilariously to exchange her husband for that of her closest woman friend, the friend delightedly marrying the discarded husband at the same ceremony. She went to a wedding which was attended by the bride's father as well as her three stepfathers. She heard an imperious old woman at a tea demanding of her son the identity of the old man who had been following her about, and heard his laughing answer, "That's my father, Mother." She heard virtuous women at a club lamenting that girls as well as men got "edged" so easily, disapproving the poker games that the debutantes often played in the spring afternoon for high stakes, discussing the sums paid by certain women to rid themselves of husbands. She knew pretty Barbara Worden, who went with her husband to Reno, where they rented an attractive house, employed a staff of servants, and shared their necessary time of residence in the divorce capital. And she heard an alarmed

mother on the telephone trying to find a daughter's where-
abouts on the morning of the day set for her debut.

"She's not with you, Miss Britton? I thought she might
have gone home with Mrs Fordyce. Great heavens, if she
doesn't come in soon I don't see how she can come out this
afternoon!"

Also revealing, where the code and ideals of this strange
world were concerned, was the general indulgent laughter
when the identity of the "Social Bandit" was finally discovered. It was just Fred Farraday, and he had always been
wild, and he had been drunk whenever he robbed anyone,
anyway, and that did constitute some excuse, and he had been
hustled off to England now, and that was the end of it. So
shut up; it hurt Sally and Tod terribly if anyone talked
about it.

Less lightly, but still with sympathy and excuses, was the
Ford case dismissed. Linda Ford had tons of money and
several servants, including a gray-caped nurse who was
reputedly paid a hundred and twenty-five dollars a month.
But all that hadn't saved the Ford baby, three years old, on
the night when Linda had given an especially uproarious
party from which everyone had streamed forth at three
o'clock to go to Dinty's for scrambled eggs. One guest, too
bewildered to move, had set the drawing-room curtains afire
with a cigarette, and at four o'clock the flames of the burning mansion had lighted all San Mateo County.

All the servants, cook, waitress, maid, governess, nurse,
had escaped. The genial cigarette-smoking guest had escaped.
But the small boy, his father divorced from his mother and
many miles away, had not escaped.

But in the crazy quilt that was this social pattern there
were a few homes that Jocelyn loved: the Carters', the
Frenches' at Woodside, the Pells'. These managed somehow
to live simply and honestly and happily in the midst of in-
sanity and confusion, and she liked to think that they were

her friends; they had elected her long before they could dream she would one day be one of them.

The weeks went by, and May was gone, and June came in on a blaze of flowers that buried the old house in beauty. Roses were everywhere, thousands, millions of roses, brilliant in the sunshine, shining darkly under the trees. Long spikes of delphinium rose like blue smoke along the borders, their bases packed with stock and foxglove and all the daisies: white, Transvaal, Shasta, Michaelmas, and the golden marguerites. Dahlias and hydrangeas were beginning; wherever Jocelyn looked, in these glowing days, her eye met the color of gardens, one garden touching another, one lawn only a more beautiful stretch of emerald than the next.

She and Philip had decided to give the world but one week's notice of their plans. His mother would be the only guest from his side of the house; the ceremony would take place very simply in Aunt Nell's parlor late in the afternoon, with the girl cousins composing the party, and the old doctor to give the bride away. Phil's car would be waiting; they would linger only long enough to be kissed and congratulated, and then go off for their long trip.

"And where do we dine that night, Phil?"

"Leave that to me. I've worked it all out."

"And who drives us? Louis or the little boy?"

"Nobody drives me. Your husband drives you."

"It sounds so delicious! To be going up into the wonderful Canadian woods, and to be able to loiter along just as we please, stopping whenever we want to. Are most people ever as happy as this?"

"I don't think so."

"And Norma is having a wonderful time," Jocelyn mused in satisfaction. "If your letter hadn't said so, mine would have been enough. It really sounds as if her mother were taking care of her. And, of course, there's always Sandy."

"Even Sandy appears to be somewhat tamed."

"I imagine Sandy got a scare. I wonder what Sandy'll

think," Jocelyn murmured, in an amused voice, "when she comes back to find me at 'Hill Acres,' to *stay?* It's too complete. It's like some old story, *Pamela* or *Evelina*."

It was nine o'clock at night, they were out on the terrace. Philip's mother had gone out to dinner; he and Jocelyn had had theirs together, and had wandered out here afterward to look at the stars and the strengthening moonlight that was whitewashing the lawns and trees and the sleeping flowers, and to talk of the announcement that was to be made on the following day, and of all that would follow it.

"She gets out then, and she stays out," Philip said, of Sandy.

"Poor old thing!" Jocelyn, who was in his arms, snuggled against him in the big garden chair, sighed sympathetically. "It's her bread and butter, I suppose," she commented.

"Bread and butter nothing! She has a pension, has had for years before she ever came to Norma the first time. She's all right."

"Oh, I love it!" laughed Jocelyn.

"Love what, sweetheart?"

"The way they all lie to each other!"

"Did it ever occur to you that truth is a very rare thing, Jocelyn?"

"Well, I suppose it is. Yet one always tries to be truthful."

"Nations don't tell the truth to each other, diplomats don't. Politicians aren't even supposed to. Businessmen don't. Newspapers don't. It's only a sort of approximation of truth—a sort of theory that we all mean to tell the truth that gets us through at all. There isn't much here!" Philip kissed the soft hair that was lying against his shoulder in a bright mass that shone in the moonlight, and laughed. "We had a funny case of lies on the grand scale here," he said. "Paul Verrinder's sister Betty Moore and Ruth Fellowes were inseparable. Ruth was crazier about Nobby Fellowes than I ever saw any woman, but she was a plain, serious little thing, and Nobby persuaded her to go to Reno and get a divorce.

She consulted me and I told her to stick it, but she didn't have a cent, and the small girl was delicate, and in the end she went. Betty Moore, who'd been through the mill, comforted her and drove them up to Reno and stayed a night or two until they got settled, and six months later, the day Ruth got her decree, Betty married Nobby."

"And what 'd the other woman do, what 'd Ruth do?"

"Oh, she was made for a while, and then she got religion of some sort and had to forgive everyone and gave Betty a luncheon. But the joke was that by that time Ruth's father was taking about a million out of Kettleman Hills, and the Felloweses had lost practically everything, so she had the laugh in the end."

"Phil," Jocelyn said seriously, after a time when complete content had kept them silent, "I don't like this atmosphere very much. Where could we go someday—I don't mean this year or any special year, but sometime? A place we could live. If we had children, if we had a garden and apples and cows, and a creek for them to fall into, and barns to hammer in and trees to climb. I like—seasons, Phil. I like to feel that winter's colder than summer, and that in the spring places get green. And here—here it's flowers and asparagus and card games and clothes all the year round. I'd love some white rambling shabby place with a hill on it, and a lot of old sheds for children to explore, and a windmill. I'd like to fuss with curtains, and cut a door through, and perhaps just have a nice colored couple, to start with, who'd talk to us while they were putting the food on the table. That isn't your way, Phil, I know that! But even after a few weeks of living here I get so—so dry inside."

"What makes you think that isn't my way?"

"Well—I think of New York clubs and first nights as your way, and a valet and the biggest suite and the slickest black car and the craziest tips to the waiter—and champagne——"

"Jocelyn," he said, as she paused, "there isn't a man alive

who wouldn't like to live the way you're describing, if he could afford it. There isn't a man alive who wouldn't like the branch of a river, and trees, and salmon hopping, and children and dogs streaming out to meet him. A couple of fishing rigs and my thirty-eight and a mountain to climb—nothing but dirty old cords and pull-over sweaters; a new kid to spoil every two or three years—my God, it sounds like heaven!"

"Oh, but then, Phil," she twisted about to show him shining eyes in the moonlight, "would you? Could we? I mean someday——"

"Honey, all next autumn after we get back we'll take week ends off and cruise around in the Lake country. And when we get the place it's going to be big. A couple of thousand acres for about that many dollars; that's what you can get if you go to the northern part of the state."

"Oh, but Phil, if people *can* do it, why don't they do it?"

"Because they like this, darling. Why, how many girls who've been stenographers in law offices wouldn't just jump at the country club and the damn messy lunches, and the eternal talk of clothes and engagement presents and all the rest of the gossip! Ninety-nine girls out of a hundred would be all for streaking it to New York, to have Metzstein design them some dresses and pick up a necklace at Tiffany's, and come back to put all the others' eyes out. Jocelyn, I knew I loved you before this," Philip said seriously, "but if I could dream that someday we'd have a place like that, and you'd be content in it, by the Lord, I'd start in loving you all over again!"

"Books, you know, Phil, loads of books, and Chinese coolie clothes, and all the girls and darling Uncle Bart too coming up with their children for holidays."

"And your Aunt Nell, too. I like her."

"Oh, she'd be up there with a grocery list before we'd got the title cleared! We'd have a big guest cabin just for them, Phil. And we'd have to order things on a tremendous scale, have a regular grocery store for emergencies."

"We'll get a place with a lake on it. Lake Jocelyn."

"Philip, we couldn't!"

"Well, I say we could, and I'm master in my own house, and I'll thank you to remember it. Jocelyn, this world would be full of families living like that, enjoying every minute, hauling wood in, looking up to see if it's going to snow, fishing for trout, if it wasn't for the women! Women have got to have clubs and movies and dressmakers and all the rest of it."

"Not all women!"

"Not all women."

"And then you know, in the winter, Phil, if it gets too cold, we can always come down here for a few weeks for the dentist, and for shows and seeing people. And to buy curry and chutney and things we couldn't get up there," Jocelyn concluded sensibly.

"I adore you," he said. "I simply and completely adore you. How'd I find you? What are you made of? Will you be glad to climb into the car with me just a week from Saturday and start off into matrimony?"

"A week from Saturday." Jocelyn was silent for a moment; her hands tight in his, his cheek resting against her temple. "I'm going to be an awfully good wife to you, Phil," she said presently. "I know all brides say that. But I mean that in spite of all the catty things I say about all this crowd, they've had the effect on me of making me want to be better. Can you understand that? They've made me feel that I don't want to drink cocktails before lunch, or lounge around smoking and gossiping and telling dirty stories, like Nita, or swearing like Olive. Olive says things when she's playing bridge that make even the men wince."

"You're telling me?" Philip murmured with a laugh.

"But even myself—the person I was a year ago, I despise *her!*" Jocelyn said confusedly, but with feeling. "It seemed to me then—I knew better, of course, for Mother was always lecturing me about girls in offices. But it seemed to me not so terrible—nothing so much out of the way—to fall in love with a married man, and go to lunches with him, and talk about how happy we'd be if his wife wasn't in the picture. And that," Jocelyn finished in a small, ashamed voice, "seems horrible to me now."

"People don't think much of that these days," Philip said. "When Tom Houston came down in his plane about a year ago everyone said 'Poor Kate!'"

"Why shouldn't they say 'Poor Kate?'" she demanded, twisting about to see his eyes.

"Because his wife's name happens to be Edna."

"Oh, Phil!" Jocelyn said with a shocked laugh. "D'you suppose," she resumed after a minute, "we'd all feel different if we'd been brought up in a strictly religious atmosphere? We never went to church at all, Mother and I."

"It doesn't always do it. Look at the—well, I could name you a dozen fellows who have died of drink and who haven't been any too careful about women either, who came of very strict families."

"Aunt Nell is very strict about church."

"Score one for church, then."

"You mean score one for Aunt Nell."

"I mean score one for church. We went to Sunday school, when we were kids," Philip mused, "and Norma was supposed to get a religious education. But it doesn't seem to take."

"Aunt Nell feels quite badly about my marrying a divorced man, Phil. I don't know what she would have felt if she'd ever known of the affair with Kent. But as it is, with Janet married since, it seems to me to—well, to take off the curse. And only a year ago," Jocelyn remembered, "I was quite complacently considering a woman's divorcing her husband so that he could marry me. But now that all seems as if it were another woman. You know, when you're in an office building where you see a man every day, you do somehow get to think that he's a superman. He's different and you're different from everyone else. You have so much in common. Every few minutes you can steal to be together seem so precious. And then, when it's over," she concluded, with a rueful little laugh, "and when he suddenly comes down with a bump to the level of other men, you do feel such a fool!"

"And then suppose you're married to him?"

"But those affairs don't end in marriage, Phil. They end with the man getting tired, nine times out of ten. I've seen other girls go through it, and cry in their lunch hours, but I never thought I would. I wish it weren't on my record. I wish I could wipe it all out."

"You haven't very much to want wiped out, my dear."

"I have that. And I have the worry of his being around— he's working in San Francisco again, and wanting a divorce and not able to get it, and wanting me and not able to get me, and wanting to succeed in his work and getting nowhere. And it all seems such a pity!"

"You've seen him again, then?"

"No. But I met Covington Keble, the man who has the little studio over in Piedmont, and he told me he was worried about Kent. And I feel so helpless about it, Phil. One can't help one's feelings changing! When it's all over it's so labored—so heavy to try to revive it. Not that I tried to do that when I saw Kent, but that I tried to remember it. And even then I couldn't! Covey wanted me to come over to Piedmont for supper and a talk with him and Kent, and how could I? I knew our engagement was going to be announced in a day or two, so I told him about it. I said to tell Kent. It seemed the only honest thing to do."

"I think that was wise," Phil said.

"I'll be glad when everyone knows. Covey seemed completely stupefied. He said that he thought of *course* I still cared for Kent, and that sooner or later his wife would have to give in. And I had to say that I had never cared for Kent, that it was all a mistake and had been over for months. I said that I had never loved him as I did you and that you and

I were actually to be married in a week. He took it like a blow—oh, the whole thing's so stupid, and it's all my fault!" Jocelyn broke off to say wearily. "Do other women have such miserable, uncomfortable times with old love affairs, do you suppose? What is it, Phil?"

He had tipped his head backward toward the dark bulk of the house behind them, as if listening.

"I thought it might be Mother," he said. "You didn't hear anything, Jocelyn?"

"I did, but I thought it was someone emptying the ash trays."

Jocelyn twisted about to look toward the dimly lighted drawing-room door, and saw a man's figure silhouetted black against the faint glow of the lamps inside. Her heart rose into her mouth with sheer instinctive terror, and she muttered to Philip, as she got to her feet,

"It *is* someone, Phil. Someone to see you."

They both were walking toward the figure now; it stood perfectly still. There was something fearful; something ominous in its immobility, its watchful silence.

"Hello!" Philip began, curious and friendly.

"Hello," the man said in a dead voice. And Jocelyn saw that it was Kent.

CHAPTER XXV

His APPEARANCE, unannounced, in this sinister fashion, robbed Jocelyn of the power of speech, and she walked into the house with the two men conscious only of fear. No possible good could come of this night visit from this pale angry specter of a man, and so much harm could come! He couldn't do anything to change her plans or Philip's, but he might give them both a bad hour; he might make her seem less desirable to Philip. He wasn't reasonable; she had seen that in their two interviews a month earlier. She had begged him then to go back to Portland, to be reconciled to his wife, to make the best of that life he had once told her was his choice. The reasonable life, the secure one, the one that meant no strain and no change for them all. Lilian was dying to forgive him, Red and Una Booth had told her that; Lilian only wanted things to be as they once had been. Why, by all that was contrary, should he begin to suffer from love of Jocelyn, suffer so deeply, just as all her suffering had so mysteriously ended?

"Hello, Dunham," Philip said. "Let's have a little more light in here. That's right, sit there. How's it happen no one let us know that you were here?"

"I didn't come to the front door. I was walking around the house," Kent explained, "and I heard your voices out here on the terrace. I sat on the steps awhile, then I walked up the other steps and went into the room and waited there a few minutes."

He looked pale and unkempt, and Jocelyn knew that he had been drinking. She took a chair opposite him at the hearth, and smiled nervously at him. Philip, with his pipe in his hand, stood between them.

"Cool enough for a fire? I should think so. And what'll you have? Want anything, Jocelyn? Nothing, eh? And you'll have a—a Scotch and soda, good. I've rung; he'll be here immediately. . . . A Scotch and soda, Lorenz, and I'll have just a glass of plain water. Nothing for Miss Britton. Well," Philip said, straightening up after touching a match to the fire, "what brings you down our way?"

"I heard the news. I suppose it's true," Kent said. The old voice, the voice that once had so thrilled Jocelyn. She only felt intensely sorry for him, and sorry for her share in making him unhappy.

"The news is true." Philip said it simply, but he could not keep the satisfaction out of his voice, and the other man's look of resentment and tension deepened. Philip, who was again busy with his pipe, and was looking into the fire, seemed unconscious of it.

Tension. That was the word Jocelyn had been trying to find. Kent was trembling with suppressed emotion; his thin hands shook; his voice shook; his lips were shaking.

"I congratulate you both," he said.

"You're the first," Jocelyn told him. "We've told nobody, not even Philip's mother. But tomorrow everyone will know."

"And then it will be very soon?" he asked steadily.

"Very soon." Philip took his pipe out of his mouth to speak, put it back again.

"What would you call very soon?"

The faintest indication of a negative movement of the head from Philip warned Jocelyn, and she answered vaguely:

"Well, we aren't sure."

"I had a letter from Lilian today," Kent said. "I am going back to Portland tomorrow."

"Oh, I'm glad." She dared not let her tone express how

glad. He was going away! The sky was clearing. "Lilian's family is there, isn't it?"

They were making talk; it was heavy going.

"Weren't you going to let me know that you were going to be married, Jocelyn?"

"You would have known if you read the papers on Saturday. But it's all been very sudden."

Kent looked down at his hands, the artist's sensitive thin hands, and cracked his knuckles as he said in a low voice, as if to himself:

"It's all very different from what I hoped. You know what I hoped, of course, Mr Fordyce. Last fall, after Jocelyn left the office, I remember talking to you. I can't believe that she's changed to me so completely. It's awful, I suppose, saying this before you, but she'll not deny that we—we had planned it all very differently. I was to ask my wife to set me free. Jocelyn knew that. She—you must forgive me, I was at a business luncheon today and we were at the table until four, and my head feels muddled—but there was an understanding between us——"

"Ah, Kent, Kent!" Jocelyn interrupted the painful, difficult flow of words. "Don't talk that way. We were friends, we made each other very happy for a little while. But last fall—you must remember this—you came into my office to say that it ought to stop. That it was distressing Lilian, that you were going away. Lilian had been miserable about it, Kent, and I was unhappy then, and now you are! We've all had a turn. Can't you believe that there was nothing in that affair that would prevent me from finding another man that I loved, and that I wanted to marry?"

She leaned forward as she spoke, the firelight and lamplight touching her aureole of hair, deepening the beauty of her shadowed eyes. Philip watched her; he did not speak.

"Hadn't I—hadn't I first right?" Kent asked hoarsely.

"You had no right. When a thing like that is over, Kent, it's over. There isn't any talk of rights. What—listen, Kent.

What do you want me to do? How can I say I love you when I don't? You wouldn't want me to give up the happiness of my life just because you and I, a few years ago, thought we were in love with each other?"

"We *were* in love with each other. Jocelyn, I don't ask you to give up anything. Just to wait. To give me another chance. Those days when we used to meet—to talk together at lunch —I've never known any happiness like them. I thought I could give it up. I thought we'd worn it out. I knew I'd never have you until Lilian freed me, and she said she never would. I know I'm talking like a fool——"

He broke off suddenly; covered his face with his hands. There was a painful silence.

"I'm sorry," Jocelyn said then, feeling the utter inadequacy of the words as she said them.

"I don't blame anyone who wants her," Philip said briefly.

"No, of course not! I'm talking like a fool," Kent said again. "I didn't mean to come down here tonight. But Covey came up to the studio about five o'clock, and we talked—I guess we talked until nearly nine. He kept trying to make me stop talking, and I kept sending downstairs for whisky and telling him—well, that's all of that."

He got to his feet and held out his hand to Jocelyn, who stood facing him, infinite distress in her eyes.

"Good-by," he said. "Good luck to you both! Anyone who gets her gets all the luck there ever was in the world."

"Write me how things go," she said, holding his hands.

He kissed her suddenly, lightly.

"I will." Philip walked with him to the door, and Jocelyn heard one of the men servants speak in the hall. Immediately Philip came back, to put an arm about Jocelyn, who was standing with her arm stretched along the low mantel and her head down on her arm.

"Gone," Philip said. "Stop trembling and pull yourself to-gether and forget him. He's lit up, for one thing, and he's the emotional sort that gets a kick out of a scene like that. He'd no business to come, and if he comes again he'll get shown out."

She took her arm down and raised her head, smiling gailantly at him, but still unable to speak.

"I don't wonder it breaks you up, darling," he said. "He looks like a ghost, and he certainly gave me a turn, too, standing there in that doorway. Want some Scotch?"

"I want nothing but your arms around me, Phil."

"That's right, keep your head down. That's the last we'll see of him. Lorenz looked outraged. 'I don't know how he got in, sir,' he said, when Dunham had gone. — My God, stand back there, Jocelyn, get out of the way!"

The sound that is like no other in the world sliced through the air. Jocelyn turned toward the door, saw the crazed reeling figure there, felt her knees buckle and her mouth taste brass. Philip shouted and sprang toward the doorway. She heard him call:

"Get upstairs!"

But the sickening swift change from safety to mortal danger robbed Jocelyn of all power of any action. The bullet rang against the lamp just behind her; there was a crashing of broken glass that died away; the sharp quick report of another bullet, somewhere outside on the terrace, followed it.

Then there was an awful silence. She and Philip, panting, faced each other in a room that had suddenly grown hostile, menacing. The quietly burning fire, the chairs and books and tables were full of horror.

"What—what——?" she whispered. She was in Philip's arms.

"You're all right?" he kept saying. Maids were heard crying out as they flew downstairs; Lorenz rushed in from the hall.

"He crashed the lamp, sir. He crashed the lamp," Lorenz said over and over. Philip put Jocelyn quickly aside and went out to the terrace, the butler somewhat hesitatingly following him. The room settled down to be itself again; Jocelyn leaned against big, comforting Agnes.

"What happened? Was he trying to kill Mr Fordyce? What happened? Was he trying to kill Mr Fordyce?" Agnes intoned.

"I was turning down the beds——" the other maid said. "Annette and me was turning down the beds."

Philip was back; he stood beside Jocelyn, gripping her hand. She had felt the bullet whiz close to her hair; she knew for whom it had been intended. But that hold on her icy fingers told her to keep still; she leaned against Philip, weak and dizzy.

"He wanted a loan. He was out of his head, I think. He'd been drinking," Philip said briefly. "Lorenz, get the police station. Jocelyn, you'd better go upstairs. You'll go with her, Agnes? I don't want my mother to hear of this until I tell her; remember, all of you!"

"Phil, is he there?" Jocelyn nodded her head toward the terrace.

"He's there," Philip said grimly. "But he won't bother us any more. That second bullet went through his head, poor fellow. He's dead."

CHAPTER XXVI

Morning came with the stilly silence and beauty of late springtime, and Jocelyn, who had not slept until the light was trembling in opal beauty on her walls, awakened late to a sense of peace and restoredness.

But immediately the events of yesterday began to form themselves again in her memory. Again she and Philip were sharing that exquisite hour of confidence and planning in the moonlight, again they had both turned at the sound of someone moving about in the drawing room and had seen it to be a man, that dreadful figure of a man silhouetted against the warm lights of the house. Kent, trembling with despair and drink and self-pity and the sense of having been bitterly wronged.

Jocelyn began to tremble again with fear and a sort of heartsickness. He had had a pistol in his pocket all the time they had been talking; at any moment he might have leveled it at Philip, killed Philip too before killing himself. He had crept about to the terrace after leaving the house, and had perhaps been a witness to her talk with Philip, had seen Philip's arms about her and her head on Philip's shoulder. Indeed, he had been near enough to hear their very words. The fearful nearness of a much greater calamity had blotted out the tragedy that had been concluded with his life.

She had not seen Philip after that. She had come hurriedly upstairs with Agnes, to stand at her window and watch the big police ambulance come in, and hear the deep voices if not

the words of the men who got out of it. Philip had come
out into the moonlight, bareheaded, to stand there talking in
low tones, and then they had come into the house, presently
to emerge carrying the covered form that had once been all
the brilliance and ambition and eagerness of Kent.

After the ambulance lumbered away, Philip and Lorenz
had gone out toward the garages, and Lorenz had evidently
gone with him to the police station, perhaps to testify as to his
letting Kent out of the house at a few minutes after ten last
night, or perhaps to drive Philip if Philip felt too shaky.

And then there had come a long silence. The big house
had been still with an unearthly stillness. Jocelyn had gotten
herself into sleeping wear, had laid an enveloping wrapper
and slippers near to be ready to go out into the hall for a few
whispered words with Philip when he returned. Hour after
hour she had watched at the dark window, but he had not
come, and now, with awakening consciousness, awakening
fear came, too. Had they arrested him? Had something gone
wrong?

She did not ring for her breakfast, but at eleven o'clock
left her room and timidly explored the upper floor. Maids
were busy with dusters and vacuum cleaner in Philip's big
room, doors and windows wide open and sunshine streaming
through; Norma's rooms were of course deserted and closed;
Mrs Fordyce's room was in its usual perfect order, with
Annette, obviously dying of curiosity but too proud to question, matching gloves that had just returned from the cleaner
at the table.

Jocelyn went on downstairs. She felt that she would go
mad if there were no word from Philip, but all the big rooms
seemed empty, and she could not bring herself to go anywhere near the terrace upon which last night's hideous drama
had been enacted.

She was going on to the small dining room, hoping to find
there some maid or man who would get her some breakfast,
when the silence was suddenly broken by that burst of words

that end any keenly contested and trickily played bridge hand.

"Yah! Take that and like it!" said Mrs Fordyce's voice triumphantly.

"I will be damned!" a lazy, pleasant man's voice responded in a tone of amazed defeat. Jocelyn could not believe her ears, but it was Philip's voice.

A confused chorus followed.

"Bert, you didn't make it! My wonder woman! Doubled and redoubled. I don't believe it! Lend me something to cut my throat! . . . Don't talk of any more suicides right here, dear. Remember where you are. . . . Partner, when I saw that nine of diamonds I knew we were saved. What a hand! What on earth did you double on, Nita? . . . That wasn't enough, honey. . . . Yes, but you'd told me about your clubs. I wouldn't play that hand again for the Hope diamond! When I saw that nine . . ."

Jocelyn, stupefied, went to that same door in which Kent had first appeared last night, that same door through which a bullet had whizzed close to her head, and wondered whether she had dreamed the whole horrible experience. A card table had been set in the rich soft green shadow of the terrace, and around were grouped Mrs Fordyce, Philip, Nita Royce, and a man she did not know. Beyond them, in a blaze of glorious color, the gardens descended, where lawn sprinklers were placidly whirling and gardeners were bending over the blooming borders. The terrace had been thoroughly washed, she noted automatically, the tiles in the deepest shade were still damp.

Philip was the first to see her, and jumped to his feet smiling.

"Jocelyn! Get a good sleep? Come over here and meet Sir Tommy Watts. Tommy, Miss Britton. Tommy arrived yesterday, Jocelyn, and the Carters couldn't put him up because they're all torn up putting some boiserie my mother stuck them with, and so Mother brought him home here."

"Hollywood papers please copy and all that," said Tommy, with his eyes upon Jocelyn.

"No, she belongs here," Philip said laughing. "And—I don't know that I've three friends I'd rather tell first," he added, as Jocelyn, her hand still in his, sat down beside him on a long bench, "she intends to take this whole place in hand sometime pretty soon. Mother's to stop drinking and smoking; Norma's to come home——"

"Oh, really?" Nita said rather faintly, in her most sophisticated tone. "I didn't know."

Tommy came over for laughing and affectionate good wishes. Mrs Fordyce said that she had known for weeks what was going on, and was perfectly delighted.

"Phil's much too nice to have every woman who asks him to supper put it in the paper the next day that they're engaged," she said.

"The papers say what they please," said Nita, who for some reason had turned red.

"Come over here and kiss me, Jocelyn," said Philip's mother. "Now you'll have that girl to raise and I wish you joy of her. Adore her, but she's as wild as a coyote. I suppose you heard the goings-on here last night, Miss Brit—— Jocelyn? Crackpot who works in the same building as Phil's office comes in to borrow money and when he can't get it shoots himself. He knocked a lamp down, too, but I never could bear that lamp. Connie Carter gave it to me, and while I simply adore Connie—— Yes, walks in on Phil with a gun. Mercy he didn't kill Phil. I got home about—when was it, Tommy? Three? Anyway, Phil was just back. He had to go to a court or jail or something. Oh no, that was the poker game, wasn't it?"

She gathered the cards in groomed, ringed hands; shuffled.

"I think it's yours, Tommy. The worst of suicides is," said Mrs Fordyce, "you can't arrest 'em. It's all over. Oh, you were down here, weren't you, Jocelyn? Your deal, Tommy. Agnes told me she went upstairs with you."

"Jocelyn was out on the terrace; we'd just said good night," Philip explained. "I'd promised to go over to Larry's for a ten-o'clock poker game. Poor Dunham didn't come to the door; Lorenz was right there. He walked up the far end of the terrace here and went in. I found him there and we talked, and Jocelyn had just come in when the shooting started."

"He must have been a good shot to miss you at that range," Nita said idly. She had been studying Jocelyn with half-closed insolent eyes all through the preceding talk, her mouth curved into a half-smile. The effect was to make Jocelyn feel that she had no clothes on.

"He was crazy, of course. If I play another, Mother," Philip said, "I'll be late. I'm making a business lunch in town."

"Try to get someone, won't you, Jocelyn?" Mrs Fordyce pleaded. "Try for Mrs Sears. And try at the club for Mr Randall—his father's funeral was at nine this morning; he may be back."

Philip followed her in to the telephone; Jocelyn squared him about in the hall.

"Philip, what happened! I waited and waited, watching for you to get back. I was so afraid something had gone wrong."

"What would go wrong?" he asked, genuinely surprised. "I was only over there fifteen minutes, then I went on to the Bickfords'."

"Oh, Philip, you didn't! You couldn't have played poker!"

"I did. Lucky, too. Sweetheart, I've got to go back. You try for Mrs Sears, or anyone she suggests. I promised my mother I'd play until someone else arrived. Now, darling," Philip said soothingly, "the easier you take these things the easier everyone else does. For a few days men will say to me, 'Nasty business, that maniac killing himself on your place,' and I'll say, 'I wish I'd let the poor devil have the few hundred he wanted.'"

"But the papers will get it, Phil! How can you possibly keep it out of the papers?"

"The papers have got it, dear, all over the front pages. But what they've got is nothing, and your name isn't mentioned. And by tomorrow it's old news and they wouldn't touch it with a ten-foot pole."

"Phil," she said gratefully, "you're so wonderful! You're the most wonderful person I ever knew. If you knew the night I had, and then to come out and see you all playing bridge on the very spot where poor Kent——" She stopped on a shudder.

"I wish I'd known you were awake. I looked up at your window, but it was dark. Don't worry about it, Jocelyn. A person who will commit suicide for one thing will commit it for another. It's the best thing all around. He wasn't happy, and I don't know that he ever would have been, and now he won't worry you again."

"What did you do with—with him?"

"I didn't do anything. They took him to the police station, identified him and his gun, and will ship the body to Portland today. Lorenz testified at the coroner's inquiry—there was an inquest at eight this morning—that he had walked in without being announced, and at his office I believe they said that he had been worried over business and was in a nervous condition."

"And that's—that's *all?*"

"That's all. Except that our announcements went to the papers this morning."

"Phil, you didn't send them!"

"Of course I sent them. So you'll have plenty to do in no time at all. Telegrams and letters and presents."

"I want to go back to my aunt today. I've little enough time, and we'll have to concentrate not only on my wedding but on Tots's, too. Things go on just the same."

"I'll take you over tomorrow. Certainly, things go on. Now I'll go back and double three hearts again. You try for Mrs Sears."

Jocelyn obediently went to the telephone.

"Wasn't that an awful thing that happened there last night?" demanded Mrs Sears, cheerfully, after enthusiastically accepting the invitation to come and play cards with Sir Tommy.

"Terrible," Jocelyn said perfunctorily, already feeling that it was little more than an awkward accident. There was something in this atmosphere that made everything seem about equally important or unimportant.

"Were you there?"

"Yes, I was here."

"Well, it must have been too thrilling!" Mrs Sears hung up the telephone, and Jocelyn went out to watch the bridge.

"Kent is dead," she said to herself, as the brisk play and shuffle and play went on. "How can she bid five diamonds on that hand? Kent is dead. How lovely and cool it is here on the terrace, even on a day like this!"

Didn't they really feel anything at all? she wondered. Did their way of life really smother all human emotion, great pain and great joy, sorrow and pleasure, quite beyond feeling? A man had lain warm and limp on these very tiles last night, panting out his life blood, and now the basket chairs were in place and the awnings lowered; oak shadows made gracious patterns on the wide flags, and the shallow steps, descending to long lawns, were lined with pots of blooming flowers.

And if wealth and amusement and the feverish filling of every hour with games or clothes or love affairs or food did dull them to human feeling, then was it a good thing? Jocelyn sat watching, drifted away into far thought, came back again

"Awf'ly nice, your marrying Philip," said Mrs Sears, picking up a hand. "His mother's just told me. Everyone's been after him, of course; but I think you're just the person for him. Two spades, partner."

"I had a French girl kill herself once in this house," Mrs Fordyce said cheerfully, while the cards were making. "Queer silent creature. They said she was in love with the Austrian butler we had helping Lorenz then. He was the only man

we've ever had who could make a Bacardi. Strange. You'd
think it would be so simple. Phil makes 'em."

"Phil makes a divine one," Nita said. "I remember when
that girl killed herself. That's one thing, positively, I'd never
do. You what? You double. I hate you. All right. Content."

The days went by. Jocelyn was at home with her aunt in
Sausalito, busy about Tots's wedding and talking of her own
plans. She was back in San Mateo for a dinner at the Wil-
sons' magnificent place; she and Phil were toasted, and it all
seemed strange and wonderful. She and Philip lunched together every day, and there were tickets, and passports with a
dreadful picture of Philip on them, and a rather slick hard one
of Jocelyn. Their laughter, their delight in their plans and in
each other's company were insatiable. No detail was too
small to fascinate Jocelyn; her smart new cards, her corre-
spondence paper with her three initials so cunningly inter-
woven; her luggage of creamy smooth leather with the tiny
letters "J.B.F." standing out boldly in black.

Did she want a maid? She laughed at the mere idea. Did
she want the Fordyce diamonds picked apart and reset in a
more modern pattern? She didn't want them at all, not for
years and years. What could Philip give her that would show
her how badly she was going to be spoiled? Nothing, nothing,
nothing! She was spoiled enough now.

They lingered over luncheon in the big hotels, and women
came up to offer them congratulations, and Phil was in-
cessantly bowing and smiling in every direction. They met
friends in shops, and laughed over china and silver. They
opened boxes filled with Arabian Nights' treasure, creamy
plates ringed with richly colored flowers, crystal from Stock-
holm, plain, beautifully molded silver from Norway, Queen
Anne saltcellars sturdy and fat, in blue glass and silver. It
was a dazzling time.

Gentle Mrs French had asked them to dine with her on
their last night but one. Jocelyn's aunt had claimed the
wedding eve; but she and Philip loved the Frenches, and

Jocelyn went down to "Hill Acres" for the appointed night, taking with her the prettiest of her new evening gowns.

It really seemed as if it might be going to happen now. It really began to seem as if she and Phil might be going to get married. The whole household knew it, and while no changing of proportions or actual redecorating had been done, a beautiful room next to Mrs Fordyce's own had already been selected by Philip for his and his wife's apartment, and Jocelyn was escorted to it on this occasion by Lena, who was all agog with excitement at the turn of affairs.

Such a lovely, old-fashioned room of which to take possession in the slanting sweet sunlight of a June afternoon! Jocelyn felt conscious of a feeling almost like a prayer as she crossed its threshold. The two beds, with their tufted cotton covers and fat taffeta comforters, were large, but they looked small in the big, airy chamber. There were reading lights, and a low chair for dressing, with a white furry rug before it; there was a coal fireplace wonderfully cozy and Victorian in its suggestion of rainy-afternoon comfort; there were six high windows draped in white, and outside two of them was a wide balcony with an awning. "Where my wife can dry her incomparable hair!" said Philip, displaying it.

The bathroom, with deep window seats set in the frames of two more windows, was a good-sized room in itself; beyond was a "den," hideous now in tasseled draperies, an oriental brass lamp whose four sides were set with colored glass; a pipe rack of Indian heads in a row; leather cushions and a big moose's head looking out from a shield-shaped board.

But Jocelyn saw this transformed into a little home study for Philip, and the two almost empty rooms beyond as a nursery someday. For they had decided that "Hill Acres" must be home for a while at least. The senior Mrs Fordyce was rarely at home, and when Norma was there her own luxurious suite was as comfortable for her as any other place could have been. "Hill Acres" was a masterpiece of turrets and bays, cupolas and window boxes, balustrades and mill-work, but it stood for all the elegance and display of a gone generation; it was in itself a little piece of California's history, and Jocelyn had come to love it.

She liked its very clumsiness and outdatedness. People did not build houses like this now. Not one line of the place was modern; the doors were high, carved from dark wood, and the enlarged photograph of Philip that hung over the mantel, Philip at six, with striped stockings, embroidered collar, and fishhook scallop of hair, enchanted her. Her aunt had found for her a picture of herself at about the same age: a pretty little girl in overalls on a fence, with a broken straw hat on a tangle of corn-silk hair, and Philip was having it framed to stand on his dresser.

There was a wide lounging chair in this room, with pillows and a rug waiting; there were bookcases; there was a writing desk in which ten times the papers Jocelyn possessed might be stored away.

"We're going to be happy in this room, Phil," she said, standing at the window and looking down at the drive.

Philip, just behind her, his arm about her, put a kiss on the tip of her ear.

"I'm kind of glad we're staying in the old place. It'll be good for Norma."

"You cabled her?"

"I cabled her today. She should have had our letters, but I thought it was a good idea. We'll have an answer in the morning. Do you want to rest or read or anything?"

"Rest! I can't rest even at night. I'm apparently wound up to the point where I can't run down."

"Then let's ride; it's cooler now. And we'll stop in at the club and see who's there and get home about seven to dress. How's that?"

"Like everything else, it's perfect."

So they walked up to the stables, and Jocelyn was mounted on the gentle bay horse she had ridden several times before, and Philip on his own big cob, and they paced their horses slowly under the trees and in and out of the patches of late sunshine, through the watered gardens, and up toward the more open country, and the oak trees in the hill meadows. Jocelyn rode merely by staying on and holding the reins, but she loved it, and was eager to learn.

"If we ever have that country place, Phil, let's ride all the time!"

"If we ever have it! We're going to find it in the fall. For a few years we'll use it as a country place. Then we'll move in."

They went in the big gates of the country club and rode up past the steps, and two men stopped them and said pleasant things of the approaching event. Water was being flung over the lawns in punctual great sprays of diamonds; the grass was very green, and the white clubhouse seemed to cling to the slope. Even at six o'clock figures were moving far away on the links; there was an air of leisure and beauty and pleasure everywhere, and Jocelyn liked it; she was long to remember this particular late-spring day, lingering so long on the gardens and hills, so sweet with flower scent and the sense that life was good.

Dressing in her big room, loitering over her bath and the arrangement of her hair, had its own charm too, and when at quarter to eight Philip knocked at her door, and she stepped forth in one of the gowns that had been originally intended for the Hawaiian trip, she would have changed places with nobody in the world.

"Jocelyn, you are so beautiful," he said. "There is something so white and pure and gold and creamy about you. Like a lily. Like a pearl."

"Anybody," she said demurely, "in this costume would look nice."

"What is it?"

"It's silk organdy, I think she said. What fun to be going to dinner together!"

"I thought we weren't going to dinners?"

"We aren't, much; we'll have much more fun at home. But now and then we'll do this. You look so stunning, and it's such fun."

"I'm going to be a proud man tonight."

"Unless they ask me to play bridge."

"They won't. Ann French doesn't play bridge; she hates it. And it won't be late; she promised me that. I told her you were going to Sausalito tomorrow early, and naturally she knows that the day before your wedding day is going to be exciting."

Mrs Fordyce was giving a small dinner, with two tables of bridge to follow, that night; and they looked into the dining room when they went downstairs, and Jocelyn, smiling shyly at the guests, thought that she would be real mistress of this home at this time day after tomorrow, and that she would be Philip's wife, and felt her breath come fast. Philip's wife, always to be with him! Even now it didn't seem true.

When they came back into the house at eleven o'clock the bridge game was still going on fiercely and steadily as Jocelyn had known it would be. The evening had been a little triumph for her, and she felt flushed with success, and happy that Philip had not been disappointed in her. They did not disturb the card players; they stood smiling and talking in one of the smaller drawing rooms for a few minutes, and then Philip put his arms about her and kissed her good night, and Jocelyn went upstairs, absolutely wearied with felicity.

"All right," he said, at the foot of the stairs, "tonight and tomorrow night you can shut your door on me, and after that I'll have something to say."

"It's day after tomorrow now, Phil. It's gone so fast!"

"It hasn't gone any too fast. Well, good night, my darling. Eight-o'clock breakfast tomorrow."

"Lena's to call me." She trailed her gauzy robes upstairs, smiled down at him from the landing, and disappeared.

Her room was in order, peacefully awaiting its occupant

for the night. The reading lamp was lighted; the bedcovers invitingly turned down; her nightdress was laid with her wrapper and slippers on a chair beside the bed.

Jocelyn went to the middle of the room, and stood there, stretching her arms above her head, watching her own reflection in the long door mirror. Then she laughed softly and went to the open French door that gave upon the wide upper balcony where Philip had said that his wife would dry her hair when she had washed it. His kisses, the touch of his hand, the sense of his protecting love was all around her as she stepped out into the moonlight. The rooftree of this old house was to be her shelter against the world from now on.

But the sight of the lawns below and the treetops all about her made her suddenly think with horror and pity of Kent— Kent not yet a week in his grave—and it was with the memory of him and her last sight of him strong upon her that she turned back to the doorway. And immediately her throat closed on a scream and she felt her whole body turn icy and faint, for the shadow of a human form was against the window casing on the outside, half crouching, one hand spread against the frame.

"Who is it?" she said in a whisper. Instantly the answer came huskily:

"Don't be frightened. It's me. It's Norma!"

CHAPTER XXVII

FOR SEVERAL SECONDS that seemed like hours Jocelyn was still too terrified to understand. She could not see the girl at first because of the darkness close to the house wall, but as Norma came nearer she recognized her, and put out a hand to clutch her and turned her to the light.

"Norma! Dear God, what brings you here now? Where have you come from?"

"Come in," said Norma in a whisper. "Lena or someone came in to turn down your bed and I came out. I've been waiting for you since—oh, about nine, I guess."

"When did you get in? Where's your mother? Norma, what has happened to you!" Jocelyn gasped rather than asked the last question, for they were in the room now, and she could see for the first time that the girl was in a terrible condition. Her hat and light coat and shoes had truly once been handsome, but they were shabby now and draggled; her face was white, she wore no make-up, and her hair hung in disorderly and shaggy locks about her ears.

She laughed without mirth—Norma's old laugh of childish bravado.

"Don't you think I look nice?" she asked. "I got in on the *Celandaria* today. A freighter, but she was bringing some Dutch school teachers and five or six Dutch maids back, and she brought me."

"Norma, you didn't come back alone!"

"Oh yes; I did!"

"But what was your mother thinking of!"

"Not about me, I guess. She has no idea where I am. Nor Sandy either."

"You didn't run away again?"

"I did. I knew one of the Dutch girls; she's been with me as a maid while Mattress was ill. Mattress was ill practically all the time; I wrote you that? Jocelyn, I'm horribly hungry. Do you suppose—— But don't tell Dad! Promise me that, not until we've talked! Then you may if you want to, truly. But not now! Promise me, Jotsy. I'm damn near dead," Norma said, with an ugly little twist of her lip that Jocelyn had never seen before, "and I'll go the whole way if you make me mad!"

"I won't make you mad." Jocelyn laid a cool hand on the child's forehead. "You've no fever," she said, "but you look as if a few days in bed wouldn't hurt you. My poor little girl!"

"C-c-cut the sob stuff," Norma said, with trembling lips, "and give me a cigarette. And could I have some brandy and maybe some eggs? I'm so damn—*tired.*"

Jocelyn went quickly and quietly about the room, extinguishing all the lamps but one.

"Get out of your clothes and into a hot bath, Norma," she said, "and I'll go downstairs and see what I can do. Your grandmother is having a card party, and there ought to be some food. Who saw you come in?"

"Nobody. I walked in. It was dark, and there wasn't a sound. The terrace windows were wide open, but I didn't see them playing cards. I came upstairs and waited."

"Then keep quiet, and I'll be back as soon as I can. That's right; get into the bath. That's the most restful thing you can do."

Jocelyn descended to the brightly lighted hot pantry. Lorenz and one of the underbutlers were there; the big nickel percolator was bubbling with fresh coffee; there were platters of sandwiches and cold meats and cake waiting the bridge players' pleasure.

"I went to a formal dinner tonight, Lorenz," Jocelyn explained, "and of course I'm starving. Could I have—yes, and two of those—and have you a little pot I could take coffee upstairs in? Perfect. Yes; will you carry it up as far as my door? Thanks."

She accompanied the man to her door, thanked him again, slipped inside with the tray. Norma had emerged from the bathroom, fresh and clean, and looking more like herself, with her slender little body enveloped in a great bathrobe, and her damp hair pushed back from her well-soaped face.

She fell ravenously upon the food, and Jocelyn watched her for a few minutes in silence. But she was too anxious to refrain long from questioning.

"Norma, you must tell me, dear. You didn't run away?"

"Oh, but I did. I'd had this Dutch girl with me, and I asked her to hide me on the boat and she did."

"Darling, you're joking!"

"No; I'm not. I went down to the dock and walked on the boat and she put me in the closet until we'd sailed. Nobody bothered me. Only I stayed six days in that room and only got out once except just to the door, and that was when she loaned me her hat and coat one hot night and I walked about the deck a few times," Norma said indifferently, with her mouth full.

"But the stewardesses——!"

"There weren't any. There were only three school teachers and these six Dutch girls; we took care of our own rooms——"

"But your mother—she must be simply beside herself!"

"No; she's not. I told her in a note that I was spending a few days with a girl friend on one of the islands, and she'll not dare move until she hears from me. Mother's much more scared of another Norma Fordyce scandal than I am or you are!"

"Norma, what a mad thing to do! We'll cable her tonight, of course. How did you get off the boat?"

"Walked off. The captain's about a thousand; he didn't see anything. I'd changed clothes with Signa; afterward we changed back. Oh, Jotsy, I'm home! If you knew how I've dreamed of getting back to you and Dad. And *food*——"

"One of the richest girls in the world," Jocelyn thought, seeing the small hand shake as Norma reached for a cigarette, and the glint of tears in her eyes. Poor forlorn little friendless thing!

"I'm so grateful—so grateful to God that you got here!" Jocelyn said aloud. "How'd you know I was here?"

"I didn't. Not until I came upstairs. I was going to hide in my room until I was sure Dad was home, and I saw this door open and your things around. So I came in and looked at everything to make sure, and just then Agnes came across the hall and I went through the window. And then I waited again."

"You had money to get down here?"

"I had a bag with everything in it, clothes and money. But the last minute someone stole it on the wharf, I suppose. I couldn't wait to find it; I was too nervous, so I walked on the *Celandaria* and let it go. So I couldn't write checks for Signa and the other girl that knew, but I will. I'll talk to Dad. Jotsy, when did you move into this room?"

"I'm not really in. But I *am* moving in to 'Hill Acres,' Norma, to stay." Jocelyn, in her evening gown, suddenly felt the color come up upon her bare shoulders and into her cheeks, and laughed with the embarrassment of a child. "Your father and I are being married day after tomorrow," she said.

Norma's face grew as red as her own.

"Oh, Jocelyn, I am very glad," she said quickly and awkwardly. "Dad—Dad must be awfully glad. But I—but I—— Look, I'm messing it all up again!"

"Oh no; you're not, don't be silly! It merely means—we can easily tell people——" Jocelyn's floundering attempts to make light of it, to make it sound merely a pleasurable addition to the plan, fell somewhat flat. She was smitten by a sudden desolating realization that this runaway girl, whose wardrobe and governess had been left behind her, halfway across the southern ocean, would not be exactly a conventional third party on a honeymoon. The vision of Canadian woods, of cool blue mountains and shady great log cabins faded away; the vision of the moving car, and her shoulder against Philip's. Here was the old problem, eternally new, of Norma. With whom could they possibly leave her now?

"Well, the first thing," she began again sensibly, "is to get you rested, and cable your mother and buy you some clothes. But there must be lots of your clothes here in this house, things we didn't send to the rummage when you went away. I'll go in, in a few minutes, and see what I can find in the way of nightgowns and things."

"I want to stay in here with you," said Norma, in her old tone of childish importunance.

"You shall. And when we go on our honeymoon—well, I suppose we'll have to take you along."

"Oh; you were going to Europe?"

"No; not Europe. We were going to Canada. We were going to drive."

"But I always get ill driving, especially if it's hot!"

"I know. I was just thinking——"

"You could leave me with Granny."

"No; she wouldn't like that. You know how she feels about responsibility. She's often out late, and she's moving up to the Rogue anyway next week."

"Well, I won't go to the Rogue. Fishing with the water up to your waist all day. I loathe it! I'd rather go somewhere else. I'd rather go to Europe. Couldn't we all go to Switzerland and take some little place?" Norma urged. Jocelyn was puzzled by her feverish manner. "I'd study, really I would. I'd work like mad at French. Mother couldn't say a word if you were married to Dad. We could get clothes in New York."

"It isn't all as simple as that. Norma, I've got to get your father in here. I don't know how to handle it. We'll see what he thinks."

"I'll ring." Norma, refreshed and fed, was almost herself again now, and was busied with rouges and powders at Jocelyn's dressing table.

"No; don't ring. I'll go. We don't want the servants talking." Jocelyn went to Philip's door. It was immediately opened to her knock. He was in his dressing gown; he had been watching the bridge for a while, he said, and was just going to bed.

"Jocelyn, how cute of you to come call me! What's up?"

"I'll tell you in a minute." She drew him into the hall. "Come into my room," she said. "I don't want anyone to hear! Norma's here."

"Norma!" he echoed in an amazed whisper. "When'd they get back?"

"Come in." They were at her door now; she opened it, and Norma rushed forward and was in his arms.

"My God, you monkey!" Philip said, sitting down with her on his knee. "What d'you mean by this? What is all this? Where's your mother?"

"She and Sandy are back in Honolulu," Norma said. Jocelyn noted with surprise that she had suddenly gone white and drooping; all her mischievous triumph in her escape faded.

"Who'd you come with?"

"A Dutch girl I knew. On a freighter."

"What Dutch girl? A friend?"

"A friend; no," said Norma, with a touch of pride. "She was third pastry cook in the palace at The Hague, and she and these others were friends of the captain, and they were on a trip. And the rest were school teachers who sang and everything."

"And you came with these girls!"

"They didn't know I was on board. We had three little

cabins aft, and I stayed in my cabin, except sometimes for a few minutes at night. Nobody knew but Signa and Frieda, and they wouldn't tell."

"But your passport! Your mother—what was she thinking about? She never wired me. I would have met you! Norma, that was a silly thing to do!"

"Mother doesn't know yet where I am. I left her a note saying I was staying with friends on one of the plantations, and I suppose she's quietly trying to find out which. It's only six days, Dad, and we can cable her tomorrow."

"I'll cable tonight, of course. Where was Sandy when you got away?"

"Asleep. She always takes naps, hot afternoons, before we swim," Norma began wearily. "I was lying on my bed reading, and she was lying on hers, and Mattress was downstairs somewhere talking to one of the French waiters, I suppose. Two of them came from Lyons, too. So I walked out, and first I was going to kill myself, and then I saw this girl on the dock and she said they were sailing on the *Celandaria,* and I asked how soon. She said any time, in about half an hour. So then I offered her a thousand dollars if she'd risk getting me back to America, and she said yes, it was only a week and she thought she could do it because the captain was so old and there wasn't any stewardess. So I went back into my room and put a few things into a bag and went out the tennis-court door, nobody was around, and went down to the dock and stood beside some lumber just looking at the ship as if I was interested, and then when I turned around my bag was gone. But I didn't mind that, I had a little money in my purse, and I knew that when Sandy and Mother and Mattress missed the bag they'd believe I'd gone off visiting somewhere."

"And what did you eat?"

"Oh, there was plenty to eat. The dining room was so hot that the girls didn't eat in there most of the time anyway, and Signa and Frieda would bring me sandwiches and cups of coffee and pineapples. It was too hot to eat, anyway!"

"Norma, why didn't you stop to think before you did a thing like this? If the newspapers get hold of this—I don't think they need, but they may—it would be just one more escapade. Why do you *do* these things, dear?"

"I wanted to get to you, Dad," Norma said, snuggling against him.

"But that's such nonsense, dear. You could have told your mother or you could have written me. Sandy must be wild with anxiety, and it isn't fair to the poor old thing. I don't know," Philip added with a sigh, "exactly what we're going to do now. But we'll arrange it somehow. You knew that Jocelyn and I were getting married on Saturday?"

"I'm so pleased, Dad." Norma seemed subdued and tired; she rested her hand on his shoulder, settled down with an echo of his own sigh. "Everything's all right now," she said. "I'm home."

"But what was this nonsense about committing suicide? Weren't you having a good time? Was somebody unkind to you?"

"Oh no," Norma said, tears suddenly in her eyes. "They were all wonderful. Parties for me and for Mother and for Spazzolari—it was one party after another! Mother never was in bed until broad daylight. I hardly ever saw her."

"But Sandy was fairly decent?"

"Yes; Sandy took me everywhere. At ship dances and beach parties there was Sandy. I hate her. But then," Norma concluded wearily, "she hates me, too."

"Well," said Philip, in a philosophical tone, "you'll be an unexpected guest at your dad's wedding, Spotty. No child can ask fairer than that. And after that I think you'll have to stay quietly with Granny here for a few weeks. We'll get some nice girl to keep you company—— Jocelyn, a bright thought! Would one of those younger cousins of yours come down here to stay with Norma?"

"Bam or Peaches? Why not? It's vacation now. Bam would go out of her senses with joy."

"And I'd trust you, Spotty, not to let us down. Then after we get back we're going to ranch-hunt. We're going to buy a place up in the Sierras——"

Norma had left her father's knee, and was standing, a singularly unimpressive and childish little figure, in the center of the floor. She spoke with sudden painful effort.

"I don't want anyone to know I'm here, Dad. That's why I didn't cable you. That's why I sneaked into Jocelyn's room. I don't want the servants or anyone to know. That—that was why I wanted to kill myself. I've got to hide somewhere— I've got to be out of everything. You see, what Jocelyn and everybody's been telling me ever since I was a little girl is true. Don't you see, I didn't believe you!" she went on impatiently. "I thought—I thought a girl could always stop— stop herself," Norma said, her voice suddenly harsh and bitter, though she did not raise it, her manner that of a child who has been deceived, "and let anyone else know that she —— that it was just fooling——"

She broke off in the middle of a phrase and stood facing them, her expression a study in appeal and fear and defiance. Philip sat staring at her like a man turned to stone; Jocelyn's first quick glance was about the room. All the doors were closed; outside the balcony windows was only the darkness and the night.

"Norma, you don't know what you are saying!" she whispered sharply in the silence.

Philip dropped his head and covered his face with his hands. Jocelyn put her arm about Norma, and they sat down together on the couch.

"Be sensible, dear," Jocelyn said soothingly, "and tell us what you mean. With your mother there, with Sandy right there, nothing could have happened to you!"

"Oh, couldn't it!" Norma demanded, in a voice she tried to make hard and scornful. She was breaking now; she began to breathe fast, and her mouth trembled. "What could that old—that old *idiot* do?"

"Some man was making love to you?" her father asked, in a quiet businesslike tone, looking up.

"Lots of them were!" Norma answered with a toss of her head. "I had two proposals on the boat!" Arrogant, stupid, limited child that she was, Jocelyn thought, she could boast even now.

"I think this is only a scare," Philip said. "Tell me what happened."

"But you can get me away, Dad? I don't want even Granny to know I'm here. Nobody must know! Josty and I," Norma said feverishly, "can go to some German place somewhere, or some school, and stay there! And I could get a wig—a yellow wig, Dad——"

"Be quieter, Norma!" her father said sternly. Jocelyn had never heard that note in his voice before. "We can't do anything or promise anything until we know what this is all about. You're trying to tell me, I think—I hope to God I'm wrong!—that you got mixed up in some love affair down there——"

"Begin at the beginning," Jocelyn said with a dry throat.

"Mother, governess, maid, old friends all on the job," Philip murmured, as if he thought aloud.

"Dad, you see this man was on the boat going down, and he was one of the ones who fell in love at first sight," Norma began. "He is much older than I am, and he was divorced, but that wasn't his fault because his wife was the most beautiful woman in Europe and she is the one who rode a horse right up the big steps of Versailles—remember? He said it was in the papers. And she wanted to marry someone else, so that wasn't his fault, was it? So Mama and I thought he was quite nice, and she danced with him and so did I."

She was launched; no matter what her personal dismay, she loved to tell long stories. This one would have its share of embroidery, Jocelyn reflected.

"Go on," Philip said, his face a mask of pain, of bitter endurance.

"He's a Hungarian prince, Dad; his name is Orgatzyk. His family have been in one castle since——"

"You danced with him, you say?" Phil interrupted harshly.

"Yes. Mama, too. But on the boat Sandy was always there. She slept in my room, and I couldn't even walk around the deck but what Sandy was walking around the other way smiling at us every time we passed. There was a crowd on the boat, Dad," Norma went on, "and we had lots of fun. And then when we got to Honolulu we went out to the Frothinghams', and Juju went too."

"Juju was this man, Spot?"

"Yes. And they had a big beach party, with ukuleles and everything—about a hundred and fifty people, and Juju had been always with Mama; I didn't think he especially liked me; two boys had asked me to marry them, but they were just kids. Juju didn't on the boat. But at this beach party——"

She stopped short. Philip had folded his arms on his chest; he did not move a muscle of his face as he said, "Go on."

"Well, it was horribly hot," Norma said, beginning to sound frightened. "And we sort of wandered along the beach and sat down on the dunes—it was night, you know. And it was so hot! And there was some others with us, and then there was no one there with me but Juju, and it was dark, and he began to say how much he loved me and all that. I'd been lying with my head on his shoulder, Dad, we all had been—and we'd been singing—and the others were right over the dunes on the sand—and I mean—if I had screamed they would have come, or they might—that's what I was afraid of—that they'd think it was just fooling, because you know how everyone screams and calls out at a picnic like that! And that he said that nothing would ever make me less wonderful to him, and that he always would love me—and I walked back and some others were strolling along, and we came to Sandy and I said I was tired and wanted to go home.

"So the next day I saw Juju at the club and we talked and

I said that I would always hate him as nobody ever hated anyone before, and that I hoped the most horrible thing that ever happened to anyone would happen to him! And then I couldn't believe it for a while, Dad, and it all seemed like some horrible thing that I'd dreamed about in the night— and you won't make me marry him, Dad, will you, because I hate him so! You won't, will you, Dad? Because he'll come up here and say we're engaged and everything——"

"You've told Jocelyn and me this," Philip said, after a long silence when she stopped on a sob. "Who else?"

"Nobody. Nobody at all!"

"Then you must forget it, Norma. It *was* all a bad dream," Philip said, his voice sharp, unemotional. "This is a thing that happens sometimes to innocent girls, as well as little fools like you! My poor little old Spot! He took advantage of you; he took the chance that you wouldn't struggle, that you wouldn't put his damned eyes out for him! Well, you'll never see him again. We'll get you straightened out here with clothes; we'll get in touch with your mother; we'll keep you with us now, you'll not be exposed to that sort of guardianship again. A man you shouldn't have been allowed to speak to! A man who knew perfectly well that if he could get you compromised there would be a comfortable income in it for him for life! It's our fault, dear," her father went on. "Sandy's and your mother's and mine, our fault as much as yours."

"He asked me to marry him afterward, Dad; he *did* do that. But I hate him! It makes me sick to have him near me. He's forty! He's nearly as old as you are, Dad. And I didn't tell him. I didn't tell anyone! I wanted to get to you and Jotsy!"

"You didn't tell him *what?*" Philip said, in a tone that frightened Jocelyn. She looked from his face to Norma's, and her heart died within her. There was no answer in words. They did not need them.

CHAPTER XXVIII

AFTER A WHILE Philip said: "What shall we do now, Jocelyn?" and Jocelyn's heart warmed suddenly to new and unexpected pride. He was in trouble and he needed her! Norma had gone to her father and was sitting on the edge of his chair, her arm about his neck, her head resting wearily against him, and suddenly Jocelyn felt that perhaps father and daughter had never been so closely united in spirit as now; she grieved at last to have hurt and shamed him, and he conscious of her need of protection and help.

"We'll think it out, darling," he had said to her. "We'll see you through." And then, to Jocelyn: "What shall we do now?"

"We have time," she said. "We have time to plan."

"Not if we're to be married on Saturday!"

"Well, we could change that."

"But not without letting everyone know that something serious had happened."

"Let me think. First, I suppose, we'll have somehow to explain that Norma ran off on a freighter," she began. "We've got to assume that—oh, I know what we can do! I know—if we could manage—we *can* manage! Listen, Phil. If we could keep it quiet that Norma is here—I suppose the servants would know, anyway——"

"Yep. There's no place she wouldn't be known. No hotel or school where they wouldn't recognize her. What would we gain, anyway?"

"The *Matsonia* gets in Saturday, don't you see? She and her maid would come in on that!"

"Without anyone knowing?"

"Without anyone knowing because she didn't want any publicity."

"But they'd know she ran away."

"To her father's wedding."

"Oh yes, that's right!" he said, his dark face brightening. "She sneaked away and didn't want anyone to know."

"And anyone who was on board, Phil, could only say, 'We never saw her. She and her maid kept absolutely to their rooms.' No newspaper could make anything of that."

"And should we meet her on the dock?"

"Oh, Daddy, you *could!*" Norma said eagerly, tremulously.

"The first time she's ever cared," Jocelyn thought, "what other people were saying about her."

"We could," her father said, hesitatingly.

"We could all three sit in the car, Phil, until th people were coming down the gangplank. Then we could suddenly appear, circling around among them, welcoming Norma. It could be done."

"But where would we tell the servants and Granny—I mean the servants in this house, Jocelyn—that Mattress was?"

"Mattress was ill. You said she's been ill. You brought another maid and let her go."

"But the newspaper men will all be there," Norma said, wincing.

"But what of it? That just gives color to it, Norma. That just lets everyone know that you came home for your father's wedding. We go right from the boat to Sausalito and are married just as we planned."

"That doesn't solve everything," Philip said. "But it saves our faces for the time being. But then—we were leaving for Canada——" he went on uncertainly.

"Suppose Norma comes back here and stays a few days

with her Granny. Then, when your mother goes up to the Rogue, she comes on and joins us."

"Well," he said, considering, approving, his face still dark and stern. "Well. And then what?"

"Then we'll have to plan on from there."

"A nice wedding day, and a nice wedding present, for you!" he muttered. "You're a wonderful woman, Jocelyn. I love this girl, Norma," he said whimsically, sadly, to his daughter.

"I do, too, Dad," Norma said in a whisper.

"But now about hiding her," Jocelyn said. "It can't be here, because the servants will be in and out of these rooms all day, getting them in order for us when we get back. They're moving your desk in, and the books—everything. So—oh, I know! You're taking me to my aunt early tomorrow; take Norma, too. I'll tell them there that she is one of the girls I knew in the office—that's true, for I did meet Norma there, three years ago, and nobody'll ever suspect who she is. They'll all be too much excited to notice anything, and on Saturday we three will come over to town and meet the boat. Do you know anyone in the shipping company who might help us out, Phil?"

"I know Von Haugermann. I know the captain, too. There wouldn't be any trouble about that. But Jocelyn, how about here? If we get my mother and Annette and all the rest of them talking——?"

"Agnes wouldn't talk. And we've not mussed the other bed, she'd not know—or Phil, why not take us both to Sausalito tonight, now? We originally talked of that. I'll slip into Norma's room and find her what clothing I can, and pack a bag, and you drive us yourself. I'll only have to wake Aunt Nell; Uncle Bart sleeps like a dead man, and I'll explain that there was so much to do tomorrow——"

"Be ready in ten minutes, then," he said, on a great sigh of relief. He looked at Norma, and his face clouded again.

"I don't know where we're going," he said, "but we're on our way!"

In Norma's beautiful rooms, where she and her wayward, willful little charge had had so many talks in the beginning of their friendship only a few months ago, Jocelyn found the furniture in slip covers, the mirrors and tables shrouded, the shades drawn. The place looked like something dead, laid out for burial.

But in the closets plenty of Norma's less popular frocks were hanging, flanked by hats of all sorts and lines of shoes. There were smart little bags and cases; in the dressing table were brushes and pots and jars of beautifying creams and powders; and in the chests were cobwebby masses of underwear; frail batiste and satin and crêpe. Jocelyn packed rapidly, opening drawers to take out stockings and handkerchiefs, mentally explaining as she did so, to some curious maid or alarmed butler who might intrude upon her, that these things were to be sent to Miss Norma.

But no one came in, and in fifteen minutes she could rearrange covers and dustcloths as nearly as possible in their original positions and go back to Norma and her father.

They were ready to go; Jocelyn delayed them only long enough to change her gown, and to scribble a note to Philip's mother:

> *Dear Mrs Fordyce, we are making a very early start for Sausalito. I've said everything I can to coax you to our wedding, but if you don't come I'll understand. Jocelyn.*

Then they were off, making the drive in forty minutes, separating with whispers in the shabby hall of the Partridge house, when a sleepy Aunt Nell took charge of them.

Jocelyn explained something of the situation to her aunt; to keep the peace with her grandmother, Norma must seemingly arrive on the *Matsonia* Saturday rather than the *Celandaria* today. Mrs Partridge nodded; Norma should be "Norah Smith" for the time being. It had been Jocelyn's thought that the name of "Norah" would save her if she absently called the girl by her own name.

"Jocelyn, how you help me!" Philip said wearily, kissing her good night in the darkness of the porch just before he went away.

"Phil, if you knew how wonderful it is to be able to!" she whispered back.

Then she went quietly upstairs to join Norma in the shabby bare spare room where she and her cousins had done so much laughing and gossiping in happy times gone by. The old house was filled with the feeling of happiness; it had long been soaked and seasoned with it. Not a girl of the radiant six who had grown up here had ever seen so sordid, so ugly a side of life as the little money princess, the world-famous heiress who was sleeping here tonight. None had known such loneliness as she, such sophistication, such hardness. The girls who had been married from this house had gone to their husbands as women should, honest and sweet and ready to begin the new life in honor and trust and self-respect. Poor little Norma never could do that now, and perhaps the saddest feature of the situation was that she would never know what she had lost; never be able to put any value on the integrity she had thrown away; never be the woman she might have been.

Hot anger against the code that had permitted this seventeen-year-old child to roam along dark tropical beaches in the escort of a calculating, unscrupulous foreigner of more than twice her age, that considered petting, kissing and fondling, cuddling in dark motorcars or sprawling on beaches as just "the way they all do, now," rose in Jocelyn's heart, and she felt, through her love of Philip, a first genuine maternal emotion for Norma, protective and sorrowful.

But she could not think only of Norma tonight. She thought of Philip, and the joy of his needing her, and her whole being was suffused with joy. Philip the magnificent, the always adequate and casual and cheerfully sure of himself, had been crushed tonight, he had not known what to do tonight, and she, the mouse, had been able to come to the lion's aid. The thought soothed away all other disturbing considerations, and warmed her to the soul as she went off to sleep.

CHAPTER XXIX

THERE WAS SUCH UPROAR in the Partridge house on the following morning over the approaching wedding, and over Sissy's well-timed return and over the now certain prospect that Jossy was expecting another baby, that family interests swept over the introduction of Miss Norah Smith like a high tide over a cockleshell. Norma was very quiet, and made no effort to attract attention to herself. She was subdued and pale this morning; wiped breakfast dishes meekly; listened eagerly to the girls' chatter, and now and then, in spite of herself, laughed her deep awkward laugh; the laugh of a girl to whom all this intimate gay sister stuff was new.

"I never saw a girl who knew so little about a kitchen," Jane confided to Jocelyn at one stage of the proceedings. "She's simply darling with the babies, but I suppose she's been in an office since high school, and doesn't know anything about housekeeping."

"She's having an awfully good time," Jocelyn said noncommittally.

"She's pretty, isn't she?"

"Yes, I think Nor—ah's pretty."

Norma went with Bam and Peaches to borrow plates from the Ridgways; she went late in the morning to the Jordans' with Jossy to get more flowers. Jocelyn's aunt had determined that the house should be just as pretty for Jocelyn's wedding as it had been for the three earlier weddings. Tots took a lively interest in the proceedings because her own wedding date was now only a couple of weeks ahead. There was a mammoth layer cake, and there were small cakes; there was to be a toast, of course, even though there would be only a score of them to drink it.

"Jocelyn," Jane said, when they were all upstairs in an enormous bedroom filled with beds and cribs and couches, and when everyone was stretched out resting after the labors of the morning, "does it make the slightest difference to you that Philip Fordyce is so rich?"

Jocelyn's eyes went instinctively to Norma's, and she felt the color in her face as she laughed. But Sissy, only two months married to a man whose income for years must be somewhere in the neighborhood of thirty-five or forty dollars a week, spoke up joyfully:

"Of *course* it makes a difference, doesn't it, Jocelyn? I mean—iceboxes and things, and looking at secondhand stoves, and simply feeling ready to die when a tire goes gently 'whoosh!' and lies down on you!"

They all laughed. Jocelyn saw Norma's eyes fixed on Sissy; Sissy, who was so lovely and so happy and so silly, and but six months older than Norma herself.

"We had about three hundred to furnish our house, but of course we're doing a lot on installments," Sissy said. "He's got that in his mouth, Jane," she said, of her seven-months-old nephew.

"Rusty's mother is sending us a lot of stuff she has had in storage," Tots said. "But I don't know how good it is. If we take a modern apartment we've no room for a sideboard and a dining-room table."

"There's only one thing I hate and loathe about housekeeping," Jossy contributed, stretching an arm from the couch where she lay, to push back into the pen the toys her nineteen-months-old daughter had thrown overboard. "I simply hate to brush up crumbs in the dining room after meals. I'll sweep the kitchen five times a day, that's all right.

But when it comes to trailing around with a dustpan, and then having to dust everything again, I hate it!"

"Use a carpet sweeper, Jossy!"

"I'm unlucky with carpet sweepers; I suppose I'm not bright. But at the last moment they always open, and drool crumbs and fluff all over the floor again."

Norma laughed her deep abrupt laugh. Peaches, fifteen years old, said firmly:

"That's nothing to gathering up the last handful out of the sink. One cherry stone and a piece of wet crust and a cigarette—ugh!"

"No, I'll tell you what I hate," Jossy contributed animatedly. "I hate grease. When Mother cooks chickens for a curry or a pie, the big pot is greasy and its handle is greasy, the strainer is greasy and the ladle and the bowls and my cuffs and the chain to light the electric light and the sink faucets, and it's all one warm greasy mess!"

"I hate onions! I'm never going to have them in my house," Sissy stated. "I've told Ned so. He was darling about it. Jane, don't you really think he's cute? You haven't any idea how cute he is. The trouble with onions is, well," she resumed, "Mother tells me to put a little onion into something. Well, then afterward, I go wash my hands, and look, no matter what soap I use—I used to use your pink dollar soap, Jane, when Charlie used to send it to you when you were engaged; it doesn't make any difference, the onion smell comes gently through!"

"Funny how you'll pick out one thing to hate," Bam, who was sixteen, said thoughtfully. "I hate peeling tomatoes and opening cans. And it seems to me Mother is always asking me to do just those two things. I can't open cans, especially sardine cans. They curl all over, and you have to hook the sardines out with a hairpin."

"Bam!"

"Well, or an ice pick. And Mother," Bam said to Norma aggrievedly, "Mother won't let you pop the tomatoes on a gas jet, you know. Oh no, that makes them watery. You have to peel them, and let them drip all over you."

"I don't mind anything," Tots, thinking of her approaching wedding day and her Rusty, said dreamily, "if I can do it alone. But when you're dressed for company, with your hair done, and you have to go out and just season something, or take it out of the oven, and then dash back to the porch and pretend that it's all going too smoothly—that makes me wild!"

All so young and gay and innocent with their trials and their joys, Jocelyn reflected, and lying in their midst the girl who was youngest of all except the two schoolgirls, and in whose heart so dark a secret rested. She tried to think ahead to tomorrow, and to what it could possibly bring in the way of a solution to Norma's problem. Would she and Philip take the girl with them when they started off in the car at five o'clock?

But she could get no further with that line of thought, for the realization that so soon she would be his, and he hers, drowned out all others, and do what she would her senses swam off into a dreamy space peopled only by their two selves, made miraculous by the fact of their loving each other.

She was to meet him in the city at three o'clock; he had to spend five minutes in court this afternoon, to resign the guardianship of a friend's son after some months of responsibility; then he and Jocelyn would wander off to do a little last-minute shopping, and finally he would bring her back to her aunt's for dinner, and leave at about nine o'clock, not to see her again until her wedding day. On that day custom said that the bride should be invisible until the very hour of the ceremony, but Jocelyn knew that they would have to flout custom for once. They would have to leave her aunt's house with Norma at about eleven; drive to the docks, wait, with the girl hidden in the car until the big ship was in, and then mingle with the crowds on board and on the dock, be photographed, give their story to the press. Philip's friend

had unsuspectingly managed a pass; they could drive close
to the ship; there would be small chance in the general confusion that anyone, seeing Norma there, would suspect her
story that she had been a passenger. Philip had decided to
give his mother a strong hint, this Friday night, that the girl
might be expected. This would have the effect of bringing
Mrs Fordyce to the arrival, and Norma would go home with
her.

"We're safe to leave her with Granny a few days," Philip
had said to Jocelyn sadly, "she's not looking for any more
mischief at the moment."

"Don't take it so hard, Phil." She had never seen him so
anxious, so sobered, before.

"I don't know what one *would* take hard," he answered
briefly.

She had joined him at the office, amused and thrilled because one or two of the girls who had been her associates
there six months ago were ready with congratulations and
eager questions about her marriage. Now she and Philip
were on their way to court. The late-spring streets looked
dry and colorless; a steady, even wall of wind moved grit and
papers along the curbs. But to Jocelyn it was all enchanted.

"I suppose if she is right, Phil—and of course she may
not be—you could persuade this man to marry her?"

"Ouch!" he said. "She need never see him again, of course.
I'm not able to believe it yet," Philip said, shaking his head
as if he shook away some buzzing troublesome insect.
"Spotty! Oh, I knew they were all young fools, and I knew
that one or two of the girls had gone too far—girls of nice
families, too—but somehow I thought she was too smart
for that."

"Cocktails, Phil, and excitement, and music, and this petting that they all do. I don't know," Jocelyn said, walking
along beside him, grave and pretty and concerned, "I don't
know where they expect it to lead! Their songs give them
away."

"Their songs?"

"If you listen to their songs, Phil, you know that they have —ideas. 'I don't want your kisses, baby, if I can't have your love,' and 'I waken in the morn to find my lover gone' and dozens of others like them. Their 'petting' goes a good deal further than—well, doesn't it?—than out-and-out lovemaking used to go. I presume," Jocelyn went on, with a rueful little laugh, "that some of these fair young debutantes know things that decent old grandmothers who had raised families of children never experienced! The theory is now that there's safety in it. But I don't think there's safety in it," she finished simply.

"One wonders why it is," Philip said, "that so often in this life everything would be perfect if we could just go back of one event, with the knowledge we have after it. If I could have kept her from just this experience! God, it seems to me her mother and Sandy might have saved her that!"

"If it is true, what she thinks, Phil, if there is really to be a child, shall you find this man and try to make him marry her?"

"There won't be any question of making him. He'll marry her fast enough! She's put herself and me too that much into his power. That's what he's after. I can see him," Philip said grimly, "discussing settlements. 'It is the custom in my country——'

"No," he began again presently, as Jocelyn walked along in silence at his side, and answered him only with a timid glance, "we aren't the first to have to face this, darling, although it's a little tough to have it come on your wedding day. We'll give the newspapers plenty of room with Norma's marriage to a prince; we'll pay him what he wants, and then we'll kick him out."

"It may be the thing that will make a woman of her, Phil."

"I don't know. There'll be the child for them to quarrel

about. As long as he holds a claim on the child there'll be trouble."

"Phil, I was thinking. If, in the autumn, we had found the place we want, a big ranch with mountains and lakes in it, and if we were building a lodge there, with open fireplaces and a game room full of guns——"

"God, it sounds good!" he said under his breath, as she paused.

"Then why not have Norma and Agnes—Agnes adores her—and perhaps Mattress up there? Let people think that Norma and her governess are traveling, have the baby there, and leave it there with some good woman and her husband who will run the place for us. Let it grow up there, swimming and fishing and riding horses, always keep an eye on it——"

"Yes, and what would we do with the prince meanwhile?" he asked, wearily despairing. "D'you think he'd stand for that? No. What he wants is the Riviera, races and roulette and women and showing off how much he was able to get out of the Americans. If she bucks, if she tells him to go to hell, then he can claim the child. Why, you've seen it over and over, Jocelyn! There are cases that come up in court every few years. The So-and-so guardianship case."

"I was thinking, Phil. Why make them marry?"

"Why——?" He looked at her amazed; stopped short in the street. "Why make them marry?" he repeated stupidly.

"Yes. The mischief's done. The sin—I suppose she never heard that word. But the sin is committed. She hates him, and she has good reason to. How does marriage help them?"

"Well, it—well, it——" he began stammering. "Anyone would say that that was the only way out," he said. "For the child's sake," he added. But uncertainly. A certain light was dawning in his eyes. The light of combat and of hope.

"God knows it is a sad enough mess, Phil. But how does tying her to this beast help it? If she doesn't marry, the child is all hers. There can't be any question of guardianship then. I don't believe a legal ceremony between those two would straighten it out in her mind. I think it would raise all sorts of hateful problems that might wreck her life. Remember that, no matter how reckless she was, this thing was not of her choosing. If Norma had wanted to carry on a love affair like this she wouldn't have chosen that man. And someday, Phil," Jocelyn said, gaining confidence, "she'll marry someone she loves, and she can tell him that before she was eighteen a man she hardly knew—she can tell him everything. And the child will be safe, growing up in the California mountains, and to Norma someday it will all come to be like a dream of youth and recklessness."

"Oh, Jocelyn, you give me hope!" the man said, holding tight to her hand, standing still in the griminess and wind of the afternoon street. "That—that lets him out entirely!" he breathed, in a deep tone of relief. "That saves us all. Nothing can make a relationship like that right; the situation is no worse now than it would be if they were married. We can protect the child; we can—I don't want to see him, and she won't. But we can find him a place——"

"Decide that when the child's here, if there is to be a child," Jocelyn said. "Meanwhile, for months, Norma can live with us here in 'Hill Acres,' and in the fall perhaps we'll travel. We'll say we are going abroad, and come back to our mountains, and take care of her there."

"If someone suspects——?"

"Phil, people aren't going to suspect. And even suspicions aren't dangerous. It may save her," Jocelyn said eagerly, "from some marriage with another titled foreigner. It may be enough of that sort of thing to last her for life! It's a great tragedy, Phil, but you can see from Norma's manner that she's not taking it lightly. She feels humiliated and shamed and shocked—I wouldn't dream that one of these modern girls who think they take life so lightly could be so horrified by reality."

"If you could know what you have done to lift the burden of worry that I've been carrying since last night——!" he began.

"So we get married tomorrow, Phil, and leave her with your mother. And then in about a week she joins us, and we can plan all the details then. And Prince—what's-his-name, Orgatzyk?—is out of it forever."

"I need never see him," Philip said, in deep thankfulness. "What a farce to think that a few words from a justice of the peace could make that wrong right! No, let him go, like the thief in the night that he was."

"And a year from now," she said, "all this will be in the past. And some good country woman will be caring for your grandchild."

"My grandchild!" he repeated, with a shake of his head.

"It seems so unfair to the baby. Norma's child should be such a welcome, such a privileged baby!"

"I know. I know. But at least you've shown me a way out. Jocelyn, I wonder if you know how wonderful you are? Such a clean, straight-thinking, reasonable party. You're going to be the mother to her that she ought to have had long ago, poor kid. We'll get her out of all this, find out what she's like, under all the nonsense and showing off. If we can slip away tomorrow—in a few months find a place to escape to sometimes——"

"Don't forget we're meeting the *Matsonia* tomorrow. That Norma's on board."

"Oh, Lord!" he sighed. But immediately he brightened. "It's too good to be true that about this time tomorrow we'll be saying our 'I wills,' " he said, "and be off into the big tree country—on and on up the coast——"

"Until death do us part!" she said, as they turned in at the courthouse. She was smiling, but there were tears in her eyes.

CHAPTER XXX

THEY HAD DULY CALLED here at the beautiful big domed building for their license to wed, a few days earlier. Today they went to a room upstairs, where there were the enormous desks and ink bottles, revolving leather armchairs and imposing high windows that only government revenues can afford. Philip conferred with a stout elderly justice who never took his eyes from Jocelyn while they talked.

There was to be a delay. Jocelyn, far from familiar with the place or its ways, yet felt sure there would always be delays here. The law moved slowly; it could not be hurried.

"I'm being married tomorrow; I'm leaving for Canada," she heard Philip say.

The dignitary at the desk could hardly have concentrated his admiring gaze more steadily upon Jocelyn, but if possible a more interested light than ever came into his eyes. He summoned a clerk; reached a fat freckled hand for the telephone.

"This is stupid, Jocelyn," Philip said, coming to sit beside her, half turning his back to the room. "My boy won't be here until half past four."

The judge had hung up the telephone.

"If you'll get Judge Troward's signature on that, there won't any trouble," he said helpfully. "We could put it through, then, without you. Isn't he your co-trustee?"

"He wouldn't be in his chambers now." Philip, who had brightened at the suggestion, looked discouraged again.

"He's trying the Scudder case, across the hall here, in his court," the other man said.

"Oh, is that right? Maybe I could catch him at the recess. Ought to have a recess any minute now. What's the case? I've not been following it." Philip was hopeful again.

"Murder case."

"Woman killed her husband?"

"Nope, he killed her. Sick-lookin' little feller that doesn't look as if he could hurt a rat. Why don't you walk in there, Phil, and just send that paper up to the desk? From what I hear, things are draggin' along in there; it won't do any harm."

"I might step in there and wait for the recess. D'you want to wait here, Jocelyn?"

"I couldn't go with you, Phil?"

He laughed.

"Well, of course you could! Ever seen a trial?"

"I don't think I've ever been in a courtroom."

"Well, it might interest you. We could wait for the recess, that 'd give you some idea of what goes on."

"The murderer won't be right there in court, Phil?"

"Certainly he will be."

"Like a play," Jocelyn said, fascinated, "like a movie!"

"It 'll probably be dull," Philip warned her. "The movies and plays only pick the high lights. You'll probably hear a medical expert testifying as to the coagulation of blood, with charts and references. That 'll go on for days."

"Oh, but Phil, I'd love just to see it!" she protested, her eyes bright.

"Well, come along then. Who's prosecuting, Judge?"

"District attorney, Matt himself. Want me to send a man in with you? It's apt to be packed, but I'll get you in the court door."

"Pleading guilty?"

"Pleading not guilty. Says he got out about midnight and was out of town entirely. Says some feller walked in there and bashed her up and he found her that way. But it doesn't look any too good for him."

"They'd quarreled, hadn't they? Isn't that the case where the woman had told her neighbors that her husband was going to kill her someday? Didn't he run away?"

"He beat it. He's a weak, miserable-lookin' little feller," said the judge. "Yes, sure he ran away. They only picked him up about a month ago; he'd changed his name; he was living in Carson City. The boys did a nice piece of work on that. Matt has him for the first degree. They found the clothes, you know. He'd taken a suit with him—he was cool enough for that—and thrown what he was wearing over Dumbarton Bridge. No, maybe 'twas the Golden Gate Bridge. Anyway, they were all blood, and they were identified. They've got 'em in court. It's a pretty straight case, but he's got a good lawyer—he's putting up a fight. Charley," he concluded, addressing a court attendant who had been summoned by his bell, "take Mr Fordyce and Miss—Britton? Thank you—take 'em over to Judge Troward's court, will you, and get 'em chairs?"

Jocelyn and Philip crossed the wide rotunda, and were admitted by the judge's door to a crowded courtroom. Jocelyn had never been in one in her life before, and in a flutter of nervousness, self-consciousness and absorbed interest she found herself seated within the railing, only a few feet away from the raised dais upon which was the judge's long desk. Above him was a portrait of some early Californian judge; above that a great flag hung straight.

His Honor was alone upon the bench; below him, at floor level, was the long table of the lawyers, littered with papers and articles of evidence, and surrounded with coffee-house chairs with comfortable round backs. In these chairs a dozen men were seated; some young, some old, all with papers before them and pencils in hand. Close to the jury box a court stenographer tapped an almost noiseless stenotyper under a velvet cloth. The witness stand was empty at the moment; a passionately earnest young man was asking that a certain small axe, clotted still with dark stains, be thrown out as evidence.

The eyes of the courtroom audience, and the jury's eyes, had focused upon Philip and Jocelyn as they had been escorted in, and even the judge had given them a sharp glance over his spectacles. But now interest in the trial had been resumed, and Jocelyn felt less conspicuous, and could feel some of the satisfaction of the privileged spectator at a scene always thrilling and always packed with an intent audience.

"Phil, when do they bring the prisoner in?" she whispered.

Philip, with a little hint of a smile, jerked his head, and Jocelyn caught an involuntary shallow breath. A man was sitting within five feet of her at the table; a quiet man whose profile she could see when he leaned to speak in whispers to the man next to him, but whose back was fully presented when he sat straight in his chair. Insignificant, with silky brown hair thinning and graying, and anxious thin freckled hands that were nervously knotted before him on the green baize of the table, wearing a cheap jacket, of shoddy brown material, that was the murderer! That was a man who could bash in the head of the sleeping woman he once had loved, and leave her to die while he made away to safety and obscurity in the greatest of the Western cities. How must he feel as here in court they unfolded the details of the drama one by one, reconstructed that terrible morning after a fight, displayed to his dull eyes the very nightgown the unfortunate woman had been wearing, the garments he had worn as he escaped?

On the wall on the jury side of the court was a scroll with a diagram; the poor little rooms in San José Avenue where this tragedy had taken place. Parlor, bedroom, kitchen; dark smudges that were blood trails crossing them; an eight-pointed star drawn where the collapsed form of the woman had been found by neighbors at six o'clock in the morning. She had been living then; she had been able to moan, to

hammer on the wall, but when they had broken their way
in she had not been coherent. Scudder had come in a few
minutes later, and had seized the now dead body in his arms
and cried and made a great scene. But when they had sent
him to telephone from the drugstore for the police, he had
hastily stuffed some clothing into a bag, and had taken—the
daughter had distinctly seen this—some money from a box,
and had gone out, not to return. An hour had gone by, and
then the women had notified other neighbors who had gotten
the police to the scene.

The neighbors were here in court; a stout, comfortable-
looking woman with a drabbled piece of cat fur about her
neck over a figured print gown; a pretty, quick-spoken girl
who remembered perfectly well that it was before Thanksgiving, because her mother had asked her brother to price
a turkey, and they had heard their neighbors upstairs quarreling that evening, and had said it was awful to quarrel
with Thanksgiving so near.

"There are lots of men in this very room that look more
like murderers than he does, Phil."

"There always are. But he's innocent until he's proved
guilty, you know."

"Phil, if they find him guilty will they hang him?"

"I believe Matt Phillips—that's Matt, the red-faced one,
that's the district attorney, says he could hang ten men on
the evidence. This man next to me was just telling me that
to him it looks like a hanging jury. But you never can tell!"

"A hanging jury?" she asked fearfully.

"That's what they say. We have to hope, of course, that
it's an honest jury."

"Oh, Phil, how important that they're honest!" She
looked at the twelve faces. To her they all seemed dull:
stolid, dull men and women. One wouldn't want to ask them
for life, against the evidence of quarrels, blood stains, fight.
"But if he's not guilty," she breathed, as Phil, resting an
arm along the back of her chair, and half twisted about,

brought his face close to hers, "then why would he run away?"

"That's, I suppose, the weakest point in his case," Phil said.

"But I would!" she confessed, and he laughed.

"If he'd come in, Phil, to find her that way, and realized that they'd been heard quarreling——"

"Come in from where? He was at home. The neighbors had heard them."

"Yes, but suppose he'd gone out—he must be trying to prove that he'd gone out, if he says he didn't do it. If he'd gone out, Phil, and walked about, walking off his mad, and then had come back, mightn't he have made off in sheer terror——"

"You're so adorable that I can't wait to walk off myself with you," Phil murmured, his lips close to her forehead. "You've cleared up this whole business of Norma's for me; I see it all now as it's going to be. I don't have to make terms with the skunk who took advantage of her; I can see my way. It's not ideal—it's a terrible thing to have come into her life——"

"Who's that, Phil?"

"That's the doctor they called in. They've just recalled him to confirm something in his evidence yesterday."

"Will they put him on the stand?"

"The prisoner? Probably. They probably have. I've not been following it. Wait a minute; I'll ask."

Philip waylaid one of the attendants who were constantly coming and going; the man went away to question somebody else. He presently returned to murmur that the prisoner was to be recalled by the district attorney as the next witness.

"You're interested?" Philip asked, glancing at her, pleased that she was.

"I'm fascinated. It's so terrible. One reads it in all the detective stories and murder books, but it's so awful when it's real. He wants so horribly to live—to walk out among men again and be interested in what he's going to have for lunch, and here he is, with a man each side of him, trapped, no getting away now from their questions and their locks and keys. Phil, mayn't we stay awhile and hear some more of it?"

"Of course we may! A little of it, anyway. I'll see Judge Troward in the recess."

"The trial won't be over then?"

"Oh no. It'll go on, perhaps for a week. And then, even if he's convicted he'll have a right to appeal, Jocelyn, so don't break your heart over him."

"It *is* breaking my heart!" Jocelyn murmured. She watched with feverish interest the slow processes that decided the prisoner should be called, heard the rustle of excitement sweep the room as he rose, saw the jury settle as the forlorn shabby little man of forty-five or -six mounted to the witness stand.

Sworn. He would tell the truth, so help him God. He sat down under the architect's drawing, close to scale in inches of the flat he and the late Eda Ripper Scudder had once rented for some twenty-two dollars a month, and had perhaps hoped to make a happy home.

"Used to hit your wife sometimes when you got mad, give her a black eye?" said the district attorney.

"She give me plenty of black eyes," Jim said miserably, and the judge was immediately justified in announcing that if there were any more laughter he would order the court cleared.

"You said yesterday," Matt Phillips said truculently, "that you quarreled with your wife at about midnight on that Saturday, that you'd been drinking, and that you lay awake awhile and then went out and got the car and went away. Was that a customary thing for you to do? You did that often, eh? Whenever you got mad?"

"No, sir, that was the only time I ever did it."

"You went to the garage for the car? See anybody there?"

"The garage is right under the house."

"And you didn't see anyone?"

"No, sir."

"Where'd you drive?"

"Round."

"You can't answer a question that way," said the district attorney warmly.

"I don't remember where I went."

"You were drunk?"

"I'd been drinking. No, sir; I wasn't drunk."

"You were so drunk you didn't know where you were going."

"I knew where I was going——"

"What did you say?"

"I said I knew where I was going. I just can't remember now where I went. I know I went across the bay."

"Oh, you know you went across the bay?"

"Poor fellow," Jocelyn thought. "It isn't fair to hound him like that. I don't believe he does remember. How could anyone remember what had happened on some casual night seven months ago?" She loathed the district attorney. Her heart beat with fierce eagerness to have him defeated.

"And the only time you ever walked out of the house and left your wife, and left the door open, some unknown person came in and killed her, eh?" said Phillips mercilessly. "Someone who doesn't wake up the five-year-old boy—who doesn't wake Bruce——?"

It was torture. Jocelyn saw him wince as the boy was mentioned. A five-year-old boy would be a little fellow indeed to leave to the mercy of the world that had sent his father out of it. One could bear death—even shameful death—but parting from an innocent frightened little boy would be something else again. That would be the turn of the screw.

"Well, but then why did he do it?" she asked herself. And instantly the following thought came: "Perhaps he didn't!"

Quite suddenly court adjourned. A gavel rapped; the judge rose and everyone in the room rose; lawyers hurried away;

the crowd drifted out. Philip drew the judge aside, they conferred, bent over papers. The prisoner shuffled off between his jailers; press men, passing near him, gave him curious and fascinated glances. To everyone else it was a show; interesting or boring, but in no way filled with terror. Everyone but Jim Scudder could now think comfortably of dinner, could walk out into the street where men and women were coming and going, free. Jim would fearfully question his lawyer—that cheerful fat young lawyer with the beefy red cheeks.

"Think it's going all right?"

"Yep. I think we're getting somewhere."

"Phil," said Jocelyn, as they drove through a windless clear sunset across the big bridge, "this establishing an alibi is a serious thing, isn't it?"

"Life or death," he agreed. "Look at the sunset, Jocelyn, Lord, what a beautiful night!"

Below them, on the silken waters of the Gate, the fishing fleet was moving out to sea. The little launches looked like a gallant school of fish themselves, heading for the west, lost in the wide expanse of the ocean's mouth. Red sunshine was glowing on the hills of the city behind them, and blazing in windows everywhere; the slopes of Sausalito's hills were already browned to summer color. The spring afternoon smelled of grass and grass fires; they had been burning the hills bare above the fort.

"Tomorrow at this time, darling, we'll be fifty miles upon our way. The Philip Fordyces."

"Jocelyn Fordyce. Beautiful name! Phil, isn't it strange that the men the law catches, the men that are cross-examined and pilloried as this poor white rat is, are the men least fitted for martyrdom! A man of any force of character would face it as just a part of the game. But this poor little meek soul is just crushed under it."

"I imagine it would crush anyone. The awful inflexibility of it. I've thought it a hundred times, in court. The guards are civil to him; he's trapped; they can afford to be nice to him. He wants to get out and mind his own business; he doesn't want women looking at him with pity, and court officers telling him to stand up, to sit down, to put up his right hand."

"He ran away," Jocelyn said thoughtfully. "That's against him. Yet he might do that in cowardice, in terror."

"He might. But we've got enough to think of tonight without him. Your last as Miss Britton. Yes 'm, I have the ring, and I have the fee, and I have flowers ordered for you and Tots, and I'm planning on picking you and Norma up in Sausalito tomorrow morning at half past ten. We'll meet the *Matsonia,* and put on our act, and come back here for—no, I bring you back here, but I don't stay. Your cousin Bam says that it's bad luck for the bridegroom even to see the bride on the wedding day, until the fatal moment, so I'll leave you here, and go over to my club and waste an hour or two."

"It's so silly, Phil, when you consider what we'll be doing all morning! However, you'll probably be just as well off in town as at Aunt Nell's, with everyone all over the place." But her thoughts were still in the courtroom, and presently she said indignantly: "I hate that Matt Phillips! Phil, don't you ever be district attorney. It's an awful job. How could anyone—least of all a brainless little nonenity like Scudder—remember what he was doing on the last Sunday in last November?"

"Ah, but he had good reason, Jocelyn. Remember that his wife was murdered that night. That might fix it in one's memory, I should think."

"Well, I couldn't for the life of me——" They were at her uncle's door now, and they descended into a boiling confusion of girls, into a jumbled welcome of laughter and kisses. Norma was here, too, but quieter, soberer than the rest. Presents had come for Jocelyn, and must be opened. There were telegrams, but those must wait until tomorrow;

there had been two reporters, but they had said they would return tomorrow, too.

Nobody noticed that Jocelyn suddenly had grown pale, and had an odd look in her eyes. Or if anybody did, it was only to think that any demonstration of emotion on her part was natural enough under the circumstances. They could not read her thoughts; she dared hardly face them herself.

Where had she been last November, on the Sunday before Thanksgiving? That had been the day following that desperate and despairing Saturday when she had tried to find Kent, had been twice to the Booths' studio, had followed him to Covey's cabin, up in the Piedmont hills.

But these memories, however unwelcome, were still her own. She could dismiss them. Kent was dead; Philip knew exactly what had happened that night; no one else but herself knew anything at all of the matter.

What chilled her spine with dawning, uneasy apprehension and seemed to stop her heart beating in her breast was the recollection of what had followed on that Saturday night. Kent, who had so hurt her, who had, while they were in the office, put her aside with his rational consideration of their affair, had been willing, that night, to fling all caution to the winds. They loved each other; that was all, he had said, that mattered. They must claim each other openly, courageously, in the eyes of the world, and take whatever followed.

And she had escaped from him, gone out trembling, breathless, to her car, driven away blindly into the black night. She had felt the car slip on a wet bank, bog itself hopelessly; she had curled down on the seat cold and frightened, to get what rest she might until morning. And in the cold dawn she had started walking briskly down the road, with the sun rising behind her, and mud underfoot, and her nervous terrors gradually fading away into the light of common day.

A little man driving a shabby small car had given her a lift. He had spoken of a turkey won in a raffle; he had told her other things; they came back to her now, etched deeply into her consciousness because of her fright and shame that day, her anxiety to leave the whole experience behind her. His wife had been "mad" at him; he had had a son named "Brucie."

Jocelyn looked at the dinner-table circle; Sissy and Ed were laughing, and all the others were in gales of high spirits. Every time Phil's eye caught Jocelyn's look he smiled at her that grave proprietary smile that set all her pulses hammering. Norma had seated herself next to Jocelyn; she was keeping close to her now, showing a trust in the older girl, an affectionate confidence that Jocelyn had found very touching in bold, shallow, arrogant Norma.

Now she could not think of it without despair. She could not think of Philip's love, of his pride, without despair. But neither could she desert Jim Scudder in his hour of need; he had carried her through hers to Philip's very arms. For it had been Jim Scudder who had picked her up in the cold dawn on the muddy, unfamiliar road. She remembered it all now, and her spirit sickened within her.

But how could she, so soon to take her honored place among his friends as Philip Fordyce's wife, tear down the whole structure of her dignity, fatally prejudice all these new neighbors, with this story of an office girl following a married man to a lonely mountain studio, running away from him in the night . . .

A wave of agonized color rushed over her from head to feet. That same married man, whose name must inevitably be brought into the story, had come down to Philip's house, had killed himself there—how long would it take the gossips to put two and two together about that?

Jocelyn could not eat; food choked her. She sat frozen with consternation. Whichever way she looked she could find no comfort, and it seemed to her that all the troubles of her life were nothing to that which faced her on her wedding day.

CHAPTER XXXI

JOCELYN AWAKENED EARLY; she had had trouble in getting to sleep and had slept restlessly; when the lavish spring dawn began to creep in at the casement and light the new green leaves of the maples outside her window, she felt as if she had not rested at all, had not stopped thinking.

It was terrible to have yesterday's tangle present itself to her again; it was terrible to go back in her thoughts to the grimy courtroom, the whispering lawyers, the packed intense crowd, the poor forlorn little man whose life had broken apart into such a flame of horror last Thanksgiving week. He had claimed, ineffectually enough, that upon the discovery of his wife's battered body he had helped the neighbors to do what he might to resuscitate her; he had laid her on their uninviting bed among the rumpled sheets and thin faded blankets, and finally beginning to realize the deadly nature of the evidence against him he had fled. She was then in partial consciousness. Five minutes earlier, before he arrived, she had moaned and somehow managed to hammer on the walls. Then the neighbors had rushed in, but far too late to do anything except witness her last breath.

Everyone except himself and one other believed him guilty. Jocelyn was that other. But what it would cost her today and all the days of her life to say so, she dared not try to estimate. This story would never die. The scandal that Philip's quick explanation had spared her when Kent Dunham had killed himself would be revived; the world would have them lovers, of course, and so Philip would face his new marriage burdened with a daughter in the pitiful strait that Norma found herself, and a wife about whom all tongues were buzzing.

Jocelyn writhed, thinking of it, thinking of the ordeal that she must undergo this morning. When Philip arrived to take her and Norma to town, she had no choice but to take him at once into her council.

"Phil, this is so terrible, dear. But I have to ask you. What time does court open?"

"Jocelyn, is your mind still running on that case? They'll not hang him if he didn't do it, dear!"

"Phil, I ought to be there this morning!"

"You ought to be there? You can't. We've got this landing on our hands. There'll be no court this afternoon."

"No court! Oh, Phil, we're lost!"

Phil looked at her, surprised and puzzled. They were driving to town. Norma had been nervous but quiet over her part of the morning's program; she understood the necessity of appearing to have come in on the *Matsonia,* of facing the ordeal of being interviewed and photographed on the dock.

"Nobody'll question it," her father had said, reassuring her. "Everyone will have too much else to think about. Landing is about the busiest thing these people do, and if anyone doubts you came—why, there you are!"

Norma, satisfied, but far from taking the mischievous pleasure she once would have taken in the situation, had subsided, only to make way for Jocelyn's first troubled outburst.

"Tell me what you mean, Jocelyn," Philip said, affectionately concerned, but not worried. "How are we lost? Can anything else possibly be crowded into today?"

"You see, Phil, he didn't murder his wife," Jocelyn said.

"Didn't!" Phil echoed, convinced from her tone that this was more than mere speculation. "How d'you mean he didn't?"

"Because he was the man that gave me a lift that Sunday, the Sunday you picked me up in Piedmont, remember?"

"Jocelyn, that's sheer nonsense!"

"But it's not. I remember the name now—Scudder. I remember what he told me about his turkey that he'd won. It all came back to me, just as we left court yesterday. I knew I'd seen him before. I couldn't ever have thought where, because he looks like every other poor little defeated soul, but when he talked of Sunday before Thanksgiving I began to think where I had been Sunday before last Thanksgiving, and then it all came to me. He couldn't have done it, Phil. He found her murdered, just as he said. The doctors said it had been done somewhere between five and six, and he was on the other side of the bay then."

"You can't be sure of that," Philip said slowly. She could see that he was deeply disturbed. "You don't want to mix yourself into this, Jocelyn. It wouldn't do any good, and it would—after all, you were over there that night with Dunham, and Dunham killed himself—we'd have people——"

"*You,* Jotsy!" Norma said, aghast.

"You see, there wasn't anyone else there that night," Philip was going on, "and it would start a lot of talk, naturally. They'd tie it up with his coming down to our house and killing himself——"

"But Phil," she said, very white, "if it's his life?"

"It isn't his life. They'll get him off. And it would be damnably unpleasant for you. After all, we're to be married this afternoon; it'd be a little thick to have you mixing up into this mess this morning. Jocelyn, if you hadn't happened to step into that court yesterday, you'd never have known anything about it. It's all very uncertain, anyway. And I think you'll have to trust me that if the poor fellow gets in pretty deep we can take it up with his attorney; Sid Napthaly—I know him. Leave it until we come back, for God's sake!" finished Phil, in one of his rare bursts of nervous irritation, "and then we can do something about it. Let's get married and settle down, and work out Norma's problem, and let people think for a few months that we're like other families! After all, Jocelyn," he added, with his own particularly kindly smile, "it's our wedding day! Let's concentrate on that. I don't want my wife involved in a criminal trial on my wedding day!"

"God knows I don't want to be involved in it," she said despairingly. "Could I write to Mr Napthaly, Phil?"

Philip turned upon her a look of enforced patience.

"Won't you trust me in this, Jocelyn? Haven't I enough on my mind now? You're not sure that was your man, and even if you were it 'd be your unsupported testimony, and you'd have to tear your reputation to shreds to give it. Matt Phillips wouldn't leave you a leg to stand on. 'You were alone with Mr Dunham in the cabin all night? You say you left him about eleven o'clock in a hard rainfall, and spent the night in your car?' "

Jocelyn shriveled under the quiet voice. She found Norma holding her cold fingers tightly.

"Dad, she didn't!" Norma said indignantly.

"I know all about it, I know all about it," said her father impatiently. "Don't meddle with what doesn't concern you. I wish we hadn't gone into Troward's court," he went on; "it's probably all your imagination, Jocelyn. And who can prove, anyway, that you were over in that part of the world that night?"

"You can," she said, her face very red, but her eyes steady. "You picked me up on the station platform when Scudder left me there."

"I don't suppose," Philip said coldly, his own face red, "that you are proposing to drag me into this?"

Jocelyn laid her hand on his arm. They had all three been riding in the roomy front seat of his car; they were at the docks now, and Norma, according to prearranged plan, crawled into the back seat and effaced herself. Philip and Jocelyn got out and began to walk slowly to and fro on the rough plank flooring of the dock. The great *Matsonia* was nosing for her place; her tremendous bulk shut off the sky at the end of the pier. A confusion of catcalls and shouts and whistles started in the quiet foggy air.

"Hello, Phil!" said some man passing him with a wave of the hand. "What you doing here?"

"Meeting my daughter," Phil called back.

"Zat so?" The man went on, and Philip said urgently:

"Jocelyn, don't worry about this. I promise you I'll follow it up later. But don't get us mixed into this now. Think what it means to you, dear. It 'd give Mother and Janet such a hold over you! It wasn't—— I know how innocent it was. But it sounds so badly. They'd have it all out of you. That you'd cared for each other, that you'd followed him there, that you'd gotten scared—as many a girl does—and run away in the night. That your car broke down—don't you see how fishy it all sounds?"

"But it's all *true*, Phil."

"I know it's all true. I know it was the purest coincidence that I happened along and picked you up, and you came to live with us, and Dunham came down there and shot himself. But it's the strangest string of coincidences that ever got together, and all it would do is mark you, and not help him. I'd deny it. I'll not get into it!"

They were making fast the *Matsonia* now, and he was watching them nervously. Stevedores, dock hands, officials went about; water churned among the piles; a gangplank came down. Men and women who had come down to welcome the ship milled in a joyous confusion about the light fence that shut off the passenger lane.

"You'd deny it!"

"I certainly would."

"Philip, if it meant his life!"

"It wouldn't mean his life! Don't get so excited about it, Jocelyn, it's all in the day's work. They'll dig out something else that frees him, you'll see."

"Phil, I don't want to, but I have to!"

"It 'd just about finish Norma."

"Norma?"

"Certainly. My mother has complete trust in you, Janet trusts you, even Sandy has to admit that you've the sort of character that most influences a girl. This pulls that all apart. Forget it, Jocelyn. Maybe we can do something later, get hold of Phillips and explain it to him. But now we've got to pull together on what we planned! Your wedding day, and you in court telling a story like that!—I think it's safe now," he added in an undertone, watching the thickening stream of passengers leaving the ship. "Any minute now we can go up and mix in."

"Philip, I'm so sorry to do anything that makes you angry."

His astonished eyes, flashing to her face, were indeed angry.

"I ask you not to," he said sharply.

"I know. But I'd never forgive myself——"

"Jocelyn, don't count on me to back you in this!"

Her heart was beating hard; she felt a deadly chill in her very vitals.

"You'd have to back me if I had them—whatever they do—call on you as a witness!"

"Listen," said Philip fiercely, "I *ask* you to let this rest for the time being. I *ask* you to! You don't know what you're letting yourself into. We'd all be in it. It might mean postponing our wedding——"

"If it did——?" she whispered, breathing hard; her eyes were steady on his own. "If it meant the end of everything, Phil. If it meant that I'm not going to let you go on and marry me, while you feel this way——"

"It *will* mean that," he said hotly, as she paused, unable to go on. "I've had enough! If you've no trust in me, no respect for my feelings or my mother's——"

They looked at each other for a long minute. Then Philip

turned and went toward the parked car. Norma got out quietly on the sheltered side and joined him, and in another moment they were a part of the confused and noisy crowd; laughing, being greeted, threading their way about among the arrivals, the friends who had come to meet them, customs and dock officials, taxi men, baggage men, waiters carrying trays of coffee, stewardesses and pursers and cabin boys.

Jocelyn, dizzy and shocked, turned the other way, found a taxi, was at the City Hall again. She was too stunned to be conscious of any particular emotion of grief or fear; she went without hesitation to the courtroom and at the door was writing a note to Scudder's lawyer when recess was called, and Napthaly and everyone else streamed out into the halls and chambers. Jocelyn saw the prisoner again, immediately saw Napthaly speaking to two scribbling newspaper men, and spoke to him.

"Mr Napthaly, could I see you on a question of importance?"

"Well, not today. If you'd telephone my office——"

"This has to do with this case today."

"Representing a newspaper?"

"Oh no." They were a little out of the current now, and alone in the crowd. "Will you give me three minutes?" she said.

"Will you tell me your name?"

"Britton. Jocelyn Britton. But I don't think you know my name."

"Aren't you going to marry Phil Fordyce?"

She hesitated over "I was going to," substituted a simple affirmative.

"I think," she said, gulping with a dry throat, "I have an alibi for Scudder. Could I see Scudder?"

He looked at her for a long minute; his expression changed.

"Sure, you could see Scudder," he said. "Come this way."

They went through a barred door, into the bareness of

iron and painted brick, of unadorned walls and uncovered floors, of a smell of carbolic acid and sweat.

Scudder, still guarded, looking wearier and more dejected than ever, was seated at a long table. There were several policemen in the room, but it was a large room, and when Jocelyn sat down near the prisoner they gave her only a curious glance, and the man sitting with the prisoner, at a nod from Napthaly, moved away. They could talk now without being overheard.

"Mr Scudder," Jocelyn said earnestly, as his faded eyes met hers without interest, "do you remember that it had been raining hard the Saturday night that your wife was murdered?"

"Sure, I remember," he said, after a silence and a dull stare.

"Do you remember you'd been over to see a man named Boston?"

The vague eyes came up with a sudden interest.

"Zat so?" the man asked, with an awakening something in his voice.

"You remember that?" Napthaly asked her sharply.

"I do remember it. Because my car had broken down, and I was walking, thinking I could telephone from the nearest gas station. And this man—Scudder—gave me a lift."

"This was—what time?"

"This was half past five o'clock in the morning." Color came into her white face. He was believing her!

"You were driving home; someone with you?"

"No; I was alone."

"But the folks you'd been with would remember your leaving 'em," the attorney stated rather than asked.

"No; because he's—the friend I was visiting is dead. He died a few weeks ago. But I can prove it, I can prove it," Jocelyn said anxiously, forestalling his interruption. "The men in the garage who went to get my car out of the mud, they'd remember. They'd have a record of it. It was about half past five o'clock on the morning of the Sunday before Thanksgiving, and Mr Scudder here was driving back to the city, and he gave me a lift. And you told me, Scudder—don't you remember?—that you had a little boy named—I think I can remember his name; wasn't it Bruce? And you said that your little girl named Florence had died——"

"Yes, sir; we lost our little girl," Scudder said suddenly, his weak eyes filling with tears as he fixed them pathetically upon Jocelyn. "She wasn't nothing but a baby when we lost her."

"He told you this?" Napthaly asked Jocelyn.

"While he was driving me down to the station."

"Think he was drunk?"

"I knew he'd been drinking."

"And how's it happen you've got this date fixed in your mind, Miss Britton?"

"Because—well, I have every reason to remember it. It was an important date to me. I was going to my aunt's for Thanksgiving dinner, and I went over that afternoon to her house."

"Tell her about it?"

"No."

"Didn't tell her you'd started home at five o'clock in the morning and your car had broken down?"

"No."

"Didn't tell anyone?"

"Yes; I did. I told Mr Philip Fordyce. The man I am going to marry."

"Say, weren't you going to be married today?" the attorney asked, diverted by sudden curiosity.

"Yes, we were. But of course—if I can do anything to help Mr Scudder——"

She felt a sudden forlornness and loneliness as she said it. She was burning her bridges behind her. Tears came into her eyes.

The attorney looked down at some penciled notes he had made.

"Know a man named Boston, Scudder?" he asked.

"Bridgie Boston, yes, sir; I do," the little man answered, pitifully eager and bewildered by uncomprehending hope.

"You said you'd won a turkey and he had it," Jocelyn prompted eagerly.

"That's right; that went clean out of my head," Scudder agreed, light breaking at last into his weary eyes. "That's right. He had my turkey, and I thought maybe if I got it and brought it home to Eda maybe she'd get over her mad. That's right. But I never seen Bridgie that night——" he added, puzzled again.

"You said you couldn't find the house. But surely he'd remember about the turkey," Jocelyn said.

"Where is he—Bridgie Boston?" Napthaly asked. "By George, we may have this case broken!" he added, half aloud.

"He and his folks have gone to Las Vegas. He's workin' on the Boulder Dam."

"You could get him?"

"Oh sure; I guess so."

"Isn't it a funny thing that you remembered Boston's name all this time?" the attorney asked Jocelyn, his eyes narrowed.

"I don't think so. My own name is Britton, and Boston being another place name, I remember it made a sort of impression. And I remembered the little girl's name because of a friend of mine whose own little girl is named Florence."

"Well, excuse me," Napthaly said, "I'll be right back."

He went away, and Scudder and Jocelyn sat on together.

"You ran away," Jocelyn said then, as simply as she might have spoken to a child.

"Yes 'm. I was frightened. I'd tried to pick Eda up," the man said. "She was moaning, and she got me all over blood. The lady from upstairs was there. I got Eda onto the bed and she sort of rolled up her eyes and groaned and I thought she was gone. They was screaming and yelling, the Garneys, and Mrs Garney said, 'You done it!' We didn't have no telephone, and they told me to run out and thought I'd find an all-night drugstore maybe and call a doctor. But then I seen my hands all red——"

He put one of these weak, freckled hands over his eyes and began to sob.

"I knew you didn't do it," said Jocelyn.

"I says I didn't do it, but I was scared!" he said. "So I took all the money we had—we kep' it in a little shell box that said 'Souvenir of Atlantic City,' and I got some clothes, and I got out. I drove on and on, and I was always thinkin' I'd give myself up, but nobody bothered me none, and this barber in Carson City had more work than he could do, and I was a barber before I was in the token and button works, so I begun to help him, and I stayed there."

"How do they know what time it happened?"

"Well, they know 'twas round five, becuz she called downstairs to Lizzie Hebbit at four. 'Lizzie,' she says, 'you've locked your dog out, and he keeps whinin' and scratchin' in the hall.' So Lizzie let the dog in, and she says to her mother, 'The poor feller has been tryin' to get in all this time and here 'tis four o'clock.' That's how they fixed it that someone went for poor Eda somewhere round half past five. I got there about half past six, cuz I know it was seven when I stopped the car and changed my clothes in the back and washed up as good as I could. I hope to God that what you say about Bridgie and all that is goin' to make some difference," the little man concluded feverishly, "for I never raised my hand to hurt a fly, and I cert'ny would feel real bad bein' taken to San Quentin and put in one of them death cells. Mr Phillips," he added respectfully, of the district attorney, "cert'ny seems to have it in for me. 'The bedroom snake,' he called me yesterday, and he says that nothin' so atrocious as this has ever happened before. He says the lethal chamber is too good for

me. But I don't feel that's much more humane than the old
way of hangin'."

"I don't think you need be afraid of either." Suddenly a
great calm and a great courage possessed Jocelyn. She felt
exhausted with emotion, yet strangely, gloriously at peace.
Her life lay in wreckage behind her; she did not care. Very
probably she would not marry Philip now; she would go alone
into the future, finding work, finding friends, beginning all
over again. It didn't matter. What mattered was that she had
not failed this miserable little fellow creature in his hour of
need. When he had thought everything lost, she had saved
him.

"I hope you are right, miss," said Scudder.

Napthaly came back; he had two other men with him. One
of them was Phillips, the district attorney.

"Is the recess over?" Jocelyn asked. "Are they going back
into court?" She had begun to feel frightened again.

"Court has adjourned. We have been dismissed until next
Wednesday," said Napthaly. He looked excited. The district
attorney sat down and asked Jocelyn questions; the other man
made notes. She told them all she could. But she was showing
the effect of the reaction already; her eyes blazed in a pale
face; she answered sometimes nervously, sometimes after
hesitation.

"I had dined with a friend, a man friend, in Mr Covington
Keble's studio in Piedmont. I had thought that other friends
were to be there. Yes; it was raining hard. I started home
about ten o'clock, but my car slipped on a bank in the mud and
I couldn't start it."

"Your friend went for help?"

"No. No; he wasn't with me. I had left him at the cabin."

"And started to drive home alone? He didn't offer to come
with you?"

"No. I didn't tell him I was going. I just—left."

"But that was at half past ten," said Phillips. "Scudder

here, you say, picked you up at half past five. Where were you all that time?"

"I was in my car. I had a blanket."

"You didn't go back to the——" He glanced at his notes. "—the Keble cabin?" he asked.

"No. I couldn't have found it. It was pitch dark and raining. And I was miles away."

"About how many miles? Guess at it. Three? Five?"

"The garage people could tell you that."

Oh, this was awful. This was cross-examination. No wonder Phil hadn't wanted her to face it! Her cheeks were on fire; her head ached. This was all shame and fear and humiliation. She hated this room, where a few minutes ago she had felt so confident and so strong!

"So you spent the night in the car, Miss Britton?"

"I couldn't do anything else."

"Ah, but that wasn't what I asked you. You did, you say, spend this cold, rainy night in a car?"

"I had a blanket."

"You had a blanket, of course. And Scudder here"——he always mentioned the cringing little prisoner with a sort of easy contempt——"told you about his girl and his boy, did he?"

"The girl, the child who died, was never mentioned in the case before, Matt," said Napthaly. The other man looked at him thoughtfully, nodded his head slowly.

"I know, I know; that's a point," he conceded. "Now! What was the name of the man with whom you dined that night?" he demanded suddenly. "I see in Mr Napthaly's notes here that he has since died."

"Yes; he died some weeks ago."

"And that was——?"

Jocelyn swallowed with a dry throat.

"That was Mr Kent Dunham."

"Mr Kent Dunham." The district attorney looked up with a sudden light in his eyes. "Didn't he—wasn't that the fellow who killed himself down on some place in Burlingame—

down on the Fordyce place?" he said. Long before he had finished his question he had answered it himself; he set the note down with a satisfied nod. "I see—I see——" he said ruminatively. "Well, Scudder," he added, "I think you're sitting pretty. If you were over in Piedmont on that Sunday morning at half past five, then you hadn't anything to do with that affair in San José Avenue. We'll see what we can do about getting hold of this man Boston——"

"He'd get a letter Monday," Napthaly said.

"Telephone him," the district attorney said briefly and magnificently. "We can't waste the People's time and money on letters. Yep. We'll wire him, and get him on the telephone this afternoon. Now, Miss Britton, where can we get hold of you if we need you, and where can we locate Mr Fordyce?"

"Mr Fordyce——" she was beginning uncertainly, when the door opened and Philip came in. Jocelyn felt the panic terror of a child caught red-handed in mischief; then her heart returned gloriously to a normal beat, and she managed a smile that was close to tears.

Philip, magnificent and browned and confident, was handsomer than ever among these homely, ordinary men. He came in like a great clearing breeze; he came over to Jocelyn at the table and sat down beside her and clasped her hand with his big warm hand.

He had given her only a friendly glance, but that was all she wanted! Now he was greeting the other men.

"Hello, Matt, got my girl in jail, did you? Hello, Sidney. How's all this going, Jocelyn?"

Joy flooded back into her soul; he wasn't angry. He was going to shoulder the whole thing, to save them all. That was all that mattered. The world came back into sunshine and safety with a great heart-shaking revolution; Jocelyn clung to Philip's hand, and drank deep of life's most intoxicating wine: sudden relief from fear and pain.

"What do you think of this, Matt?" he asked conversationally. "Doesn't this give this fellow a pretty good break?"

"Well, it does, Mr Fordyce; it does, Phil," said the district attorney cautiously. "That is, if we can check on these dates. I wish you'd come in with this evidence before. We've got this thing started; we've got our jury and everything. This would have made a difference. This would have made a big difference. We've got the time of that murder fixed at five o'clock. Now you and Miss Britton say you met while she was waiting for the six-o'clock train. How d'you happen to remember the time?"

"I remember the time I took my car out of the garage at the Wahneta Club. And I suppose the garage would have that down, wouldn't they, Matt?"

"The man's bringing the book from the other garage here now. I'll call the Wahneta."

"Someone said the trial would be put over until Wednesday."

"Why, hell," Matt said pathetically, with great simplicity, "there won't be any trial now. We've got to go at this from another angle. We've got to take the whole thing from another angle. I'll get right onto this and see how soon we can turn Scudder loose. I hope you get that, Mr Scudder? You can thank this lady for saving your life; do you get that? She came through with what you needed just when you needed it."

The prisoner was far from grasping the situation. But he knew that matters were turning in his favor, and he cleared his throat preparatory to speech.

"I don't know that there's any way I can thank you, miss. I don't clearly remember that it was you I gave a lift to that morning, but it comes back to me that I did see a lady walking along in the mud, and I appreciate that you felt like you wanted to be so loyal."

These were not exactly the words Jocelyn would have chosen in his place, but she looked at him seriously and said that she was happy to be of service to him.

"You understand, Matt," Philip said, "that it was the

merest accident that Miss Britton and I came into Judge
Troward's court yesterday. I was turning over the guardianship of young Leslie Baker; his father made Judge Troward
co-guardian with me, you know, and Miss Britton came into
the court with me to wait until I could speak to the judge.
Something that was said made her remember what had happened last November; otherwise she never would have known
of Scudder's trial at all! So we'll be here now if you want us.
You have her statement? You'll want one from me. It's just
to the effect that I happened to pass the Piedmont station at
six o'clock that Sunday morning, picked her up, and heard
from her the same story she's told here."

"That's all you'll have to say, Phil."

"We're being married at four o'clock today, and we'll go
off somewhere near—Del Monte, probably. I'll keep in touch
with you. I'd have been here with Miss Britton," said Philip,
"but I had to meet my daughter. She just got in on the
Matsonia."

"I hope to God I can do something for you folks someday!" Scudder, by degrees assimilating the meaning of all
this, said with sudden passion. Jocelyn, standing now, with
Philip beside her, laughed with tears in her eyes. "I hope
you'll never know what it is to stand in the shadow of death,"
added the little prisoner feelingly.

"I hope I won't," Jocelyn said. She looked at Philip. "I
hope I'm not standing there now," she said significantly.
Philip laughed, and she laughed back. Wherever she stood,
he was beside her now. Nothing could go very wrong while
they two were together.

"I'll bet you folks were going away on a honeymoon," said
the district attorney, with compunction. "Seems a shame to
keep you here. I'll tell you, you wait here a minute, Phil. Step
over to court and wait, until I see if I can get in touch with
Mahoney. Lynch," he said to one of the officers, "I think
very probably this prisoner will be discharged this afternoon,
if I can get in touch with Judge Mahoney. If not they'll prob-

ably let him go on Monday. I'll be back in half an hour."

He went away, and Jocelyn said shyly to Scudder:

"Where is your little boy now?"

"He's with my sister in Chico, miss. I didn't want for him to see his father in any of this mess. I cert'ny," said Scudder, with his characteristic little nervous clearing of the throat, "will be pleased to see him again."

"I wish you luck!" she said cordially, extending her hand.

CHAPTER XXXII

SHE AND PHILIP WENT BACK into the courtroom and took two of the round-backed coffee-house chairs. The place was empty now, except for two men cleaning; they both looked like Scudder, Jocelyn thought. She wondered if he would go back to Carson City and his barber's chair; she wondered what the little boy would think of this story someday when his father told it.

"I know how he feels," she said.

"You!" Philip had lighted a cigarette; she knew that he was happy.

"I knew, the minute you opened that door, Phil, how poor Scudder felt. It was salvation, when I thought I was drowning alone in a big cold sea. To have you come in, so easy, so sure of yourself—but then you're always that!"

"I don't remember being so decent, down on the wharf, Jocelyn."

"You had reason, then. And believe me, I wasn't enjoying it," Jocelyn said. "I think while I was coming up here in a taxi I would have given my life to get out of what I had to do. My life! That wouldn't have worried me. But one's life never counts in those times. I had to go on and drag myself down and drag you down, and Norma, and give your mother and Sandy and Janet just the weapons they've been wanting. I had to lower myself to Norma," Jocelyn went on, very close to him, one hand holding to the button of his overcoat, her beautiful eyes raised to his own. "I was to be the influence in her life that was going to steady and protect her, poor Norma, and now she'll know that I am pointed at myself, that I did just what we've always warned her not to do!"

"But you came up here," he said, with his slow smile, "you faced the music. You don't know how I loved you for it, how my heart went to you when I saw you walking away. I knew I was wrong when I said we'd wait and see how the case went. We couldn't have waited. We had to see him through. Coming just when Norma's news came, coming the very day of our wedding, it upset me. I've had lots to worry about, Jocelyn; things sprung on me make me nervous. Did you think that they'll tie all this in with Dunham's death?"

"That was the first thing I thought of."

"And that was the first thing I thought of. But we'll face 'em together, darling, and maybe they'll whip us through the market place and tear every rag of clothing off us, and we'll live through it. And then we'll get Norma away and get her business over, and live through that, too. And then you'll be Mrs Philip Fordyce of Burlingame, raising a family of kids, liking a few families and being bored by most of 'em, going to New York with me, deciding to dash on to Europe, giving dinners, and thumbing your little nose—that is your nose that I just kissed, isn't it?—at the whole crowd."

"Oh, Phil," she said breathlessly, "if you feel that way, I'd *rather* have it start like this! I'd *rather* let them know that we aren't afraid. It was only when I thought I might lose you —I thought you were angry at me——"

"You're never going to lose me."

"Then I don't care!" His arm was about her now; they were in one chair. Jocelyn looked dreamily at the empty bench and the empty jury box, the portrait of a pompous-looking old man and the flag that hung above it, and thought that justice was a wonderful thing, that when the atmosphere of a court was not hideous and menacing, it was a substantial and protective air to breathe.

The district attorney came back with another, older man, and Philip stood talking with them for a few minutes in a low tone. Jocelyn watched; was relieved to hear Philip presently laugh. Then all three turned to her.

"I wish you all the luck in the world, Miss Britton," Phillips said. "I've known this boy since he was in law college, and you certainly are getting one prince of a husband."

"Thank you," said Jocelyn, radiant.

"They think they won't need us any more," Philip said. "Matt here says that we can make for the Canadian backwoods this afternoon without being followed by a posse, which is always nice on a honeymoon. And that's that, Jocelyn," Philip added, when they had come out into a world miraculously bright and friendly and safe, and were in his car going to Sausalito; "that's all, I believe, we'll ever hear of that. They'll put it on the record; they'll throw the charge against Scudder out, and we'll be in Banff, the happiest people in the world. Of course, someday," he went on, "someone may dig up the story, some woman may ask you how well you knew Dunham and if you didn't testify in the Scudder trial——"

"And all I'll have to do is laugh," Jocelyn said, resting against his arm in complete content.

"Exactly."

"Phil, I am so glad I did it! I hadn't any idea it would be so important, but I knew I had to do it."

"I knew it, too, as soon as you were gone. I only waited until a few people had seen me welcoming Norma, and the press had taken some pictures of me welcoming Norma, and then I turned her over to Mother and beat it after you."

"Your mother was there?"

"Oh yes; she turned up—late; she's going to be at the wedding, trust her! She's carried Norma off to lunch—my Lord, Jocelyn, we've not had any lunch, have we? We've got just two hours before we're married. Will you lunch with me at Fisherman's Wharf, Miss Britton? This is the last meal I can buy you, because after this I'll have to have my wife along."

"I hear that your wife is crazier about you than any human being ever was about anyone before," Jocelyn suggested, thoughtfully.

"If she isn't now," he said seriously, "you can bet she's going to be. Twenty-five years from today I'll prove it!"

The fog was gone now, and an afternoon of rare warmth and brilliance was shining over the hills of the city, and the stretches of the bay. Philip turned the car toward the water front and Fisherman's Wharf, and the steep streets fell away below them, and all the world looked washed and bright in the glory of the sunshine.

THE END